MURDER IN HONOLULU

A Skye Delaney Mystery

R. BARRI FLOWERS

D1520069

ALSO BY R. BARRI FLOWERS

PRAISE FOR R. BARRI FLOWERS

"Even hotter than its exotic Hawaiian setting. A police procedure of the highest order, mixing equal parts Sue Grafton and Jeffrey Deaver with a sprinkling of Patricia Cornwell at her best Sure to make both Kahana and Flowers household names." — Jon Land, author of Strong Justice on MURDER IN MAUI

"A masterful thriller set in the dark underbelly of Maui, with lots of fine action, down and dirty characters, and the vivid details of police procedure one would expect from an author who is also a top criminologist. A terrific read!" — Douglas Preston, co-creator of the bestselling Pendergast series of novels on MURDER IN MAUI

"A gripping and tightly woven tale you won't want to put down. Author Flowers neatly contrasts the natural beauty of a tropical paradise with the ugliness of murder and its aftermath." — John Lutz, Edgar winner and bestselling author of Night Victims on MURDER IN MAUI

"A combination of grit, action, and incredibly realistic police procedure. That's the recipe that keeps me turning pages until the sun comes up. A tale so genuine that even I was tempted to call for backup a couple of times." — Lee Lofland, former detective and founder of the Writers' Police Academy on MURDER IN MAUI

"Flowers delivers the goods. An exotic setting, winning characters, and realistic procedural details make MURDER IN MAUI a sure hit with crime-fiction readers." — Bill Crider, Edgar award winner and bestselling author of Murder in the Air on MURDER IN MAUI

"Gripping writing, wonderfully rounded characters you really care about, and vivid locations—this novel is a real and rare treat." — Peter James, international bestselling author of Dead Simple on MURDER IN MAUI

"From one of the best true crime writers around, R. Barri Flowers now has combined his impressive criminology credentials and literary talents to create Maui homicide detective Leila Kahana, a fascinating and complex heroine. Fans of CSI and Hawaii 5-0 will love this one and scream for more!" — Deborah Shlian, award-winning co-author of Double Illusion on MURDER IN MAUI

"A thoroughly puzzling mystery to solve. If you love Hawaii or a good head-scratching mystery, you'll enjoy this book. Very entertaining." — William Bernhardt, bestselling author of Capitol Betrayal on MURDER IN MAUI

"A steamy, non-stop thrill-ride through the seamy underbelly of Hawaii. R. Barri Flowers writes with the passion and knowledge of someone who truly knows his craft." — Allison Leotta, Federal Sex Crimes Prosecutor and author of Law Of Attraction on MURDER IN MAUI

"Starts with a bang—literally—and drops you right into the deep end of murder. A by-the-book mystery that keeps the suspense taut and edgy." — Joe Moore, bestselling co-author of The 731 Legacy on MURDER IN MAUI

"A gripping account of the murders committed by husband-and-wife serial killers Gerald and Charlene Gallego. Top true crime author and criminologist R. Barri Flowers provides his keen insight and expertise into what made these killing partners tick. Compelling reading." — Gary C. King, author of Blood Lust on THE SEX SLAVE MURDERS

"It gets no better than this! R. Barri Flowers has written another thriller guaranteed to hold onto its readers! It was so gripping that I forgot to breathe a couple of times!" — Detra Fitch of Huntress Reviews on DARK STREETS OF WHITECHAPEL

"A compelling and powerful account of Jack the Ripper.... Flowers has captured the sights and sounds of New York City and London's East End in 1888.... The action is fast paced; the suspense building to a peak to the finale." — Barbara Buhrer of MysteryAbout.com on DARK STREETS OF WHITECHAPEL

"A page-turner legal thriller that begins with a bang and rapidly moves along to its final page. He has filled the novel with believable characters and situations." — Midwest Book Review on STATE'S EVIDENCE

"An excellent look at the jurisprudence system...will appeal to fans of John Grisham and Linda Fairstein." — Harriet Klausner on PERSUASIVE EVIDENCE

"A model of crime fiction.... Flowers may be a new voice in modern mystery writing, but he is already one of its best voices." — Statesman Journal on JUSTICE SERVED

"An interesting blend of classic film noir and rough, modern cinema.... Quick action and tight dialogue make it a jolting thriller, but it's also got the psychological tightness of a good mystery puzzle." — Robert A. Sloan, author of Raven Dance on DEAD IN THE ROSE CITY

* * *

CHAPTER 1

The name's Skye McKenzie Delaney. I'm part of the twenty-first century breed of licensed private investigators who live by their wits, survive on instincts, and take each case as though it may be their last. The fact that I double as a security consultant for companies in and around the city of Honolulu, where I reside, gives me financial backup not afforded to all private eyes. This notwithstanding, I take my work as an investigator of everything from cats stuck in trees to missing persons to crimes the police can't or won't touch very seriously. If not, I wouldn't be putting my heart, soul, and body into this often thankless job.

I also happen to be happily divorced—or at least no longer pining for my ex—and not afraid to get my hands dirty if necessary in my business. I get along with most people, but won't take any crap from anyone should it come my way.

Before I became a security consultant/private eye, I used to be a homicide cop for the Honolulu Police Department. Stress, fatigue, burnout, and a real desire to get into something that could provide more financial security and flexible hours, without the downside and depression of police work and know-it-all authority figures, convinced me to change careers.

During my six years on the force, I spent my nights earning a Master's Degree in Criminal Justice Administration. I'm hoping to get my Ph.D. someday when I no longer need to work for a living and can devote my time to further educating myself. In the meantime, I'm getting an honorary doctorate in private detectiveology, where every case can be a real learning experience.

On and off the job, I carry a .40 caliber or 9-millimeter pistol Smith and Wesson—depending on my mood. And I'm not afraid to use either one if I have to, as it sure beats the alternative of ending up as just another private dick on a cold slab in the morgue.

If I were to describe myself character-wise, the words that come to mind are feminine, adventurous yet conservative, streetwise though I often rely on intellect to get me over the hump, and kick-ass tough when duty calls.

I've been told on more than one occasion that I'm attractive—even beautiful—and sexy as hell. I leave that for others to decide, but I'm definitely in great shape at five-eight, thanks to a near obsession with running and swimming, along with not overdoing it with calories. I usually wear my long blonde hair in a ponytail. My contacts make my eyes seem greener than they really are.

I recently celebrated my thirty-fifth birthday. All right, in truth, it wasn't much of a celebration. I spent the entire day holed up in my house with my dog, Ollie, contemplating the future and happy to put much of my past behind me. That included my ex-husband, Carter Delaney, whose greatest contribution to my life and times was making me realize that no man was worth sacrificing one's own identity and integrity, even if it meant losing him in the process.

I did lose Carter five years ago, after deciding I had no desire to share him with his mistress (and probably others I didn't know about). It was a decision I firmly stand by today and am definitely the better for.

At least I convinced myself that was the case even as I came face to face with the subject in question on a muggy afternoon at the end of July. I had just filed away some papers when he walked into my office literally out of the blue. It was his first visit to my office since I joined the ranks of private eyes. I had once worked for the man as a security consultant. That turned into lust, sex, love, marriage, and divorce, and now we were little more than distant acquaintances.

The tremulous half-smile that played on Carter's lips told me that he was not entirely comfortable being there. I felt just as awkward for probably the same reason: the *ex-spouse syndrome*, which would forever keep a wall of regrets and painful memories between us, thick as molasses.

Never mind the fact that Carter Delaney was still every bit the physical specimen I had fallen in love with another lifetime ago. Tall, fit, handsome, and perennially tanned with dark hair and gray eyes, he almost looked as if he had just stepped out of the pages of Good Looking Digest. Though it was hotter than hell outside, he was decked out in an Italian navy designer suit and wing-tipped burgundy leather shoes. He glanced at the expensive watch on his wrist as if he needed to be somewhere else.

At thirty-eight, Carter Delaney was a successful businessman. A former Honolulu prosecutor in the career criminal division, Carter had walked away from the job after excelling at it for the lure of cold hard cash in the world of commerce. He had turned his smarts and acumen into a successful Internet-based international trade company.

It was during the early stages of this success that I entered the picture. Carter had hired me, wanting to have the best security devices for both his home and business. The rest, as they say, is history.

At least it was.

We had managed to avoid running into each other for nearly a year now, which suited me just fine. I wasn't looking for history to ever repeat itself, so quite naturally my curiosity was piqued as to why he was here now. Rather than appear too overeager, I decided to wait and let him take the lead.

"Hi," I said tonelessly as I eased back into my chair and scooted it up to my gray workstation desk. I shuffled some papers to at least give the guise of being busy. In fact, I was going through somewhat of a dry spell right now with the sluggish economy and all. This was particularly true on the private eye side of things, where potential clients seemed more willing to go it alone or rely on an overworked criminal justice system to solve their problems.

I wondered if Carter was here for a social call or if he was looking to hire me as a security consultant again.

"Nice office," he said, though the words seemed to squeeze through his tight-lipped smile.

I agreed with his assessment, as I'd paid enough for the roomy one-woman, air-conditioned unit in a high rent downtown office building that had all the tools of the private eye trade.

Carter hadn't taken his eyes off me since entering the office. It made me just a little uncomfortable. I wondered if he was trying to undress me with his penetrating gaze, as if he hadn't seen the merchandise before.

Either way, it was not winning him any brownie points, if there were any left to win.

I glared at him and said dryly: "Glad you like what you see."

He immediately turned his eyes downward, as though searching for something. When he looked at me again, Carter's smile had faded as he said, clearly for my benefit: "I've been meaning to stop by, see how things were going, but between work and—"

I was only too happy to bail him out in this instance, though I had the feeling he was stalling. For what, I had no earthly idea.

"Don't torture yourself, Carter," I told him. "It's a little late for a guilt trip. Or have you forgotten that we're not married anymore?"

At least not to each other. Six months to the day after our divorce was finalized, he and the mistress tied the knot. Rumor had it she was pregnant at the time. Rarely did I take rumors seriously but, sure enough, the newlyweds did produce a baby girl shortly thereafter. I didn't want kids—at least not until I had done the career thing first. Carter didn't want to wait for me or my career.

To this day, we've never discussed whether that was the beginning of the end or just the beginning of his wandering eyes. Either way, it did little to erase my self-doubts, what might have been, or what had transpired since.

"Like it or not, a part of us will always be married, Skye," he declared, "at least in spirit."

"I don't think so," I said, sneering. "In spirit or otherwise. What's done is done."

"Maybe you're right." He rubbed his chin thoughtfully.

"Do you plan to tell me why the hell you're here?" I decided to be blunt, since he seemed willing to take his own sweet time. And in my business, time was money. He didn't have to know that it was only trickling in at the moment. "Or am I supposed to guess what reason my ex-husband might have for paying me an office visit?" I asked.

I honestly couldn't think of any reason for him to be there. Other than maybe to check out my office digs out of curiosity or get a glimpse of what he'd given up back in the day.

He chuckled. "Still as impatient as ever, I see."

I frowned. "Guess some things never change..."

We eyeballed each other for a moment or two of stubborn reflection. Finally, he asked coolly: "Mind if I sit?"

I indicated either of two brandy-colored cluster armchairs. He sat down and for some reason I was glad that my desk separated us.

Carter sat there staring blankly at me, as though in a trance. I stared back and waited with uneasiness at this unlikely get together.

I suddenly felt compelled to ask: "So how's your wife and...?"

At about the same time he was saying: "I'd like to hire you..."

My question could wait. If I hadn't known better, I thought I just heard Carter Delaney actually say he wanted to hire me! If the notion wasn't so absurd, I might have burst into laughter at that moment. Instead, I forced myself to say: "I'm listening—"

He shifted in the chair unsteadily. "I think Darlene is cheating on me..."

He was referring to wife number two. I'd always detested the idea that someone named Darlene took my place in his life. It was as if her name was *darling*—somehow making her more endearing than I ever was to him.

Apparently, a certain someone must have concurred.

I resisted the urge to say what goes around comes around. *Oh, what the hell*, I thought. *Let's hear what else he has to say.*

"Really?" I said. "Now isn't that a terrible thing to suspect—" I couldn't resist smiling when I said it, in spite of myself.

Carter peered at me beneath thick, dark brows, clearly annoyed and perhaps embarrassed. "I'm not looking for sympathy or amusement," he said.

I got serious again. "Could've fooled me." A well-timed sigh. "Exactly what is it you want from me?" I dared ask, almost afraid of his answer.

He recomposed himself, and after a moment or two said: "I'd like you to follow her around, see where she goes, who she talks to..."

I suddenly found myself laughing, almost hysterically, probably to keep from crying. When I finally stopped, I said: "You can't be serious!" But something told me he was. "You don't really expect me, of all people, to spy on the very bitch-slash-bimbo you left me for, do you?"

His brow furrowed. "Can you lay off the name calling? I was hoping this would be a bit more civilized—"

I was almost enjoying this. *Almost.* "Get real, Carter. You didn't come here for civility. That ended between us the day you decided I wasn't enough for you."

He gave me a quizzical look. "Remember who kicked out who? It's not like I'm asking you to do something illegal. Isn't this the sort of work a private investigator does? Or is my money not green enough for you?"

I leaned toward him; anger building up that I thought had been buried for good. "Don't patronize me! It's not about money. It's about respect! You've got a hell of a lot of nerve showing up in my office and asking me to snoop on your wife. I'm afraid I don't come *that* cheap—" I took satisfaction in making that abundantly clear to him.

He actually seemed shocked by my reaction, and maybe even hurt. "Dammit, Skye, I didn't come here to insult you. I came because I need your help." He batted those charming eyes at me emotionally. "You think it was easy for me to come to you with my, uh, problem? Hell no, it wasn't, but I did because I thought you'd understand."

"Sure, I understand all right," I told him. "You're feeling betrayed, humiliated, and agony over your suspicions. Am I right?" I was sounding like a still bitter ex-wife and found it to be oddly refreshing.

Carter sighed, sounding exhausted. "You're never going to give up the spiteful ex-wife routine, are you? What happened between us is history. Right or wrong, I can't do a damned thing about it now." He hoisted to his feet so fast he nearly toppled over. "I guess it was a mistake coming here. I thought you were professional enough to take on *any* case without letting your personal feelings get in the way. Obviously I was wrong." He turned his back to me and headed for the door.

Carter always had an incredible way of being able to manipulate people—especially me—into seeing things his way. Not this time! I was not about to be conned into feeling guilty or unprofessional because I refused to take a case that was far too personal and could only stir up feelings that I would just as soon forget, if that was possible.

I stood and asked what seemed like a legitimate question under the circumstances. "Why me? Surely you could have found some other private eye in Honolulu to follow your wife around—one who didn't happen to be your ex-wife."

He turned around and gave me a look that implied the answer should have been as obvious to me as it was to him.

"Do you even have to ask why?" He clenched his jaw. "The last thing I want or need is to make public to already jittery investors *my* private business...or the fact that I think my wife—the mother of my three-year-old little girl—is cheating on me. You're the only private detective I felt I could count on for a *discreet* investigation that wouldn't come back to haunt me." He lowered his head. "I guess in some ways it already has—"

I suppose I took it to heart that he trusted me enough to feel that I would handle such an investigation with the utmost discretion. But, all things considered, I wasn't sure that I could trust myself as much.

"I can recommend someone—" I offered as a goodwill gesture.

"Don't do me any favors," Carter muttered irritably as he turned toward the door, gave me a final heated glare, and vanished much the way he had appeared.

I slumped back down into my chair, angry that he had put us both in an unenviable position. In truth, things had not been all that great for us even before the other woman entered the picture. Carter's obsession with getting ahead at all costs and his insistence on meticulousness in every aspect of our lives clashed heavily with my somewhat lower aspirations and lack of perfect order in my life. And our differences over when children should become part of the picture hadn't helped matters either.

The final straw came when I learned of Carter's affair and the reality that he didn't really seem to give a damn that the cat was out of the bag. It was more like a big relief to him. And when confronted with the option of me or the other woman, he was unable or unwilling to make what I believed to be the intelligent choice.

I sought to hold my ground where it concerned my ex. It had been over between us for a long time. I owed him nothing but the painful memories of days gone by. Neither of us had even pretended to be friends once our relationship had officially ceased. (I even turned down a generous divorce settlement, preferring to leave the marriage with only what I brought to it. At the time, it seemed like only a clean break could allow me to regain my dignity.) What was the point when we had gone too far beyond friendship to go back?

As far as I was concerned, that overused cliché applied perfectly when I thought of Carter Delaney. He had made his own damned bed and now had to lay in it—but not with me!

* * *

The privilege of sharing bed space with me in the post Carter Delaney era currently belonged to Ridge Larsen. A homicide detective for the Honolulu Police Department, Ridge had transferred from the Portland Police Bureau in Oregon just after I had gone into early retirement. He was forty, divorced, and handsome in his own rough-hewn, square-jawed way with crafty blue eyes, a shaven bald head, a thick dark moustache, and six foot three inches of solid muscle.

Ridge and I had been dating for the past six months. I wouldn't exactly call what we had serious, insofar as my wanting him to put a ring on my finger. Being on my own for some time, I had become extremely possessive of my independence and privacy and was in no hurry to share my space with anyone on a permanent basis. Ridge seemed to understand and fully accept this, being of the same mind after a disastrous marriage, which probably accounted for half of why we seemed to work so well together.

The other half was that he tolerated my infrequent but not very pretty mood swings, knew when to leave me alone, was a great cook, and an even better lover.

An added fringe benefit of having Ridge around was that he came in handy during those not so rare occasions when I needed official snooping or able-bodied assistance in the every day and sometimes dangerous world of private investigations.

"I've never had the pleasure of meeting the current Mrs. Carter Delaney," hummed Ridge in bed, his strong arm holding me close to his taut body, "but from what I've heard, the former prosecutor's wife is hot stuff."

I jammed my elbow into his ribs and watched him wince. "I wouldn't know about that," I said tartly. "And now is *definitely* not the time for you to fantasize about my ex-husband's wife."

The afterglow of making love for the past hour was dimming quickly.

Ridge groaned. "I wouldn't dream of fantasizing about anyone but you these days." He planted a nice kiss on my lips. I enjoyed the taste of him. "I only go for pouty ones with long blonde hair and a smokin' hot body."

I soaked in the compliment and felt my annoyance beginning to wane.

Ridge sat up and asked nonchalantly: "So are you going to take the case?"

I looked at him dumbfounded while partially covering myself with a satin sheet, as if he hadn't already gotten a bird's eye view of every inch of me. "What case?"

"Delaney versus Delaney," he said cutely. "Sounds like pretty routine stuff to me." He grinned. "Let's face it, it took guts for him to come to you of all people for help."

I couldn't believe my ears. "Give me a break! Guts or not, why the hell would I want to find out for poor Carter if his wife is fooling around on him?"

"What are you afraid of?" Ridge asked.

"I'm not afraid of anything," I insisted. Except for maybe not being in full control of my own life at all times, I thought. But I knew it didn't work that way in the real world. We were all victims of circumstances for which we often had little to no control.

Ridge eyed me suspiciously. "You don't still have the hots for your ex, do you?"

I stared at his chest, then into his eyes, rolling mine. "What do you think?" He gave me that look all men have— the one that says they need to hear the words of reassurance. "No, I'm *not* still hung up on Carter Delaney," I said with an edge to my voice. "You of all people should know that, Ridge. I don't make a habit of sleeping with one person while fantasizing about another—" I hoped that would erase all doubts.

It didn't.

"Prove it," Ridge challenged me, "if only to yourself and maybe to Delaney. Take his case just as you would any other client. After all, it's just business, right?" He twisted his lips and added: "Who knows, you might even find it therapeutic."

I sneered at him. "Thanks for the advice, Dr. Phil."

He grinned crookedly. "Just wait till you get my bill. I don't come cheap."

I could vouch for that, as his expensive tastes included having a sometimes difficult girlfriend.

Reluctantly, I climbed out of his king-sized bed and gathered up my clothes that were scattered about the floor as if a tornado had passed through.

"What are you doing?" Ridge asked with a frown.

"I'm going home," I told him.

"Why? I hope it wasn't anything I said or didn't say."

I slid into my jeans and zipped them. "It wasn't. I have to feed my dog—"

He got out of bed. "Can't it wait—maybe for a couple of hours?"

"No," I said. "Ollie starts to get antsy when he goes practically all day without eating." I looked around, but couldn't find my cami, which seemed to work to Ridge's advantage.

He came up behind me and wrapped massive arms around my waist. "Are you sure you aren't just a little pissed at me?"

I wriggled out of his arms and gave him a sincere look. "There's nothing to be pissed about."

At least not with you, I told myself, reserving that for my ex at the moment.

Ridge looked relieved. "Good. I just don't want you to throw away Delaney's money for all the wrong reasons."

He was starting to press his luck and my patience.

I sighed and told him: "This may come as a surprise to you, but what's wrong for one person may be totally right for another—"

So maybe I was a little pissed at Ridge for seeming to represent the typical male in sizing up the situation. It was as if there was no room in the scheme of things for emotional baggage or ethical principles where it concerned making money. I wasn't sure I bought into that or if he really did.

I found my top, which had somehow ended up beneath Ridge's black denims. He gathered up his clothing.

"Any chance we can start the night over?" he asked lamely.

I couldn't help but smile at the thought. "Don't ask more of yourself than you're capable of delivering."

"Try me," he dared.

Though a repeat performance was pretty damn tempting, I grinned and said, "Isn't that what I just did?" while glancing at the wrinkled bed coverings that betrayed the hot and heavy activity that had taken place there tonight.

"At least let me drive you home," Ridge offered.

"My car will get me there just as quickly," I said, and kissed him lightly on the mouth. "You can walk me to the door, though."

He grumbled and hugged me as we walked in step through his ranch style home on Keeaumoku Street in the Makiki section of Honolulu that wasn't far from my office.

I could never be upset with Ridge Larsen for very long. His intentions were usually anything but self-serving. Yet I couldn't help but wonder if by pushing me into this case, he was more motivated by his own insecurities than any self-doubts I may have had.

My instincts told me that both were likely to be tested before this thing was over.

CHAPTER 2

I left Ridge's house at eight o'clock, feeling a bit worn down for a day that had begun with Carter and ended with Ridge. At the moment, I was happy to be going to my own little piece of paradise, where I did my best thinking alone.

I had a one-year-old Subaru Forester that fit quite nicely into my current monthly payment budget. I drove to Waikiki, where I owned a nice house on a palm tree lined, dead-end street not far from the beach. I purchased the two-story plantation style home shortly after my divorce was finalized from an elderly couple who decided to move back to the mainland. It was my good fortune to be in the right place at the right time to get the property, which had been well maintained and reminded me of the home where I grew up on the island. My parents had been beach bums who island hopped before settling into Oahu and having me.

I could hear my dog barking when I pulled into the driveway. Ollie was a five-year-old German Shepherd, named after my late uncle who was as mean as a junkyard dog and ornery as ever. In fact, more often than not, Ollie was just the opposite—sweet and gentle as a lamb, as long as he was not provoked.

Opening the front door was all he needed to make me eat my thoughts, as Ollie literally attacked me. Okay, so it was just his way of playing and asking me "Where the hell have you been all day?" Or maybe "I'm hungry as a dog. What's for supper?"

We ended up wrestling for a few minutes before I turned on the ceiling fan in the living room, then fed Ollie his favorite dog food. He wanted more, but I wasn't about to let him get fat on me. That wouldn't help either of us.

After freshening up and changing into a sleeveless shirt and denim shorts, I allowed my sore feet some freedom from footwear, padding barefoot across the hardwood floor and into the kitchen. I made myself a salad and ate it with two slices of wheat bread and a glass of red wine. Ollie loved to hang out on the kitchen's cool ceramic tiles more than anywhere else in the house.

However, the kitchen floor still took second place to the backyard. When he began to grow restless, I got the picture, letting him out of the house to run around in our nice sized, fenced in yard. I joined Ollie a few minutes later and tossed a Frisbee around for him to chase, making sure he stayed clear of my vegetable garden.

Back inside, I watered the flamingo flowers, vanda orchids, and heart leaf philodendron I kept throughout the house, which helped give the place a Hawaiian botanical garden look.

By the time I was ready to call it a night, I had tucked Ollie in his basement hideaway, read a couple of chapters of a John Lescroart novel, and watched the news.

Before drifting off to dreamland, I had more or less decided that, for better or worse, I would take on the task of spying on the current wife of Carter Delaney. Business was business, I convinced myself, even if it happened to involve my ex-husband and his ex-mistress. I still hadn't decided if I wanted his suspicions to prove false or right on the money.

Only time would tell...

CHAPTER 3

Every morning at five o'clock, Ollie and I ran on the beach for an hour or so. While he was comfortable in his furry body, I preferred a loose T-shirt, shorts, and running shoes. Staying in tiptop shape was becoming more and more difficult for me as gravity and age became natural obstacles. Fortunately, I had determination and powerful legs on my side. Ollie also had determination and strong legs, matching me step for step on a short leash.

It was seven o'clock when I called Carter's office. His voicemail picked up so I left a message for him to call me. Oddly, in not having to speak directly to the man I once could never get enough of, I somehow felt as if I had been given a reprieve.

Maybe this wasn't meant to be after all, I thought.

Somehow, I had a feeling I wouldn't be let off the hook that easily. As if on cue, the phone rang and it was Carter on the other end.

"Aloha kakahiaka, Skye," he said, which meant good morning in Hawaiian.

If you say so, I thought, but responded nicely in kind: "Aloha kakahiaka back at you."

"Hope I didn't wake you," he said, sounding like he really meant it. Apparently Carter wasn't returning my call.

"You didn't," I told him, giving him the benefit of the doubt that he'd somehow forgotten I had always been an early riser.

He paused. "Look, I wanted to apologize about running out on you like that yesterday. Guess I just let my frustrations and suspicions get to me."

That was about the most I could expect from Carter Delaney as far as groveling. And it was enough for me, considering I'd already had a change of heart.

"I'll take the case."

"Really?" There was a note of surprise in his voice that was clearly more for my ears than anything.

"I charge two thousand a day, plus expenses," I informed him. What I didn't say was that I had raised my normal fee by five hundred dollars, figuring I deserved it from my rich ex for what he wanted me to do.

He didn't argue the point.

"When can you start?" he asked anxiously.

Was he that desperate to find out if his wife was sleeping around? Or was I missing something here?

I decided not to think so much and just do the job he was paying me handsomely for.

"If you can stop by the office this afternoon to go over some details," I told him, "I'll be happy to begin right away."

"How does eleven sound?"

"Perfect. I'll see you then."

I remained seated on my sofa for several minutes after hanging up, second-guessing if I was doing the right thing in getting involved in my ex-husband's marital problems. I had to admit, there was a certain amount of irony and a lesser degree of curiosity in taking this case. My bottom line wish was that it was over and done with as soon as possible with minimal casualties along the way.

* * *

"Where do I begin?" Carter asked as he sat before me in my office. As usual, he was impeccably dressed in a sharp suit, as if to wear anything else would somehow spoil his image of the consummate successful businessman now than he no longer had to get his hands dirty as a prosecutor.

I looked down at my desk nervously and started counting the dust particles, as though about to go on my first date or something. I realized that, in effect, we were starting all over in communicating with each other in the post marriage era. And I had a feeling it wasn't going to get any easier.

"Why don't you start by telling me why you think your wife is cheating on you," I suggested with a straight face.

Carter reverse-crossed his legs clumsily. "There are a number of reasons. Darlene's never home for one, and when she is, she's usually bitchy, lies about where she's been and who with, and"—he forced himself to look at me—"we haven't made love in months..."

I colored a little in that moment where it seemed like our own intimate past had come back to haunt us. He had certainly given what seemed to be legitimate reasons for his suspicions. I took notes, attempting to treat his case as I would any other client's.

However, that seemed to be asking the impossible.

"I take it she doesn't work?" I'd heard that through the grapevine. Not that she needed to work, since she was married to a man who appeared to be more than capable of supporting his wife. Of course, that hadn't stopped me from wanting to do my own thing when I was married to him back in the day. But then that was just me.

"Not on this planet," Carter moaned. "Hell, not even in this city! The word *work* is not in Darlene's vocabulary."

Strangely enough, one of Carter's pet peeves in our relationship was that I *did* work (never mind the fact that it was his hiring me that led to our romance in the first place). It had something to do with the balance of power most men prefer to have in their favor. Had he changed his tune over time? Or was this really only about Darlene doing something with her time other than maybe having an affair?

Another one of those awkward moments between us left an eerie silence that hung in the air like thick smoke.

"What about your child?" I asked. "I thought most mothers had their hands full just getting through the day."

Carter's brow creased in the center. "One of the advantages of being independently wealthy is that you can afford hired help," he bragged. "Darlene has made an art form of it. Usually the only time I can get her to live up to her responsibilities of being a mother is when she wants something."

A sad statement, I thought, if true. "Have you confronted her about your suspicions?"

He paused. "Yes."

"And?"

"And she denies it." He curled one side of his mouth into a sneer. "She says I'm jealous, paranoid, and way off base."

I had never known Carter to be jealous or paranoid in our marriage, probably because I gave him no reason to be. On the other hand, the word *possessiveness* did come to mind.

"Well, where does Darlene claim she's been when she goes out?" I asked.

"Shopping or at a girlfriend's."

"What makes you think she's lying?"

He scowled. "She never shows me anything she bought during the times in question, though she never has any trouble doing so the rest of the time whenever she decides to run up the charge cards." He sighed. "As for friends, I've never known Darlene to have *any* female—"

We were interrupted by the untimely, irritating presence of a giant whitefly that invaded my office and seemed to take particular delight in watching us squirm. It finally had the decency to land in a most appropriate spot. I kept an insect swatter in my desk drawer for such routine occasions and didn't hesitate to use it when I thought I could nail the critter.

"Don't move!" I ordered Carter, who had apparently lost sight of the insect. Fortunately, I knew exactly where it had landed. I raised the swatter, took two looping steps, and lowered the boom right between Carter's legs.

Bull's-eye!

Or right on the money, pun intended.

Carter buckled, more from sheer embarrassment than anything else.

"Oops," I said, and managed to suppress a giggle. It felt better than I could have expected. "Let me clean that nasty little creature off you..."

I yanked a couple of tissues from the box I kept on the desk and scooped up the victim's remains.

Carter grimaced. "Dammit, Skye! Couldn't you have waited for it to land somewhere else? This suit cost me a pretty penny!" He grabbed two tissues to finish wiping his pants—which turned into smearing what was left more than anything else.

"So have them professionally cleaned," I uttered half sympathetically, "and send me the bill." I made a feeble attempt at justification. "Sometimes they just won't leave on their own. Sorry."

"Yeah, I'll bet you are," he grumbled, and now seemed to find humor in it himself. "I suppose I had that one coming—long overdue." He chuckled. I smiled, but kept my mouth shut. "At least it was that poor bastard," he said, glancing at the wastebasket, "who got the worst of it."

The incident appeared to break the tension in the room that had been palpable. A moment later, it was back to the business at hand.

I asked: "Do you have a picture of your wife?"

I had never had the pleasure (or lack of, was probably more like it) of meeting or laying eyes on his former mistress, having chosen to spare myself the indignity.

Carter removed a five-by-seven picture from his suit coat pocket and handed it to me. It was a wedding photograph of him and his bride.

"It was all I could find," he said guiltily. "We haven't taken many pictures—"

I hated to admit it, but Carter's former mistress and current wife was beautiful. It wasn't surprising really. If nothing else, Carter Delaney definitely had an eye for attractive women, present company included. It was the fact that he couldn't seem to settle for one woman at a time that pissed me off. At least it had back in the day.

Darlene Delaney looked at least ten years Carter's junior and she was several inches shorter. She had short blonde hair, blue eyes, and a shapely body in what looked like a very expensive wedding gown. Or certainly much more than what I paid for mine. Whether I chose to acknowledge it or not, Carter and Darlene were a nice looking couple. But then so were we and look where it got us.

I wondered if Carter and his present wife were headed down the same path toward divorce.

"This will do," I said evenly, putting the photo on my desk. "I'll also need your address, the type of car Darlene drives, and some idea of what time she likes to go out."

"No problem." Carter dug into his wallet and pulled out a snapshot. Sporting an uneasy smile, he said: "Thought you might like to see what my daughter looks like—"

Silently, I took the picture of a baby not more than a year old, with beautiful blue eyes and curly blonde hair.

"Her name is Ivy," Carter said proudly.

I tried to imagine this pretty little baby as mine—ours. That thought quickly gave way to reality. Ivy was the product of Carter and the woman he essentially gave me up for and now questioned her faithfulness to him.

I bit the inside of my lip, but managed a smile while handing him back the photo.

"She's cute," I said honestly.

Carter beamed. "You should see her now—"

It was something I was understandably in no hurry to do. I changed the subject by handing him a yellow notepad. Apparently, he got the message.

"So what happens if your wife is cheating on you?" I asked more out of curiosity than anything else.

Carter shrugged. "Probably a divorce..." Our eyes locked, and he said: "Guess I really never knew what I had with you until it was too late—"

"Don't, Carter—" I said quickly for both our sakes. "Let's not go down that road. Just keep this *strictly* professional."

He seemed to contemplate it for a long moment before asking: "What made you change your mind about taking my case? Or is that privileged information?"

"There's no hidden agenda here," I assured him. "I felt there was no reason why I couldn't work for you just as I would anyone who came into this office and requested my services. It's as simple as that!" To suggest anything else would only complicate matters, I thought. Including the added pressure Ridge had given me to take the ball and run with it rather than give in to past demons.

My response seemed to irk Carter, but he tried hard not to show it. "So how much of an advance do you want?" He pulled an envelope out of his briefcase and removed a batch of crisp bills. "Will ten thousand do for starters?"

He put the cash down in front of me. It was certainly a nice way to begin an investigation, though I couldn't help but feel he was flaunting his wealth. Or reminding me of what I'd missed out on financially.

I picked up the stack of hundred dollar bills. Though I was very tempted to take it all, as he apparently wanted me to, I didn't bite the bait. Since I figured it should take no more than two or three days at the most to get the goods on his wife, if there were any goods to get, I counted out five thousand dollars and handed him back the rest.

"This should be fine for starters," I told him, choosing professional ethics and personal pride over a more than generous advance. "I'll bill you if you owe me more."

He nodded. "You make the rules..."

I stood. "I'll be in touch as soon as I have something for you."

Carter rose almost reluctantly, and favored me with a grim look. "Thanks for your help, Skye. If you run into any roadblocks, don't hesitate to let me know. Darlene may be giving it up to someone other than me, but she sure as hell isn't going to spread her legs for *you* without fighting tooth and nail to hold on to what she thinks is rightfully hers."

CHAPTER 4

I was still pondering Carter's parting words as I sat in my car outside his house. By the looks of it, I could see what Darlene wanted to hold onto. The oceanfront home was located on Kaikuono Place in one of Honolulu's most exclusive districts, Diamond Head, and screamed *fabulous*. On the slopes of the world famous volcanic crater by the same name, the mansion was two stories and boasted a combination of stone, stucco, and rich woods with arched windows, steep gables, and wrought iron. There was a masonry garden wall and an entry blocked from the street by an electronic gate. Palm trees and high shrubbery surrounded the property like guards sworn to protect its occupants.

A touch of envy overcame me as I remembered the nice but modest place we called home when we were married. Carter had obviously moved up quite a bit in the world since then. And so had Darlene as a result.

My thoughts turned to the reason I was there gawking at my ex-husband's exquisite accommodations. At precisely ten a.m., Darlene Delaney emerged from the house with her daughter. With the telephoto zoom lens of my digital camera, I honed in on the two.

With her hair in pigtails, Ivy was wearing an pink dress and matching shoes. She held her mother's hand seemingly under protest.

Darlene looked relaxed and stylish in an olive pantsuit and high-heeled mules. Her shoulder length hair hung loose. She removed sunglasses from an oversized purse and covered her eyes before heading toward a bright red BMW in the circular drive.

I disappeared from view as the car sped past the gate and onto the street, whizzing by me as though my comparatively inexpensive vehicle was insignificant. Was she in a big hurry or what? I wondered while starting my car. Or was this just Darlene's normal reckless way of driving with her daughter in the car?

In any event, I had to put on the burners just to keep up.

During my surveillance, I considered the irony that Carter may well have been getting a major dose of the same medicine he had once dished out to an unsuspecting me. After sulking for some time, I finally got past it and on with my life. So had he, and apparently never looked back.

Till now.

Then I found myself wondering what Carter would think of Ridge. And vice versa. They were about as different as night and day, but had enough common ground to get involved with me. At this stage of my life, I couldn't help but think I was much better off with Ridge.

These musings drifted away as I followed Darlene to a day care center on Ala Aolani Street, where she literally dropped Ivy off before going it alone to some unknown destination. For a time, she seemed to be driving just for the sake of driving. Or maybe to see how many heads she could turn in the cars she left in the dust.

This exercise in tire wear came to a head when she turned onto Kalakaua Avenue and parked at the Royal Hawaiian Center, a four-level shopping mall in the heart of Waikiki.

I parked not far from her and waited while Darlene took extraordinary pains to redo her face and hair, primping for someone apparently other than her husband. Normally I had a feel for whether or not a spouse was having an affair. But in this case, my instincts were undoubtedly flawed. Spying on your ex-husband's current wife probably nullified any objectivity. But something told me there was more to it than that. Judging by Carter's complaints about Darlene, the marriage seemed more or less doomed whether she was having an affair or not.

Or was that perhaps wishful thinking on my part?

I doubted it. Why on earth would Carter want to stay married to someone who mistreated him and apparently neglected their daughter? On the other hand, if Darlene was willing to fight me "tooth and nail" to keep the life and luxuries she had, why would she risk it all by having an affair that she seemingly did not give a damn if her husband was privy to or not?

It didn't add up, making me even more suspicious, even though I knew as well as anyone that marital triangles rarely added up to everyone's satisfaction. I was living proof of that.

Darlene left her car and headed inside the mall. I followed from a safe distance, dressed in my foot surveillance inconspicuous attire of a blazer over a mock halter and slim leg pants. I wore casual flats for practicality and brought along a nondescript handbag with all the essential elements of the trade.

An unlikely place to meet a lover, I thought, but not impossible. Maybe Darlene would surprise me and meet with someone in the back room of one of the fashionable boutiques. Or maybe even out in the open in the food court.

If that was the case, she certainly was taking her own sweet time about it. Darlene spent nearly three exhausting hours at the mall. At least it was exhausting for me, in spite of my fitness routine. This was one time in which the lady did take full advantage of her credit cards. She left the mall overloaded with bags, but no lover.

Her next stop was a manicurist on Woodlawn Drive. A young woman gave Darlene the full fingers and toes treatment. Seemed innocent enough, I thought, ruling out for the moment that the affair was with another woman. I took pictures anyway just for the hell of it.

Things finally began to get interesting when I tailed Darlene to a community park on Aala Street. She walked hurriedly to a shaded area, where she met with a thirty-something Hawaiian man of medium build with a short dark ponytail. My first thought was: *Gotcha, Darlene!*

But it looked like I'd jumped the gun.

They exchanged a few words before she handed the man an envelope. I captured it on digital and watched through the telephoto lens as he riffled through what could only have been money. More words were exchanged before he reached into his pocket and quickly—his eyes darting left and right as though scared to death that someone might catch them in the act of committing a crime—placed a small plastic bag into Darlene's palm, and curled her fingers around it for good measure.

My guess was that I'd just witnessed a drug transaction between a dealer and the wife of a former prosecutor and now wealthy businessman. Suddenly this case had far greater implications than merely a wife who was having an affair. I found myself almost wishing it had been something as simple and non-criminal (unless it happened to be your own spouse) as adultery. Was this the essence of Darlene's "affair"? Drug abuse? Did Carter even have a clue that his wife was doing drugs and willing to go to risky lengths to get them?

CHAPTER 5

My favorite place to unwind was at a Waikiki watering hole on Kuhio Avenue called Clyde and Bonnie's. Named after the infamous bank-robbing couple from the 1930s, the walls were lined with images from a time gone by. The music piping out was also vintage jazz standards, featuring the likes of Sarah Vaughan, Frank Sinatra, Ella Fitzgerald and other great crooners of that era.

I sat with Ridge at a small table near the window, sharing a pitcher of beer. His brow furrowed as he studied the photograph I'd just handed him.

He turned his eyes to me. "Looks familiar," he said. "I think I'll run it by the guys in vice."

I grabbed the picture of Darlene and the man she had met at the park. "Strictly *unofficial*, remember?" Against my better judgment, I had shared with Ridge my suspicions about Darlene and her probable drug dealer. "I can't really be sure what I saw," I said waveringly. I'd held back the more incriminating pictures. "The last thing I want to do is betray the confidentiality of a client—particularly one who was once a top prosecutor in this city—by providing dirt for every cop on the police force who may have had, or still has, a beef against him."

Not to mention those nervous investors Carter mentioned. And just plain old media folks who like to jump on any story that seems remotely newsworthy. At the very least, I figured that Carter deserved to hear it from me first if there was any substance to my suspicions.

Ridge put the beer mug to his mouth and flashed his deep blue eyes at me drearily. "Do I detect some sentiment for Carter Delaney and his female problems?"

I stared at the tricky question while tasting beer. "I'm not going to pretend we were never married"—as if that was an option—"or that there aren't some lingering feelings that come with the territory," I conceded, hating to admit it. "But right now my only interest in the man is as a client who entrusted me with a job—one that doesn't include smearing his name and reputation. Or, for that matter, his wife's reputation at this stage."

Ridge drank more beer and studied me thoughtfully. "Whatever happened to the woman who just two days ago wouldn't touch this case with a twelve foot pole?"

I fixed him with a narrow gaze. "Do I need to remind you *who* talked me into taking the case?" *Or at least he helped push me in that direction*, I thought.

He smirked. "I just hope my big mouth doesn't get you in over your head. Looks like Delaney may end up with a hell of a lot more than he bargained for."

I put the mug to my lips, spilling beer down my chin, and concluded painfully: "Most clients do."

The only real question in my mind was just how much more dirt was there to find concerning Darlene Delaney? And was Carter prepared to deal with the fallout?

* * *

I got up at the crack of dawn for my morning run with Ollie. For some reason, he seemed more out of it than me. I half-expected him to call it quits about halfway through and get his ass back home, but he managed to keep pace with me.

When we returned home, I noticed my housekeeper's dark blue Chevy Malibu in the driveway. Natsuko Sasaki was a twenty-five-year-old Japanese graduate student with bold sable eyes and a stylish black bob. She was petite, sassy, sarcastic, and often too damn opinionated for her own good. She also had a strong anti-male philosophy in life, but insisted that it had nothing to do with her sexuality. Who was I to argue with that?

Natsuko cleaned my house once a week after I convinced myself that I had neither the time nor desire to keep up with my housework, much less pet projects. She also happened to be great with Ollie, which in itself made my life a whole lot easier.

We found Natsuko in the kitchen where she had managed to get rid of last night's dirty dishes by way of the dishwasher, and had actually fixed breakfast.

"Aloha kakahiaka," she said.

"Hey," I responded.

Ollie gave her his unique brand of good morning by jumping up on her, nearly knocking Natsuko down. She recovered nicely, maintaining her balance by grabbing the counter.

"Ollie, I missed you too," she claimed. "I made some toast and scrambled eggs to go with orange juice and coffee. That all right?" She regarded me with uncertainty.

In fact, I wasn't too big on egg yolks these days and their cholesterol, preferring to use only the egg whites for cooking. But I wasn't in the mood to spoil Natsuko's good intentions. Besides, my nearly empty stomach was ready for just about anything.

I grabbed a piece of toast, bit into it, and said with a smile: "Thanks, Natsuko. It's great."

She gave me a toothy grin and turned to Ollie. "I didn't forget about you either, boy—" She led him to his bowl that was filled with tasty looking dog biscuits.

"I just signed up for a course in self-defense," Natsuko said in the breakfast nook where she had only black coffee. "One can never be too careful these days."

I forked some scrambled eggs into my mouth. "I think a self-defense course is a good idea," I told her while trying to imagine Natsuko on the attack. "Let me know how it goes..."

In the police academy, I learned my fair share about self-defense strategies. Even took up boxing a few years ago, mainly as a way to increase my upper body strength. Although I'd like to think I could kick anyone's ass who messed with me, the reality was that most confrontations were not about hand-to-hand combat, but who had the more powerful handgun. Nine times out of ten, the thugs seem to be better equipped these days, which was a problem for everyone. Including Natsuko if she happened to encounter the wrong assailant.

I took a shower and dressed before stepping into some comfortable slip-ons. I had just tied my hair back when Natsuko walked into the bedroom. She was holding a dust rag that didn't look particularly dusty.

"So what are you working on these days?" she inquired, moseying over to the window. "Anything interesting?" Her eyes bulged with fascination while she casually ran the rag across the faux wood blinds.

"Not really," I said and added unenthusiastically: "Just your standard cheating wife case—" There certainly was no need to go into the details concerning my ex and his drug using wife. As it was, I had no evidence yet that she was cheating.

"Not the worst thing that could happen," Natsuko said.

I agreed, were Darlene's actions confined to that. Nevertheless, having been the victim of a cheater, it still left a bad taste in my mouth. "I can think of a lot better things to do with your time," I told her.

Natsuko's face flushed. "It's not that I believe in adultery, but men have been getting away with it for years. Maybe it's time *we* put the shoe on the other foot—"

I frowned and said: "Just who do you think the vast majority of men have been, as you say, *getting away with it for years* with?"

She looked stumped. "So women can be bitches just like men can be bastards," she conceded. "No one ever said we were perfect."

"Far from it," I admitted, putting on some lip gloss. "That doesn't mean we can't try to be." I grabbed my purse, and told Natsuko: "I've got to go. Don't forget to lock up when you leave—"

"No problem," I heard her say as I headed out the door, all the while thinking about Darlene Delaney and the trouble she appeared to be in.

* * *

Another day, another two grand, I thought while staking out Carter's impressive estate. Once again, Darlene left home bright and early, whizzing by as if it was her last day on earth and time was of the essence. And, once more, she was dressed to kill, figuratively speaking, in what could only be described as provocative designer clothing. Only this time Ivy was not with her.

I followed Darlene to a hair salon on Dillingham Boulevard, where she emerged an hour later with a new look. Her hair was shorter, lighter, and curlier. I liked the old look better. But it was doubtful my opinion would count for much. I found myself wondering if Carter's opinion would matter to her.

Darlene went from the hair salon to a motel on Nahua Street called Palm Tree Lodge. There were a few palm trees on the property, as if strictly for effect. Something told me that Darlene had not come there to meet Carter. But who? Perhaps the drug dealer she'd met the day before at the park.

I eased into a parking spot inconspicuously on the other side of the lot. I'd barely noticed the shiny black Mercedes that Darlene had parked next to. I was too busy watching her take one more look at the new hairdo, put on a fresh coat of lipstick, and get out of the car.

She sauntered to a first floor room where the door opened before she could knock. A man greeted her. Definitely not the drug dealer from the park—or Carter. This man looked to be in his early to mid forties, and was tall and well built with thick graying hair. He was wearing a kimono style robe and apparently nothing else.

Through the telephoto zoom lens of my camera, I snapped pictures as the man in question greeted Darlene with a big, juicy kiss. She was more than reciprocal as she kicked the door shut. So much for the freebies! Not that I hadn't already seen enough to earn my pay. Carter's suspicions about the wife were right on the money. Darlene had a lover.

In that moment, I actually felt sorry for Carter. If the truth be told, I suppose part of me had hoped his qualms were not unfounded. Perhaps I wanted to make him feel renewed guilt for cheating on me, but not the pain of being cheated on. None of that seemed to matter now. Only the hard reality that Darlene Delaney was seeing another man and very likely doing drugs at the same time, if not the same place.

An hour or so later, the two emerged from the room. He had ditched the robe in favor of a dark suit. They barely exchanged words before she went to her BMW and he to the Mercedes. I was left to wonder what he did with his time when he wasn't bedding Carter's wife, given that the man could obviously afford to drive in style.

I realized that I was perhaps overstepping my bounds in speculating on the man's net worth and source of income. My only interest here was to confirm that Darlene was having an affair. She was. That should have been the end of it.

But, knowing Carter, he'd want more than merely confirmation. I needed to find out who the lover was. I took down his license plate number as Darlene left the lot. He drove off in the opposite direction, as though their worlds together began and ended at cheap motels. I followed him while dialing Ridge at work on my cell phone, putting it on speaker.

"Detective Larsen—" his voice boomed.

"Hi, Ridge—" I said in the cozy tone I used whenever I needed a favor. "Got a minute?"

"Barely..." he said. "What's up?"

"I need you to run a make on a license plate." I cursed silently as I pressed on the brake at a red light while the Mercedes disappeared down the street.

"Let's have it," Ridge said. "Just remember, you owe me one."

"Just one?" I joked. "I'm sure a repayment plan can be worked out to your satisfaction, Detective Larsen—"

"Yeah, I'm sure it can, and I plan to hold you to it," he replied.

I could only imagine what he might have in mind. "The plate is EHA 849."

"Okay, hold on," Ridge said. "The car is registered to Edwin Hugh Axelrod of 813 Onaha Street," he informed me in short order.

"Axelrod..." The name sounded familiar. And with good reason.

"He's a criminal attorney," Ridge said, filling in the blanks. "The man defends some of the city's low life elite who can afford the best that money can buy, even if the money is soiled."

He was also having an affair with the wife of a former prosecutor and current success story in town who happened to be my ex-husband, I thought. Was it a coincidence? Or was there something more to it?

This was something Carter would have to sort out himself, along with his wife's apparent drug use.

For me, the hard part was serving to my ex on a somewhat less than silver platter the preliminary results of my investigation.

CHAPTER 6

The bar was not his usual watering hole, but a place Carter Delaney had been to before a couple of times. Then, like now, he had wanted to drown his sorrows in liquor without running into anyone in his business or social circles. These days he didn't even know who the hell he was anymore. Yes, he was a onetime successful prosecutor in Honolulu, where crime had run amok and the pressures of the office were more than he could handle. And, yes, he had gone into business for himself and ended up making far more than he could have ever dreamed. Then there was the fact that he was married to a beautiful woman and was the father of the prettiest little girl in all of Hawaii.

But that hardly got to the root of who Carter Douglas Delaney really was. In better times, he was a young ambitious lawyer, wanting only to do his best to put the bad people where they belonged: behind bars. Once that stage of his life had run its course, he had turned to the business world to make his fortune.

But his life hadn't truly begun to take shape till he met the former Skye McKenzie Fairchild. She was the complete package: brains, beauty, and sexual appeal. It was probably love at first sight, though he hadn't known it at the time.

There was no doubt that what he felt for Skye was the real deal when they got married less than a year later.

At first, it looked like a Cinderella love story where they both got what they wanted from each other and would live happily thereafter. But real life was never a fairy tale. He'd learned that the hard way. They saw the landscape differently. Though Skye impressed the hell out of him as an ex-cop turned security consultant who he would have gladly recommended to anyone, at the end of the day he wanted a stay at home wife and mother to a bunch of kids.

Skye had other ideas. She wasn't about to give up what she'd worked so hard to achieve. And he was too stubborn and impatient at the time to respect her for who she was, especially when other women were at his beck and call, tempting him left and right. He went to the cookie jar too many times and paid the price when Skye walked out on him. With that went the marriage and probably the best thing to ever happen to him.

Carter put down another vodka. His third. He admitted to being an alcoholic and, he believed, with good reason. He had screwed up his life big time. He had screwed up his business, and his second marriage was going to hell. The walls seemed to be coming down around him and all he really wanted was for things to go back to how they were when Carter felt like he was on top of the world.

Maybe there was still hope, he thought. Yes, maybe he could find a way out of the mess he had made of his life and look at the glass half-full rather than half-empty.

Skye had asked him to meet her this afternoon to discuss her findings. She'd sounded tense, as if the news was worse than he'd imagined. Was that possible?

Carter ordered another vodka and used the time to reflect on seeing Skye in her office that first time the other day. She was actually better looking now than when they were married, if that was possible. She had obviously taken good care of herself over the years—both physically and professionally. He'd heard that she not only was a top security consultant locally, but one of the best private investigators around.

But that wasn't why he had hired her. His reasons were far more personal than that.

He immediately downed the drink that had been placed before him. It was time to find out what Skye had learned about his current wife. Then maybe he'd have a thing or two to say to Darlene.

Carter Delaney burped, and put a brand new fifty-dollar bill on the counter.

He stumbled out of the bar and onto the street, managing to get to his car.

CHAPTER 7

Carter had agreed to meet me at my office at four o'clock sharp. I had hoped to close this case by five and have dinner with Ridge at six, but as of four-thirty, Carter had not shown up for our appointment. Punctuality had never been his strong suit. But that hardly justified putting my life on hold while I waited for him to set foot in the door only to hear things he may not want to know.

I finally called Carter's cell phone, but got his voicemail. I reminded him about our scheduled meeting, then decided to try his office. He was not there.

"Did he leave a message for me?" I asked his secretary.

"I'm sorry..." she said insincerely. "Nothing."

I hung up, feeling hot under the collar. *Where are you, Carter?*

I found his wife's cell phone number, which Carter had given me as a possible tool to use in obtaining her phone records to identify a potential lover. I suspected Edwin Axelrod's number was on the list and likely the drug dealer's as well.

At the moment, I was itching to call Darlene Delaney, though I knew it wasn't a very good idea. What the hell was I supposed to say to her? *"Hi, I'm Carter's ex-wife, Skye. He hired me to find out if you're having an affair. You are, and you're also buying illegal drugs. Now I need to locate your husband so I can give him the good news..."*

I nixed the idea and instead phoned Ridge and told him I would be a little late for dinner, which he was cooking. He seemed to accept it; though, reading between his sighs and mutters, I could tell he was pissed. Couldn't really blame him. I would make it up to him later.

I knew exactly who to blame for messing up my plans.

By a quarter after five, it was obvious that Carter was not going to keep our appointment for whatever reason. I was in no mood for excuses from him nor was I particularly anxious to reschedule our meeting.

When I left the office, I had more or less planned to terminate the investigation. I didn't have time to play games with Carter or his cheating, drug-abusing wife. I would leave him a voicemail summing up what I'd learned. If he wanted more dirt on Darlene, he would have to get someone else to dig it up.

* * *

I went home to feed Ollie and freshen up before heading to Ridge's place. I got my first clue that something was wrong when I drove up to my house and heard Ollie barking like the dog from hell. There was no sign of Natsuko's car. Instead, there was a silver Cadillac DeVille in the driveway. Carter's car. I recognized it from the second time Carter visited my office. I'd watched from the window as he climbed in and drove off in style.

Why is he at my house? I wondered, knowing I certainly hadn't invited Carter to conduct business at my private residence. In fact, he'd only been there once before. It was shortly after I'd moved in and we were no longer married. He'd stopped by to pick up some of his precious books by Ernest Hemingway and F. Scott Fitzgerald that had inexplicably gotten mixed up with my own books.

Had Carter somehow believed that I wanted to meet him here instead of at my office for the final report on his cheating wife? And how the hell had he gotten in? The last I knew, I hadn't given him a key for safe keeping. He also did not have the codes to my security system, which seemed to have been deactivated.

Was Natsuko still here when he came? I wondered. Maybe she let him in.

I peeked inside Carter's car. There was no sign of anything unusual. His leather briefcase was on the front seat, passenger side. There was a newspaper folded neatly on the back seat and a suit coat stretched across the back of the front seat. The car was not locked.

Neither was the front door to my house, which was slightly ajar as I stood there inspecting it. I wondered why Ollie, who was still barking ferociously but from a distance, hadn't come out. I pushed open the door cautiously while calling out Carter's name. If he was there, he was not answering or showing himself.

The whole thing was very bizarre and unnerving, to say the least.

"Carter, where are you?" I asked nervously, but still got no response. "Ollie, come here, boy..." He too failed to show, though I continued to hear his somewhat muted barking.

I entered the foyer at which point I half-expected to see Carter sitting in the living room, looking wearily at his watch, and wondering if he'd have to wait all night to hear what I had to say. Instead, there was no indication that I had company. To be sure, I took one quick glance around, looking for signs of life. My eyes passed over the French provincial furnishings, area rug, decorative art, and plants.

Carter was definitely not in the room.

On impulse, I reached for the 9-millimeter handgun in my purse still strapped across my shoulder. Had I been anywhere other than home, my instincts would have kicked in long before now. But, for some reason, the comforts of familiar surroundings caused me to let my guard down.

If Carter was an uninvited guest, he was starting to scare the hell out of me. He'd better have a damned good explanation for being here and not bothering to respond, I thought as I moved cautiously through the house.

I followed the sound of Ollie's barking through the kitchen and down the hall till I came to the utility room door that was closed. I could hear Ollie jumping up against the door, trying to get out. When I opened it, he practically attacked me.

"Whoa, boy, what's wrong? Who put you in there?" Carter seemed the obvious choice, as he had never been an animal lover, but Ollie wasn't confirming it in so many words. I was taking no chances, keeping the gun out, just beyond Ollie's reach.

He was barking like crazy, clearly trying to tell me something.

"What is it, Ollie?" I asked, my heart skipping a beat. "Where's Carter? I know he's here, his car's in the driveway. Is he hurt?"

As if he understood me, Ollie darted away and headed down the hall toward the stairs leading to the second floor. I followed, not sure what to expect, but somehow fearing the worst.

At this point I still had no reason to believe there was real cause for alarm, other than my dog's follow-me routine. I called out to Carter again, hoping he had simply failed to hear me while snooping around my house, which I really did not believe. There was no response.

I watched Ollie dart in and out of the bathroom, urging me to go in. As I approached, I could hear the jets of my Jacuzzi bath churning. I sucked in a deep breath and, with my gun drawn, turned the corner to come face to face with what had really spooked my dog.

Nothing could have prepared me for what I saw.

Carter was in the bath, his head was under water, and water was spilling out onto the ceramic tile. I noted that his clothes and shoes were tossed about the floor, getting soaked, as though he could care less.

Not knowing if he was alive or dead, I immediately rushed to his aid, screaming Carter's name frantically. I turned off the water and the jets and lifted his head up, trying to make sense of this. His naked body was cold and rigid and it looked like there were scratches on his legs.

It was one of those times where in the space of a heartbeat your entire world took an inexorable left turn into the depths of hell.

The sheer grief of the moment took on an added dimension when I noticed between barks that Ollie, who had never left my side, had blood dripping from his mouth. Had he bitten someone? Carter? Or was Ollie the victim of an assault?

Returning my attention to Carter, I noticed that there was something protruding slightly from his grayish blue lips. Carter's eyes were wide open, but it didn't take a forensic examiner to know that they had lost their sight forever—

* * *

The jury was still out on Ollie. I avoided cleaning him up so I wouldn't destroy any possible evidence before the police arrived, took pictures of the dog, and then took him to the vet for treatment. The verdict on Carter was far more ominous and conclusive. The former attorney and ex love of my life was dead! Almost as unsettling was the sight of him as a corpse. Drawing on my police training and common sense, I managed to refrain from further corrupting what I believed to be a crime scene once I determined that Carter was no longer amongst the living.

In my mind, this was a homicide perpetrated by an unknown assailant in my house. Unfortunately, the early indications suggested otherwise.

Inside Carter's mouth was apparently a suicide note, according to police, who had taken over my house—routine for incidents that could at the very least be described as suspicious circumstances. The note was typed and read:

"Skye, sorry to have to dump myself on you like this, but I really didn't feel like I had much choice. At least with you, I knew I could count on a decent burial. Recently, my life's been going to hell! Between the pressures of work and home, it just got to be too damned much. This—killing myself—seemed like the only halfway dignified way out. I'm sorry for everything...

Carter"

At this point, I was like a walking zombie. If Carter really did write that note, not only was his death undignified, but the apology was totally unacceptable. In my gut, I was sure there was far more to this than met the eye.

But that was to come later. For now I was still grief stricken and waiting for Ridge to arrive, whom I'd called right after calling 911. I needed him now more than ever to get through this.

CHAPTER 8

"Dammit!" Ridge Larsen cursed after he learned that Skye had found Carter Delaney in her bathtub, the victim of an apparent suicide.

Why the hell would he commit suicide and at Skye's house of all places? Ridge thought as he drove his department-issued dark sedan to the house.

He felt awful for Skye. She was the toughest woman he'd ever known when dealing with adversity. But this was different. This was a man she had once been married to. And she had been working for him, with Ridge's encouragement.

It wasn't going to be easy to simply push it out of his mind, as cops tended to do in the course of routine homicide investigations of nameless strangers. This figured to be an investigation that was far more personal than Ridge was used to.

Especially since it involved the woman he was currently seeing. They seemed to get along as well as anyone could expect, and certainly much better than he got along with his ex-wife. He had no idea how long things would last between him and Skye. Maybe months or even years. They hadn't placed any parameters or prerequisites on their relationship. All that really mattered at the moment was that they enjoyed each other's company, were a perfect match in bed, and left the door wide open for whatever the future may bring.

Now he'd been assigned the investigation into a possible homicide that took the life of the man who had been lucky enough to marry Skye then, like a damned fool, threw it all away. Ridge contemplated how this set of dynamics might play in taking on this case, rejecting any thoughts of a conflict of interest. He would treat the case like any other insofar as being professional enough to see it through.

* * *

Ridge pulled up to the curb in front of Skye's house. There were already squad cars there and an ambulance. He got out of the vehicle, thought a moment longer about what he would find inside, and went up to the front door. He was wearing his usual cheap navy suit, loafers, and a deadpan look. He identified himself to a young uniformed officer, and went inside.

The first thing Ridge noticed when he got to the bathroom was the only thing he couldn't miss—Carter Delaney's nude body partially slumped over the side of the now empty Jacuzzi. As he assessed the former prosecutor's remains, it was hard to imagine this stiff being Skye's ex-husband. But death did that to you, he realized. It took away your physical stature and vitality, and left nothing but a pitiful shell. This was made even worse if it came by way of a criminal offense.

Ridge closed his eyes for a moment. When he opened them, he saw one of the crime scene investigators who indicated that they had finished collecting the evidence from the victim and his immediate surroundings.

He stepped into the hall where a team from the medical examiner's office was standing by. "Get him the hell out of here," Ridge ordered them.

"Will do," muttered one tonelessly.

Ridge bypassed them and approached a young female officer who was standing guard to prevent any tampering with evidence.

"Where is Ms. Delaney?" he asked her anxiously.

"In her bedroom, sir."

Ridge headed in that direction. He wondered if anyone at the scene was privy to his relationship with Skye. They hadn't exactly tried to keep it a secret. But Skye seemed in no hurry to let the cat out of the bag, as if it would somehow complicate his sometimes-unofficial assistance with her private detective work. From his standpoint, he would be happy to be the man in her life for the whole world to see.

But, for now, there were more important things to be concerned about, starting with Skye's well being.

Then he could turn his attention to the mysterious death of Carter Delaney.

CHAPTER 9

"Why would Carter kill himself?" I cried out to Ridge as the reality of this tragedy really began to sink in. "It just doesn't make any sense..."

Certainly not where it concerned the Carter Delaney I knew. But perhaps he wasn't the same man anymore. Maybe his personal and professional demons had driven him over the edge.

Or not.

Ridge had been assigned the case as a possible homicide. In walking a tightrope, he was also playing the role of sympathetic boyfriend. Though I hadn't always embraced the idea of our romance being public, for reasons that were more professional than personal, it had to take a back seat to my overwhelming need to feel connected to someone after such a tragedy.

"I've never heard of a suicide that did make sense," he replied in his detective-like voice as we sat on the comforter atop my Queen Anne bed, away from the activity outside the room. "But that doesn't stop people from taking their own lives all the time, Skye—" Ridge said, putting a comforting arm around me. "Obviously Delaney was having some marital problems. Maybe he just decided it wasn't worth the aggravation."

Maybe. But I wasn't buying it. Not in my house.

"If so," I said, "why would Carter go through the trouble of hiring me without giving me the chance to give him the information he paid for?"

Ridge scratched his chin, as if searching for answers there. "The note said he had work pressures. Maybe he had reached the point where he no longer gave a damn what you found out about his second wife—"

Even in my hour of grief, I couldn't help but think like a private detective and ex-cop. My mind kept coming back to the alleged suicide note. I had never known Carter to type anything in his life, especially when there was always someone to do it for him. Why start now?

I looked into Ridge's deep eyes, which were already trained on me, and asked: "Don't you find it just a bit odd that Carter chose to leave a *typed* suicide note rather than a handwritten one that would be easier to verify? After all, he was a former prosecutor who had to know what suspicions this note would leave behind."

Ridge thought about it for a moment or two, then said: "Have you considered that he wasn't thinking like a onetime prosecutor who wanted to leave no room for doubt?" His arm tightened around me. "If this was a suicide, I'd say your ex was thinking more like a desperate man whose only intention in coming here was to die...and for *you* to find his body."

I broke away from Ridge's warm embrace and looked at him with annoyance. "Is that why Carter agreed to meet me this afternoon at my office? To keep me preoccupied so he could break into my house and drown himself in my bathtub with a suicide note stuffed in his mouth? I don't think so..."

Ridge seemed to reflect on my argument against suicide, while lightening up. Unfortunately, his counter argument was even stronger. "The spare key you kept under the plant holder on the porch was on the kitchen counter," he pointed out. "There was no indication of forced entry. Hell, apparently your alarm wasn't even set, practically inviting anyone to come in. And you admit yourself that it's at least possible Delaney might have thought your meeting was supposed to be here."

My body tensed as I contemplated this against my better judgment. I still wasn't sure why the security system wasn't on. At this point, I had to assume that it had been tampered with.

Ridge looked me in the eye and said evenly: "I'm talking to you right now as a cop. And I'm telling you that right now it looks like Carter Delaney planned to kill himself when and where he did..."

"What about the blood we found on Ollie?" I asked, still doubtful about the suicide angle. "Was Carter planning to kill him too, but for some reason decided to lock him in the utility room instead?"

"We don't know yet if Ollie bit Delaney or even if Delaney bit the dog," Ridge offered humorlessly. "For all we know, Ollie's injuries may have been self-inflicted. Dogs can get stressed out too when they encounter unexpected situations. Maybe he got a little crazy there."

I had to admit even in my despondency that the circumstances surrounding Carter's death did not as yet add up to murder. But the part of me that felt I knew him deep down inside refused to believe he would take such a macabre means to end his life. I told Ridge as much.

He rolled his eyes at me and said: "Maybe the man you knew, or thought you knew, died a long time ago."

We were interrupted by a knock on the door. Ridge got to his feet almost instinctively in that moment. I felt obliged to do the same. The last thing either of us needed was to let our personal relationship compromise the investigation in any way.

A thirty-something crime scene investigator walked in. "We're about ready to dust this room for prints," he told us. "You know, standard procedure and all..."

Ridge frowned. "Can't that wait? I doubt you'll find anything useful in the lady's bedroom."

"It's all right," I told Ridge, knowing this was a reaffirmation of our relationship that Carter was strictly in the past where it came to intimacy. But since the issue on the table was his death and possibly a homicide, I didn't want to stand in the way of progress. I turned my attention to the investigator. "Do whatever you have to. The sooner this thing is over with, the sooner I can reclaim my life and house."

He nodded and went for help.

Ridge looked a little embarrassed at the notion that the very real possibility existed that the only prints they would find in the room belonged to the two of us, and Natsuko. He put a hand on my shoulder. "Until we get this thing sorted out one way or the other, I think it's probably a good idea for you to stay at my place."

I had no doubt that this was the homicide detective speaking and not the man I was seeing romantically. Either would have been warmly received under the circumstances. I nodded at him and said: "I accept your offer. I'll just grab a few things..."

Ridge gave me a pleased look before saying: "I'll be outside—"

I watched him close the door and wondered what this whole mess meant to our future, if anything. *I have to try to keep a level head here and not allow my emotions to get too off track*, I told myself. Then my thoughts turned to Ollie and the fact that the extent of his injuries was still not known.

* * *

"Has anybody notified the wife yet?" Ridge asked a burly detective as I watched the covered body being carted out the front door, giving me the chills.

"We haven't been able to reach her," he answered.

Ridge gave me an *I'm-not-surprised* look and told him: "Well keep trying! She must be *somewhere* in this damned city!"

Yes, somewhere, I agreed. But where and with whom? Her lover or her drug dealer?

I seriously wondered if Darlene Delaney would even care that Carter was dead. That he was an apparent suicide victim. If Carter really had killed himself, I couldn't help but think she had driven him to it.

Right now, I still had far more questions than answers.

As if the nightmare of having my house turned upside down by the people I used to work with wasn't enough—in addition to the trauma associated with seeing your ex-husband go from a strong man to a soft corpse—waiting outside was more unexpected grief. The overzealous media had gotten hold of the breaking news story and were out in droves.

One hulk of a man in a Hawaiian shirt and denim jeans said as though he really cared: "My heart goes out to you, Ms. Delaney. Can you tell us exactly what happened here?"

I met his eyes and responded tersely: "I think that would best be answered by the authorities. Now if you'll excuse me..."

He backed off respectfully with a nod and another inquisitive journalist quickly took his place.

With an overnight bag in hand, I successfully managed to "no comment" my way through all but one particularly persistent reporter—a tall, slightly built male in his mid thirties with curly dark hair, intrusive gray eyes, and a crooked mouth.

"Ms. Delaney," he said, matching me step for step in a wrinkled brown suit as I headed for Ridge's official cruiser, "why did Carter Delaney kill himself in your house?"

I shot him an angry glare. "I think you'd be wise to wait for the autopsy before you start drawing conclusions as to the cause of his death."

Regardless of what I thought about Carter's death, I was not about to let some hotshot reporter looking for a story turn speculation into fact.

He persisted to irritate me. "Is it true that *your* ex-husband, Carter Delaney, hired you to spy on his current wife?" he asked.

How the hell did he find out about that? I wondered, feeling bile begin to rise in my throat. I could imagine him replying, *"I have my sources."*

Which didn't tell me anything. All I knew was that Carter's life was about to become an open book and there was little I could do about it, except try to limit the damage where it concerned me.

I pinned my eyes on the reporter and told him: "What a client hires me for is privileged information."

He stood in my path as though determined to get an answer that he could make something out of. "So, is that a *yes* then?"

I sucked in a deep breath while glancing at his press badge that identified him as Liam Pratt. "Look, Mr. Pratt, if you know what's good for you, you'll get the hell out of my face!"

We got into a brief staring match before he backed off. I had put it down as a victory until I realized I had been assisted by the intimidating presence of Ridge who had come up behind me.

"Is there a problem here?" he asked toughly.

"Nothing I couldn't handle," I told Ridge with a scowl as the reporter wisely walked away.

Liam Pratt stopped for a moment and said over his shoulder: "The truth is going to come out one way or another, Ms. Delaney—"

CHAPTER 10

He watched from amongst the reporters as Skye Delaney sidestepped questions about Carter Delaney's mysterious death like she was dodging bullets. She put on a good show as one tough lady PI.

She was hot to trot. He liked the way she walked. You could tell she was a runner by the strength of her stride and the grace of her strut. He found himself getting turned on just by watching her thighs rub together inside those tight jeans as she moved toward the detective's car.

No wonder Carter Delaney had reintroduced himself to her. He probably figured if he couldn't have her all to himself again, might as well have his ex work for him.

He wondered how Skye Delaney felt seeing her onetime lover boy husband drowned in her bathtub. Not a pretty sight.

He could see the headlines now: FORMER PROSECUTOR AND PROMINENT BUSINESSMAN KILLS HIMSELF IN EX-WIFE'S BATHTUB.

That should get people talking, he though with a laugh. And he'd listen, along with everyone else, till he got his fill of it.

He watched as Skye Delaney and Detective Ridge Larsen got in the car and drove off, leaving reporters scrambling for neighbors and wherever the hell else they could go for information on this breaking story.

He could only imagine what the two lovers were talking about. They were probably on their way somewhere to check on that damned dog's condition. She was almost certainly asking Larsen why this thing had happened on her turf. He was probably asking her the same thing.

They could ask Carter Delaney, except dead men didn't talk.

CHAPTER 11

In the car, Ridge cautioned me when he said: "The going could be a bit rough for you for a while. After all, it's not every day that something like this happens to a fairly well-known figure in this city—who also happens to be a man you were once married to."

I didn't need to be reminded of that, but I heeded the warning nevertheless. Carter's death was not going to go away—at least not until I knew why he died. And why in my house?

We arrived at the veterinarian's office where Dr. Garth Nishimura, chief veterinarian, greeted us. He was in his early fifties, but looked younger with short, fine black hair. He had done wonders putting Ollie back together a year and a half ago after he broke his leg fighting a neighbor's dog, so I felt totally comfortable with him in the vet's hands now.

When he returned to the waiting room after about thirty minutes, I stood up anxiously.

"So, how's Ollie?" I asked.

"Couldn't be better, Skye," he said. "A slight abrasion above his right eye was all we could find to complain about." He led us to the room where Ollie was waiting enthusiastically and apparently not the worse for wear. "I'd say he still has many good years left in him," Dr. Nishimura said while Ollie licked my face like it was a lollipop. "But I'm not so sure the same can be said for whoever he took a chunk out of—"

Ridge and I looked at each other before re-facing the doctor. "Are you saying Ollie bit someone?" I asked.

"Yes, that's exactly what I'm saying."

I gave Ridge another look. No one had said anything about any dog bite wounds on Carter. If that someone was not Carter, then it would mean another person was in the house around the time he died.

"I understand there's a police investigation underway," Dr. Nishimura said.

I reintroduced Ridge as Homicide Detective Larsen and he filled the vet in on the circumstances surrounding Carter's death. Dr. Nishimura seemed genuinely shaken up by it.

"Will you be all right?" he asked me.

"I haven't really had enough time to think about it yet," I answered truthfully, and glanced at Ridge.

"Doctor, what can you tell us about the person Ollie bit," Ridge said.

He shrugged. "Not much, really. I sent the tissue samples to the crime lab—" He scratched his flushed cheek, then added: "It definitely was a human rather than an animal, I can tell you that—and enough of an injury that medical attention was likely required—"

"Unless, of course," Ridge remarked thoughtfully while stealing a glance my way, "the person didn't plan to be alive long enough to bother—"

* * *

It was deathly silent in the car en route to Ridge's house. Even Ollie seemed unable or unwilling to muster his normal vociferous barks. I couldn't read Ridge's mind, but mine was occupied with more whys about Carter. Why did he really hire me? Why didn't he show up at my office as scheduled?

You stupid bastard. Why did you have to die in my house, leaving me to remember you like that? I thought, nonplussed.

The silence was broken when Ridge got a call on his car radio. "We finally got in touch with Carter Delaney's old lady," the voice crackled. "She seemed to take the news of his death really hard—"

Both Ridge and I had serious reservations about that, knowing what we did about Darlene Delaney. At the same time, I felt an instant bond with Carter's widow. After all, we were both married to him, for better or worse. Even a cheating wife must have had some feelings for the husband and father of her child that she had now lost forever.

Needless to say, Ridge's home-cooked meal was ruined, as was our date. I was now a temporary houseguest, and food was the last thing my stomach craved. And any musings about sex were even further away.

Ridge didn't make a fuss on either score, understanding that right now all I needed was some time to grieve and deal with the tragic turn of events.

Sleep came easier than I thought it would. I wasn't sure if it was due to the comforting embrace of Ridge's muscular arms or the sheer exhaustion of a day that could not have ended soon enough.

* * *

In the morning, I fixed breakfast in a country style kitchen where I felt like a stranger. It was the first time I had been there in the capacity of, well, almost a wife. Ridge seemed quite comfortable at the prospect, playing the would-be husband role to perfection. Surprisingly, so did Ollie, who gobbled down his portion of waffles and maple syrup as if he was in dog heaven. I could tell it was going to be difficult to get him to return to his regular cuisine.

Too bad.

I had made up my mind that I would go back to my place sometime today to face the music. I was not going to be driven out of my own home by a dead body, not even Carter's. And I certainly wasn't ready to change the nature of my relationship with Ridge any time soon, even if he made it awfully tempting.

Ridge didn't have to talk me into accompanying him to the Honolulu Police Department's crime lab. He couldn't have kept me away. I had to know firsthand if the police had found any signs of foul play in Carter's death. Ollie had definitely greeted someone rudely. My guess was that it was someone other than Carter, though those scratches I had seen on Carter's legs bothered me.

"What type of man was Carter Delaney?" Ridge asked during the drive, and added before I could answer: "I actually met him once when he was still a prosecutor."

"Oh, really?" This was news to me.

Ridge shrugged. "It was no big deal. He attended a community policing seminar in Portland when I was on the force there. I never really got a feel for the man one way or the other, except that he seemed pretty hard-assed about wanting to get violent criminals and other troublemakers off the streets and behind bars where they belonged." Ridge paused. "Evidently somewhere along the line, his priorities took a serious hit."

I looked at Ridge after that last comment, wondering if he somehow resented Carter's success in the business world. I quickly rejected those thoughts. Ridge was as down to earth as anyone and believed in everyone succeeding in life to the best of their ability, as long as it was legal. This included Carter. Still, I sensed that Ridge, a man who had been in law enforcement much of his adult life, found it difficult to understand how Carter could walk away from the legal profession, leaving it behind for greener pastures.

Truthfully, I wondered the same thing myself at times, but never questioned his decision since the Carter Delaney I fell for had already established himself as a confident and successful businessman when I entered his world.

I took a moment to think about the type of man Carter Delaney was, which proved to be more difficult than I cared to admit. There was something about describing a person—Carter—in past tense that was unsettling, especially when just yesterday he was still very much alive and seemed in control of his life to some extent.

I regarded Ridge's handsome profile behind the wheel, and said levelly: "The Carter I knew was sweet, kind, smart, ambitious, opportunistic, and sometimes demanding of those around him."

I wasn't sure if I had said too much or not enough.

Ridge seemed to weigh my words while staring straight ahead. Finally, he looked at me and said: "Sounds like a guy who had it together—" He paused again. "Where do you suppose it all went wrong?"

I fluttered my lashes at him with minor annoyance. "Who said it did?"

I knew that I was defending my ex just for the sake of defending him. It was obvious that something was deeply wrong in Carter's life, and it had taken a deadly turn.

Ridge rounded the corner rather sharply. "Everything I know so far about Carter Delaney says it," he said. "For starters, he definitely went wrong when he let you get away. His second wife was screwing around on him. Then he ends up in your Jacuzzi—only it wasn't for a bath. Something or someone led him to that point. Seems to me that every move he's made lately somehow blew up in his face..."

"I never said Carter was a saint," I snapped, though agreeing that my ex had erred in cheating on me and ruining what had been a good thing by and large. "He had his faults just like anyone else. If you're asking me if I believe his problems drove him to commit suicide, I would say you're probably asking the *wrong* Mrs. Delaney. Carter's death is as much a mystery to me as it is to you. But that doesn't mean it was inevitable, especially at my house."

We stopped at a red light and Ridge planted his eyes on my face. "Everybody's death is inevitable," he said. "It's just a question of when, why, and who's responsible. If Delaney didn't do himself in, we'll know soon enough." He glanced at the light and back to me. "Either way, Skye, the last thing you want to do is blame yourself for his death—"

Ridge left it at that, and held my hand as if for reassurance. I squeezed his fingers and offered a nod of appreciation. Inside, part of me couldn't help but feel that if I had only been there or maybe if he had never left, Carter might still be alive...

CHAPTER 12

I had visited the state of the art crime laboratory frequently in my other life as a police detective. Fortunately, I had maintained a certain degree of respect in the department, in spite of some lingering sore feelings both ways, which allowed me access to areas normally off limits to civilians. It didn't hurt to be accompanied by a well-respected homicide detective either.

"Aloha, Skye," said Sumiyo Ishimoto, a forensic specialist and ten year veteran of the force. She almost looked like one of those TV forensic specialists complete with the white jacket. Her jet-black hair was in a loose chignon and she was several months pregnant with her third child.

"Hey, Sumiyo," I said.

"Nice to see you again," she said and then frowned. "Wish it were under different circumstances, though."

"Me, too." I flashed Ridge a quick look of despair.

"Sorry to hear about Carter—" Sumiyo seemed unsure what to say after that. Ridge came to her rescue.

"It's a shock to everyone in the department," he said, adding: "And probably lots of other people on the island." He scratched his pate and asked her: "What did you come up with?"

Sumiyo sighed. "Not much in the way of fingerprints, I'm afraid." She put on her gold-rimmed glasses and opened a folder. "The only legible prints lifted from the house belonged to Skye, the housekeeper, and"—she looked directly at Ridge—"we matched an index finger and thumb to you, Ridge..." She batted her lashes and he seemed to cringe before recovering quickly.

"That's it?" Ridge asked.

"Of course, we also found prints from the victim—"

Ridge gave me a disappointed face. I returned it. To Sumiyo, he said: "Mind if I take a look at that?" His eyes lowered to the report in her hand.

She offered it to him.

I read the report over his shoulder while Sumiyo was saying: "The hair strands we have appear to be consistent with those from Carter's head, and dog hair. Of course, DNA tests will confirm it."

The evidence for suicide seemed to be mounting. Short of the autopsy results, which weren't due until tomorrow, it now appeared that the person Ollie bit (assuming it wasn't Carter) offered the best chance for a case of murder.

Sumiyo seemed to be reading my mind. "I did come up with something interesting on the blood samples we got from the vet," she said looking at me. "And those taken from your bathroom—"

"Lay it on us," Ridge said eagerly.

Sumiyo led us to a table where the results of her lab work still lay. She lifted a clipboard. "First of all, the preliminary DNA results show that the samples almost certainly came from the same source," she said. "And, secondly, it seems that your dog bit someone with a rare blood type."

"How rare?" I asked.

"Very rare," she said. "Someone is walking around this city with AB negative blood and a very painful dog bite. I'm guessing it's a shoulder wound or a defensive wound on their arm or hand—"

Ridge wrote something down and then glanced at me. "Hmm... Rare blood type. That should narrow things down for us."

"I'll call the medical examiner's office to get Carter's blood type," Sumiyo said. "If only to rule out—"

"That won't be necessary, as far as ruling out goes," I interjected. "If I'm not mistaken"—and I was not—"Carter's blood type is AB negative."

I was starting to believe that Carter's death was a suicide, and that Ollie must have bitten him. Maybe that also accounted for the scratches I'd seen on Carter's legs. I deduced that Carter probably surprised Ollie when he entered the house without my presence and Ollie thought he was an intruder, which he was, and bit him.

But that still didn't tell me why Carter would kill himself. Nor did it end my suspicions as to the timing of his death. I found it more than a little shaky that Carter died before I could tell him that his wife was seeing another man and doing drugs.

Was that merely coincidence of the worst kind?

Then there was that reporter who seemed to know Carter had hired me, even though Carter had seemed to go out of his way to keep his suspicions from becoming public knowledge. What was that all about?

There was one more thing that just didn't sit right with me about Carter's death. Other than some scratches on his legs, I didn't recall seeing anything that looked like a dog bite on his body or any wounds with blood. Could there have actually been someone else in the house with the same rare blood type as Carter?

What were the odds of that?

Admittedly, the odds did not seem very good that Carter had been the victim of anyone other than himself. But I never allowed long odds alone to sway me one way or the other.

I withheld judgment for now, wishing I didn't have a sinking feeling that this was more the beginning than the end of the mysterious death of Carter Delaney.

Ridge dropped me off at my house at three-thirty. The police had completed their investigation of the premises and departed. I would pick up Ollie from Ridge's place later.

Right now, it was time for me to regain control of my life, hard as it would be. Alone. Ridge, bless his heart, did not argue the point. But he did offer to stay over. Or, at the very least, check on me often.

"I'll be all right," I promised, and made myself believe it.

He flashed me a doubtful look from the car. "Just do me a favor. Keep your gun loaded and close by. Just in case—"

I assured him I would, all things considered.

"I'll let you know when the autopsy report comes in," he said before driving off.

It now seemed as if the results would be a mere formality, which, in and of itself, left me weak in the knees with concern.

* * *

I went for a swim in the ocean. It beat swimming pools any day of the week. As with jogging, it was my answer to relaxing my mind and working out at the same time. I also used exercise as an opportunity for solitude when getting away from my world and all its troubles seemed a necessity. Only something was missing. It was Ollie as my constant companion for staying in shape. He also happened to be a very good swimmer. Ridge was still dog sitting for me. I'd have to suffer alone this time.

After an hour or so, I returned home exhausted with much work to do and precious little time to heal my emotional wounds. My house had been left a mess by the city's finest. All in the line of duty, they would say. I called it a bit overzealous, knowing they would get to go to their own orderly homes when they were done messing up mine.

I called Natsuko and asked her to come over for an extra day this week. I could use the help. She was only too happy to offer her assistance and also satisfy her huge appetite for curiosity, not to mention a free meal.

"It must have really freaked you out," Natsuko said with a contorted look on her face. "Seeing him in the tub like that and all..." She shivered.

It was ten times worse that you could ever imagine, I thought.

"I've definitely had better days—" I moaned, and gazed pensively out the kitchen window.

I considered the ineffectiveness of my security apparatus, which had apparently allowed Carter to enter uncontested, even with a key. The alarm seemed to be working perfectly now.

Natsuko shuffled her way into my periphery. Glancing at her, I asked: "Did you forget to activate the alarm when you left yesterday?"

"I don't think so," she responded defensively. Then in an about face, said: "I was late for a class and had to run back home for a minute. Maybe it did slip my mind...but I'm still pretty sure I set the alarm."

"All right," I told her, though feeling less than certain. It could explain how what was supposed to protect the place from intruders, or at least notify the security company, had not. I wasn't sure if this made me feel better or worse.

Natsuko was off the hook this time, as there were other issues to deal with.

"I couldn't believe it when I read in the paper that *the* Carter Delaney was *your* ex," she exclaimed. "I know you had the same last name and all, but—"

But you just can't imagine the wealthy and charming Carter actually being married to me, I thought, slightly amused. Giving her the benefit of my gaze, I muttered: "It was a long time ago. Before he became *the* Carter Delaney—"

We both took a moment to collect our thoughts before Natsuko asked: "Was he your first love?"

"Yes," I told her.

"And were you his?"

"I think so," I said while thinking that Carter had always hinted at that without coming right out and saying it. Later, it made no difference one way or the other. Especially when he decided that he had enough loving to go around.

"Did he want you back?" Natsuko asked, moving to the other side of me so that she could see my eyes, having apparently recovered from the shock of my marriage to Carter.

I made it easier for her by looking directly at her. "No! He was married to someone else."

Natsuko must have missed that in the paper, judging by her reaction. Never mind the fact that their marriage had hit a few bumps in the road of late.

"I'll bet he never got over you," she said mischievously.

If that were true, Carter sure chose a rotten way to make his point, I thought. I preferred to believe—suicide or not—the circumstances went well beyond his feelings for me.

I told Natsuko: "We both knew going our separate ways when we did was the best thing at the time. I doubt anything had changed since then."

Not for me it hadn't.

"One thing has changed," Natsuko said solemnly. "Your ex is dead—"

I left the kitchen on that depressing note. Natsuko followed, saying: "When the police came for my fingerprints and told me what happened, I realized I had just missed him—"

I regarded her with a raised brow. "What makes you say that?"

"I remember passing his car when I left," she said. "He almost hit me. I wondered why he was in such a hurry to—" She stopped on a dime.

"How do you know it was Carter?" I asked bluntly, knowing I was grasping at straws here.

Natsuko looked at me as if it were obvious. "He was driving a silver Cadillac DeVille like he owned the road or something. The police described his car to me."

"I see." After sucking in a deep breath, I told her unenthusiastically: "I think it's time we got to work in here."

For the next three hours, we cleaned up everything the police had left in disarray, and then some. But there was no cleansing away the memory of Carter in the bathtub. Whether the house could ever truly be the same again remained to be seen.

Natsuko had disappeared to who knows where when the doorbell rang. Since I felt relatively safe answering the door in broad daylight, in spite of being unarmed, I didn't bother to check to see who it was before opening it.

Standing before me was Carter's widow...

CHAPTER 13

Observing her up close, face to face, Darlene Delaney was thinner than I realized, but definitely not gaunt. There were no outward signs of drug abuse. In fact, she appeared remarkably healthy, with a clear and enviable complexion, while sporting her new haircut. She was dressed rather ostentatiously in a paprika skirt suit with a matching hat, an off-white French cuff blouse, and high heels. The shoes made us about the same height as I stood there in flats. At the moment—wearing my cleaning jeans and a baggy old tee shirt—I felt somewhat diminished in stature.

"You don't look like a private investigator—" Darlene said as we stood on opposite sides of the entryway.

It sounded more like an accusation than an observation.

I sneered, thinking sarcastically: *Well, you don't look like a woman in mourning. Or, for that matter, an adulteress and drug abuser. Obviously, looks can be deceiving. Or maybe not.* "PI's come in all shapes and sizes," I told her.

She touched the brim of her hat. "I guess."

I studied Carter's widow, curious as to the nature of her visit, which she revealed before I could beat her to the punch.

"I could never do that sort of thing," Darlene told me. "Carter wouldn't have allowed it, even if I'd wanted to. It wouldn't fit his idea of the 'good little wife'...at least not the second time around—"

The man hadn't been dead for forty-eight hours and his widow was wasting no time drawing unflattering comparisons between us.

"I guess people change," I said resentfully, not sure whom the resentment should be directed toward. Truth be told, I was the one who had changed more than Carter. Yet he clearly seemed to be in the middle of some major turmoil in his life—before it ended.

Natsuko chose this well-timed moment to resurface. "I have an exam in the morning I need to prepare for," she advised me, practically squeezing between us to get out the door. She eyed me with a good-luck-you'll-probably-need-it look, and said: "I'll see you next week, Skye—"

"Mahalo for coming to help," I told her.

She smiled. "No problem. I can always use the extra money." Then Natsuko added: "If you need someone to talk to..."

"I have your number," I finished for her, smiling appreciatively.

As soon as she left, Darlene said unevenly: "If this is a bad time..."

I gave my uninvited guest a sarcastic look. "I wonder what gives you that impression."

Her mouth became a straight line. "Look, I really didn't want to come here to—"

"Then why did you?" I felt I was entitled to ask.

Our eyes met. "It seemed like it was time for us to meet," she uttered, licking the gloss on her lips, "under the circumstances. I'm guessing if I hadn't come to see you, it was only a matter of time before you showed up at my door."

The lady was slick, I thought, and obviously brighter than I'd made her out to be. Made me wonder just what she was up to. Did she come to gloat over stealing Carter, several years too late? Or to solicit sympathy from someone who could relate to her loss?

I gave her the benefit of the doubt and decided to play along for now. "You're right, we were going to have to cross paths sooner or later," I said coolly. "Now is probably as good a time as any."

She took that as her invitation to come in and it was.

In the foyer, Darlene flashed me what looked like a practiced smile and put out a perfectly manicured hand. "Carter has told me so much about you," she gushed, "I feel as though we've already met."

We had, in a roundabout way, but I wasn't ready to show my hand just yet.

"So do I," I hummed.

I shook her hand. It felt moist, and I wondered if it was from the heat or nervousness beneath her cool exterior. It occurred to me that drug addicts were prone to perspiring while in need of a fix.

We stood there staring at each other in silence for a few moments of where-do-we-go-from-here before I broke the ice. "Can I get you something to drink?" I asked her. "I've got beer, wine, papaya juice, coffee, tea..."

She shrugged. "I'll have what you're having."

Two glasses of papaya juice coming up, I thought. I went into the kitchen, half-expecting her to follow. She did not. At the last moment, I had a change of heart and poured some red wine into two goblets.

I found Darlene in the living room, which was the last room Natsuko and I had worked on. It was presentable, but there was still the distinct smell of death in the air, as Carter's corpse had passed through here on its way to the morgue. We would both have to deal with it in our own way.

Darlene seemed fascinated by my ceiling fan, as though it were spewing out air crookedly or something.

"Your wine," I said, startling her.

She took the glass and sat on the sofa. I joined her.

She met my eyes and asked bluntly: "Why did Carter choose to kill himself in your tub? I mean, couldn't he have chosen a more dignified way to commit suicide?"

I wondered why she was so sure he had taken his own life. Granted, the tide seemed to be leaning in that direction, but it was almost as if Darlene knew more than she had apparently let on to the police.

I sipped my wine. "The exact cause of Carter's death is still under investigation."

She gave me a doubtful gaze. "Something tells me you don't believe he killed himself."

"It doesn't really matter what I believe," I told her warily. "What makes you think he killed himself, other than what you've read? Was Carter suicidal?"

Darlene hesitated. "He was a little depressed, but I didn't think it would come to this."

"It *has* come to this!" I argued. "Carter was your husband. Why the hell don't you tell me why he's dead now, Darlene?"

She sighed and looked away from me. "Sure, I'll tell you—" After drinking some wine, she turned back to face me. "If you really want to know, I think Carter killed himself in *your* house to punish and humiliate me."

I nearly choked as though I had a chicken bone lodged in my throat. "You've got to be kidding. Why in the hell would Carter come into my house and drown himself because he wanted to punish and humiliate you? Excuse me, but you didn't find him. I hardly think—"

Darlene didn't flinch. "If you knew Carter the way I did, you'd understand why. He's never been happy with me or his daughter, who he never wanted brought into this world. I was never good enough for him, no matter what I did or tried to do. He wanted to make me pay for taking him away from his precious Skye, who could do no wrong—"

I was shocked by her assertions. The Carter I was married to never held me in such high esteem. He certainly found enough faults to go elsewhere for his sexual needs...and his desire to father a child.

I viewed his widow's words with a healthy dose of skepticism.

"With Carter, everything had to be dramatic," Darlene continued bitterly. "And what better way to kill himself than somewhere where *you* would be sure to find him, knowing that I would have to live with it for the rest of my life." She sighed. "That no good bastard!"

In that moment, I couldn't help but sympathize with her to some degree, having been on the receiving end of Carter's deep betrayal. Was Carter really so unhappy with his life that he would end it at a time when he was searching for answers?

Answers that I could have provided for him had he kept our appointment.

Could the man I had once loved actually have been so spiteful as to commit such a violent act in order to hurt his wife and daughter? Did that make me—the one who literally mopped up his remains—any less a victim?

Whatever else was going on with Darlene, I couldn't help but think that she too must have loved Carter in some way, shape, or form, in spite of her transgressions.

"I'm sorry about Carter," I told her sincerely. "At this point, I don't know why he died at my house, but the last thing either of us needs is to blame ourselves or each other."

Now was not the time to play on my suspicions, not to mention facts, surrounding her.

"You're right, of course," Darlene said, and offered me a tearful smile. "You, if anyone, should know what I'm going through—" I wasn't sure if I needed to read between the lines. She put the glass to her lips, sipped, and then said: "I guess I'd better be going. I still have to make the funeral arrangements. And I haven't found the courage yet to tell my daughter that her dad is dead..."

I didn't envy Darlene in that sense. Carter had truly loved his daughter. Now the girl was fatherless, and would probably suffer as a result.

I couldn't really offer the widow any advice, since I had never walked in her shoes. However, I did say a silent prayer for Darlene in the hope that her own actions wouldn't result in more grief for her daughter.

I watched through the blinds as Darlene Delaney screeched away in her red BMW and couldn't help but wonder how much of her ordeal was self-inflicted. Another side of me wondered if in some strange way I was just as culpable.

CHAPTER 14

He watched from the cluster of palm trees as the housekeeper left the residence, got in a car, and drove off quickly, as if she had somewhere more important to be. She never even bothered to look in his direction. Not that she would have seen him behind the cover the trees provided around Skye Delaney's property. That was just the way he wanted it. There was no reason to draw suspicion at this point.

He was much more interested in the meeting taking place inside between Darlene Delaney and Skye Delaney. He imagined that Carter would love this. His ex and his widow sharing bedroom stories and other dirt on the former prosecutor, businessman, and royal screw up. If either woman only knew the half of it.

He could almost hear them pointing their damned fingers at each other threateningly. *"Carter killed himself because of you,"* he said mimicking Darlene. Then he responded as Skye: *"The hell he did. He killed himself because he couldn't bear knowing that his wife was a damned whore and a drug addict."*

A brawl could ensue. He'd put his money squarely behind Skye, who was definitely fitter and just plain tougher when push came to shove.

Yes, Skye Delaney was definitely his type of woman. He was glad he had finally gotten to meet her—kind of. The problem was she didn't know it as such. And he planned to keep it that way until it was time for them to meet formally.

Darlene came out the front door. He couldn't tell if she was pissed or satisfied that she'd covered her ass. She got into that red car that Carter had given her, started it, and, just like the housekeeper, zoomed off to a destination unknown. That didn't mean he couldn't hazard a guess as to where she was headed. He'd bet it was to see that asshole lawyer she thought was her *secret* lover boy.

Secrets are made to be exposed, he thought.

He pondered that for a moment of glee, and then noted it was Skye's turn to emerge from the house. He quickly ducked behind a tree. It wouldn't be smart if she caught him snooping around. There might be questions.

Then more questions.

And he wasn't about to do any talking. Not yet anyway.

He waited out of sight until he heard her car drive off. For a moment, he considered entering the premises while the lady and her dog were away. Then he decided not to press his luck.

Not like Carter Delaney had pressed his luck. Until he ran out of it...

He made his way through more palm trees on the dead-end street until he arrived at the next street where his car awaited.

CHAPTER 15

Murder was the Medical Examiner's official conclusion as the cause of Carter Delaney's death. Ridge stood there with his mouth agape in the examining room where Carter's remains lay on a table in front of us. In spite of being repulsed by the idea that the discolored corpse in front of me was once my husband, I felt somewhat relieved that he hadn't taken the easy way out by committing suicide. He had been the victim of foul play, but it was still a hard pill to swallow.

Dr. R. Mitsuo Isagawa was the Chief Medical Examiner for the City and County of Honolulu. The rather frail, black-haired man in his early fifties had personally conducted the autopsy. Because the decedent happened to be a former lawyer for the Department of the Prosecuting Attorney and one of the city's most prominent businessmen, there could be no question as to how he died or who determined such cause.

Mitsuo had probably seen just about every type of death there was. He gave me a fatherly look with irregular furrows lining his brow. As a cop, I had spent more than my share of time listening with difficulty to the results of autopsies he had performed. This time would undoubtedly be the hardest.

"Are you sure you want to hear this, Skye?" Mitsuo asked in a gravelly voice, glancing at the body, "And see Carter like this—?"

I cleared my throat and said with determination: "I'm a big girl, Mitsuo. I have to know how Carter died, no matter how hard it is to listen to."

The three of us exchanged looks before Ridge eased his fingers between mine, and Mitsuo said: "Carter died from neck compression..."

"So he didn't drown then?" Ridge asked.

"No," Mitsuo said flatly. "He was already dead before his head hit the water—" He looked me in the eye and continued: "Carter's neck was crushed while he was in a horizontal position—likely on a hardwood floor, judging by the scratches and dust particles found on his body. I'd say someone who was very strong used either a knee backed by their full weight on his neck, or maybe even their bare hands..."

Mitsuo tilted Carter's limp head from side to side as if to illustrate his point. "Whoever did this probably knew exactly what they were doing, if the plan was to inflict a great deal of pain, commit murder, then try to make it look like suicide by putting his head under water." Mitsuo squinted. "But, by then, the lethal damage had already been done."

"You okay?" Ridge whispered to me worriedly as Mitsuo pulled a sheet over Carter's body.

I nodded even though I felt a little lightheaded. I reached deep within to keep myself from passing out, not wanting to let this get to me in a way I couldn't control. Satisfied that I had shaken it off, I asked Mitsuo: "So you're saying that Carter was *definitely* killed by a man?"

Mitsuo regarded me and Ridge with one eyebrow cocked. "I don't recall saying that. The only definite thing about murder is that someone is dead." He sighed. "Yes, the killer was most likely a man, though an enraged or strong woman probably could have done the same thing, especially if she used something like a barbell or some kind of heavy object to assist her."

Ridge rubbed his chin and asked skeptically: "Could a woman have also carried Delaney up the stairs after possibly killing him on the main floor and then put him in the Jacuzzi?"

Mitsuo pondered the question. So did I. After a few minutes, he said: "That's one you'll have to figure out, Detective Larsen." He paused, planted his gaze on my face, and said: "Of course, no one ever said the killer acted alone..."

One of Carter's arms suddenly dropped from the table. I gasped as the lifeless, pale limb dangled. Was it a post-mortem reflex? I wondered. Or was it a cry of help from the other side?

Instinctively, I lifted the arm and noticed no sign of Ollie's handiwork. I asked Mitsuo: "Did Carter have any wounds that could have come from a dog bite?"

His eyes widened. "No." He put the arm back under the sheet. "Why do you ask?"

I told him about Sumiyo Ishimoto's speculations regarding the dog bite.

Mitsuo flipped through his autopsy notes. "There was no indication that Carter was bitten by a dog." He gave Ridge, then me, a puzzled look. "If your dog bit someone with AB negative blood, I'm afraid it wasn't Carter. DNA tests should confirm that."

Then it must have been Carter's killer, I told myself. Carter's death had suddenly taken on a whole new dimension—beginning with the reality that we were no longer dealing with a suicide, but cold-blooded murder.

"By the way," Mitsuo said to both of us, "this probably doesn't have any bearing on your investigation, but I thought you should know that Carter was legally intoxicated at the time of his death—"

Ridge and I pondered that information.

* * *

"That could explain how Delaney ended up at your house instead of your office," Ridge said when we were back in the car.

"And," I suggested, "it could explain how someone may have been able to murder Carter apparently without much of a struggle."

Even to the end, Carter looked like he was in pretty good shape. He had always prided himself on being mentally and physically prepared for any trouble that dared come his way. Obviously both had failed him when he needed them most.

"Sorry I ever doubted your woman's intuition or whatever the hell it was about Delaney," Ridge said, breaking a stony silence. "Maybe in his own way the man was trying to tell you something," he added, changing lanes.

"Maybe in his own way, Carter was," I agreed. "Only he never got the chance to finish what he started."

"We'll see if the DNA sample Ollie took from the presumed killer matches anyone in the CODIS database," Ridge said, referring to the Combined DNA Index System, a national DNA databank that can help identify persons involved in criminal activity.

"That would certainly simplify things," I said, "at least in terms of telling us who we're looking for." I knew that actually finding the suspect would not be as simple.

"Don't get your hopes up," Ridge told me. "It could go either way."

At this point, I wasn't willing to bet the house that it would go my way. "Maybe we'll get lucky," I said, sounding less than optimistic.

"Yeah, maybe," Ridge said. "In the meantime, I don't suppose I can persuade you to stay out of this, can I?"

My eyelids fluttered at him defiantly. "I wouldn't even want you to try—"

He sighed. "This is a police matter, Skye. We're talking about the murder of your ex. You'll only get in the way if you go around asking questions to the wrong people—and that includes Delaney's widow."

If only it were as cut and dry as letting the police do their job, I thought. Since Carter was my ex-husband and client, I felt a moral obligation to do my own investigation into his death. I owed him that much for what we once had.

"Carter was murdered in my house, Ridge. Until I know why, please don't ask me to look the other way." I softened my tone and added: "Meanwhile, I'll do my best to avoid stepping on the toes of police detectives...or at least one in particular—"

Of course, I could offer no guarantees. Wisely, Ridge never asked for any.

* * *

After I got to my office, I went over my recent case files with a fine tooth comb. I couldn't rule out that someone with an unfulfilled grudge or perhaps extreme dissatisfaction with my work might have wished to do away with me. I wondered if somehow Carter's death might have tragically been a case of being in the wrong place at the wrong time.

The problem with that theory was that he should not have been at my house in the first place. So why was he? If the killer had meant to kill me, why kill Carter instead and keep me alive for another day to be better prepared for the next possible attempt?

My search produced nothing viable that I could give to the police, much less send my own warning bells into high alert. I made a couple of calls to clients where the conclusion of the case had caused particular grief and resentment to others. They gave no indication they were in fear of their lives and doubted I had any reason to be as it related to them.

I kept the possibilities open and would keep backtracking on the small chance that I was a marked woman. But my better half believed that the intended target was Carter, and the mission had been accomplished.

Not waiting around to see if there was a DNA match with a known offender, I spent the next two and a half hours trying in vain to locate a clinic or hospital where someone with AB negative blood had been treated for an injury, possibly a dog bite, in the last few days. So far, the results had been pretty much the same with statements such as: "We have no record of anyone with that blood type or dog bite being treated recently."

I put the bottled water to my lips in frustration and thirst, while viewing my computer screen and the dwindling number of medical facilities left in the city. Had Ollie's bite been deep enough for the person to require treatment? I wondered. I also considered that the victim could have gone to a private physician or somewhere outside Honolulu.

Luck was always a welcome friend in the private eye business, especially if it came quickly and conveniently. That did not seem to be in the cards this day, until a ray of hope suddenly emerged...

"Yes, someone with type AB negative blood was treated at the Honolulu Medical Center two days ago," said the nurse informatively, "and released..."

"What can you tell me about the patient?" I asked hopefully.

A pause. "I'm afraid, not much," she said. "All patient records are confidential."

I posed as an investigator with the Centers for Disease Control, and explained that we were tracking individuals with this rare blood type who may be susceptible to a potentially deadly bacteria strain.

"All we really need is some basic information on the patient," I said smoothly. "Race, age, and gender can usually give us a good indication of whether the person is a high or low risk candidate. And, of course, a name so that we can get in touch with him or her to be tested, if necessary—"

The nurse seemed to be biting the bait. "Well, let's see..." she mumbled. "Does a seven-year-old Filipino girl sound like a high risk candidate?"

"No," I told her, and slouched in my chair. Damn. Unfortunately, I was back to square one.

CHAPTER 16

Ridge stepped into the office of Honolulu Mayor Lloyd Newman, who had requested to speak to him personally as the detective in charge of the Carter Delaney murder investigation. Ridge had tried to get around this, not wanting or needing the mayor to tell him how to do his job. But when the mayor wants to see you, you go. So ordered his boss Captain Felix Chu, who was also present, along with Detective Henry Kawakami.

They were seated around a square glass table. This was to be the sixty-something mayor's last term in office, with an eye supposedly on the governorship.

But there was still some unfinished business.

After some small talk, mostly by the mayor, he got serious and said to Ridge in a tough voice: "I don't think I need to tell you, Detective Larsen, that it's imperative we get to the bottom of Carter Delaney's murder as quickly as possible."

"I understand that, sir," Ridge responded tightly, looking him right in the eye.

"Do you?" Newman asked before glancing at Captain Chu, a thirty-year veteran on the force.

"What's not to understand?" Ridge asked, hoisting a brow, as if he hadn't a clue. "You want the case solved. So do I."

Newman sucked in a breath, looked at Homicide Detective Kawakami who was a thirty-seven-year-old native Hawaiian, and back at Ridge, before saying: "When you were assigned this case, Detective Larsen, the assumption was that we were looking at a possible suicide." He paused, eyeing all the parties present. "Now that we know Carter Delaney was a victim of foul play—"

Ridge's brows came together, not liking the implication. He decided to speak up before this went any further. "Are you saying you don't think I'm qualified to run this investigation?"

"Not at all, detective," Newman said calmly. "You're a damned good cop. At least that's what everyone keeps telling me. But Delaney was a good friend of mine, and active in the community. It's important to people in this city that we don't give the impression of dragging our feet in bringing his killer to justice. For that reason, we think you should have as much help as you need, leaving no stones unturned in conducting this investigation."

He stopped and deferred to Captain Chu, who said flatly: "It's still your case, Ridge. But I'm bringing in Detective Kawakami to help run the investigation. Hopefully, together, you two can make everybody happy by getting some hard evidence and arresting whoever is responsible for Carter Delaney's death." Sighing, he faced Ridge and asked: "Any questions?"

Ridge felt as though he was being put on the spot. He could rant and rave about this conspiracy to undermine his authority in investigating Carter Delaney's death. But what good would it do, when he was clearly outnumbered by those who counted? He decided to make the best of the situation and try to put this case behind him as soon as possible.

"None whatsoever," he told his boss.

Chu nodded agreeably, as did Newman.

Ridge regarded the muscular Henry Kawakami, whom he had worked with briefly once before, and said: "Welcome aboard."

Kawakami nodded and asked: "I understand you ran a DNA sample of a suspect bitten by Skye Delaney's dog through the national database?"

Ridge pursed his lips. "Yeah. There was no match," he said. "Whoever the dog bit, they aren't in the system. But it did indicate that the DNA belonged to a male." In fact, he had already assumed this to be the case, given the nature of Delaney's murder. But Ridge wasn't ruling out female involvement in the homicide, with the victim's widow a prime suspect, considering recent circumstances.

"So we'll have to rely more on good old-fashioned detective work to get the bastard," Kawakami said, running a hand through his coarse dark hair.

"Yeah, whatever it takes," Ridge said.

Everyone seemed in agreement on that.

"There is one other thing..." Newman said, looking directly at Ridge.

Isn't there always? Ridge thought to himself, sensing what was coming.

"I've heard rumors that you're involved with Carter Delaney's ex-wife—" Newman looked uncomfortable mentioning it.

Ridge thought about denying it, especially with Captain Chu looking on, but then figured what was the point? Especially when he wanted their relationship to become public knowledge. The fact that he was seeing Skye had nothing to do with this case, per se. Or his ability to conduct the investigation.

"They're more than just rumors," Ridge admitted. "Skye and I are dating, so..."

"I understand she's an ex-cop turned security consultant and private eye," Newman said.

He's obviously done his homework, Ridge thought. Or more like he'd gotten someone else to do it for him.

"Right on all counts," Ridge said, wondering where this was going.

Newman scratched his nose. "Will she be a problem?"

Ridge raised a brow. "A problem...?" He knew damned well what the mayor was talking about, but he wanted to force him to say it.

Newman adjusted in the chair. "The last thing we need is for Ms. Delaney, with her background and professional skills, interfering with this investigation. Think you can keep her in line?"

Ridge thought about it for maybe one second, then said: "With all due respect, Mayor, it's not my job to keep Skye Delaney in line. I have no control over what she does as a private investigator or citizen for that matter—"

Newman frowned. "Don't get me wrong, Detective Larsen, I don't give a damn about who you're sleeping with. This is about *not* jeopardizing this case for any conflicts of interest. I hope I'm making myself clear."

Ridge composed himself before responding. "You are. But, just for the record, there is no conflict on my part. I intend to treat this case like any other and Skye completely understands that. She'd never ask or expect me to compromise the investigation in any way." *Not that she's above asking for favors*, Ridge thought, which he was happy to give, as long as they both understood where to draw the line.

Captain Chu seemed satisfied and so did Detective Kawakami. Mayor Newman gave a polite nod and said: "Glad to hear that." He stood. "I guess this meeting is over. The sooner you wrap this case up, the better for all of us."

Ridge took the words seriously, believing that the longer the investigation dragged out, the greater the pressure to solve Carter Delaney's murder, particularly with Skye just as determined to get at the truth.

CHAPTER 17

It was my turn to pay Darlene Delaney a visit.

This time it was anything but a get-acquainted house call. Whatever problems she and Carter may have had, there was no escaping the fact that the woman he had chosen over me was having an affair at the time of his death and was also involved with a drug dealer. In my mind and experience, that was more than sufficient reason to make her a leading suspect in Carter's murder before, during, or after the fact.

Whomever Ollie bit had no DNA record on file with CODIS. But the person did have AB negative blood, which would help narrow the field. Since the suspect was believed to be a male, that would rule Darlene out. However, she got no free pass from me for possibly being complicit in Carter's murder.

The electronic gate was open when I arrived. Darlene's BMW was parked in the driveway. It looked like it had just been washed. *At least she has her priorities in order*, I thought cynically. Or maybe she had something to hide. Noticeably absent was Carter's Cadillac, currently impounded by the police as possible evidence in his murder.

Professionally dressed in a periwinkle suit and sandals, I moseyed up to the arched double doors and rang the bell three times before someone answered. It was not Darlene, but a forty-something dark-skinned female.

"Yes?" she asked in a non-friendly voice.

"I'm here to see Ms. Delaney," I said, unsure of how to address the woman with whom I shared a name and, for a time, the man behind it.

The woman batted brown eyes at me and said: "*Mrs.* Delaney is mourning the loss of her husband and isn't seeing anyone she doesn't have to—"

"I think she'll see me," I said firmly. "Tell her it's Skye Delaney—"

She gave me a disbelieving look, as if I somehow did not measure up to the name, then finally said: "Just a moment..." before closing the doors behind her.

When they opened again, it was Darlene who stood there. She was a far cry from the stylish woman I was used to seeing. She wore no makeup and had on an oversized sweater, jeans, and was barefoot.

"Elberta is our housekeeper," Darlene told me. "With the press hounding me since Carter's death, I've found it easier to have her screen visitors."

I understood, but said bluntly: "We need to talk!"

She regarded me coldly. "I think you're right," she spat, "considering that my husband was *murdered* in *your* house—"

It was a reality I was still trying to wrap my mind around, even as I considered what role, if any, his widow may have played in his death.

Once inside, I glanced around at the spacious, immaculate setting with high-beamed ceilings, walls painted in earth tones, French doors, and plantation shutters. The architecture was exquisite and the bamboo floors were accentuated with Oriental rugs. I marveled at the Great Room's contemporary furnishings.

All in all, the place seemed to represent everything Carter had dreamed of in a home, right down to the neoclassical art and collectibles. I got a glimpse of Elberta moving from one room to another, but not before she pinned me with her glare. She seemed to resent my presence.

Might as well get used to me, I thought, *because you and your employer are going to be seeing a lot of Skye Delaney until Carter's murder has been solved and the killer or killers are brought to justice.*

I followed Darlene into the huge study. It had a wet bar and an impressive wall-length wooden ornamental bookcase filled with Carter's law books. That part of his life had apparently always remained with Carter, even if it had taken a back seat to his strong desire to become a force in the business world.

"I'd give you the grand tour, but..." Darlene left it at that.

"Don't knock yourself out," I told her sarcastically. "I didn't come here to see what Carter left behind."

We settled into leather accent chairs around a glass top coffee table, facing a floor to ceiling window with a magnificent view of the ocean beyond a swimming pool.

Darlene frowned. "He left behind a wife and a daughter who will never really get to know her father..."

Although I concurred with her, especially regarding the daughter, I said tersely: "Carter didn't *leave* either of you intentionally. Someone *chose* to snuff out his life."

She stared at that reality for a moment, and said in a monotone voice: "Yes, that is what the police are saying." Darlene drew in a long sigh. "I think I need a drink..." She rose swiftly and headed for the wet bar. "Can I get you something?"

Three o'clock in the afternoon was usually way too early for me to indulge, particularly when investigating a murder, but I found myself borrowing her words from our previous meeting: "I'll have what you're having."

She made two martinis. Handing me one, Darlene said: "Carter told me that I drink too much. Funny, but I often accused him of the same thing..." She put the glass to her mouth. "I guess that makes me a living alcoholic, and him a dead one—"

It was hard for me to believe that Carter was an alcoholic, but when I thought about it, the signs were there long before the medical examiner told me that Carter's blood alcohol level was excessive at the time of his death. The man I was married to had always been able to carry his liquor. Now I strongly suspected he had carried it way too far.

Darlene put her glass on the table and looked at me. "So what is it we need to talk about? Other than the fact that the man we both married just happened to be at your house when somebody decided to kill him." Her eyes shifted distrustfully at me. "Maybe you can tell me what the hell Carter was doing there. Or am I supposed to guess?"

I tasted the martini and took a moment to try and figure out if this woman was actually implying that I had reversed the tables and was having an affair with Carter. I would never have stooped to her level, but I let Darlene consider the possibility just a while longer, fully aware I could be looking at an accomplice to murder.

I took a deep breath, then said levelly: "Carter hired me as a private investigator—"

Darlene's eyes widened and she licked her lips. "Well, this ought to be interesting—"

"Oh, it is," I assured her, and wet my throat with more drink. "He suspected you were having an affair..." I watched Carter's widow suddenly grow tense. "He wanted me to verify it. At four o'clock on the day Carter died, I was supposed to meet him at my office to tell him what I had learned in my investigation. Only he never showed up. He must have decided to meet me at my house. That's where I found him—"

Darlene's eyes became slits. "That bastard!" After sipping her drink, she asked accusingly: "So, what were you going to tell my husband?"

I un-crossed my legs and sat erect in the chair. Looking her in the eye, I said: "Well, for starters, that you were—*are*—having an affair..."

She was silent, apparently fuming inside at the thought that I had discovered her dirty little secret. Of course, that wasn't the half of it.

Darlene's nostrils flared. "It must have been quite a perverse thrill for you—his ex-wife—to discover that I was cheating on him just like he cheated on you."

I sneered. "Don't flatter yourself. It was strictly business on my end—nothing more." I had the feeling she wasn't buying that, so I added: "To be perfectly honest, my marriage to Carter was over long before *you* came into the picture, for all intents and purposes—"

I had managed to convince myself of that when I looked back now.

Darlene's brows contracted as she gave me a look that wavered between uncertainty and edginess. She asked cautiously: "And so you're here to tell me what? You think because I was cheating on Carter, I had something to do with his death?"

"The thought crossed my mind," I replied honestly.

She set her jaw defiantly. "Well I'm sorry to disappoint you, but you're wrong—at least about my being responsible for Carter's death." She paused. "Okay, I won't deny that I was having an affair...what's the point? But that doesn't make me a murderer—" As if it made a difference, she added: "Not my own husband...the father of my daughter—"

I went back to the "doesn't make me a murderer" part. "What does it make you?" I dared to ask, having my own ideas.

Darlene finished off her drink in one fell swoop. "It makes me a normal, healthy woman who was damned sick and tired of being rejected by a husband who was too critical, too busy, and too womanizing!"

Darlene caught my attention with those last two words, and she knew it. "Are you saying Carter was having an affair?"

She peered at me. "Figure it out yourself. You're the detective *and* former wife. Once an asshole, always an asshole! He didn't know the meaning of the word *faithful*—certainly not with me, and obviously not with you. I swear, I don't even know why he and I ever got married in the first place—"

I could think of two very good reasons. One was the thrill of the chase, which clearly wasn't that thrilling once Carter had caught and married Darlene. The other was the very real possibility that Darlene was pregnant, which would have been all the more reason for Carter to do the right thing, in his mind, and marry her.

Then I thought of one other reason. Darlene had coined the phrase rather aptly: *Once an asshole, always an asshole!* But that was beside the point at the moment.

Darlene leaned back in her chair. "His latest fling was a hula dancer. Carter was spending most of his nights and a fair share of his days with her for the past three months."

Despite being well aware that Carter had trouble keeping his pants on, this revelation caught me completely off guard. It was as if I had expected him to treat his new wife with the respect he should have given me. But why would a zebra change his stripes with a change of scenery?

"Sorry to shatter your illusions about Carter, if you had any left," Darlene said with a self-satisfied grin. "I accepted his faults for the sake of our child. But I'm only human with needs that he was either incapable of or unwilling to fulfill."

"Does that include doing drugs?" I asked point-blank.

"Excuse me?" Darlene said with a look of bewilderment.

"My guess is crack—"

She fixed me with hard eyes. "What the hell are you talking about?"

I lifted two photographs from my purse. One showed her with the Hawaiian drug dealer, the other was a close-up shot of the packet he handed her.

I passed Darlene my photographic work. "Maybe these will help jog your memory of what the hell I'm talking about—" She gazed at the prints and colored. "Look familiar?"

She grimaced. "Where did you get these?"

"The same place I got these—" I added to her collection the telling photos of her and her lover, Edwin Hugh Axelrod. "Remember, I'm a private investigator. I was supposed to hand these over to Carter, but someone murdered him first."

Darlene shot to her feet and threw the pictures on the table while glaring at me. "You had no right!"

A natural reaction, I thought. Was it defensive? Or apprehensive?

"I was only doing my job," I informed her with a touch of regret, as if I'd done something wrong in exposing her secrets. "Did Carter know about the drugs?" I had to ask, partly out of curiosity, but more as a possible motive for his death. "Maybe your drug dealer friend freaked out after Carter confronted him or something."

She licked her lips nervously. "Kalolo had no reason to kill Carter. He didn't know we were married and Carter never knew about Kalolo or..." Darlene hesitated while favoring me warily. "Should I have a lawyer here, or what? I mean I wouldn't want anything I say to you to get back to your cop friends. Or is that what this is all about? You're just here to set me up."

"I'm not here on behalf of the police," I promised her. Not that they were too far behind me in trying to connect her to Carter's death, I thought. "I work for and by myself." I chose to forget for the time being that Ridge was heading the investigation into Carter's murder, making us unofficial partners in this case. "My only interest is in finding out who might have killed Carter, and why. Anything else you tell me won't leave this room."

Darlene flashed her blues eyes at me for a moment or two of, no doubt, reluctance, fear, anger, maybe even betrayal—before seeming to decide it was better to tell me than my so-called cop friends. She made herself another drink without offering me one this time, and sat back down.

"I've been using cocaine recreationally for a couple of years," Darlene admitted. "Ironically, I was introduced to the stuff at a party Carter took me to—" She put the glass to her lips. "He was too damned busy doing whatever with whomever to notice. Kalolo—the guy in the picture—is just someone I met at a club. He knows me only by my middle name. Amber." She wrinkled her nose. "He isn't a big time drug dealer or anything. If I need something, he knows where to get it. We only meet maybe once a month—"

That's one time too many, I thought. I wanted to tell *Amber* that, in light of her obvious alcohol and drug abuse, she might consider entering a treatment program. But I decided it wasn't my place to tell her. Besides that could be the least of the troubles she faced.

Assuming Kalolo was not involved in Carter's death, it still left Darlene's attorney-lover as a suspect, which I relayed to her.

"Edwin couldn't have killed Carter," Darlene was quick to come to his defense. "Yes, we've been having an affair, but we were both married. Neither of us wanted anything more than sex—" Her eyes met mine. "Carter may have suspected, but he never had any proof..." She rubbed her nose and sighed heavily. "Whatever you think of me, you've got to believe that, in spite of our screwed up marriage, I never wanted Carter dead."

Her argument was convincing, if not altogether airtight. It was too soon to eliminate suspects—especially one who, on the surface, seemed to have the most to gain by her husband's death.

"Someone obviously did," I told her with a catch to my voice. "You have any ideas who that could be?"

She ran a hand through her hair. "As I told the police, Carter kept his professional and personal life totally separate. He was not the ex-prosecutor or the sharp businessman in our relationship." She took another sip of her martini. "I honestly don't know who would want to kill him..."

Perhaps, I thought guardedly, watching her eyes watch me. But Ollie had taken a piece of someone and I couldn't help but think that Darlene knew more than she was letting on.

"Did you know Carter's blood type was AB negative?" I asked curiously.

"Yes," she said coolly. "Why?"

"My dog bit someone with that blood type. Only it wasn't Carter."

Darlene shrugged. "I don't know what to tell you. I don't make a habit of asking people their blood type. And, in case you're wondering, I'm O positive—"

Looks like you're off the hook on that one, I thought, knowing that the victim of Ollie's bite was an unknown male. *But it still doesn't let you off the hook completely. Not till some missing pieces of your puzzle fall neatly into place.*

"That wasn't exactly on my mind," I told her truthfully. "But it's something the police may want to know, just for the record."

The phone rang twice before stopping. Momentarily, Elberta entered the study.

"Your attorney's on the line," she informed Darlene, and eyed me sternly. "Do you want me to tell him you'll call back?"

"That's not necessary," I answered for Darlene, wondering if her attorney was Edwin Axelrod, the same man she was sleeping with. I got to my feet. "It's time for me to go home and let my dog out for some fresh air. He just hasn't been himself lately since witnessing Carter's death—" If Darlene was involved, I thought, that just might shake her up a bit.

"It's better that your dog saw it, believe me," Darlene said as if she could vouch for this. "How frightening would that have been if you or I saw Carter murdered?"

"Pretty frightening," I admitted, though feeling no less sorry that Ollie had been there to see it. Except for the fact that he'd probably taken a chunk out of the probable killer, which would ultimately lead to the person's arrest.

Darlene walked me to the door. "My daughter just started piano lessons," Darlene said. "I was never any good with musical instruments, but she really seems to like it." Her face became downcast. "I'm seriously contemplating having Ivy stay with relatives until this thing blows over. It's really been terrible for her. She keeps asking me when is her daddy coming back. She doesn't understand that he isn't—"

I did, only too well.

* * *

Ollie wasted no time scampering out into the backyard. Though the vet had given Ollie a clean bill of health, I had a feeling he would never be at peace until Carter's killer was apprehended.

That went double for me.

"Ollie," I called out to him after he chased the Frisbee to the end of the fenced-in yard. He quickly brought it back to me. "What would I ever do without you, boy?" I hoped I didn't have to find out anytime soon.

While Ollie playfully licked my face, I told him: "You may be the only one who can identify Carter's killer." Once a dog had that blood scent in his nostrils, he would never forget it. "If only I could take you inside and out of every damned house in the city to snuff out a murderer—"

Later that evening I paid a visit to my neighbors, hoping they might have seen someone or heard something. Fat chance. One of my neighbors was an eighty-five-year-old woman whose sight and hearing had deteriorated to the point that her daughter wanted to put her in a nursing home. A younger couple just down the street claimed they were too busy fighting with each other to have noticed that a man was killed practically in plain view of their residence, were it not for the palm trees.

One neighbor thought she might have seen someone lurking around my house, but she couldn't remember if it was before or after Carter's death. Then she decided that maybe the whole thing had just been in her head.

What I was left with was the undeniable fact that at least one person had managed to break into my house without the alarm sounding, murder Carter, then put his body into the tub—all without being noticed, or leaving behind any clues to point the finger in their direction. Except for one. A very rare blood type...

It occurred to me that Carter could have actually come to my house with his killer, unaware that his life was about to end...and, as such, not feel he would need to defend himself. Not until it was too late.

That night I put my thoughts down in my computer as I normally did for any investigation, detailing everything I had so far and what was missing. It read like a chronicle of frustration, question marks, helplessness, and the real feeling that there was no end in sight in getting to the bottom of Carter Delaney's untimely death.

CHAPTER 18

The funeral took place on what felt like the hottest day of the year in Honolulu. It seemed as if half the city's dignitaries and business leaders were present, along with a healthy dose of representatives from law enforcement, to pay their respects. As a former prosecutor and self-made success story, Carter Delaney had obviously made a lot of friends.

And likely just as many enemies, I thought.

The widow was dressed in traditional black and gave every indication that she was distraught. Beside her was Carter's daughter, Ivy, who probably would suffer the most in the long run in being denied a father as she came of age and beyond. I stood next to Ridge somewhere in the middle of the rows of mourners. Not being invited to take a spot amongst family members was a bit dampening, but actually preferable. After all, it was senseless to have Carter's first and second wives standing side by side like we were some big, happy family, which clearly wasn't the case.

Ridge, whose new partner was scouting the area for a possible brazen appearance by Carter's killer, whispered in my ear: "If the widow played any part in your ex's death, it won't be easy to prove. Witnesses at a popular spa back up her claims of being there at the time the medical examiner says Delaney was killed." I could feel Ridge's warm breath on my cheek as I took in his words, which were more of a relief than disappointment. "The boyfriend's alibi is even more solid," he said. "Edwin Axelrod was in San Francisco on business the day Delaney checked out. Looks like we might be barking up the wrong tree on those two, no pun intended—"

That was both good and bad news, I thought. The good news was a love triangle may not have cost Carter his life after all. The bad news was it went against my gut feeling that Carter hiring me to prove his wife was being unfaithful had in some way, shape, or form figured into his death. I still wasn't fully convinced that Darlene Delaney was free and clear as far as playing a role—directly or indirectly—in Carter's demise was concerned. Alibis and corroboration had strange ways of being manipulated and arranged by people who wanted to cover their asses.

"Where do we go from here?" I whispered to Ridge.

"How about my place," he said suggestively. "I'll ditch Kawakami and meet you there—"

I elbowed him in the side and watched him wince deservedly. "I hardly think this is the time or place," I said under my breath. "I'm talking about the case—"

Ridge appeared to regret his weak attempt at seduction. Finally, he said: "Who the hell knows? Right now it's anybody's guess who murdered Delaney. We're taking the investigation one step at a time."

Knowing Carter, I honestly think he felt he would live forever. Or at least long enough to go gray, white, then bald, before spending his days on a chaise lounge reading the classics, and lying on the beach. However, fate had intervened. The thought bothered me, especially when I had serious reservations that his death was set in stone. Whoever had murdered Carter was not God, but a cold-blooded assassin.

"If only Carter hadn't gone to my house," I muttered lamentably to Ridge. Even then, it was becoming obvious to me that Carter had been targeted for execution whether he had gone to my house or not.

I honed in on the pastor, a heavyset man with thinning gray hair and a resonant voice that seemed made for such occasions.

"...Carter Delaney will be sorely missed. Not just as a public servant and a business leader in our community, but as a husband and father. Darlene and Ivy Delaney face the very difficult task of having to rebuild their lives. But, God willing, and with our help, they will do just that—even as Carter watches over them from above..."

In that moment, I was grateful that my life had already been rebuilt since Carter and I split up. But that still hadn't taken away my own unexpected feeling of loss.

My eyes wandered about the cemetery until they latched on Detective Kawakami. He appeared to be eyeing everyone suspiciously. I knew him from my days on the force. We actually went out on a date once, but I quickly realized he wasn't my type. He didn't necessarily agree, but never argued the point.

Other familiar faces were present, including that reporter who had gotten in my face on the day Carter died. Not far away was Edwin Axelrod. I wondered if the man had shown up to pay his last respects or to move in on the widow now that Carter was conveniently out of the way.

Farther away from the crowd was a man who looked very much like Darlene's drug dealer associate, Kalolo—the one who supposedly never knew her as *Mrs. Carter Delaney.* So what the hell was he doing here? I didn't like what I was thinking.

My eyes left him for a moment to scan the faces and profiles of other mourners. I had an eerie feeling that there was a good chance whoever was responsible for Carter's death would not be satisfied until they saw the dirt covering his casket.

By the time I looked back to where Darlene's drug supplier was standing, he was gone.

CHAPTER 19

He paid his last respects to Carter Delaney, just like all the other assholes who showed up, as if they really gave a damn about him when he was alive. It was like a game. Everyone played it, some better than others. Even he had to go through the motions and pretend to be all broken up about the late ex-prosecutor turned successful businessman, soon to be six feet under. In truth, the bastard didn't deserve to be alive. He had done the world a favor by dying.

It didn't make one bit of difference if the police had labeled his death a homicide. The bottom line was that Carter Delaney might be alive today if he'd cooperated.

If you don't play, you pay, he thought.

He gazed at Darlene Delaney. The good-looking widow was giving the performance of her life, dabbing at those teary eyes for the entire world to see. What was that old saying? *You can fool others, but you can't fool yourself.*

She sure as hell didn't fool him at all! He knew that she wanted Delaney dead as much as Delaney had wanted her dead. Only Delaney didn't have the balls to go that far. But his widow's wish had come true. Darlene had it all now, and there was no more Carter Delaney to tell her what to do with it—including that hot body of hers.

He watched Skye Delaney as she sat beside Detective Ridge Larsen. They were far from the perfect couple, even if they may have looked the part. The sexy private eye deserved a lot better man than the detective. Or, for that matter, Carter Delaney.

Why the hell couldn't they have just accepted Delaney's death as a suicide? It had been so carefully planned and executed. Now things had gotten complicated. An investigation was underway to find the bastard's killer. This could be dangerous for him. Very dangerous.

He had to be careful and watch his back. No one else was going to. If he made one wrong move, they would be onto him like white on rice.

He couldn't let that happen.

He kept his eyes steady as the detective named Henry Kawakami—even in plain clothes, he could easily spot a cop a mile away—passed by him looking for a sign that he had something to hide.

Which, of course, he didn't to the naked eye.

CHAPTER 20

"She's the cheating wife you were hired to catch in the act?" Natsuko flashed me a wide-eyed look of interest.

We were in my garden picking everything that was ripe. Natsuko had volunteered to help as a break from her household chores. For me, it was a respite, or so I thought, from the ongoing investigation into Carter's tragic and very mysterious death.

I wiped sweat from my brow, and said to her: "Who?"

"Your ex-husband's widow!" She raised a thin brow whimsically. "Am I right—?"

I figured what the hell, if inquisitive minds really wanted to know, there was no reason at this point to deny it. "Was I that obvious?"

Natsuko ate a handful of sugar peas and said: "No—*she* was. After I thought about it, it didn't take much to put two and two together," she said. "Isn't that what men do best? Use one woman to get what they want from another woman, and vice versa? The way I figured it, Carter Delaney needed someone to get the goods on his adulterous wife. What better person than his ex-wife who does that sort of thing for a living and probably still had the hots for him."

I pursed my lips, thinking, *aren't you miss know-it-all.* I told her: "You've been watching too much TV, Natsuko. I gave up the hots for Carter a long time ago, and he damn well knew it."

"Uh huh," she responded doubtfully.

"It's true," I said louder than I meant to. I brushed away more perspiration from my face. It seemed to be getting hotter by the moment.

"I'll just keep my mouth shut then," Natsuko said as her way of apology. "I don't mean to pry into your business. The man's dead and buried..." She ate some more peas and decided it was time to open her mouth again. "His wife had some nerve coming here the other day to check you out." She rolled her eyes. "Wonder what he saw in her anyway?"

"You'll have to ask Darlene sometime," I responded dryly. But I knew exactly what Carter saw in her: youth, beauty, sex appeal, immaturity, and a new person he could mold and shape into the person he wanted.

Natsuko was not exactly subtle in her views, which sometimes got her into trouble. In fact, I was one of the few people she seemed to approve of. Don't ask me why.

I gazed at her with a soft smile, pulled out a carrot, and said: "Let's go in for something cool to drink."

Five minutes later, we were in the breakfast nook downing strawberry-guava nectar like it was going out of style. Natsuko was back at it once more, asking me: "Are the police any closer to finding out who killed Carter? Or aren't they talking?"

"The police only talk in circles," I said, speaking from experience. "If they've got anything concrete, they aren't saying."

Even Ridge had been unusually quiet about it. Since the funeral, all he really had to say about the investigation was that they were doing their best to solve this high priority case.

I found myself regarding it in precisely the same manner.

CHAPTER 21

There were four messages on my answering machine when I arrived at the office the next morning. One was from Liam Pratt, the pesky reporter.

His message said: "Ms. Delaney, I'm still interested in following up on the allegations that Carter Delaney hired you to spy on his second wife...and what that might mean, if anything, regarding his untimely death. If you'd like to meet with me and talk about it you can reach me at..."

This guy doesn't know when to give up, I thought, irritably. Who the hell was his source? I didn't recall reading anything about Darlene's affair coming to light. What did he really want?

Though the better part of me wanted to stay as far away from Liam Pratt as possible, my curiosity got the better of me. Maybe he could shed some light on how he found out about my investigation of Darlene and who else was privy to this information.

I gave Liam Pratt a call, but got his voicemail. "This is Skye Delaney, returning your call. I'd like to talk to you—"

He returned my call almost immediately, as if waiting by the phone, and we agreed to meet for lunch at the Whaler's Club on South King Street. I've never gotten along very well with reporters, dating back to my days on the force. Probably because too often they are rude, arrogant, insensitive, aggressive, prying assholes—a lot like some private investigators I know.

The reporter was already seated when I entered the restaurant and lounge, a half-filled mug of beer in front of him as though a prop on display for my benefit.

"Ms. Delaney—" he said, and stood.

He seemed taller and somewhat heavier than our previous close encounter.

"Glad you could make it," he said.

"Let's just say you aroused my curiosity," I told him, which was only partly true.

"Ditto," he said.

"Look, Mr. Pratt—" I began, intending to set some ground rules.

"Call me Liam," he insisted. "Mind if I call you Skye?"

"Suit yourself," I responded, and glanced at my watch. This wouldn't last any longer than necessary, I decided, and the clock was ticking.

We sat across from each other in a booth. "What would you like to drink?" Liam asked, and put the mug of beer to his mouth.

"Coffee," I told him laconically, and watched the surprised look on his face, as though he expected me to share his beer with him.

I called the waitress over. She filled my cup and left menus for us.

Peeking over his menu, Liam asked point-blank: "So, is it true Carter Delaney hired his ex-wife to follow his second wife around town?"

I noted a small recorder on the table, which was on. I took the liberty of shutting it off. "I'll decide what's on the record," I told him.

He cracked a smile and nodded. "Okay, fair enough."

I gazed at the oddly attractive face across from me and said: "Maybe you should tell me where you got your information before I confirm or deny it."

He seemed prepared for this and responded smoothly: "Straight from the horse's mouth, as they say. It was Carter Delaney himself."

My eyes hit him with skepticism. "I don't mean to sound flippant, but why in hell would Carter tell *a reporter* anything about his personal life? Especially if he knew it could potentially be used against him and his family." I sipped my coffee while maintaining a steady gaze at him.

Liam kept a placid look on his face. "People talk a lot when they've had too much to drink." He gulped down more beer as if for effect. "It was one of those days when Delaney apparently had a hell of a bad day. I happened to be a listening ear at the bar as he droned on about the pressures of being a big shot in Honolulu...and his growing frustrations with his wife. I got the distinct impression that she wasn't putting out in the bedroom—at least not for him..."

The waitress returned and we ordered.

I was disturbed by what I'd heard so far. Had Carter been careless enough to have actually aired his dirty laundry in public to, of all people, an overzealous reporter who seemed to be looking for his own fifteen and a half minutes of fame?

"I guess we all have a weakness for something," Liam continued. "Darlene Delaney's weakness seemed to be anything but her husband."

I wondered if Liam knew about her drug use apart from her infidelity.

"So what's your weakness, Skye?" he asked intently.

"Whips and chains," I responded cynically, "if it makes you feel better."

He grinned. "The real question is does it make *you* feel better?"

Time to change the subject, I thought. "Let's just stick to Carter and what he told you, okay?"

"All right," Liam said. "Delaney mentioned that you were his ex and a security consultant/private eye. It was almost as if he was bragging about both. He said he was thinking about hiring you to check out his wife to see if she was being faithful to him." Liam paused. "Did he hire you?"

I was pretty good at lying, and certainly wasn't going to give him a juicy story he could use to draw inferences and possibly ruin people's lives. Least of all Carter's, though he was no longer around to feel the rippling effects.

"Sorry to disappoint you, but you've wasted your time—and mine," I said with a straight face. "Carter hired me as a consultant to do some background checks on people he was thinking about hiring. Nothing more—"

Liam regarded me thoughtfully. "Too bad. Not exactly the stuff movies of the week are made of."

"Maybe you should try writing fiction for a living," I suggested unapologetically. "That way you can create any trashy tale you want."

He reacted as though I'd punched him. "I'll keep that in mind."

The food arrived at the same time my appetite left. I tried eating anyway for the sake of my health, nibbling on grilled mahi-mahi and stir-fried vegetables.

Liam took a bite of his sautéed shrimp and said: "When I heard Carter Delaney was found dead in your Jacuzzi, I figured he must have followed through on his threat to see what his wife was up to and paid the ultimate price for it."

My fork lifted as if it had a mind of its own and pointed threateningly at him. "Get a grip on reality," I scoffed. "You're a reporter. Even though Carter may have spouted off to you in a drunken state, there's no proof it had anything to do with his death." On the other hand, I thought, it was still too early to rule out a connection. And too early to rule out Darlene being involved in Carter's death.

Liam seemed to agree with my stated observation. "Okay, so maybe I'm just grasping at straws here..." He bit off another piece of shrimp, then said: "But aren't you the least bit curious to know if the second Mrs. Delaney was *really* getting it from another man?"

I looked at him and said convincingly: "Why should I be? That was between Carter and her." I hoped my downplaying it might be enough to convince him to leave well enough alone, though I wasn't sure why I cared. Perhaps it was because I was overly sensitive where it concerned Carter and adultery, even if he happened to be on the other end of it this time around. It occurred to me that Darlene had accused him of fooling around on her as well. I didn't doubt it, all things considered.

"I guess it's a dead story then—figuratively speaking." Liam chuckled at his own sick sense of humor and watched for my reaction. There was none.

I forked a piece of broccoli and told him: "As far as I'm concerned, the story was never really alive—"

Liam wiped his mouth. "Too bad the same can't be said for the late Carter Delaney." He stared at me lasciviously. "So I was thinking that maybe we could get together sometime for a drink, the theater, or whatever. You name it."

Now the conversation had gone beyond the boundaries I always set when dealing with people who were supposed to be professionals.

I tasted some water and said: "I don't think so." Then I added for the record: "To tell you the truth, you're not my type." Not that I had a problem dating snoopy reporters, per se, only those who rubbed me the wrong way.

He shrugged. "That's cool. No harm in trying."

I took out my wallet and removed some bills, setting them on the table. "That should cover us both."

"You don't have to—" he started.

"I know I don't," I finished. "It's no big deal. I'm taking it as a business deduction. Good-bye, Liam—"

I walked away without looking back, hoping he got the message that there was no reason for us to see each other again. That said, something told me we would.

CHAPTER 22

He watched Skye Delaney sashay out of the restaurant like she owned the place. Whatever else he may have thought of her, there was no denying she was one hot-blooded, easy on the eyes woman.

He could only imagine what she was like in bed. Maybe, if he played his cards right, he could take his imagination to the next level.

Right now, there were more important things on his mind, like what the hell was she up to? How far was she willing to go with her nose for snooping? Did she think she was dealing with a moron?

Think again, bitch! he thought.

He would be watching her like a damned hawk. If she got too close to the truth, she'd pay dearly for it.

He finished his drink at the bar and left.

Outside, he was careful to make sure he wasn't being followed. He walked two blocks to his car. Confident that no one was onto him, he drove home.

The place wasn't much, but when you didn't have much to begin with, you didn't know what you were missing. Well, he had some idea. Trouble was every time he had something in the works, it always backfired. Tough damned luck.

He grabbed a beer from the fridge and went to his dark room. On a table were some eight by ten black and white close-up photographs of Skye Delaney. He took a swig of beer and picked up a picture of her in a teddy with a low-cut ruffled trim bodice that revealed lots of leg.

He found himself getting aroused at the image, wishing he had her all to himself.

Maybe someday soon.

He took a moment to relish the thought.

CHAPTER 23

It seemed like it was time for me to pay the "other man" a visit. Although the police had more or less eliminated Edwin Axelrod from their list of suspects, I still felt he was worth checking out. He was, after all, intimately involved with the wife of a former prosecutor, potentially compromising his law practice. If that wasn't enough, there was the simple fact that he was sleeping with a married woman whose wealthy husband was now dead.

Murder was one way to eliminate a problem before it became unmanageable.

I looked him up on the internet. His office was located on the ninth floor of the Harbor Towers Building on Bishop Street. I didn't bother to make an appointment after phoning his secretary and being told he was booked solid until four, after which time he would be out of the office for the rest of the day.

Instead, I made myself comfortable in the small lobby area of the ninth floor near the elevators while I waited for Axelrod to emerge from his office. He did so at five minutes to four, holding hands with an attractive redhead who looked young enough to be his daughter. She was tall and had the ultra thin body of a fashion model in a bright yellow tank dress. High heels made her nearly as tall as him. They kissed openly while they waited for the elevator.

I wondered if the woman Edwin Axelrod could hardly take his hands off was actually the wife that Darlene had alluded to. Or was he actually bold enough to fool around with another mistress right there in his office building? I chose to go with the former. Obviously, Axelrod had a thing for young women, including Darlene. It didn't seem to matter if he was married to them or not. My instincts told me that the Darlene-Edwin Axelrod affair was not really about grass being greener on the other side, but at whose house the grass happened to be growing. In this case, it was the residence of the late Carter Delaney, with his wife still very much alive.

I hated to break up the lovebirds' preoccupation with each other's mouths, but duty called.

"Mr. Axelrod—?" I said, getting their attention. I approached them, and said tersely to him: "We need to talk—"

He cocked his brow. "Do you have an appointment?"

"Not really," I said. "But I've been waiting for close to an hour now, if that counts for anything. It concerns the Carter Delaney murder investigation. I understand you knew the victim..."

This caught his attention and it appeared that I had gained his respect that had previously been lacking. "Uh, yes, of course—" he said clearly for the benefit of his companion. He told her: "This shouldn't take long. Why don't you wait for me in the car?"

She seemed less than thrilled at the prospect. "Just remember, Edwin, we have reservations at the restaurant at four-thirty." She hit me with a dirty look and pressed the elevator button.

"Come in," Axelrod said as he opened his office door. He closed it when we were both inside, then said rudely: "What the hell is this about?"

It took me only an instant to study the man more closely. He seemed anxious yet careful as his deep, dark eyes gazed back at me beneath thick brows. He wore a navy designer suit and what looked like expensive leather shoes. All in all, I supposed he could be classified as handsome—at least in Darlene's eyes.

Handsome men were also just as capable of committing murder as their less than handsome counterparts. Adultery went without saying and, in some minds, was just as bad.

"My name's Skye Delaney," I began, figuring the common last name of his lover would likely cause a stir within him. Simultaneously, I presented my I.D., adding: "I'm a private investigator looking into Carter Delaney's death—"

Axelrod took a long look at my credentials, then my face. "How can I help you?" he asked as if he had no idea.

"I'm not sure, really," I admitted, and took a sweeping glance at the spacious and expensively furnished art deco office, before returning my focus to the attorney. "Maybe you could start by telling me about your affair with Darlene Delaney."

His brows knitted. "I don't know what you're talking about. If she put you up to this, you've wasted both our time—"

"I think it's time well spent," I responded curtly. "I'm afraid it's *you* who's wasting it—" I pulled a few snapshots out of a folder, calmly walked over to his large teak desk, and placed the photos side by side across the top of it. "You might want to take a look at these," I said with a catch to my voice.

Axelrod hesitated, as though he knew it was something he'd rather not see, before moving across the plush carpeting and looking down.

"Correct me if I'm wrong," I said smugly, "but that is *you* with *Mrs.* Carter Delaney, isn't it?" I watched as a startled look of resignation crossed his face. "I believe the place is called the Palm Tree Lodge."

He gathered the pictures together and tried unsuccessfully to squeeze them into a ball. "Where the hell did you get these?" he demanded, glaring at me.

I met his eyes head-on. "Believe it or not, I took them with my very own camera. Carter Delaney hired me to find out if his wife was having an affair. Those pictures—and there are more—prove it. Problem is, my client ended up dead before he got the chance to see them."

I picked up a framed photograph from the desk. It was a picture of Axelrod and the model-like beauty he obviously couldn't wait to get back to. It looked like it had been taken recently. Gazing at the real life Edwin Axelrod, I said nonchalantly: "As an attorney, doesn't that strike you as just a wee bit suspicious *and* coincidental?"

He yanked the frame from my hand like it was more precious than gold and set it back on the desk. "Not particularly." He curled his lip. "So I had an affair with Darlene Delaney. Sue me. It wasn't even fulfilling, to tell you the truth. There certainly was no reason for me to want to kill her husband—"

Stranger things have happened, I thought, while taking note of the past tense nature of the affair. I assumed Darlene was of the same mind, considering her rather precarious situation.

"Anyway, the police already know I was out of town when Delaney was killed," Axelrod pointed out. "I'm sure even you're smart enough to know you can't be in two places at the same time, detective—"

Beneath that cool façade was definitely a cold, arrogant son of a bitch, I thought. Not to mention patronizing. He was confident in his denials. Perhaps a little too confident. But did that make him guilty of anything other than poor judgment and a desire for someone outside his marriage?

"Yes, you're right about that—no one can be in two places at once," I had to agree. Yet something still didn't seem right about this one. I decided to apply the pressure a bit more to see how he reacted. "Just out of curiosity," I said, "how do you think Carter Delaney would have reacted had he found out you were involved with his wife?"

Axelrod seemed to weigh his response carefully, then said: "I don't suppose he would've been too happy about it."

"Is it a fair assumption that he might have been angry enough to do you bodily harm?" I asked dramatically. In reality, the Carter I knew was non-violent. It was the Carter I didn't know that worried me.

Edwin Axelrod's patience seemed to be running thin. "I can't answer the question if I don't know the answer. Can I, Ms. Delaney?"

He stepped closer, bearing down on me with eyes that could best be described as menacing. Was he trying to intimidate me, or cover his ass by playing tough guy?

I took a step or two backwards. "I guess not," I replied curtly. "Unless, of course, Carter knew about you and his wife, threatened you with maybe more than bodily harm, and you decided to do him in before he followed through on his plan. But first, you had to conveniently arrange to be out of town and leave the dirty work to some hired assassin. Does that sound about right?" I knew I was overstepping my bounds and in the process exaggerating the chain of events. Still, the scenario struck me as entirely plausible.

Once again Axelrod approached me, and once again I backed up, feeling somewhat threatened. "You have a very overactive imagination, Ms. Delaney," he said tautly. "If you can prove your tale, I suggest you take it to the police. Now get the hell out of my office!"

I gave him a nasty look, realizing I had overstayed my welcome. "All right, I'm going..." I took a few steps toward the door, stopped, and asked, as if a harmless afterthought: "Just for the record, mind telling me what your blood type is?"

Axelrod stiffened where he stood. "What for?"

I tried to put it in a way he could relate to. "You might say I have a fetish for certain blood types..."

Being a clever attorney, he wasn't buying that for one second. But Axelrod could hardly refuse to answer the question without giving the guise that he had something to hide.

"A positive," he said casually. "Not all that unusual, really. Dogs don't go for blood that's too tart. Sorry." He flashed me a crooked grin. "I know all about you, Delaney, and your self-appointed mission to single-handedly bring your late ex-husband's killer to justice. Well, you won't find him here—"

I batted my eyes at this man who was evidently even smarter than I gave him credit for. But he wasn't as smart as he may have thought he was.

"Who said anything about Carter's murderer definitely being a male?" I doubted that the police had made it public knowledge that the AB negative blood Ollie took from the assailant belonged to a male. That gave me another opportunity to put the squeeze on Axelrod for his reaction. Directing my attention to the framed photo on his desk, I asked what seemed obvious: "Is that your wife?"

Axelrod acknowledged it indirectly. "Leave her the hell out of this!"

Did he know something I didn't? I wondered. At the very least, perhaps the wife was involved indirectly, I thought. "I assume she doesn't know about you and Darlene."

His temples swelled. "That's none of your damned business. This meeting is over!" He grabbed the damaging photos. "And take these with you..."

"Keep them for your archives," I told him. "I have them on a flash drive in case I need reprints—"

I left him brooding over our conversation. In the elevator, I wondered if Edwin Axelrod's wife did know about the affair and, if not, what lengths he might be willing to go to in order to keep his sordid little secret from his young wife.

CHAPTER 24

I woke up the following morning feeling really stressed for some reason. Perhaps it was the company I'd been keeping recently. Or not so recent. I decided to go jogging to burn off the stress and try to keep things in a proper perspective. Including the fact that Carter was gone and there was nothing I could do about it other than try to find his killer, if the police didn't do it first.

As usual, jogging worked like a charm. Ollie and I pounded the sand and got in some good exercise at the same time.

An hour later, I did my cool down, stretched, and took a long, hot shower. Feeling somewhat refreshed and reinvigorated, I chased Ollie around the house—actually I think it was the other way around—for a time, before we both decided to call it quits and find something more productive to do with our time.

For me, it was doing my weekly grocery shopping that was already two days overdue. The cart was stuffed with mostly healthy food as I made my way down the cereal aisle en route to the checkout lane. I stopped in the middle when someone called my name from behind.

"I thought that was you..." said Lily Yokouchi, a butcher at the store and former neighbor when I was Mrs. Carter Delaney. She wore an apron that was splattered with more blood than I cared to ponder.

"It was the last time I looked in the mirror," I said lightheartedly. I always seemed to miss seeing Lily whenever I came to the store, but not deliberately. Neither of us could help it if, as an attractive divorcee, she seemed to get along better with Carter than me back in the day. I tried not to take it personally.

She gave me a strained smile. "Pehea 'oe? she asked.

"Maika'i no au," I responded in Hawaiian, meaning I was fine. "And you?"

"O ia mau no," she said, or the same as usual. She wiped her hands on her bloody apron and I hoped she didn't plan to shake mine. "Keeping busy. You know how that is."

I did and told her so.

Furrows formed on her brow. "Heard about Carter. I wanted to call, but...I really wasn't sure what to say—"

"Don't worry about it," I told her, feeling the same way and trying to remember that Carter was my ex-spouse, not current lover. I glanced at my frozen foods that were beginning to thaw.

"You never really believe something like that can happen to someone you know, until it does—" Lily said.

"There are no guarantees for any of us," I muttered. "Life can go as quickly as it comes."

Lily saw right through me. "But there should be guarantees against being the victim of violent crime." She gulped. "If such a terrible tragedy can happen to one of the most well respected, successful men in this city, how can the rest of us feel safe from harm?"

Her point was well taken. Carter didn't deserve such a fate, even as my ex-husband with problems beyond the cool, calm façade he presented.

"I know," I muttered. Especially when one or more people were still on the loose after murdering Carter

Delaney, I thought. To Lily, I said: "Fortunately these things don't happen all the time—at least not in Honolulu."

I was hoping to leave it at that and get my groceries home before they melted or withered away before my very eyes, when Lily asked: "Will they be making an arrest soon for Carter's murder? Or is this going to turn out to be one of those unsolved mysteries that will end up on a television crime show someday?"

"We can only hope for the best," I suggested lamely, the thought of Carter's murder never being solved unnerving me. My eyes lowered to my cart, and back to her. "I've really got to get going. Nice to see you again, Lily."

"I'll call you—" she said as a parting shot, which we both knew would never happen.

I made it through the checkout line in no time flat. The sliding doors parted for me and the young male clerk who insisted on carting my groceries to the car for me. I allowed it, still preoccupied with finding Carter's killer.

At home, Ollie was only too happy to see me and, even more, his dog food. I had just finished putting the last of the groceries away when Ridge phoned. His voice always provided welcome relief from whatever was ailing me, even if his presence was not always the answer.

That didn't stop him from trying a back door approach to getting together. "What you need is a head to toe massage, which just happens to be something I specialize in," he hummed suggestively.

"Sounds wonderful," I said, speaking from past experience. "But today I really need to be alone... Tomorrow," I added hopefully, "I may be in need of some serious massage therapy—"

Ridge seemed to accept this without sounding hurt, even if he was. "Any time, any place," he said. "Just say the word—"

I kept that in mind and switched subjects. "Any new news on Carter's murder investigation?"

Ridge hesitated before answering. "We don't have anyone in custody," he said, then added with assurance: "But no one around here is going to get any rest till we do—"

That was a comforting thought, if not the same thing as having the case solved. I was still left with several questions about Carter's death and determined to get some answers. If not for his widow, then for the daughter Carter had left behind.

I downplayed it to Ridge when he probed me about my unofficial investigation into Carter's murder. At this point, I wasn't prepared to share any information, especially since he seemed in no hurry to do the same. Not that I had much to share. But he didn't have to know that.

We were both fully aware that this case was different from others Ridge and I had helped each other with. Carter's death had almost become larger than his life ever was. Until the public and I were satisfied that justice was served, there would be no business as usual. And that included the private business between Ridge and me, even if a part of me wanted to run into his arms.

I cuddled up with Ollie on the sofa and fell asleep.

CHAPTER 25

The investigation into Carter Delaney's death was round the clock. Ridge felt the pressure from both the top and bottom. Every lead had to be checked and double-checked. Even the usual crackpots and assholes flooding the department lines with so-called tips and sightings of potential suspects couldn't be ignored.

Not this time.

The last thing this city in so-called paradise needed was an unsolved case involving a man who some almost worshipped for his successful prosecutorial days and even greater success in the business world. Between the press hounding them and concerned citizens demanding that an arrest be made, Ridge was starting to believe that if they didn't have a bona fide suspect in custody soon, they may well have a damned near riot on their hands.

Fortunately, Ridge got along well with Henry Kawakami, who was currently shuffling some papers at his desk. He doubted they would ever be best buddies, but they respected each other and, more importantly, knew their temporary partnership could make or break them insofar as career advancement.

Kawakami told Ridge about his one date with Skye before Carter Delaney ever came into the picture. He said it fell apart after that and Ridge never asked why. What happened in Skye's romantic past was none of his business, unless she wanted it to be.

Except where it concerned Carter Delaney, now that he had met his maker. He had resurfaced in Skye's life, and Ridge had perhaps rather foolishly encouraged it. Consequently, they both had to see this through, even if it put a definite and unavoidable strain on their relationship.

Ridge blamed himself for that. He was under orders to avoid talking to Skye about the case as far as anything useful, in spite of the fact that she had a right to know where things stood in the investigation if for no other reason than Carter Delaney was still unofficially her client. Until satisfied that her case had no bearing on his death, Skye would keep digging till she could draw her own conclusions.

Ridge feared that this could only end up putting her in danger. He didn't believe for one second that she couldn't take care of herself just as well as any male private eye with a background in police work. But that didn't stop him from being worried about her. He couldn't rest while a killer who knew where she lived was out there.

Maybe when this was over, he and Skye could escape to one of the other islands or Las Vegas for some romantic time together.

Right now, any such vacation seemed a long way off, Ridge thought. Especially when there were more pressing matters to keep him awake at night.

CHAPTER 26

I went to a luau on Waikiki Beach. Scantily clad, shapely island girls moved their hips gracefully to sensual Hawaiian music while hunky male hula dancers performed choreographed, athletic moves in the background. Bordering them were Samoan fire knife dancers, daringly and skillfully twirling knives of fire.

I honed in on a Polynesian dancer named Leilani Mahaulu who, according to Darlene, was having an affair with Carter right up to the end of his life. Maybe she knew something that could shed some light on his death.

It didn't take much to understand what Carter saw in Leilani. She was gorgeous and exotic with long, silky black hair and a curvaceous body that I could only dream of.

I recalled seeing Leilani at the funeral, looking miserable. Now she looked like a hula dancer who hadn't a care in the world other than pleasing her audience, which included me. I was less interested in the show than sizing up the woman Carter was alleged to have been involved with and who may have intimate knowledge of why he was murdered. Admittedly, there also was a morbid curiosity on my part about her as the other woman who came after the woman who had succeeded me as Carter's romantic interest.

I was baffled as to why Carter had hired me to prove Darlene was being unfaithful if he was also up to his same old dirty tricks in bed.

After the hula performance was over, I wasted little time catching up to Leilani. She was still in costume, but seemed eager to change into street clothes.

"Nice dancing," I told her and meant it, while wondering if I had what it took to master the technique.

She grinned. "Mahalo."

"My name's Skye Delaney," I said calmly. "I'm a private investigator."

Leilani looked at me curiously. "What do you want with me?"

"I'm investigating Carter Delaney's death."

She gave me the once-over. "Who are you? His sister?"

I made a face. "No, I'm his ex-wife—"

This revelation clearly took her by surprise. Leilani wet her lips. "I'm sorry, about Carter," she said. "But what does his death have to do with me?"

This was where it sometimes got sticky, I thought. "Maybe nothing at all," I said carefully. "Or maybe everything..."

She raised a brow. "I'm afraid I don't follow you."

I narrowed my eyes at her calculatingly. "You were having an affair with Carter, weren't you?"

Her expression grew tense. "Who told you that?"

"His widow, Darlene Delaney."

"Well, she's wrong," Leilani insisted. "Carter and I were just friends. Nothing more..."

I had no proof to contradict her story, except for my usually razor sharp instincts. And they seemed right on target in this instance.

"Look, I didn't come here to make accusations," I told her truthfully. "Remember, I'm the *ex*-wife. Whatever was going on between you and Carter is your business. Mine is to try to find out who murdered him." I lowered my voice. "I was hoping you could help—"

Leilani did not bite the bait. "I'm sorry, but I don't know anything," she said sharply.

I didn't buy it. She looked nervous, even scared. What or who was she afraid of? I wondered. "Did Carter ever talk to you about any problems he was having?" I pressed.

She stiffened. "Only that he wasn't happy in his marriage." Her dark eyes met mine. "Obviously, that was the story of his life. And probably his death..."

A muscular fire dancer interrupted the conversation. He seemed barely cognizant of me when he asked Leilani, "You still need a lift home?"

She looked at me as though weighing her options before telling him: "Yes. I'll just be a few minutes."

"Okay." He gave me a long look and walked away.

I wondered if that was the new man in her life—or old one—now that Carter was permanently out of the picture.

"Just a friend," she said as if reading my mind.

"Right, like Carter," I said sardonically.

She didn't seem amused. "I have to go change now."

I got the message. I took out a business card and handed it to her. "In case you happen to remember something that might help your other friend rest more peacefully, give me a call—"

She took the card, but said nothing. I had a feeling that I might hear from her sooner than later.

I headed to my car, left with more questions than answers. What did Leilani know that she was not telling? Darlene had seemed so certain that Leilani and Carter were lovers. Was she right? Or were they truly just friends with other types of benefits?

What interested me most was whether or not either had any bearing on his death. If anything, friends usually made far better confidants than lovers, I mused, while imagining Carter trying to get the most out of any type of relationship he was in. Maybe he had confided in Leilani that his life was in jeopardy. Or maybe not.

I began to wonder if I was getting too deeply involved in my ex-husband's personal business. I had to consider that his murder might have had nothing to do with his private life. Being a millionaire certainly was reason enough for someone to want you dead. Especially if you'd made your fortune by walking over others along the way. I knew I had to keep every possibility on the table, including a random act, even if I didn't believe that for one minute.

* * *

I drove to Ridge's place, in desperate need of his company. He welcomed me with a deep, long kiss. I wasn't complaining.

After our lips unlocked, I gave him the rundown on Leilani Mahaulu. Or rather, my speculation about her. I figured I owed him that much since he was my eyes in the Honolulu Police Department and the detective heading the investigation into Carter's death.

"So you think this Leilani was having her way with Delaney?" Ridge asked, glancing at me sideways. "Or maybe it was the other way around?"

I shrugged. "I believe Leilani knows more about him than she's willing to admit."

"Like why he was murdered?" he asked.

"That's something you may want to ask her yourself—" I responded with a definite edge to my voice.

"I think I'll do just that," Ridge said. "So what was it about Delaney anyway that seemed to have women falling at his feet?"

I chuckled. "Sorry, but I can only speak for myself. While I certainly didn't worship the man, being good-looking and charismatic probably didn't hurt matters any," I admitted, and left it at that, refusing to get caught up in exploring Carter's sexual conquests.

That didn't stop Ridge from speculating further. "With Delaney bedding so many women and worrying about getting a dose of his own medicine, I just wonder where the hell he found the time to make his fortune."

With a weak attempt at humor, I suggested: "I think it's called managing one's time wisely."

Ridge wasn't laughing. "I can think of some other things I'd call it," he said. "Anything else interesting you've discovered about your ex that you'd like to share?"

"I might ask you the same thing, Detective Larsen," I tossed back at him. "Or do teamwork and cooperation only work one way in your book?"

"I think I'll take the Fifth on that one—"

It seemed more like a brush off to me. Was I expecting too much from him for this case? Or was he expecting too much from me? I wondered. Both were probably true, under the circumstances.

Silence fell between us at the worst possible time, just as things seemed to be heating up following our passionate kiss. Suddenly, I could wait no longer to speak my mind: "Why the Fifth? I've got a right to know what's happening with the investigation other than what I hear on the news. And we both know they only report what they're told, not what they aren't..."

As he usually did when cornered, Ridge looked away contemplatively before meeting my eyes again. "This one is a little too close to home—for both of us," he said unevenly. "My ass is on the line here, Skye. Everyone knows about us and about your past with Carter Delaney. If I leak out anything to you and it gets back to my superiors, I'll be on permanent desk duty and you'll lose your license to legally investigate Delaney's death outside the department."

I remained mute, prompting Ridge to ask flatly: "Do you get my drift?"

I nodded meekly. "Yes, I understand where you're coming from, Ridge. And I don't want any information from you that will jeopardize your career—or mine." I paused. "But can you at least tell me if the investigation is proceeding along nicely insofar as getting solid leads? Or is there something else going on that you don't want to talk about?"

Don't ask me why, but I had a gut feeling that there was more to the case in finding Carter's killer than met the eye. It was obviously bigger than the fact that Carter was a self-made millionaire and somewhat of an icon in the community. I glared at Ridge and waited to see if he would at least give me a clue.

Ridge hesitated for a long moment before saying: "I'll just say this much and we'll leave it at that. Although Delaney had walked away from the legal system some time ago, apparently he had not stopped working for the prosecuting attorney's office altogether—"

Of course, I couldn't simply leave it at that without further clarification, so I asked: "Are you saying that Carter was working with the prosecuting attorney *while* we were married?"

"Yeah, I think so," Ridge replied awkwardly. "From what I understand, Delaney was a high-powered consultant with the P.A.'s office ever since his retirement as a prosecutor. He dispensed advice behind the scenes and was effectively a hand's on person in some of the county's biggest cases, without actually getting his own hands dirty."

I listened with shock, taken aback that Carter had managed to keep this from me throughout our marriage and after, clearly not trusting me enough to confide in me. It made me wonder what other secrets he may have taken to the grave.

"So you think his death had something to do with his work for the P.A.?" I asked straightforwardly.

Ridge chewed on his lower lip. "We're not sure, to tell you the truth. It's just one angle we're working on. But, yes, it's possible...along with something related to his business empire or his private life, including the wife or mistress—"

In other words, I thought, Ridge seemed to be saying that they still did not have enough to know what or who they were looking for, and why.

And I was in the same predicament.

* * *

"Why the hell did Delaney pick this time to invite you back into his life?" Ridge asked me later in bed. His tone was anything but conciliatory.

The same question gnawed at me. None of the possible answers was satisfactory. My head was resting on Ridge's chest as I responded dryly: "I'd ask him, if I could—"

"Seems to me he not only wanted the cake and frosting," moaned Ridge, "but the damned leftovers as well—"

I lifted up and glared at him, appalled. "Is that all I am to you, Ridge—damned leftovers?"

"Of course not," he said. He smiled, clearly regretting his choice of words. "I think you know me better than that."

"I'm not sure I do," I protested, still fuming at the thought of being anyone's leftover.

Ridge gently took me into his arms and kissed my forehead. "Oh, don't get all bent out of shape, Skye. You're anything but leftovers in my book—you're more like a five-star meal." He paused. "That said, I've got a murder to solve. Until I do, neither of us can ignore the possibility that Delaney's motives for hiring you may have had little to do with your amazing detective skills or his wife's extracurricular activities—"

I wanted to speak, but the words would not come out. Instead, I started to cry. They were the first tears I'd shed since Carter's death. As a cop, I was taught that emotion was a no-no or a sign of weakness, at least if you wanted to be treated as an equal. But I was no longer a cop, bound by cop's rules, no matter how sexist and antiquated they could be. I was reacting as a woman and the ex-wife of a man I was just getting to know in death and didn't necessarily like what I was discovering. I feared what was yet to come. To hell with holding back tears that needed to come out.

Only it was not Carter I was crying for as much as those he left behind. Whoever he was inside, and whatever made him tick, his life was over now. But life went on for the rest of us. And I fully intended to stick around until I was old and grumpy, regardless of what emotional baggage I had to sort out and dispose of in the process.

CHAPTER 27

I took my case straight to the prosecuting attorney's office, expecting resistance in my attempt to learn what, if anything, Carter had been involved in that may have led to his death. Even when I was on the force, such information was hard to come by when it involved their own, or their inner circle—except when used in the courtroom.

Bradford Rennick was the First Deputy Prosecuting Attorney for the City and County of Honolulu. He was in his late forties and much shorter than I expected. His hair was definitely died jet-black and he had a cleft in his chin. Rennick had made the difficult and obviously successful move from the police force to the office of the Prosecuting Attorney. I had never had the pleasure—or displeasure—of working with him in either capacity.

"So, you were the *first* Mrs. Delaney," Rennick remarked as we walked side by side down the long corridor on the tenth floor at Alii Place, where his office was located.

"I still am, as far as I know," I responded wryly, looking up slightly into his brown eyes.

He tugged at the jacket of his gray suit. "Carter's death hit us all hard. I keep expecting him to call me and say this whole damned thing was just a bad dream..."

More like a *very bad* nightmare, I thought. Only it was real and nothing on earth could change that.

We entered Rennick's large, carpeted corner office, bypassing the walnut desk and floor to ceiling matching bookcases in favor of a rectangular table surrounded by cranberry-colored leather chairs. There was a coffee pot, paper cups, cream, sugar, and a bowl of fresh fruit on the table.

"Help yourself," Rennick said as he reached for an apple.

Though tempted, I passed on the fruit, but did pour myself a cup of coffee while pondering what direction the investigation by the P.A.'s office into Carter's death had taken.

After taking a generous bite of the apple, Rennick commented: "Heard you were one hell of a cop way back when, Skye..."

"Funny," I replied without laughing, "heard the same thing about you—"

He chuckled. "I wonder if we have the same mutual admiration society."

I seriously doubted it, but didn't tell him that. Instead, I cut to the chase. "I understand that Carter was working for your office before he died. Is that true?"

Rennick did not seek to deny it. "He never really stopped contributing to law and order in this county," he said. "Delaney's expertise and insight were invaluable to us."

I tried not to let it show that I was taken aback with his confirmation that Carter had continued to work as a lawyer, even while making his mark as a businessman. I assumed Carter had his reasons for maintaining the secrecy.

As though reading my mind, and perhaps sensing the awkwardness of the moment, Rennick said: "When Carter left the P.A.'s office, I think he'd had enough of the politics of the legal system. But he never turned his back on fighting for justice. He just didn't want to do it in the public arena anymore. He agreed to be a consultant when we needed what he brought to the table, as long as it was strictly unofficial and did not encumber his private or professional life. It seemed to work out well for all parties concerned—"

Except for Carter, I thought. His secret deal with the prosecuting attorney's office might have cost him his life.

Meeting Rennick's eyes, I asked him directly: "Do you think Carter's death was related to whatever he was working on for you?"

He stared at the question before responding. "I never like to say never, but I doubt it." He poured coffee into a cup. "We don't really have anything concrete at this point that links Delaney's murder to this office."

"Do you have anything non-concrete?" I asked, sensing there may be something he wasn't telling me.

Rennick gave a long sigh. "Anyone following the news in recent months knows that the P.A.'s office has been trying to nail Kazuo Pelekai—also known as Chano—for some time now."

I wasn't very good at following the news. There never seemed to be enough time in the day, or night, for that matter. That didn't mean I wasn't familiar with Kazuo Pelekai. He was like the Hawaiian version of Al Capone or maybe John Gotti: a reputed kingpin in Honolulu's underworld of drugs, prostitution, and murder, with strong ties to the local street gangs. Only, unlike Capone and Gotti, Pelekai always seemed to stay one step ahead of those who wanted to see him spend the rest of his life behind bars.

Rennick continued: "As a prosecutor, Delaney was one of the leading forces in trying to build a case against Pelekai. But nothing seemed to stick. He still believed it was possible, even as a consultant. We were just beginning to zero in on nailing Pelekai's ass when Carter was murdered..."

"Are you saying Pelekai may have ordered a hit on Carter?" I looked at Rennick wide-eyed.

He hunched a shoulder. "Not that we can prove. At least not yet..."

The idea that Carter may have been the victim of a sleaze bag like Kazuo Pelekai made my skin crawl. I tasted the coffee while wondering if an arrest was imminent or just wishful thinking.

"Of course, there are other possibilities we're following." Rennick gave me the type of look my father used to when he was about to accuse me of something he already knew I was guilty of. "Did Delaney come to your house the day he was killed for any reason in particular?" he asked. "Or did your ex often drop by?"

I wasn't sure what he was getting at, but felt relieved that Ridge hadn't spilled the beans about my work for Carter until it became absolutely necessary in relation to his death.

Still, I felt compelled to set the record straight right now about certain issues. "Since our divorce, Carter and I hardly ever saw each other," I said, "and certainly not socially." More bitter coffee went down my throat as I walked the fine line between eliminating myself from apparent suspicion and protecting the confidentiality of a client. "I'm a security consultant *and* private investigator," I told him, though I was sure Rennick knew everything there was to know about me, including my relationship with Ridge. "Carter had recently hired me. On the day he died, we were supposed to meet at my office. But I think there was some sort of miscommunication, and he went to my house instead—"

Rennick took another bite out of the apple, and chewed for a few moments while gazing at me. "Tasty. Sure you don't want one?"

"I'm sure," I told him. I was in no mood to be buttered up with fruit.

He got back to the real issue on his mind that I preferred to dodge for the moment. "Do you mind telling me what you were working on for Delaney? And please don't tell me it's privileged information, even if it is. Need I remind you, we're dealing with a *homicide* here—"

Caught between a rock and a hard place, I used quick thinking to say with a straight face: "It's not privileged information—at least not to this office. Carter asked me to do some investigative work on Kazuo Pelekai."

Rennick did not convince easily. "I've been working closely with Carter on this case. Why the hell would he go outside the P.A.'s office without consulting me?"

"Hey, I have no idea what went on inside Carter's head." I batted my eyes innocuously, while knowing at least that much was true. "I'm sorry if he stepped on your toes, Bradford, but maybe Carter figured he needed a fresh perspective. Someone who would report only to him—"

"Yeah, right..." Rennick muttered with uncertainty, and then appeared to give me the benefit of the doubt. He ditched the rest of his fruit, and asked as if it were a test: "Well, what did you come up with? We can use all the help we can get—"

"I'm afraid I don't have much to offer. I was just getting started on my investigation into Pelekai's financial wheelings and dealings, when Carter was killed—"

At that moment, I was suddenly struck with a weird vision of Carter dead in my Jacuzzi tub. I quickly drank more coffee to try to pull myself together.

"Too bad," Rennick said, giving me the evil eye. "And too damned convenient."

"Death is never convenient," I told him. "I wish Carter was still alive and working with you to nab Pelekai. But it just didn't work out that way."

Rennick still seemed less than convinced that I wasn't holding back on him. "What about *your* enemies?" he asked suspiciously. "All private eyes have people who would love to see them dead. Maybe someone went to your house looking for you, and found Delaney instead?"

I had asked myself that same question a thousand times. And 999.9 times the answer came back the same. I told Rennick: "If someone was looking for me, I'd be a much easier target at my office or during my daily jogs than at home—" I finished off the coffee and made a face as the bitterness stuck in my throat. "Besides, I've gone back and forth through my case files and came up with no one who fits the bill and timing."

"All the same," Rennick said sharply, "I'd appreciate it if you'd provide us with a list of your clients for the past year and the nature of each case—"

I flashed him an "excuse me?" look, not so much for the unrealistic request, but that he apparently expected me to buckle from the weight of his stare. I replied candidly: "I can't do that. What you're asking for is confidential information that I believe has no bearing on your investigation. You'll just have to take my word on this one."

He frowned, then seemed to back down, but still made his position clear. "I try not to take *anyone's* word when it comes to murder." Standing, he said: "I hope you don't have any travel plans, Ms. Delaney"—he made his voice sound intimidating—"just in case we need to talk to you again."

I lifted to my feet. "I wouldn't dream of taking a vacation, Mr. Rennick. There's no other place I'd rather be than Honolulu." A tiny smile played on my lips. "Oh, and just for the record," it seemed worth saying, "I came here voluntarily. Thanks for the crummy coffee—"

I felt as if I'd just dodged a bullet after leaving Rennick's office and making my way outside the building. For how long was anyone's guess. Right now, I was glad to have come away with more information than when I went in. The question was whether or not Kazuo Pelekai was just another hard-to-corner thug. Or was he the man behind Carter's murder?

CHAPTER 28

It wasn't like I expected to extract a confession from Pelekai. But stranger things had happened. I had to find out for myself if this man who had people in the Prosecuting Attorney's office sweating was the one I should be going after for the murder of Carter Delaney. I brought Ridge along for the ride in a nonofficial capacity.

He was less than thrilled with my determination to take on Kazuo Pelekai. "This isn't a man you want to screw around with, Skye—" he insisted from the passenger seat.

"That's not what I had in mind," I quipped, though I took the matter very seriously.

Ridge lowered his brows. "Then what the hell do you have in mind?"

"Just a few questions, nothing more," I replied laconically.

Ridge was still leery. "Pelekai is already under investigation for this case and a dozen others that I know of. If we had anything we thought could stick, he'd already be behind bars. In the meantime, if he is somehow involved in Delaney's death, he wouldn't think twice about doing you in too, if it meant saving his own ass—"

"Carter was murdered in *my* house," I said, as though he had forgotten. "If the killer had wanted to kill me too, I'd already be dead." I knew this was a sorry rationale for feeling I'd be able to walk in on Pelekai's turf without putting my life in jeopardy. Even if I hadn't been the intended victim, that hardly meant I wouldn't become the next one. I looked at the road and back at Ridge, this time giving him a smile. I took one hand off the steering wheel and put it on his. "Besides," I added cutely, "isn't that why you're here? To protect me from harm's way?"

He wrinkled his nose. "Yeah, well let's just hope it doesn't come to that."

Though I had the utmost confidence in Ridge's ability—and my own for that matter—to get physical, I had brought along my 9-millimeter just in case it was needed.

Kazuo Pelekai lived in an impressive Mediterranean villa on Poipu Drive in East Honolulu. It stood out like a palace even in an upper middle class neighborhood that was known for its upscale and gated properties.

A gate attendant let us in after Ridge flashed his badge and told him we were here on official business. I drove onto a circular driveway and parked next to a late model Lexus and Mercedes.

Before we could ring the bell, Kazuo Pelekai opened the door himself. This was somewhat contrary to my image of crime bosses being layered with bodyguards and first cousins. I recognized Pelekai, whose reputation in the city preceded itself. In his mid forties, he was of medium build and had short black hair parted on the side and ebony eyes. Apart from his run-ins with the law, he had often appeared before television cameras as an upstanding, charitable member of the community. But the police and prosecutors seemed to believe that much of what he gave away was nothing more than blood money and hush money.

Pelekai furrowed his brow and peered at me. "What's this about?" he asked.

I sucked in a breath and said concisely: "The late Carter Delaney—"

Pelekai didn't even flinch. "Yeah, I heard about his death. What does it have to do with me?"

Ridge replied: "Mind if we come in?"

Pelekai looked at him distrustfully. "Yes, I mind. Do you have a warrant?"

We didn't, but I wasn't about to let that deter us. "Why, do you have something to hide, Pelekai?" I asked. "We just want to ask you a few questions, that's all."

He shifted his eyes from me to Ridge and back. Displaying a slight grin, he said: "All right. Come in—"

We guardedly followed him into the house that looked even larger on the inside. Two very big muscular bodyguards greeted him and glared at us.

"It's fine," he told them. "They want to ask me some questions about Carter Delaney—"

Pelekai's associates remained tense, but did not speak or appear as if they were ready to present a problem without Pelekai's say so. We were led across a hardwood floor past the traditionally furnished living room to a formal dining room, where a long wooden table was loaded with a variety of traditional Hawaiian foods. At the far end sat a thirty-something, attractive Asian woman with shoulder length dark hair.

"This is my wife, Shizue," Pelekai said, introducing her as if we were the new neighbors. To her, he said: "We've got some visitors. Detective Larsen and—" He looked me in the eye.

"Skye Delaney," I told him. The name seemed to draw everyone's attention.

"Would you like something to eat?" Shizue asked politely.

Before I could decline, Ridge said: "We didn't come here for dinner."

Pelekai kept his cool. "Okay, then let's go to my study to talk." He looked at his wife and said: "Start eating. I won't be long."

She looked disappointed, but complied.

Pelekai raised his hand to halt his bodyguards. "I'll do this alone," he told them. "Sit and eat."

They did as he asked and we followed Pelekai down a curving hallway and past several well-appointed rooms, until he pulled open double doors leading to the study.

Once we were inside, he leveled his eyes at me. "Let's get this over with. Ask your questions..."

He was clearly a confident man who was no stranger in talking to the police, and probably private investigators as well. Ridge and I looked at each other and realized that since this visit was not part of the official police investigation, Kazuo Pelekai was within his rights to talk or not. Obviously, he had made up his mind to say something, but we weren't holding our breath that it would be an outright confession.

"Okay," I said, "did you have anything to do with Carter Delaney's murder?"

"You his wife?" he asked curiously.

"Ex, which is beside the point," I told him.

Pelekai seemed to let that sink in before saying: "Like I already told the other cops, I don't know anything about Delaney's death, other than what I heard on the news—"

"Cut the crap, Pelekai," Ridge said with an edge to his voice. "We both know you've had it in for Delaney since his prosecutor days. It was just a matter of time before you and your crime syndicate cronies were on your way to the state pen, thanks to some of his efforts that continued to put the squeeze on your operations. So maybe you started feeling the heat and figured you would be better off just getting rid of the man who was giving you nightmares, once and for all."

Pelekai's nostrils flared. "You come into *my* house and make such wild accusations, while offering no proof? If you expected some type of confession to a made up story, you've wasted your time and mine. I had no part whatsoever in Carter Delaney's murder and don't know who did!"

He showed no sign of buckling under pressure, which was still far from making him an innocent man. I decided to come at him from a different angle.

"There are rumors flying all around town, Pelekai, that you *did* play a role in Carter's murder," I told him. "I would think that kind of negative publicity of killing a former prosecutor would be very bad for business. Is that what you really want?"

He glared at me. "Ms. Delaney, rumors mean nothing without solid evidence to back them up. I'll be honest when I say I'm not shedding any tears over Carter Delaney's death. But that doesn't mean I had anything to do with killing him. No respectable businessman, which I am, would take out Delaney in this city. As you say, it would be very bad for business..."

If nothing else, Pelekai impressed me with his poise and façade of innocence. But was it reverse psychology? Or was it an indication that he truly was the wrong person to point the finger at for Carter's murder? Even if that were that the case, it didn't mean someone from his inner circle hadn't done the dirty deed, with or without Pelekai's knowledge, having just as much to lose if he went down.

In spite of his attempt to distance himself from Carter's death, something told me that Pelekai knew more than he was letting on. So, grasping at straws, I asked: "If you had nothing to do with Carter's death, then who did? Give us a name—"

He chuckled. "I'm not a psychic, Ms. Delaney. Sorry, but I can't help you."

"Can't or won't?" I tossed back at him. Then I threw in another angle that was worth a try, even if out of my control: "Giving us something to work with now might give the P.A.'s office a good excuse to find someone else to go after—"

Pelekai seemed to ponder the notion, but refused to budge from his position.

"Let's get the hell out of here," Ridge told me. "We're not getting anywhere with him." He issued a warning to Pelekai: "Next time you see me, it won't be a voluntary chitchat—"

Pelekai clasped his hands together. "I'm always willing to cooperate with the authorities," he said, "as long as it doesn't become harassment."

It was hard to argue the point, so I didn't. I decided it was best to save that for another day when we were better equipped to back up our suspicions that Kazuo Pelekai was a key part of the puzzle that resulted in Carter's premature death.

CHAPTER 29

After we left Pelekai's place, Ridge asked me: "So, other than being a well positioned drug dealer, illegal firearms dealer, pimp, and all around son of a bitch thought to be involved in organized crime throughout the islands and on the mainland, what was your take on Pelekai?"

As if those things weren't bad enough, I answered bluntly: "He knows something about Carter's murder. Don't ask me what. Call it women's intuition."

"Maybe," Ridge said, sounding less than convinced. "Try taking that to court."

"I didn't say he killed Carter," I told Ridge. "I'm pretty sure Pelekai wouldn't do the dirty work himself, but that doesn't mean one of his bodyguards or other associates couldn't have done the deed."

"Yeah, I agree," Ridge said. "We've had our eyes on the so-called bodyguards for some time now. Alfonso Takemoto and Masakazu Miyoshi. A couple of scumbags who are suspected of drug dealing and assault, among other things. They're also suspects in a drive-by shooting that killed a snitch named Frankie Pokipala."

I wondered what Ridge meant about the cops having their eyes on the bodyguards. Either they believed Kazuo

Pelekai and his comrades were involved in Carter's death or they didn't, apart from their other alleged criminal activity. I steadied the car over a bumpy stretch of road, then inquired innocuously: "Does the P.A.'s office, or your office for that matter, really think it has a case against Pelekai in Carter's death? Or is that just wishful thinking on my part?"

Ridge ran a hand across his head, which also seemed to give him time to consider the question carefully. "Sure would wrap things up in a nice, neat little package if we could arrest Pelekai and his cronies for Carter's murder," he admitted. "And, to be quite honest about it, it would make our job in the department a hell of a lot easier if they were all locked away—"

I flashed him a look of skepticism. "Does *easier* mean looking for a scapegoat instead of finding the *real* murderer?" I had to ask, though I already knew the answer.

"We're doing the best we can," Ridge said defensively. "Carter Delaney, like him or not, left his mark on this city and many of the people in it. No one in the department wants to pin his death on the wrong person or persons. If Pelekai had nothing to do with it—and I'm not sure I buy that—he'll be dropped from our list of suspects and we'll go on from there."

"Sorry," I told him sincerely. "Guess it's easier being a cop when you're not one anymore." This seemed especially true when it happened to be your ex-husband's murder that was being investigated.

"Hey, there's nothing in the rule books that says a cop who retired ahead of schedule can't rejoin the force," Ridge hinted. "I think it would be fun working with you officially for a change."

"Don't hold your breath," I warned him. "There's no amount of money or other enticements that could get me to give up my freedom to return to the grind of the rank and file. Besides, I'm not sure you could handle dating someone you had to work side by side with on a daily basis."

He must have agreed, given his sudden loss of speech.

* * *

Ridge and I went to dinner at a place on Ala Moana Boulevard called Yoshio's Bar & Grill, where we ordered smoked salmon and fettuccini.

I took a sip of red wine before asking Ridge: "So how the hell does someone with Carter's same rare blood type follow him to my house, strangle him, dump him in the Jacuzzi tub, lose some flesh and blood to Ollie's fangs, and then manage to apparently go underground—all without being seen or heard by anyone? It can't be that easy to hide in Honolulu."

If that was a mouthful, Ridge seemed able to digest it with one even swallow. "Obviously, the whole thing was well thought out and executed without a hitch, except for Ollie's ferocious appetite. And maybe it wasn't so ferocious after all. Unless he bit a doctor, it couldn't have been much more than a flesh wound, since there's no indication the person was treated anywhere on the island."

A thought occurred to me as I tasted more wine. "Do you remember reading about that clinic in Manoa on Punahou Street that was shut down a few weeks ago due to unsanitary conditions?"

"Yeah, why?" Ridge asked.

"I think I heard they were back in business while they appealed their case," I told him.

"So?"

"So," I said, "whoever Ollie bit could have gone there for treatment..."

"That's assuming they knew the clinic existed, much less reopened," Ridge said skeptically.

"But it makes sense," I said. "The clinic isn't far from my house, and just about every other medical facility in the city has already been accounted for. Being under the radar, it would have been the perfect place to get patched up."

Ridge dribbled his fingers on the table pensively. "Seems like a stretch, but I suppose it's worth checking out."

That told me the cops hadn't checked it out yet. It was a surprising oversight for a police force that was supposedly checking every nook and cranny to find Carter's killer. I didn't blame Ridge, per se. He may have been in charge of the investigation, but he was only one man dependent on the professionalism and dedication of his partner and their subordinates.

Meaning I needed to check out the clinic myself and see if it led anywhere.

The conversation turned to topics more suitable for two people who were seeing each other socially, if not sexually of late. The timing for intimacy hadn't been right, and the mood had definitely been all wrong ever since Carter's death, as if he were somehow sabotaging my relationship with Ridge even from the grave.

This night was no different, as I dropped Ridge off at his house and went straight to my own, favoring my company over his. He didn't press it, and I hated putting him in a position where he had every right to press. I didn't want to lose him, but was afraid I might do just that if he got tired of waiting while I sorted out what I needed to.

Sleep was my escape—but it came at a price. In a dream, Carter came back to haunt me in the image of how I had last seen him dead in my tub. I awoke in a cold sweat and went to the kitchen for a glass of water. It seemed like Ollie was also having a restless sleep. I found him half-draped over a living room chair, whimpering.

"It's just a bad dream, boy," I said, gently running my hand across his head. "Maybe water will work for you, too?" He licked my hand. I took that as a yes and put my glass to his mouth where he quickly lapped up the rest of the water with his tongue.

Back in bed, with Ollie on the floor beside me, I was ready to give sleep another try. When it finally came, I was spared the nightmare of Carter's death. But I had a feeling that it was merely waiting for another time and place to strike again.

CHAPTER 30

Manoa was less than a mile from Waikiki and home of the University of Hawaii at Manoa. It was also where the Manoa Aloha Clinic had recently reopened its doors.

It was nearly noon when I stepped inside the clinic. The place was crowded with people waiting to be treated and in various stages of health. I headed over to the reception counter, where I saw a thirty-something receptionist with thick dark hair and blonde highlights.

"Can I help you?" she asked.

"I'm not sure," I admitted. "I need some information—"

"What kind of information...?" She gave me a serious look of distrust, as though I might be a spy from the Health Department.

I explained in an improvisation of fact and fiction that someone had broken into my house about a week ago and stole some jewelry. In the process, my dog bit the person before he or she got away. Due to the amount of blood left behind, I figured the wounds were probably deep enough to require treatment and since this was the closest medical facility...

"One piece of jewelry taken was a family heirloom given to me by my grandmother," I said, pretending that I was

147

about to cry. "I'd like it back—that's all. But first, I need to know if I'm on the right track—"

Lying was almost an art form in the private investigation business. If you were good at it, you were far more likely to net positive results, even if you felt bad about it afterward. So far, for me, the outcome had been mixed.

The receptionist hesitated before saying: "You need to talk to Doctor Zeller." Her eyes scanned the patients waiting in chairs and on foot. "I hope you aren't in a hurry because it's first come, first serve—"

I was in no position to argue. I settled for an adequate smile and a searched for an empty seat, which I never found.

Nearly two hours later, a tall, gray-haired man of around forty approached me. "I'm Dr. Zeller," he said.

"Skye Delaney." I stood and met his dapple-gray eyes.

"Come with me please," he said in a tired voice.

I followed him to a small and cluttered back office, where he offered me a seat in one of two vinyl chairs. I couldn't help but notice the framed medical degree from the University of Hawaii at Manoa's John A. Burns School of Medicine awarded to Andrew Gavin Zeller.

Dr. Zeller regarded me after following the path of my eyes, and sat down at his glass-topped desk. "Yes, I received my degree locally and am proud of it, but it doesn't mean much to most people who come to this clinic. Many haven't even graduated from high school, much less gone to college, and they don't always know how to take care of themselves."

I got the feeling he was defending the need to have such a clinic available to poor, uneducated, and uninsured people. I wasn't prepared to debate the complex issues of health care and impoverishment, so I said simply: "It's nice to know some of us do go on to college and are able to give something back to those less fortunate."

I couldn't tell whether he agreed or not, since he gave me a deadpan look. Finally, he said: "The receptionist told me your sad story about the family heirloom. Sorry to hear it was stolen—"

"It happens," I responded guiltily.

"And you think the thief your dog attacked may have come here for treatment?"

"I was hoping you could tell me—"

He hesitated. "That all depends..."

I frowned. "On what?"

Narrowing his eyes, Zeller responded: "Whether or not the wounded thief is the same person who killed *your* ex-husband." He watched my surprised reaction, then said: "You did say you were Skye Delaney, didn't you?"

I nodded reluctantly.

"And Carter Delaney was murdered at your home, right?" He leaned back in his chair. "It doesn't take a detective to be able to put two and two together, Ms. Delaney."

I agreed and tried to soften the blow. "My ex-husband really has—"

"What is this really all about?" he cut in sharply.

There seemed no point in stringing this out any further, so I sighed and said what he had likely already heard. "I'm a private investigator." I got no particular reaction from him, so I continued. "I need to find out if anyone came in here with a dog bite on the day Carter was killed."

Zeller stared at me for a moment or two, then said: "Yes, as I recall, there was a man we treated that evening who had a dog bite on his shoulder. I patched him up and he left in a hurry, after refusing a tetanus shot. There's not much more I can tell you about him than that."

He had already told me something. Was the wounded party Carter's killer or was it just a cruel coincidence?

I gazed at the doctor eagerly. "Did you by chance happen to keep a sample of his blood?"

He shook his head. "There was no reason to. Sorry."

I sighed. "I suppose that also means you don't know his blood type."

"Afraid not," Zeller said.

"Can you describe him?" I asked.

Zeller shrugged. "I'm not really good at describing people. He was Caucasian, average height and build, probably in his late thirties. Wish I could be of more help, but I don't have the luxury or time—being only one of two doctors on staff with more patients than we can handle—to pay much attention to those who use our services, aside from treating them as best we can." He paused, then asked: "You think he was the man who killed Carter Delaney?"

I considered the question and could only come up with one answer. "I'm not sure—" I stood up. "Thanks for your time."

He rose. "No problem."

As an afterthought, I asked: "Do you know if he came here by himself or maybe with a woman?"

Zeller shook his head. "Couldn't say. Sorry."

Not as sorry as I was.

I left the clinic feeling as if I had actually made progress on the case, though I was no closer to the who's and why's of Carter's death. If this man was Carter's killer, it still left more questions than answers.

I called Ridge and told him: "I suggest you get someone down to the Manoa Aloha Clinic right away and talk to Dr. Zeller. Mug shots and a sketch artist would probably be helpful, too."

* * *

I went home and had some lunch. Then I did a bit of neglected gardening, swam with Ollie, and showered. By three-thirty, I was at a boxing club on Palolo Road called Kurt's Gym. It was where many of the up and coming boxers in the city trained in hopes of hitting the pugilistic jackpot someday. Others were simply interested in getting a good workout.

The gym was named after its owner, Kurt Butler. Once a promising middleweight contender in Philadelphia who fell prey to drug addiction, he was now a middle-aged, well-respected trainer and drug free. Having lived in Honolulu for over a decade, Kurt also happened to be a man with big eyes and even bigger ears. He had been my source for information that I couldn't get anywhere else ever since my days on the force, and he was also my personal trainer in boxing techniques that came in handy at times. He called it settling his debt for my role in helping him stay out of prison when he was knocking at the door. I called it a nice and lasting friendship.

I walked through the place that reeked of body odor and sweat, worsened by the humidity that hung in the air like a cumulus cloud. Boxers worked out in rings for that one big shot, while others had taken to the bags in developing arm strength and quickness.

I found Kurt holding a bag unsteadily as yet another young hopeful was pounding away at it with everything he had.

I commented: "Hey, take it easy there on the old man. He's on your side."

Kurt smiled broadly, his bald head gleaming with perspiration. He had on a Kurt's Gym jersey and gray sweats. "Damned right I am," he uttered, absorbing a couple more punishing blows before saying to the puncher: "Take ten, kid..."

"Is he as good as he looks?" I asked Kurt while his finely sculpted, glistening protégé walked off.

Kurt chuckled. "Thinks he is. Like all young boxers—and sometimes us old ones—he's got a helluva lot to learn." Kurt took the towel off his wide shoulder and dried his face. His smile returned. "So how you doin', girl? Ain't seen you in a long time." His eyes scanned me from head to toe. "I see you're still taking good care of yourself."

"Have to if I'm going to keep up with you," I told him proudly. In fact, he looked as good as I'd ever seen him.

He laughed. "Ain't always easy, but I do all right." He sucked in a deep breath. "So what brings you down here? You ready to go a few rounds with me in the ring?"

Under other circumstances, I would have welcomed that with the master, but replied: "I'll have to take a rain check on that." I sighed and summed my visit up with two words: "Carter Delaney..."

Kurt's gray-brown eyes lit up. "Your ex," he said. "Heard he took it on the chin, so to speak."

"You could say that," I muttered, then said in earnest: "I need your help, Kurt."

He looked at me curiously. "What you got in mind, girl?"

I glanced around the gym and back at Kurt's face, before answering. "I need you to help me find out who murdered Carter." I knew it was a long shot, especially if the killer was beyond Kurt's network of underground contacts. On the other hand, if there was one person outside the police force who might be able to yield something useful, I was looking at him.

He wiped away more sweat from his face, which seemed to have increased in the last few seconds. "Why don't we step into my office?" he said. "It ain't too comfy, but it's quiet..."

And away from listening ears, I mused.

Kurt's office was small and carpeted, with paneled walls. The stench of cigars permeated the air, in spite of a corner fan that was on. A large TV sat on a stand next to an old metal desk that was cluttered with papers. Two wooden folding chairs leaned against one wall, and another wall was covered with framed photographs of Kurt with such boxing greats as Joe Frasier, Muhammad Ali, George Foreman, and Sugar Ray Leonard.

Kurt closed the door, unfolded a chair and said: "Sit." So I did. He sat on the edge of the desk, and gazed at me warily. "You know I love you to death, Skye, but I don't see how I can help you."

"Ask around," I suggested, "and see if there was a hit on Carter or anyone who may have had a strong reason to want him dead."

Kurt pursed his lips. "Ain't that what us taxpayers pay the cops for? Or are you trying to beat them to the punch cuz it's personal?"

"Let's just say I want to see justice done more than usual," I told him. My eyes rested on his scarred chin where boxers had left their mark. Looking into his eyes, I said: "If it means solving a case for the cops, so be it—"

He tilted his head to one side. "Carter Delaney was pretty well known in this town, and not always for the right reasons, which I'm sure I don't have to tell you. If someone put a hit on him, the dude must be pretty powerful. Course, there's always some lone rangers out there to settle old scores..."

I considered both of those possibilities, along with a few others.

Kurt leaned toward me. "I owe you, Skye, always will. Can't make no promises, but let me ask around—see if I can find out anything. Just know that askin' the wrong questions to the wrong people can get me killed—"

A wave of guilt washed over me. "I wouldn't think of asking you to put your life on the line, Kurt," I stressed. "It's not worth that for either of us, and it's too late for Carter. If you come up with something that won't put your nose out of joint, fine, if not, I can live with that—"

He smiled and then stood. "We'll be talkin' real soon."

I was counting on it. I got up and smiled at him. "You know where to reach me."

Kurt nodded and said: "Look, if you've got time, what say we do a little workout—keep those skills I taught you sharp as a knife."

"What about your protégé?" I asked.

"He can take another ten or fifteen. I don't think he'll complain."

It was an offer I found hard to pass up. "I've got the time," I told him.

"Good," he said. "Let's go."

My heart was already pounding with anticipation. As we headed into the gym, I told him: "By the way, in case I forgot to tell you, whatever debt you feel you owe me, you paid up in full a long time ago." I winked. "But feel free to keep believing otherwise if you want."

* * *

Nearly an hour later, I stepped outside Kurt's Gym feeling exhausted, but ready to rumble. The fresh air was like a slice of heaven. I wondered if it was smart to allow myself to become so wrapped up in a murder that hit so close to home.

It took me until I was halfway home to accept that I really had no choice but to see this thing through come hell or high water. The fact that I was operating as my own client, in essence, for a case that seemed anything but open and shut, made it all the more challenging.

Following a shower, change of clothes, and babying Ollie, I headed to my office. I was two minutes away when I suddenly felt lazy and decided to forego work for the rest of the day. Whatever had to be done could wait. A trip to the bookstore before it became extinct sounded much more inviting. Maybe diving into the latest Mary Higgins Clark or Devon Vaughn Archer novel was just what I needed to take my mind off real life horrors.

I couldn't think of a better way to spend the rest of the afternoon.

CHAPTER 31

He followed her to the bookstore just for the hell of it.

She was so wrapped up in looking for the perfect book that she never even noticed him, even though he practically went out of his way to block her path so she would bump into him. He imagined her saying, as though it was her fault: "Excuse me," then he'd been prepared to say humorously: "Don't I know you? Aren't you Skye Delaney? At least now I know you can read..."

Then he would have given her his charming smile and asked her out. Who knew where they might have ended up from there...if he had his way?

But no, before the fantasy could play out, she went the other way—straight to the cashier with three books in hand, and was soon out the door.

The mood had definitely been broken.

Next time, Skye Delaney, there may not be an easy out, he thought. He tossed the book he'd been holding on a table, and left.

* * *

By morning, he was back to his old confident self again. He followed Skye as she ran from her house to the beach, all by her lonesome. Must have been too early for that damned dog of hers to come along.

He took some pictures of her. And more pictures, enjoying each and every image she conveyed so gracefully.

Skye never failed to get a rise out of him. He could see everything that Carter Delaney saw in her, and probably more.

You hear that, Delaney? a voice in his head shouted. *Your ass is six feet under and your ex old lady is very much alive and ripe for the taking, even with that damned Detective Ridge Larsen in her life. Think about it, while you rot in hell.*

He ran out of film at about the same time Skye got tired of running.

Time to go develop these, he thought eagerly. He slipped away, and Skye Delaney never even knew he was there.

CHAPTER 32

Ridge studied the sketch of the suspect from the passenger seat of the car as Kawakami drove. They'd just come from the clinic, where Doctor Andrew Zeller had described a man who had been treated for a dog bite around the same time Carter Delaney was murdered.

"What's your take on him?" Kawakami asked.

The man in the sketch was white, approximately thirty-five to forty years of age, with close dark eyes, straggly blonde hair, medium build, and about six feet tall.

Before Ridge could respond, Kawakami said: "He could be our man."

Ridge looked at the sketch again. "I don't think so," he said confidently, wishing to hell he felt otherwise. Especially since it was Skye's legwork that had sent them to the clinic in search of a killer.

Kawakami glanced his way. "Why not? We can place him in the vicinity of the crime when it was committed and he was bitten in the shoulder by a dog, but didn't hang around long enough to answer any questions... Seems to fit—"

Ridge frowned. "Anything's possible, but I'm just not feeling it. I'd hate to put too much focus on the sketch of a man Zeller admitted he couldn't even be sure was an accurate depiction. We've got no DNA, fingerprints, or anyone to back up the doctor's statement. My guess is this patient was bitten by a dog other than Ollie and had his own reasons for leaving in a hurry."

"So you're saying we should eliminate him as a suspect before we even track him down?" Kawakami asked.

"I'm saying I think there are others who make much stronger suspects, as far as I'm concerned," Ridge said, trying not to step on any toes. "Could be Zeller was mistaken in his description of the man, if not lying altogether, for whatever reason. Or Delaney's killer may not have needed treatment by a doctor. We just need to keep all possibilities on the table."

After a moment or two, Kawakami asked Ridge: "What were you doing when Delaney was killed?"

Ridge cocked a brow in surprise. "Am I a suspect now?"

"You tell me," Kawakami replied brusquely. "You're involved with Skye Delaney and the deceased happened to be her ex who may have been gone from her life, but was definitely not forgotten. Maybe that mile long jealous streak in you snapped like a twig and you went after Delaney so you'd have Skye *all* to yourself."

Ridge resented the insinuation. As far as he knew, he did have Skye all to himself, when she gave in to romance. Even if part of Skye had still pined for Delaney, Ridge felt Delaney had his hands full with enough other women that he didn't need to try and win her back too. *I would never have killed Carter Delaney or anyone else to eliminate the competition,* Ridge thought angrily.

Then he sucked in a deep breath and realized that Kawakami was just being Kawakami, trying to push his buttons for the hell of it. Still, Ridge felt obliged to defend himself. "I was on a hostage stakeout/homicide investigation on the other side of town *all* afternoon until I got a call that Carter Delaney was found dead at Skye's house. At least a dozen other cops were on the scene at the time. You want their names *and* badge numbers?"

Kawakami grinned and then chuckled. "Lighten up, Larsen," he said. "I'm just messing with your head, man. No one's accusing you of offing Delaney. You're not that stupid or reckless." Kawakami paused. "But Skye is definitely worth fighting for. I only wish she'd seen in me what she obviously sees in you."

Ridge forced a grin, though he was not amused by Kawakami's sense of humor. "Yes, Skye's worth fighting for, but not murdering for out of jealousy without due cause. As for what she sees in me and didn't see in you, you'll have to ask her that." Ridge had a few ideas, but didn't want to mention them to Kawakami.

That notwithstanding, he couldn't help but wonder if Skye's interest in him was waning. Things clearly hadn't been the same between them on the romantic front since Carter Delaney's death. He wanted to be patient with Skye, but he needed her to be willing to meet him halfway, even as they pursued separately and together the culprit for her ex-husband's murder.

Ridge looked once more at the sketch and basically dismissed him as the person they were after, believing it simply didn't add up to be credible enough to pursue. Which meant that they were essentially back to square one in many respects. *Nice try, Skye,* he thought.

CHAPTER 33

Leilani Mahaulu walked into my office clutching my business card in her hand as if it was more precious than gold. It was early Friday morning and the coffeemaker was still dripping.

"Hey," I said from my desk chair, masking my surprise, and hoping to make her feel comfortable at the same time.

"Aloha," she said in a shaky voice. "I kept your card and—"

"Please, have a seat..." I told her, offering a welcome smile.

Unlike the performer I last saw, this Leilani was much more down to earth in appearance. Her long hair was in a ponytail and she wore no makeup. Casual attire replaced the hula dancer outfit.

"I was just about to have some coffee," I said. "Want some?"

She nodded. "Sure."

I filled two mugs, adding two packets of sugar to hers.

"Mahalo," Leilani said and put the cup to her mouth.

I sat back down and did the same. Neither of us said anything for a moment or two as I waited for Leilani to say what I suspected weighed heavily on her mind.

Finally, she asked unevenly: "I was wondering how the investigation into Carter's murder was coming along?"

"Not very well, I'm afraid," I answered honestly, insofar as my own investigation. "Few people seem willing to talk, if they know something..."

I had a feeling that was about to change.

Leilani put down her mug and admitted: "I was romantically involved with Carter at the time of his death—"

Chalk up one for Darlene, I thought. We both did more sipping of coffee while I wondered just how many other Leilanis might be out there waiting to surface.

"It wasn't serious," she claimed. "He didn't want it to be. Neither did I. Serious relationships usually end in disaster, especially when one party is married." Leilani's face suggested there were more serious feelings than she was willing to admit. "With us it was great sex, laughs, and comfort when one of us needed it. When I heard Carter was dead, all I wanted to do was distance myself from him."

"Why?" I asked, even though the answer was crystal clear.

"Why do you think? I'm a hula dancer," she said, as if they were dirty words. "He was a powerful, married businessman who seemed to have everything going for him—well, almost. I didn't want or need any tabloid type publicity or trouble—"

"What type of *trouble*?" I asked, favoring her with wide eyes.

Leilani put the cup to her mouth. "When I first met Carter at a club, he was with a man he introduced as Nellie. Later, he told me the guy was his bookie. Carter loved to gamble..."

She wrinkled her nose as if this should come as no surprise to someone who had been married to him. The Carter I knew played the horses on occasion, but never bet anything more than a few bucks here and there.

"Go on..." I prodded with interest.

"He owed a *lot* of money on lost bets and was afraid he might not be able to come up with it and what might happen if he didn't." She rolled her eyes. "Then Carter winds up dead. What was I supposed to think?"

"Probably just what you've been thinking," I admitted, though shocked at the notion. I was aware that people had been known to lose their lives when they were unable to cover gambling debts in a timely manner. But Carter was supposed to be worth a bundle, or so I'd read from time to time. Unfortunately, I had divorced him before he really hit his stride as a millionaire. Could he have been in such hock that he couldn't raise the money to pay his debts? I was equally disturbed by the idea that Carter had been addicted to gambling.

Leilani interrupted my thoughts when she said: "I'm only telling *you* this, because it seemed like something I should do. But no police! I don't want to spend the rest of my life having to look over my shoulder—"

I couldn't make her talk to the police. For that matter, why would I want to? She didn't have to come to me with what she had. From where I sat, if the police wanted her statement, they would have to get it on their own.

"No police," I promised, and hoped it was a promise I didn't have to break anytime soon.

Carter's dirty laundry seemed to be getting dirtier with each passing day. My only interest was to find out who killed him and why. It was best left to a higher authority than me to pass judgment on him or anybody else.

I gazed at Leilani. "Do you happen to know what Nellie's last name is?"

She shrugged. "Nellie was all he called him—"

So much for being able to zero in on the man, I thought, while believing it shouldn't be that hard with a little help from a friend. Finding Nellie had suddenly become a priority.

* * *

"I'm looking for a bookie by the name of Nellie," I told Kurt at the Coconut Club on Kona Street, where drinks were on me.

He scratched his pate. "Nellie, huh?"

162

"You know him?'" I asked over the rim of my beer mug. "This could be important—"

"Yeah, I know him." Kurt downed a swig of beer and licked his lips. "His name is Nelson Lewinski. He's got a place on Auahi Street. Smalltime bookie with big connections."

I took the information down. "Thanks," I said.

"You lookin' to bet or borrow some money?" Kurt asked.

"No," I assured him. "I only gamble on sure things with my own money. I need to see Lewinski for a case." I left it at that and he didn't ask for more. I saw no need to make Carter's gambling issues public knowledge, while assuming they already were to some extent. My mouth dove into more suds, then I asked: "Did you come up with anything on who may have had it in for Carter?"

Kurt's brows united. "There's all kinds of rumors goin' around, but nobody to point a finger at and still have it attached to your hand."

I barely suppressed a giggle, but got the drift. "You mean the finger is pointed at someone in particular, like Kazuo Pelekai?" I asked.

Kurt hedged and looked around the bar cautiously. "Now don't go puttin' words in my mouth," he said, gulping beer. "Let's just say not everybody is as torn up over your ex's death as you. Having him out of the way is good for business for some people, if not bad news for Carter Delaney. But being the one to put him out of commission is something else..." Kurt's eyes fixed me carefully. "I'll be sure to let you know if I hear 'bout anything that ain't gonna get either of us killed—"

"And I thought tough ex-boxers weren't afraid of anything," I said.

"Who said anything 'bout being afraid?" he scoffed. "It's a matter of survival, girl. I wanna be around to see my nephews and nieces graduate from high school. College, too."

I could relate, even though I didn't have any nephews or nieces. Finishing off the beer, I told Kurt: "You know where to find me when and if you need to."

He nodded and said: "Yeah, I do."

I thought about the potentially perilous road that may lie ahead for both of us.

CHAPTER 34

I found Nelson Lewinski just where Kurt said I would. He practiced his trade on the second floor of a building that also housed a loan shark and massage parlor. I definitely found some symmetry there for people who made their living in the underbelly of society. The sign on the door said simply Business Services. I opened it and entered the cramped office. Sitting at an L-shaped wooden desk was a fifty-something man of medium build with a receding reddish hairline. He had a cell phone to his ear and was shouting profanities to some poor sucker on the other end of the line.

I glanced at an overflowing wastebasket and a ceiling fan that was struggling to operate in the stuffy office. I looked again at the man. He was staring at me while telling someone to call him before nine if he valued his life, and then he ended the conversation.

He looked at me lasciviously and said: "What can I do for you, sweet lady?"

"Are you Nelson Lewinski?" I asked, to be sure, adding: "Nellie?"

"Yeah, that's me. Who are you?"

"Skye Delaney," I said. "I'm a private investigator—"

A thoughtful expression formed on his face. "Delaney, huh? You wouldn't happen to be related to the late Carter Delaney, would you?"

"Not that it matters, but we were married once," I replied.

He sighed. "Believe me you're better off without him!"

I had to agree, but said somewhat resentfully: "I'm not here to talk about my private life."

"Too bad," he moaned and gave me the once-over. "Exactly what are you here to talk about?"

"You—" I said and stepped toward the desk.

He lifted a thick brow. "What about me?"

"I want to know about the gambling debts Carter Delaney amassed and how far you were willing to go to collect them."

Lewinski flinched. "I have no idea what you're talking about," he claimed.

I planted my hands solidly on the desk and leaned at him with a scowl. "You and I both know you were his bookie, so let's cut the crap—"

He grinned, showing me his yellow teeth. "Okay, so I took bets for Delaney. Big deal! He liked to bet on college and pro football, boxing matches, and more. If wasn't me, it would've been someone else to take his money."

"But it was *you* who Carter placed the bets with—and now he's dead," I pointed out. "I'm sure the police would be very interested in talking to you about it."

This seemed to unnerve Lewinski. "Now don't get your feathers all ruffled, sweet lady," he said. "If you're suggesting I had something to do with Delaney's death—"

"I am unless you can convince me otherwise—" I told him, wanting to keep the pressure on just in case it was warranted. "I know Carter was in over his head. Even slime like you can resort to murder, if the shoe fits."

His nostrils expanded. "It doesn't."

When he reached for a top drawer, I clutched the gun in my purse and said: "I wouldn't, if I were you. I'm not about to take a bullet—at least not before giving up one or two myself."

Lewinski raised his hands, as if in surrender. "Hey, take it easy. I was just going to get my ledger out." His hands lowered slowly. "Delaney's debts were paid in full while he was still alive to place bets—"

He went again for the drawer.

"Careful..." I said, watching him like a hawk as he removed a red ledger.

"Delaney was into me for one mil, until just recently..." Lewinski said, flipping through the pages. "Lucky for me and his widow, the account was paid up before he met his maker." He stopped flipping. "Here, see with your own eyes—"

He handed me the ledger and I honed in on some scribbling on several pages that included Carter's name, various wagers, and a debt totaling one million dollars. Stamped across the last page were the words PAID IN FULL.

Needless to say, I was floored that Carter had gambled and lost so much money. Of course gambling of any kind, including bingo, was illegal in Hawaii, but that didn't prevent people from doing it. I wondered if Darlene was aware of his betting excesses. How could she not be? But then I considered that Carter had fooled me for years into thinking he was someone that he wasn't. Why should Darlene be any smarter?

Lewinski was saying: "I'm old-fashioned when it comes to record keeping."

Not to mention a ledger is easier to get rid of if the authorities come calling versus having the info on a computer, I thought, glancing again at what certainly appeared to be proof that Carter was in way over his head as a gambler.

"So you see, I had no reason to want Carter Delaney dead," Lewinski contended. "Just the opposite. I was sorry to see him go. He was the type of person any bookie could learn to love: a big time gambling addict who always found a way to pay up at the end of the day."

I studied the last page of Carter's entry in the ledger. The debt paid was dated two days before he was murdered. Did Carter have a premonition of his death? I wondered. And what had he had to do to come up with the money, since apparently his business income still left him strapped for hard cash.

I looked down at Lewinski and asked: "How did Carter pay you?" I closed the ledger and gave it back to him.

"He didn't pay me," Lewinski said, running a hand across his mouth. "His wife Darlene Delaney did. Paid off the balance due with a cashier's check—"

The plot thickens, I thought in surprise. Why would Darlene pay off the debt—and why two days before Carter was murdered? She'd clearly been holding out on me, and likely the police as well. But did that make her an accomplice in Carter's death?

In my preoccupation, I was caught off guard when I suddenly realized that Lewinski was now on his feet and scant inches away from me. Instinctively, I reached inside my purse, but Lewinski was faster, grabbing my wrist in a viselike grip and pulling the purse away with his other hand.

He tossed it on the desk and said leeringly: "Now that we've finished our business, let's get to know each other better on an intimate level..."

He was several inches taller and pressed his body against me, still holding one wrist. Unfortunately for him, he left my other arm free. I was still fresh off my one-on-one with Kurt and was only too happy to put practice into real time use.

When Lewinski overconfidently moved in for a kiss while slowly inching his hand up my thigh, what he got instead was a hard fist slammed against his nose. While yelling and trying to recover, he released my arm and I went to work, pounding his face with rapid lefts and rights till my fists were sore. Then I planted a knee squarely between his legs, figuring that since he was looking for some action there, I'd be happy to oblige.

Nelson Lewinski fell to the floor writhing and moaning in pain, his face a bloody mess.

I looked down at the man who made a living off other people's misery and had overstepped his bounds with me, and said with satisfaction: "Hope it hurts like hell! If I were you, I wouldn't press my luck much further. Sooner or later the debt collector will come looking for you and you may not be able to pay the price—"

CHAPTER 35

Elberta led me to Darlene, who was swimming in an Olympic-sized pool in the backyard. The pool area had a spa, lagoon, waterfall, and accent rocks, and was surrounded by lush Hawaiian landscaping. Not to mention the mesmerizing ocean as a backdrop. She completed a lap expertly while I waited for her to arrive at my feet. It was obvious she was not expecting company, or should I say *my* company.

"Ms. Delaney insisted on seeing you," Elberta said apologetically.

"It's okay," Darlene said with a pasted on smile. "Nice to see you again, Skye. I think..."

"I need to talk to you—" I told her, skipping the pleasantries.

"No problem," she said, leisurely floating on her back. "How about joining me in the pool? I'm sure Elberta can find you a swimsuit that fits."

I kept my cool under the hot sun. "No, thanks," I said. "I prefer wearing my *own* suit." I gave her a dirty look. "Anyway, I didn't come here to swim—"

Or, for that matter, I thought, *to watch you show off how you're living the good life while your husband lays six feet under, though apparently now debt free.*

She finally climbed out of the water, her tanned body barely covered in a skimpy leopard print bikini. Elberta handed Darlene a long mint green towel and received an eye-to-eye cue that her outdoor services were no longer needed.

Darlene studied me while drying her face. "Have you learned something more about Carter's death?"

I sighed before responding with a catch to my voice: "I was hoping you could tell me."

Our eyes locked. She fluttered her lashes and said: "I don't understand."

"Neither do I," I said, and probably confused her even more. Squinting and sweating, I asked: "Can we get out of the sun?"

I followed her to an acrylic table under a market-style umbrella. A pitcher of iced lemonade and tall glasses waited invitingly. We both sat in pine Adirondack fan back chairs.

Drying her hair with the towel, Darlene inquired curiously: "So what is it you were hoping I could tell you?"

"How long have you known about Carter's gambling habit?" I asked bluntly.

Her eyes grew. "How long have you?"

"Since Leilani Mahaulu told me—"

Darlene's reaction was a mixture of anger and affirmation. "I should've known," she grumbled. "That bitch! She had Carter wrapped around her finger and he loved every moment of it."

You've got some nerve, lady, I thought. *Talk about the kettle calling the pot black*. "That's between you and her," I stressed. "I'd rather talk about the million dollars you paid to cover Carter's debt—"

Darlene shot me an annoyed look. "Is that what that little bitch told you?"

"No, Nelson Lewinski happily volunteered the information..." I announced and watched her shrink back into the chair, while I thought about the way I left him in a heap on the floor. "I find it just a tiny bit suspicious that the wife of a man who was up to his eyeballs in heavy gambling debts managed to cover those debts just days before he turns up dead—"

She tensed. "Yes, I paid off his bookie, but only because I wanted to protect myself and my daughter from something that could have destroyed Carter, and ultimately us." Darlene met my eyes. "I had no idea Carter would be killed!"

I held her gaze. "Are you telling me that Carter was being blackmailed?"

"No... Um... I was," Darlene stammered, catching me by surprise. She sipped some lemonade and continued. "Lewinski approached me and said that Carter owed him a million dollars. He told me if he didn't get his money, he'd see to it that the tabloids and anyone else who'd listen would find out that the former prosecutor and businessman had illegally gambled away damned near everything he had and could get his hands on—" She sucked in a deep breath. "I scraped up the money by dipping into Ivy's trust fund, selling some stocks and mutual funds in my name, and anything else I could turn into cash. Carter was so wrapped up in his own little world and big problems, he never even knew—"

And never would, I lamented. Carter's gambling addiction had nearly ruined him and had taken away from his daughter's financial future, while tainting all of the positive things he stood for in life. Was his death somehow related to the gambling, I wondered, not really sure about anything anymore where it concerned my ex-husband and what was going on inside his head.

I regarded the second wife. In many ways, she was probably more than Carter deserved and in other ways, less. "For what it's worth," I told her, "I probably would've done the same thing, given the same circumstances—"

Darlene licked her lips. "For what it's worth, I'm glad you never had to."

I reflected on that while glancing at the suddenly inviting pool. "Someday it might be nice to go swimming in your pool."

"Anytime you like," she offered, and seemed to mean it.

CHAPTER 36

It turned out that Carter's death was only the start of a trail of untimely demises in Honolulu that may or may not have been connected. Right now, my interest was solely on discovering why Carter had been left head first in my Jacuzzi tub, the victim of foul play.

Ridge provided one possible suspect. "Kalolo Nawahi," he told me during a video phone chat, revealing the name of Darlene's drug supplier. "He's been arrested a couple of times on drug charges, but was released for lack of evidence."

I gathered as much, since the person Ollie bit had no DNA on file in the CODIS database. Was Nawahi just lucky? I wondered. Or was there more to him than dealing drugs, like having AB negative blood and committing cold and calculated murder?

"Could be Nawahi discovered the lady he knew as Amber was really Mrs. Carter Delaney, wife of the millionaire businessman," Ridge suggested. "If that isn't enough, it just so happens that when Delaney was a prosecutor, he put Nawahi's half-brother, Julio Estrada, away for attempted murder. Maybe Nawahi was trying to blackmail Delaney about his coke-using wife and it went sour. Or maybe he just decided he wanted revenge on behalf of Estrada, so Nawahi killed Carter—"

I looked at Ridge's face on the small screen, digesting his words and the surprise about Nawahi's half-brother. This notwithstanding, the facts and figures still didn't add up in my mind and I told Ridge so. He agreed, sort of.

"Okay, so maybe revenge wasn't the most likely motive," he conceded. "But finding out that he could make a hell of a lot more money from the husband than the wife might have been more than Nawahi could resist."

"Possibly," I said, knowing that greed and murder often went hand in hand, along with opportunity.

"Kawakami and I are going to pay Kalolo Nawahi a little visit," Ridge told me. After a pause, he added thoughtfully: "You want to meet us there?"

"Are you inviting me?" It wasn't every day that he allowed me to ride along for an official visit with a suspect. But this wasn't a run of the mill case where the stakes weren't high for both of us.

"Just this *one* time," Ridge said cautiously. "Maybe your women's intuition or something can tell us if Nawahi is our man, assuming he doesn't volunteer the info..."

"Why not," I hummed, not wanting to press my luck with this sudden cooperation in the investigation. "Where to...?"

I took down the address, and headed there, hoping to put my women's intuition to work.

* * *

It was three o'clock when I arrived at the apartment building on Kukui Street where Kalolo Nawahi lived. Located in a part of the city known for drug dealing and prostitution, Kalolo's unit was on the third floor. I knew something had happened when I saw a number of people milling about outside, a scene I was all too familiar with and was usually associated with tragedy. If that wasn't enough of a clue, the flashing lights from several cop cars were a dead giveaway, figuratively speaking.

I realized the trouble involved Kalolo when Ridge greeted me in front of the suspect's apartment building.

"What happened?" I asked, noting the yellow crime scene tape already in place.

"Nawahi's dead," Ridge said glumly. "Someone called in, reported hearing gunfire in his apartment. Looks like he was shot once in the back of the head—execution style."

I winced at the thought, as well as the irony. "First Carter, now Kalolo..." I sighed. "It's almost as though he was silenced before you could talk to him—or maybe before he could talk to you..."

"Let's not jump to conclusions, Skye," Ridge urged, keeping his voice level. "Nawahi was a known drug dealer and probably had more than his fair share of deals gone sour. Anyone could have had it in for him."

Including Darlene Delaney, we were both no doubt thinking but kept to ourselves. We parted to allow the body to be removed by members of the medical examiner's office.

I followed Ridge inside the victim's apartment. I saw Detective Kawakami, along with several others from the department, combing the place for evidence. Kawakami glanced at me and smiled, almost as if to say: *"Don't worry, Skye. Everyone knows you're working this case. Just stay the hell out of the real cops' way and no one will bother you."*

I smiled back at him and just as quickly wiped the grin off my face, knowing that joviality aside, someone had been murdered who was, at the very least, indirectly associated with Carter and directly connected to his widow. The distinct sweet and sour smell of fresh blood permeated the air in the tiny apartment. I could see blood and brain matter where the body had been. I couldn't help but wonder if his blood happened to be AB negative.

Ridge was reading my mind, which he'd done so well of late. "Nawahi's blood type will be analyzed right away," he told me. "My guess is he didn't have anything to do with Delaney's death. Other than the common link between the two, there's no evidence to indicate Nawahi took a bullet as a result of his association with Darlene Delaney—"

Wearing a pair of protective, disposable gloves, I carefully picked up a folded newspaper on the coffee table that the techs had ignored. Unfolding it, I noted the headline: FORMER PROSECUTOR CARTER DELANEY FOUND DEAD IN JACUZZI. The article was accompanied by a picture of Carter and Darlene. The paper was dated the day after Carter's death.

"Take a look at this," I said to Ridge, handing him the newspaper. "If nothing else, Kalolo probably recognized his cocaine customer *Amber* as Darlene Delaney from the photograph and article..."

Or, I wondered, had he already known the relevant facts in the article before the paper was even printed?

* * *

"Kalolo Nawahi's blood type was O negative, which also matched the blood in his apartment," Ridge informed me the following day. We were enjoying an early morning jog on the beach, while Ollie tagged along.

I moaned, though not surprised, and said: "It would've made things so much easier if Nawahi's blood had been AB negative and his DNA was a positive match with the blood Ollie took from Carter's presumed killer."

"Yeah, well, homicides are never that cut and dry," Ridge muttered, sidestepping a clump of seaweed.

I yanked on Ollie's leash, pulling him away from the seaweed he suddenly seemed very interested in. Then I told Ridge: "If you're still interested in what my women's intuition is telling me, I'd say that Kalolo was somehow involved in Carter's death, and it may have cost him his life—"

"We're double and triple checking every possibility surrounding Delaney's murder," Ridge assured me. "That means we're not eliminating any suspects, including Kalolo Nawahi."

Ridge was beginning to huff and puff. Jogging was not his forte; he preferred the gym, lifting weights, or getting his workout making love. I had no problem with any of those where he was concerned.

He looked at me and said: "I don't think I'm giving anything away by telling you that there are others who may have had a stronger motive than Nawahi for wanting to see your ex dead..."

"You mean like Darlene?" I asked, perspiring in a sports bra and matching shorts.

He wiped his brow. "Yeah, like Darlene. Strictly from a financial point of view, she had at least a couple million reasons that we know of to benefit from the death of her dearly beloved."

I regarded Ridge as if I hadn't heard him correctly. "What are you saying...?"

"Darlene took out a two million dollar insurance policy on Delaney just a month before he died," Ridge informed me. "Either she's psychic or the lady had good reason to believe Delaney might not be around for long—"

"Hmm..." I mumbled aloud while thinking about the million dollars Darlene said she raised through liquidating assets and her daughter's trust fund to pay off Carter's mounting gambling debts. Obviously his business fortunes had taken a serious hit along the way, making the hefty insurance policy all the more unnerving.

I was still split on my feelings about Darlene Delaney. While she was clearly no saint with more than a few skeletons in her closet, there was still a big stretch between infidelity and drug abuse and cold-blooded murder. Frankly, it was hard for me to imagine that Darlene could have masterminded Carter's murder for the love of money. I wanted to believe, if only for the sake of their child, that Darlene wouldn't have knowingly conspired to kill Carter.

But that was not a declaration of innocence, I thought. Money had a strange way of corrupting even the noblest person, which Darlene clearly was not. It also represented just one reason why people commit murder. That seemed especially true when talking about the man who, two weeks ago, had the world—or at least Honolulu—believing he walked on water and was drowning in success.

Now it was evident that both were far from the truth, which still had to be sorted out and a killer apprehended.

CHAPTER 37

He watched as they jogged along the beach: Skye Delaney and Ridge Larsen, along with her dog. They seemed to be caught up in their own little world. He imagined that they were comparing notes on their respective investigations into the death of Carter Delaney, under the guise of a leisurely jaunt.

Well let them try to put the pieces together all they want, he thought. It wouldn't get them anywhere, except maybe in their own graves...right beside Delaney.

He continued to stare at the private eye and police detective as they moved farther away. The dog was practically running around them in circles, as though he had lost his sense of direction. He should've killed that damned mutt when he had the chance. Instead, it had nearly killed him. Or so it seemed when the dog lunged at him, looking for blood. But he'd managed to fight back and overpower it enough to force the dog into the utility room, while keeping his eye on the primary objective: making sure Carter Delaney got everything he had coming to him.

He took a few more pictures of Skye Delaney and the detective, before heading to his car.

He had to be very careful these days, even more than usual. They could be on to him quicker than he was on to Delaney that day if he did something dumb. He couldn't allow them that satisfaction.

In the car, he sat there for a couple of minutes plotting his strategy, knowing there was still work to be done. He put the car in drive and took off, still thinking about Skye. That was replaced by the real deal as he actually passed by her, Larsen, and the mutt, who were now on the street. He was careful not to make eye contact, but watched them through his rear view mirror. As far as they knew, he was just another driver on his way somewhere, having nothing to do with Carter Delaney.

Well, think and think again.

He wondered if he'd thrown them off sufficiently by killing Kalolo Nawahi. Would that drug freak's death satisfy them that they had Delaney's killer? Or would they force him to take out more deserving assholes to cover his tracks?

See, Delaney, he thought, *this is what happens when you renege on a deal, man. People die. But you already know about that, don't you?*

His lips curved into a self-satisfied grin.

CHAPTER 38

Darlene Delaney walked into my office wearing dark sunglasses, a red, short-sleeved dress that contoured to every curve on her body, and white pointed-toe mules.

She looked around in no particular direction. "This place was really hard to find," she complained.

"I would've been happy to give you directions if I'd known you were coming," I said dryly from my desk, barely able to hide my surprise at this unexpected visit.

"It was impromptu," she said nervously, licking her ruby lips, before asking: "Mind if I sit?" She answered her own question as she planted herself in a chair.

It was our fourth face-to-face encounter since Carter's death. In spite of the fact that we happened to have married the same man, I saw no reason why we should be acquaintances, much less friends. This was particularly true while she remained a bona fide suspect in playing some role in Carter's murder.

Physically, I doubted Darlene was capable of killing Carter all by herself. But that didn't rule out her involvement, if not direct participation, I thought, in spite of her alibi that suggested otherwise.

Which brought me to why she had decided to pay me a visit in the middle of the week on a hot, humid afternoon. Was she on a guilt trip? Maybe she wanted to confess to something...like how two million dollars can pay for a lot of tears.

"I need your help—" she said finally.

"Excuse me?" I let my mouth hang open for effect.

She removed the sunglasses and rolled her eyes. "I want to hire you. Or do you only work for people who didn't happen to steal your man?"

I was stung by those last words, as if I needed to be reminded that she was the cause of my breakup with Carter. Of course, deep down inside, I knew that it took two to unravel a relationship. It didn't include the faithful spouse. I doubt that she'd had to put a gun to Carter's head to get him to cheat on me. Just as Darlene got to see the shoe on the other foot of betrayal when Carter turned his attention to Leilani Mahaulu.

But none of that seemed to matter at the moment. Admittedly, I was curious as to why Darlene needed my services.

I kept my cool as I responded: "What can I do for you?" *This ought to be good*, I thought.

She squirmed and took a deep breath. "I want you to find out who murdered Carter—"

I cocked a brow at the odd request, especially considering that I had already made this my personal mission, much to the chagrin of Ridge and those he worked for.

"That's a police matter," I responded nevertheless, hoping to draw much more out of her. "And my cop days are long over—"

"Oh, don't give me that—" Darlene snapped. "This is a *private* matter to me, and you're a private cop. Whether you approve of my life or not, I'm asking for the sake of whatever Carter once meant to you to take the case..."

I could feel my nostrils grow with vexation, even as my mind noted the irony of the request. It seemed as if I'd been down this road once before with her husband, who had sat in that very seat. I'd had nothing but grief since making the mistake of taking on a client whose personal life I wanted no part of. So why in the hell would I want to make the same mistake *twice*? I asked myself.

"Whether I approve of your personal life or not is beside the point," I stressed, knowing that was very much at issue in the scheme of things. "Murder investigations are outside of my jurisdiction, especially when the victim happened to be *my* ex."

"And *my* late husband," Darlene said, seeming to take pleasure in reminding me. "Carter came to you when he needed help. And now he's dead, and they'd like nothing better than to lay the entire thing on my lap—"

"Who are *they*?" I asked pointedly.

She sighed. "I think you know. The police—"

I knew nothing of the sort, and told her so, leaving out the reality that she remained a person of interest in the case for obvious reasons. "I doubt very much the police are interested in anything but—"

Darlene broke in: "Trying to make me a scapegoat for something I didn't have anything to do with—other than being married to the man. You aren't being hounded by the cops at every turn..." Her eyes narrowed suspiciously. "But why would you be—when the man you're sleeping with is heading the investigation into Carter's death?"

The fact that she knew about my relationship with Ridge was less surprising than her insinuation. I drew in a deep breath and said tartly: "I'm not even going to dignify that last comment—"

Again, she interrupted with: "Carter kept a file on you—" She hung onto to that last word long enough to watch the obvious shock written across my face. "He liked to think that in some strange way you were still *his* private property. He had to know who you dated, socialized with, even what time you went to bed—and who with... One of his fetishes was comparing himself sexually to the men in your life since you kicked him to the curb. Of course, Carter always rated himself superior in that department."

I shivered with embarrassment, disbelief, and, frankly, disgust. "Even if Carter did keep this so-called file," I sputtered at her, finding it hard to accept, "what the hell possible difference does it make now? Especially when Carter can't defend himself from this crap."

Darlene stiffened. "I just thought you'd like to know what type of man you divorced and I married," she stated simply. "Yes, I probably should've divorced Carter and, yes, maybe sometimes I wished him dead because of the way he treated me..." Her voice broke. "But I also loved him and really wanted to try and make our marriage work."

"Is that why you had Carter insured for two million dollars one month before his death?" I asked bluntly. "Out of love *and* devotion?"

She shook her head. "It was *his* idea. He had me insured for the same amount. That was on top of a million dollar policy Carter already had on himself. He said the additional amounts were a hedge against what he called the laws of nature. He wanted to make sure neither of us would suffer greatly financially if either died prematurely—"

If what she said was true, could Carter have somehow anticipated his death a month before, prompting him to put an additional two million on his life? Equally baffling was why he would want a woman he suspected of cheating on him, and probably would have divorced had he lived long enough, as his beneficiary.

I gazed at Darlene with a great deal of uncertainty. "Have you told this to the police?"

"I'm telling it to you," she snapped. "They hear only what they want to. There seems to be a well orchestrated effort by the authorities to make me out to be my husband's executioner."

"Aren't you being overly melodramatic?" I asked, knowing that Carter's actual executioner was a male with AB negative blood.

"You tell me—" Darlene tossed back.

She gave me a conspiratorial look, which seemed to once again lead to my involvement with Ridge. This made me very uncomfortable. Ridge continued to be fairly tightlipped about where the investigation was going, except for their suspicions concerning Darlene and possibly those connected to her. Could there be a cover-up of some sort within the department? I wondered. And, if so, for what reason?

"All I know," I told Darlene truthfully, "is that the police are investigating whether or not the death of your friend Kalolo Nawahi could somehow be tied to Carter's murder."

A shadow of regret and deliberation crossed her face. "I heard about Kalolo. I'm sorry he's dead." Our eyes met. "But to connect that to Carter's death—"

I told her about seeing Kalolo at the funeral when he supposedly never knew her as Mrs. Carter Delaney.

"So he wasn't as dumb as I made him out to be," she rationalized. "That doesn't prove I put him up to murdering Carter—or that Kalolo did it all by himself to try and get something out of me!"

I agreed with her, but said anyway: "It's not me you've got to convince, Darlene—"

"Isn't it?" she charged, flipping her hair to one side. "This is *my life* we're talking about here. I don't want to see it messed up any more than it already is when I'm innocent—" Her eyes fixed me with desperation. "If you have any feelings left in that heart of yours for Carter, you'll prove my innocence in his death by using your detective skills to track down the real killer."

She made it almost sound as if being a private detective was a game or TV show, where private dicks always got their man or woman at the end of the day. If only it were that simple to track down a real killer or killers, I thought. All the detective skills in the world offered no guarantees of success. Complicating matters was an ongoing police investigation, possible cover-up, the growing questions about Carter and his dual life, and his chameleon widow, whose own issues and question marks made her less than convincing as a person who was being unfairly targeted.

"I'll pay you whatever you want," Darlene said as added incentive.

I was sure she would and obviously could. In this case, it was definitely not about money, whether I could use it or not, but an obligation on my part to do the right thing.

"I can't accept your money," I told her succinctly, then added in a more conciliatory tone: "But I will follow up on any leads I come across to try and find out who killed Carter, even if the trail leads right to your door—"

She nodded and actually looked relieved. "I wouldn't expect or want anything less."

"Good to know," I made clear.

"Mahalo," Darlene said, as she stood up.

It was hard to dislike Carter's widow, no matter how much I may have wanted to. "A hui hou kakou," I told her, or *until we meet again*, knowing full well that the circumstances may be anything but pleasant.

Darlene stood up and removed what looked like a journal from her purse. Pushing it halfway across the desk, she said: "Even if Carter was still alive, he'd have a hard time defending himself on some things. It's all there. He certainly won't be needing this anymore, and neither will I—"

On that note, she turned and strutted out of the office. I lifted the thick, gray journal, which I had a feeling I would regret reading, yet was compelled to.

CHAPTER 39

Darlene had not exaggerated. There were times, dates, places—some that I'd forgotten or wanted to—that were logged stretching back to when Carter and I had first separated. He knew when Ridge and I met, our first date, when we first made love. When we last made love prior to Carter's death, which was the day before he died...and seemingly every aspect of my personal and professional life that he no longer had a right to know.

Why, Carter? I wondered, hoping that somehow he could hear me from beyond the grave. *Why the hell would you do this? What did you hope to gain by prying unnaturally into my life and times?*

I could only wonder if this obsessive behavior had existed long before he became involved with me, or Darlene for that matter. I even started to consider if it was somehow tied to Carter being a control freak; as well as his gambling addiction, history as an attorney, and business practices.

I read on, finding myself unable to put down the journal. It was like reading my unauthorized biography. Even my caseload as a private investigator had been detailed. In Carter's words, I was "brutally efficient, clever as a fox, had skills I never dreamt she possessed when we were married, and was as good as any man I knew in solving even the most difficult of cases..."

This apparent flattery hardly enamored me, considering the source in which he chose to express himself, noting at one point that "she gave as much as she received, and then some, in bed and out of bed...only I never truly appreciated it till it was too late to turn back..."

He talked of plans to hire me to "get the goods on that whore" who seemed to take delight in being a major embarrassment to him and all he stood for. That way he would have the ammunition to get rid of Darlene without being taken to the cleaners or giving up his daughter—the one thing worthwhile in his life.

I closed the journal on that note, disgusted and intrigued at the same time. I wondered if Darlene had bothered to read it before she gave it to me, sensing she had. It suggested Carter had already made up his mind to divorce her once he could prove her unfaithfulness. I assumed that was what he meant by "get rid of her." If so, it was also incentive for Darlene wanting to see him dead before she lost everything.

But it still didn't add up to murder—at least not by my calculations. Darlene wanted to hire me to disprove perceived police attempts to railroad her for Carter's death. Even going so far as to part with what amounted to Carter's last known thoughts, some of which gave her good reason to destroy this potentially incriminating evidence. In my mind, this either made her a complete lunatic or perfectly sane in her beliefs that the police were on a witch hunt, but targeting the *wrong* witch.

Far more disturbing was the fact that I was the central character in Carter's journal, as though a dark novel. What was going on in his head that possessed him to violate me in a way no common criminal ever could? It was more bizarre than I was prepared to contemplate on an empty stomach.

I locked the journal in my desk, grabbed my purse, cut off the lights, and left the office for an unknown destination. I drove around in circles for what seemed like hours, having been affected more than I cared to admit by the unfolding drama of my ex-husband who was as much a mystery to me as his death.

* * *

It was a quarter past five when I showed up at Ridge's door. He stood there barefoot in a striped T-shirt and shorts. Mayonnaise trickled down from the corner of his mouth, a reflection of the half-eaten chicken sandwich he held precariously in one hand.

He took one look at me and said: "You look like you've been to hell and back—"

I hadn't meant for it to be so apparent. Since he was right, I saw no reason to deny it. "I confess my day hasn't gone too well..."

That was probably the biggest understatement I'd ever made.

Ridge frowned with concern. "I can see that." He bent over and kissed me on the cheek, then hugged me with his free arm. "Come on in and tell me all about it. I've got nothing but time."

I wondered if I could ever tell him that my ex-spouse had been keeping a play-by-play account of *our* love life, among other things. Maybe there would never be a reason to bring it up as long as it had no bearing on his murder. It was not something I wanted to share with Ridge or anyone else if I could help it.

Instead, I turned my attention to the hunger pangs that stabbed at me. Grabbing the sandwich from Ridge's hand, I asked: "Do you mind?" Before he could answer, I helped myself to a generous bite of his sandwich. "I'm starving!"

"I'll go you one better," he said, somewhat bewildered. "You can have the sandwich—what's left of it—and I'll make us both another..."

We went into the kitchen and he fixed more sandwiches while I made a salad. All the while I was thinking about Darlene's allegations concerning the police, and the fact that

Ridge was spearheading the investigation into Carter's death. What did it all mean? Did it mean anything?

Ridge had managed to keep his curiosity in check during my musings.

At the table, I told him of Darlene's visit to the office, minus the journal. Ridge responded with a little laugh and shook his head in disbelief. "That woman's a real piece of work. Did she *seriously* expect you to be on her payroll?"

"Why not?" I replied, playing the devil's advocate. I was a little pissed at him for so easily dismissing the notion.

A dumbfounded look appeared on his face. "You're asking me? Last I knew, she was still a legitimate person of interest in her husband's murder for one thing, technically speaking. And I'm assuming you haven't forgotten the lady's bad behavior was the reason Delaney hired you in the first place."

I dug my teeth into the sandwich and chewed. "Just because Darlene was cheating on Carter doesn't mean she's not entitled to learning the truth about his death," I said.

"There's a damned good possibility she already knows some version of the truth," Ridge said brusquely, and stuck his fork into the salad.

"And as good a possibility that Darlene knows nothing more than she's already admitted to," I suggested, surprised that I was now suddenly defending a woman who cost me my husband and had not been totally exonerated of his murder, even in my mind.

Ridge refrained from putting the salad in his mouth. "What *exactly* has Darlene Delaney been telling you?"

Since he asked, I related her feelings of being unjustly persecuted by the police for lack of a better suspect. Then I put in my own two cents about a possible police cover-up, though I didn't have a shred of evidence to back it up or any real reason to think that the authorities had something to hide regarding the investigation into Carter's death.

As expected, Ridge defended the department. "There's no cover-up," he insisted, adding, "at least not that I'm aware of.

Believe it or not, no one's trying to protect Carter Delaney's reputation or prevent a scandal. If there was any indication that evidence was being disregarded, tampered with, or otherwise mishandled in this case, I'd go to internal affairs myself and let the chips fall where they may."

One of the things that had attracted me to Ridge was his way of convincing you that he was always on the right side of the law. I wasn't so sure this time, but felt if he was aware of anything that wasn't above board in the investigation, he'd risk his own neck to have it resolved through the proper channels.

"If Darlene Delaney thinks we're being too aggressive in our investigation of her, that's her problem—not yours," argued Ridge. "It's called police work. We've got to be as aggressive as we can without stepping over the line, especially when a prominent figure is murdered and, as far as we know, the killer is still walking the streets. You know the routine, Skye..." He chewed on a piece of lettuce. "Until we solve the mystery of who murdered your ex, no one is going to get a free ride—and that definitely includes the newly wealthy widow."

Ridge had spoken and I had to respect his position. He was really trying hard, even though he didn't know half the story about Carter and the bizarre behavior that may have contributed to his death. Darlene would never win the award for the most admired woman in the world, particularly by those who saw her as the big winner in Carter's death, including myself. But sometimes winning came with a price. She had lost a husband, respect, and a part of herself. In my mind, that was enough for one lifetime and not worth any amount of money.

Besides, from what I understood, most of what Darlene stood to gain came in the form of insurance payouts, pending completion of the criminal investigation. It appeared as though Carter had squandered away most of his fortune through gambling and bad decision-making. The fact that Darlene might still come out of it smelling like a rich rose was not something that concerned me. I had already given up any claim to Carter and whatever he was worth, and felt I was better for it.

Ridge gave me a serious but seemingly relieved look, and said nicely: "If there's anything else you'd like to get off your chest, I'm listening—"

I wiped my hands with a napkin, thought about it, and responded with a smile: "Yes, there is one other thing. What's for dessert?"

He raised one of his brows. "That's up to you. What would you like?"

I could think of a few things, but none more inviting than the man my eyes gazed upon. He looked quite scrumptious at the moment with that crooked smile, shiny bald head, and firm body staring back at me. I leaned over and kissed him. The warmth of his mouth on mine seemed to release me from the demons that had played with my mind since Carter's death. My libido suddenly came alive and I wanted Ridge more than ever right now.

We got to know each other again in bed, rediscovering what worked and what did not, making love with passion and energy that left us both thoroughly content. We cuddled together afterward as if neither of us wanted to be anywhere else. The thought of Carter somehow spying on us from another dimension gave way to the reality of here and now with the person who currently meant more to me than anyone. I wasn't about to allow Carter to deprive me of that one bit of satisfaction.

CHAPTER 40

Ollie and I went for our morning jog on the beach. We huffed and puffed for a good hour and a half before making it back home in a sweat. Ollie had more or less returned to his normal feisty self. That told me he had apparently gotten over the trauma of witnessing Carter's death and the confrontation with an as yet unknown assailant.

I only wished the same could be said for me.

I was having lunch today with a good friend whom I had managed to neglect recently, all in the name of the hectic life of a private investigator and security consultant. Not to mention the time spent with a certain police detective. Whitney Quinn was a psychologist who got half her business courtesy of the Honolulu Police Department. A psychological evaluation was both routine and mandatory for cops who had stepped over the line, been suspected of such, or experienced extreme psychological stress on the job.

It was the latter circumstance that first brought me before Whitney. I had only been on the force for two weeks when I shot and killed a burglary suspect, who would have shot and killed me had I not been a hair quicker to the trigger. I had been warned that the first fatality was usually the hardest. That did not prepare me for just how hard it really was to deal with killing another human being.

I was fully cleared of any wrongdoing, but the psychological burden was a whole different matter. That was where Whitney came in. Not only did she do wonders in helping me overcome the guilt and self-blame, but I also ended up with a lifelong friend.

It was as a friend that I hoped to get some informal counseling in an attempt to help me understand the inner workings of the man I was once married to. A man who left behind a legacy that was as baffling as it was tragic.

We met at Harry Woo's, a restaurant on Kapahulu Avenue in Chinatown. Spending too much time trying to decide what to wear, I was a little late getting there for the one o'clock date, whereas Whitney was her usual punctual self.

"Sorry," I said lamely. "The time got away from me."

"Don't worry about it," Whitney said, smiling brightly as she looked me over. I was wearing a lavender scoop neck top, gray pencil skirt, and black open toe pumps. "It's good to see you."

"You, too," I said, and gave her a hug.

When we pulled apart, I quickly surveyed the thirty-nine-year-old psychologist who looked much younger. She was just under my height with blue eyes and blonde hair in a short pixie style. She had on a white pantsuit, yellow cami, and brown sandals.

"Has it really been what, six months?" I asked in disbelief while hiding my regret.

"More like seven or eight," she said, "but who's counting?"

I certainly wasn't, but wondered how we'd managed to miss each other during that stretch.

We sat down, and Whitney said: "I have to admit, I was a little surprised to hear from you—"

She wasn't making this any easier, but I tried to keep it lighthearted for starters. "Well, you just never know when an old friend will call and invite you to lunch," I said.

"I suppose..." She lifted her cup of coffee. "In my line of work the unexpected means never quite knowing what's coming next. Sometimes that can be dangerous."

"Don't I know it," I said, thinking that my own profession as a private eye had more than its fair share of unexpected dangers.

She regarded me curiously. "How are things going with you, Skye?"

I picked up my glass of water and took a sip before looking at her and admitting: "Not as well as they could be."

The menus came, allowing me time to collect my thoughts and gather my words. Even in an informal setting, it was hard to share my anxieties and anger concerning Carter. But for the sake of my own mental health and well-being, I owed it to myself to get this off my chest.

I told Whitney about the journal, which I'd read more of, much to my mortification. This was followed by my thoughts about the bizarre circumstances surrounding Carter's death and how they'd left me drained, confused, and unsure of what the hell it all meant.

Whitney seemed to listen with compassion and understanding even as I tried to read her mind. "I know this was a few years ago," she said, "but how did Carter take it when you told him the marriage was over?"

"Like any man who wanted the best of all worlds," I said, remembering it as though only yesterday. "He tried hard to convince me he'd made a mistake and wanted a second chance to make it right."

She peered at me. "But you would hear none of it?"

"Would you, if you were in my shoes?" I challenged her.

Whitney hit me with a remember who's the psychologist look and said: "This isn't about me or what I would do, Skye."

I got the picture. Still, a sneer appeared out of nowhere. "All right, so I didn't need a man I couldn't trust, much less one who wanted more than I apparently was capable of giving him, either sexually or emotionally."

The waitress brought our lunch.

Whitney tasted her kung pao chicken, then gave me a stern look and asked the obvious question: "Why in the hell did you let this man you wanted nothing more to do with back into your life, even if it was only for professional reasons?"

I had probably asked myself that a thousand times since Carter's death. Was it to prove my growth and objectivity? Was it to reassure Ridge that he had nothing to worry about? Or was—as I imagined Whitney must have thought—I still in love with Carter?

It took me only a moment to come to the conclusion I had reached from the time I'd agreed to work for him. "It had *nothing* to do with my personal feelings for Carter," I said firmly. "It wasn't about hoping for a second time around love connection—which wasn't there, for my part. Or," I added, "a desire to reopen the lines of communication between us." I drank some tea, watched Whitney watch me, and told her in the most succinct terms what I truly believed. "I was providing a professional service for Carter with the clear understanding that this was a onetime deal with no emotional or any other strings attached—"

Whitney's razor thin brows twitched. "I almost hate to say this, Skye, but you *did* want my professional opinion..."

I bit into a spring roll and felt my heart skip a beat while waiting to hear what came next.

"It seems pretty clear to me that, at least from Carter's perspective, the emotional ties had never really gone away," she said levelly. "The journal was his way of holding on to you, if only in his own mind. Keeping tabs on your every move allowed him to fantasize that he was still an integral, intimate part of your life, while maintaining control over you from a safe distance by knowing every which way you turned and anything else that he deemed important—"

If that was true, I thought, and I had no reason to doubt it, I could only feel sorry for Carter. Aside from a cheating, drug-abusing wife, and his own gambling addiction, he seemingly had everything going for him. He certainly didn't need me to make his life whole. So maybe that life was less than perfect. It didn't give him the right to retreat back to something that was no longer his for the taking. If only I'd had a clue at some point of Carter's unbalanced behavior, I might have been able to do something before things got out of hand.

"My guess is Carter hired you as an extension of this dangerous game of obsession he was playing," Whitney said, now clearly on a roll, "even if his reason for coming to you was perfectly legitimate." Her eyes widened at me. "The truth is I could hardly blame his second wife for looking elsewhere for attention. From what you've told me, I doubt she ever had a fighting chance with Carter. Not when he seemed to have channeled all of his feelings of love and devotion in your direction."

Her interpretation of Carter's mindset left me even more confused and angry. I wasn't sure I bought it, but unless a better explanation came along, I had to go along with Whitney's psychological autopsy of Carter.

The conversation shifted to small talk—a welcome change.

It wasn't until we were finished eating that I asked Whitney what had most been on my mind regarding Carter's peculiar disposition and his demise. "Do you think Carter's death could somehow be tied to his, for lack of a better description, obsessive behavior toward me?"

Whitney contemplated the question for a moment. "Yes and no," she responded. "His obsessive behavior could have impacted his ability to reason as both a businessman and a husband, which may have led to his death." Whitney gave me that look you give someone when you're about to say something you want the listener to embrace, and said: "If you're asking me if *you're* somehow to blame for Carter's unnatural feelings toward you, the answer is absolutely not, Skye! No one can control what goes on inside another person's head. In my opinion, Carter was a walking time bomb, waiting to explode. Whether that was directly related to his death or not is something for the police to figure out—"

I felt a certain amount of relief with Whitney's professional opinion and her friendly support. But I continued to have a problem with where the bomb went off, so to speak. And why?

As for the journal, I decided to keep it in cold storage for now. At least until I was satisfied that it was not somehow instrumental in Carter's death, rather than merely the bizarre reflections of a sick man who was once my husband.

CHAPTER 41

I returned home to find that tropical fire ants had invaded my house! Or should I say that Ollie had discovered the little creatures milling aimlessly about the floor and on the walls. He seemed to be as spooked as I was by the unwelcome company.

I didn't even want to hazard a guess as to where they had come in, knowing it could have been anywhere. My only concern was getting rid of them so I could reclaim the house and some peace of mind.

I phoned Natsuko and asked her to come over to help me deal with the fire ants, a pest common in Hawaii but actually helpful to sugar cane farmers with their crops. Ollie did his best to avoid the menacing little insects that weren't afraid to bite him, or me for that matter, if we tried to get in their way. As if there weren't already enough of them, even more suddenly seemed to come out of hiding, as if welcoming the challenge they presented.

Natsuko arrived shortly thereafter and made light of a bad situation. "They're really friendly once you get to know them," she said jokingly.

I sneered, hardly in a joking mood. "I can do without their friendship, thank you."

I think she got the message. She had brought some organic fire ant control products that she wanted to try before calling the pest control company.

With the jury still out as to whether we had gotten to the root of the ant problem, Natsuko was gracious enough to take Ollie home for the rest of the day and night. I packed an overnight bag to stay at Ridge's, sure he would welcome the company.

I went to the office first to pay a few bills and catch up on some work that I'd left undone or half done. It had been this way ever since putting my energy into solving Carter's murder. I had just gotten started when my cell phone rang.

It was Ridge. "I thought you'd like to know," he said, "that we're looking into two people of interest who possibly had reason to want Delaney dead."

"I'm listening—" I told him, leaning back in my chair.

"As a prosecutor, Carter put away Adam Ramirez for life. He was convicted of murder and armed robbery," Ridge said. "His brother, Antonio Ramirez, thirty-six, swore he would seek revenge against Carter at the time. Allegedly, he's never gotten that out of his system. Then there's Norman Mitchell, forty-seven, a former business associate of Delaney's, who accused him of cheating him out of money and has supposedly wanted payback ever since."

"Have you spoken to either of these guys yet?" I asked, believing they were legitimate suspects in the absence of others who had so far come up flat.

"We're about to go talk to them right now," he answered. "You can run with us on this one and, if we're lucky, help nab Delaney's killer—"

Ridge had made me an offer I couldn't refuse. I figured that maybe one of these men had AB negative blood and had gone after Carter. Or, at the very least, could be eliminated as a suspect.

The bills and catch up work would have to wait.

* * *

I was in the back seat while Ridge drove and Kawakami sat in the passenger seat. I couldn't help but notice that Henry Kawakami's once thick black hair had begun to thin and I wondered if it had anything to do with this case. Fortunately, with Ridge regularly shaving his head, I would never know if going after Carter's killer was causing him to lose hair.

During a pause in the conversation, Kawakami turned around and winked at me. I wasn't quite sure if it was a come-on, a stamp of approval of my dating Ridge, or his tacit support of my accompanying them on official police business. In any event, I winked back, and left it alone. There were far more pressing matters to occupy my thoughts, such as Antonio Ramirez and Norman Mitchell.

"Ramirez is gainfully employed at a construction site," Kawakami said with a cynical lilt in his voice. "He's been there for the past month. Lives by himself in an apartment on Ala Wai Boulevard."

I took mental notes, occasionally looking at Ridge's profile, and asked: "What's Mitchell's story, apart from his business connection to Carter?"

"He's continued to fall on hard times," Ridge said. "His business recently filed for bankruptcy and he foreclosed on his home. Mitchell is currently living with a divorcee named Ignacia Horikami and her daughter."

I wondered if times were hard enough for Norman Mitchell to resort to murder.

"So maybe his girlfriend and her daughter weren't enough to cure Mitchell's blues," Kawakami suggested. "Losing his home and business may have been the last straw and sent him over the edge straight to Delaney."

I winced at the thought. At this point, I wasn't ruling out anything or any person, especially someone who had an axe to grind with Carter.

We drove to a construction site in midtown Honolulu, where luxury condominiums were being built. The foreman led us to the skeletal building where Antonio Ramirez was working on the second story.

"Ramirez!" the foreman screamed. "Some people here to see you—"

This was normally where a guilty person either made a run for it or tried to play it cool, only to flee later. Ramirez did not run, which made sense considering he was about twenty feet off the ground. After he came down, we quickly surrounded him like flies on rotted meat. Even then, at around six-five and of muscular build, he didn't exactly seem intimidated by us.

Ridge took the honor of identifying each of us, flashing his badge for effect. "We'd like to talk to you—" he said.

"About what?" Ramirez asked as he ran a hand across his bald head. His unblinking dark eyes peered at me.

"Carter Delaney—" I told him.

"Carter who...?" he asked, playing dumb.

"The man who put your brother Adam away for armed robbery and murder," Ridge reminded him.

"Oh, yeah," Ramirez said with a scowl. "Delaney, the prosecutor... So what about him?"

Ridge snorted with irritation. "I think you know damn well what this is about. Delaney was murdered not too long ago—"

Ramirez cracked a grin. "Awe, that's too bad. But what's it got to do with me?"

"Don't jerk us around, Ramirez," Kawakami said with narrowed eyes. "You expect us to believe you've forgotten the threats you made against Carter Delaney after he sent your brother to the state pen?"

Ramirez grimaced. "Ain't you ever done something you wish you could take back, man? I was pretty angry back then that he railroaded Adam. But I can't change what happened to him any more than you could what happened to Delaney. I'm just trying to get on with my life—"

I studied Ramirez's face while trying to read his mind. Was he toying with us? Had he been in my house and confronted Carter? I noticed a partially healed wound on his bulging upper arm that extended to his shoulder. The aftereffects of a dog bite, I wondered.

"I'm sure you have an unbreakable alibi for the day and time Carter Delaney was murdered," Ridge said to the suspect.

Ramirez paused. "What day and time was that?" he asked.

Ridge told him.

Ramirez suddenly seemed to be relishing the attention as he hovered over us. "Let me look into it and get back to you," he said.

"Where the hell were you when Carter Delaney was killed?" Kawakami demanded, getting into Ramirez's face. "Or do we haul your ass in right now for suspicion of murder?"

Ramirez did not buckle, staring down at Kawakami. "Don't waste your time, detective. You got the wrong man. Actually, I was in church that day—all day—getting closer to Jesus. And lots of other believers saw me." He looked at me and said: "Maybe you can come to a service with me someday..."

"Not in this lifetime," I told him.

He grinned lasciviously. "Your loss."

I doubted that seriously. I looked at his arm and said: "Nasty looking injury you have there. How did you get it?"

Ramirez flinched. "I was in the wrong place at the wrong time," he said simply.

I wondered about the time and place. "What's your blood type?" I asked him, figuring it was worth a shot.

He shrugged. "Got no idea. What's yours?"

"Never mind," I told him, not interested in playing games for his amusement.

Ridge asked Ramirez: "Where is this church?"

"It's on Nehoa Street," Ramirez said, then added smugly, "Be sure to tell Pastor Owens I said Praise the Lord!"

"We'll check it out and see if someone at the church can vouch for his whereabouts," Ridge said as we headed toward the car.

"If you ask me, I think he's full of it," Kawakami said.

"Or he's just another dead end in the mystery surrounding Carter's death," I grumbled.

CHAPTER 42

Next, there was Norman Mitchell to contend with. We drove to his address, which turned out to be an expensive home on Kolohala Street in the Waialae section of town.

"Are you sure we have the right address?" I half-joked, wondering how a man in bankruptcy and foreclosure wound up in one of Honolulu's most exclusive neighborhoods.

"It's the right place all right," confirmed Kawakami. "Guess Mitchell picked the right rich lady to shack up with."

I couldn't help but think that Darlene had pulled off the same trick when she married Carter. Only she ended up with more problems than not as a direct result. I wondered if the same could be said for Norman Mitchell. Had he found someone to support him in style, including committing murder?

There were no cars visible as we drove onto the property, but a closed three-car garage suggested someone could be home.

Ridge rang the bell. A peephole allowed us to be seen. After a second ring, a woman's voice yelled out: "What do you want?"

Ridge identified himself as a police detective, holding his identification up so she could see.

A moment later, the door opened. An attractive Hawaiian woman in her mid forties with black hair in a loose chignon stood there.

"Are you Ignacia Horikami?" Ridge asked politely.

"Yes," she said.

"We'd like to talk to Norman Mitchell," he told her. "Is he here?"

She eyed each of us suspiciously before saying in a calm voice: "No. He went to the store and will be back shortly. May I ask what this is about?"

We looked at each other before Kawakami said: "I'm afraid it's official police business, Ma'am."

"All the more reason I have a right to know if Norman is in some kind of trouble," Ignacia said determinedly, her small brown eyes darting between us. "He's my fiancé. We're getting married next month—"

Ridge and Kawakami made eye contact, and then Ridge asked: "May we come in?"

"Please do," she replied.

It was an open, luxurious setting by any standard with a cathedral ceiling, floor to ceiling windows, and ivory wall-to-wall carpeting—all accented with fine European furnishings and expensive collectibles. But we weren't there to admire the accommodations.

"We just need to ask Mitchell a few questions," Ridge said, "regarding a homicide."

Her eyes shot wide. "You think Norman killed someone?" she asked.

"We just want to eliminate him as a suspect," he told her. "Strictly routine."

Ignacia looked at me and asked, "Who was murdered?"

"Carter Delaney," I said. After a pause, I told her what I thought might help: "I'm Skye Delaney. We were once married."

"I'm sorry for your loss," she said, "but Norman had nothing to do with that. You see, the day he was killed, Norman was right here with me—"

Ridge, Kawakami, and I exchanged looks of doubt in what seemed just a little too pat.

"And what day was that?" asked Ridge.

She told him as if it were ingrained in her memory.

"Exactly what *time* of the day was Mitchell here?" Kawakami asked.

"All day *and* all night," she said without wavering. "Is that *exact* enough, detective?"

She was clearly a woman who wouldn't back down for two tough male homicide cops and one equally tough female private eye. She seemed determined to give Norman Mitchell a solid alibi whether we wanted him to have one or not.

Ignacia folded her arms. "We were in bed, making love—the whole time." She glanced at me unabashed, and then took a longer look at Ridge. "At about ten that night we turned on the TV and heard that Carter Delaney had been found dead. Norman recognized the name immediately as a man with whom he had bad business dealings. But he would never have wanted him dead—"

I watched Ridge and Kawakami give each other that lascivious conspiratorial look of men who were stricken with the notion of a superwoman in the bedroom. I resigned myself to the fact that boys would be boys, even during a murder investigation.

I brought them back to the real world when I asked: "How old is your daughter?"

"Twelve," she responded.

"And where was she during this marathon day in bed?" I asked. It seemed like a reasonable question, all things considered.

"Spending the day with her father," Ignacia said coolly. "We have shared custody."

It seemed like the lady had every base covered, I thought. But that still didn't mean Norman Mitchell was out of the woods, especially if he had a different story to tell.

As if on cue, we all turned our heads toward the door when we heard sounds on the other side of it. Kawakami instinctively went for his .38 Smith and Wesson revolver that he kept in a shoulder holster. It wouldn't have been the first time a murder suspect came in firing.

Opening the door and entering was a short, thin girl with long, dark hair. She was followed in by a man of average build with gray hair. He held a paper bag stuffed with groceries close to his chest.

"Mom..." the girl uttered fearfully as she looked at the gun pointed in their direction.

"It's all right," Ignacia said, opening her arms and beckoning her to come forward. The girl obeyed and ran to her mother. Ignacia announced: "This is my daughter, Elisea."

The man remained standing just inside the door, as though his feet were stuck in cement.

"You Norman Mitchell?" Ridge asked tensely.

"Yeah," he said in a non-threatening manner.

"They're police detectives," Ignacia told him quickly, "investigating the death of Carter Delaney. I told them you were here with me—"

"Now we'd like to hear it from you," Kawakami said, keeping the gun drawn. "We just need to ask you a few questions. Why don't you put that bag down?"

"No problem," Mitchell said, frowning. "I've got nothing to hide..."

Elisea suddenly bolted from her mother toward Mitchell, wrapping her arms around his waist.

"They won't hurt me," he promised. "Take the bag."

She obeyed him. Only then did it become apparent that Mitchell was missing an arm—or three-quarters of it. His sleeve was wrapped loosely below the shoulder. He looked up self-consciously. "I was in a car accident six months ago," he said sullenly. "Lost my arm, but I'm dealing with it. As for Carter Delaney, we had our differences, but I certainly didn't kill him. From what I heard, the way he died would be pretty hard to do with two good arms and it would be damn near impossible with just one—"

No one in the room could argue with that logic, I thought. Especially those of us who knew exactly how Carter had died. Obviously, the investigation into Norman Mitchell had failed to uncover the fact that he was missing an arm, and therefore was not the most likely candidate as Carter's killer. I also saw no reason at this point to believe Mitchell was part of a larger conspiracy to do Carter in.

We left the house essentially back where we started, although there was still follow-up work to do on Antonio Ramirez's alibi.

In the meantime, Carter's killer or killers remained very much at large.

CHAPTER 43

Edwin Axelrod was the third person connected to Darlene Delaney, and indirectly to Carter, to end up dead. Axelrod was found slumped over his desk, a bullet wound to the side of his head. The possible murder weapon was in plain sight. Right now, the police were calling it a probable suicide. I was calling it one damned coincidence too many.

Upon hearing the news, I raced to the scene of the crime. Axelrod's office building was crawling with police personnel. I flashed my private detective credential to get through. Sometimes it worked, other times I was dismissed as a pain in the ass who was playing a game way out of her league.

Fortunately, the young male officer who stood guard at the entry was a sucker for a private investigator with nice legs. Once past him, I was home free. I made my way to Axelrod's office, careful not to contaminate any possible evidence. It looked as if it had been hit by a hurricane. More things were displaced and dispersed than not.

The victim had already been carted off to the morgue. His desktop was splattered with blood, as was his chair, and seemingly half the wall behind the desk. Crime scene investigators were finishing up after the detectives had moved on.

I wondered about Edwin Axelrod's final moments of life. Like Carter, he did not seem like a man who was willing to give up on his life without one hell of a fight. It certainly seemed very possible that a struggle had taken place.

"Do you have business here?" a voice asked from behind me.

I turned to see a red-haired, tall female from the CSI team.

"Used to," I said. After showing my I.D. and stating my name, I continued the lie. "I did investigative work for Mr. Axelrod from time to time. So what the hell happened here?"

She shrugged. "Suicide. Murder. Too soon to tell—"

"Any witnesses?" I asked.

"From what I understand, he was found in here alone," she said.

I looked around the office and told her: "My guess is he had company who left in a hurry, but not before searching and probably finding something worth killing for." If not, I thought, it was made to look that way.

"I'll have to ask you to leave now," the CSI said. "Unless, of course, you have something solid to back up your theories—"

I smiled faintly and said: "Nothing but good old-fashioned speculation."

She seemed disappointed, but let it pass while leading me out of the office.

Down on the main floor, I nearly ran into the reporter Liam Pratt. He seemed just as surprised to see me.

"What the hell are you doing here?" were the first words to come from my mouth.

He half-grinned, putting his hands in the pockets of his trousers. "I could ask you the same thing, Private Detective Delaney."

"You first," I said.

He seemed to think about it, then said smoothly: "Fair enough. But only if you let me buy you a drink."

"Not a good idea," I told him. I had a firm policy against making the same mistake twice.

"Just one drink is all I'm asking," he pleaded. "No harm in that." He looked me over as if my clothes were too loose. Or maybe too tight. "What do you say? There's a little bar just down the street—"

Just how familiar was he with the area? I wondered. *Did he live around here?*

It seemed like a harmless enough outing, I told myself, even if he reminded me of some of the creeps I dated after Carter and before Ridge. Not bad looking, but too cocky and conceited for their own good. Besides, I was curious as to what business, if any, Liam had in the building where Edwin Axelrod had bitten the dust. Could he have known Axelrod?

"One drink," I told Liam. "And *one* drink only!"

He chuckled as though merely to placate me. "Yeah. I hear you."

We walked to the bar on Bishop Street called NiteSpot. I can't say it was a place I could get used to. There was a creepy element about it and a musty scent in the air. Cheesy Hawaiian music was playing in the background as we sat at a table against the back wall.

We both made beer our drink of choice.

"So why were you there?" I got right to the point, having no desire to socialize with the man merely for the sake of it.

"I heard an attorney was found dead in his office under suspicious circumstances," Liam said evenly. "It's my job to follow the news—"

If that was all, and I had no basis to believe otherwise, I was not about to fan the flames. I tasted the beer and leaned back in my chair.

"Why would a private eye be at the scene of a routine murder?" he asked, and then answered himself. "Unless it had something to do with a case she was working on. Am I right?"

He seemed to know the answer ahead of time, making me a little uncomfortable. "Guilty," I pled, but saw no reason to share any more than that.

Liam stared at me. "Well...did you find what you were looking for?"

Wouldn't you like to know, I thought, wondering if this was idle curiosity or inquisitiveness with a purpose.

"I found all I needed to—" I said simply.

"Which was?" he pressed with those reporter's eyes looking back at me.

"A prominent attorney is dead and the cause is still under investigation," I responded. "Why don't we just leave it at that, Liam?"

"If you say so, detective..." He drank more beer and studied me thoughtfully.

I put the onus back on him. "So what do you plan to write about regarding Edwin Axelrod's death?"

"I'm not sure yet," Liam said. After a moment, he said: "How about a headline that reads Crooked Attorney Edwin Axelrod Dead—Was it Self-Inflicted or Murder?"

I raised a brow. "That's a bit over the top, don't you think?"

"You tell me," he said with a catch to his voice. "Is it?"

I put the mug to my mouth and then asked curiously: "What makes you think Axelrod was crooked?"

"That's easy," Liam said flatly, "because he was. Everybody knows Axelrod was on the payroll of some of Honolulu's top crime assholes, making it almost impossible to keep his own hands clean."

"You mean like Kazuo Pelekai?" I couldn't help but ask.

"Who's bigger?" he confirmed.

I met Liam's eyes. "Then you do think Edwin Axelrod was murdered."

"Don't you?" His mouth hung open. "The poor bastard probably knew way too much—"

Knew too much about what? I wondered. Or who? Had Edwin Axelrod gotten in so deep that he had become more of a liability than an asset to Pelekai? I could imagine one of his muscular cronies doing the honor of snuffing out Axelrod, making Pelekai's life a little easier.

Suddenly, I could see some scary patterns emerging. If Edwin Axelrod had been in Pelekai's hip pocket, it could be connected to Axelrod's affair with Darlene. Maybe Axelrod had been using her to get information that could help Pelekai in a criminal proceeding in which Carter's consultant work with the prosecuting attorney's office could have been compromised. Or, at the very least, I mused, a mistrial would have been a given, had the defense shown a conflict of interest on the part of the State's case, considering that Carter's wife was having an affair with Kazuo Pelekai's defense attorney. That Carter and Axelrod were now dead could be all Pelekai needed to walk away scot-free from his troubles. It was a lot for me to digest.

"Some of my sources tell me Axelrod was a womanizer," Liam said as he refilled his mug. "You got an opinion on that?"

"Not really," I said with a straight face. "I didn't know the man." Which, of course, was only a half-truth. What I did know left me less than impressed with Axelrod as a husband and attorney, as far as faithfulness and ethics went.

"I thought private eyes had a sixth sense for that sort of thing," Liam said, favoring me with steady eyes.

"Only in the movies," I responded dryly. "Real detectives aren't psychic." *Was he toying with me?* I wondered. Or viewing me as a toy he could wind up whenever he wanted to?

"Well reporters *are*, in a sense," he declared. "And my vibes tell me that Axelrod was definitely a ladies' man, except where it concerned his wife—"

"I don't see what any of this has to do with—" I argued.

"Maybe Axelrod was murdered by a scorned woman," Liam suggested, "if he was murdered at all. Point is, you can't rule out anything."

"I suppose not," I responded nonchalantly. Was he insinuating that Edwin Axelrod's mistress killed him? Could he know that Axelrod had been involved with Darlene?

I was obviously not bosom buddies with Carter's widow, but making her out to be a vindictive murderess seemed like a stretch, especially since I was under the impression that things had ended between her and Axelrod. But had they? Though I realized Darlene still had not been officially eliminated as a suspect in Carter's death, I somehow convinced myself that there was a distinction between killing one's no good lover and one's cheating, gambling husband.

I finished off my beer and decided I had better quit while I was ahead or at least on neutral ground.

"Thanks for the drink, Liam."

"Thanks for the company," he said with a boyish grin. "It's hard to find people to have an intelligent conversation with these days."

"Maybe you're looking in all the wrong places," I said sardonically.

"Maybe," he said, eyeing me as though that was about to change.

Liam insisted on walking me back to my car. I insisted that it went no further than that.

"See you around," I told him routinely after starting my car, but not meaning it.

"That a promise?" he asked eagerly. I couldn't tell if he was serious or not. In fact, there was a lot about him that left me uncertain and uneasy. Maybe I was making too much of nothing. Could be he was simply a damned good reporter given to some harmless flirting. Problem was I found myself buying into it to some degree.

I hated to burst his bubble, but there was no interest on my part in engaging in such conversations with him when there was nothing else on the table. I was more than satisfied with Ridge where it concerned intelligent conversing and otherwise spending time together.

I drove off without answering his question.

* * *

I ran some of Liam's theories and innuendoes about Edwin Axelrod's life and death by Ridge during dinner that evening. More specifically, the part about Axelrod being on Kazuo Pelekai's payroll.

Ridge listened with interest while chewing on barbecued chicken right off his own grill. "I knew that," he said as if no big deal.

"How long have you known?" I asked.

"Since you first had me run a check on Axelrod's license plate," Ridge answered.

I wasn't sure whether to be angry or wait until I heard his explanation. "Did it ever occur to you that I might be interested to know that the man Darlene was having an affair with just happened to be the attorney for Kazuo Pelekai—a man Carter spent years trying like hell to send to prison?"

Ridge nodded. "Yeah, it occurred to me—"

"And—?" I asked, assuming there had to be more.

He drank some wine and seemed to consider his words carefully. "I didn't want to involve you in this case any more than necessary, Skye. Hell, if I'd told you about the connection between Axelrod and Pelekai, you might have ended up way over your head in something that may have had nothing to do with Carter's death, but everything to do with putting you on someone's hit list." Ridge sipped more wine, and then said: "As it is, we haven't been able to tie Delaney's murder to Pelekai or Edwin Axelrod—"

I nibbled on a dinner roll. My disappointment was tempered by the fact that Ridge was a cop first and foremost, bound by cop rules. He also made a judgment call of a personal nature. I had to respect that, given our personal relationship and his wanting to protect me from harm.

"So what do you make of Axelrod's death?" I asked. We were sitting at a picnic table in Ridge's backyard. "Don't you find it strange that he wound up dead when he may have known who killed Carter—possibly burying his secret with him forever?"

Ridge ate more chicken before responding. "Having an affair with the wife of a former prosecutor doesn't mean it was part of a greater conspiracy against Carter Delaney," he said. "More likely, Axelrod took on one crook too many and paid the ultimate price. That said, I'd say suicide is still a damn good possibility. I heard the suicide rate is unusually high for attorneys. Must have something to do with job stress—"

Was he returning to the theory that Carter's death might have been a suicide, in spite of the evidence to the contrary? I wondered. Carter had not practiced law in years when he was killed, which would seem to debunk such a theory where it concerned him. Yet I could not deny that he was under a great deal of stress from more than one source. But, in my mind, this still did not add up to suicide. I was sure that Ridge and I were on the same page here; whereas the circumstances surrounding Edwin Axelrod's mysterious death were still very much up for debate.

My thoughts turned to Liam Pratt's suggestion that Axelrod's death was related to his cheating ways. It made me wonder if Darlene had, in fact, resumed their affair and the wife found out. Perhaps it was she who decided to pay her husband back by putting a bullet in his brain. Admittedly, it seemed farfetched, but it was totally plausible in this day and age where murder amongst married intimates occurred much more often than one might imagine.

Ridge's cell phone rang. He grabbed it from his jacket pocket and gave me one of his excuse me smiles before answering.

I watched as he listened mostly to the caller. Ridge hung up with a grim look in his eyes.

"What is it?" I hesitated to ask.

Ridge swallowed hard as he muttered: "Kazuo Pelekai was just found in his Lexus with half his face blown off—"

CHAPTER 44

He kissed her breasts. They were soft with hard nipples.

His lips moved to her mouth, which was waiting for him, attacking it with hot kisses as they had sex.

It was over in about five minutes. He spent another half hour listening to her tell him how great it was.

Not for him. He could think of any number of women he'd rather be with and who could satisfy him. One in particular. But he could only play the hand dealt him, which at the moment was putting up with the one he was with.

While she dozed off, the alcohol and sex apparently making her tired, he grabbed the remote and cut on the TV. He recognized the face that filled the screen.

He sat up and listened as the reporter said: "Reputed crime boss Kazuo Pelekai, also known as Chano, was found dead in his car last night. He was shot in the face at close range. So far there are no leads or suspects—"

He grinned. No leads? No suspects?

Good, he thought. Keep them guessing.

As far as he was concerned, it was one less person to pollute the streets of Honolulu.

Rest in a million pieces, Pelekai, he thought gleefully.

Suddenly, the one he was in bed with looked inviting again. He woke her up and was all over her like a cheap suit. He put his imagination in high gear and pretended she was the sweet, sassy and sexy private investigator named Skye Delaney.

CHAPTER 45

With Kazuo Pelekai dead, I was quickly running out of suspects. At least living ones.

Not quite sure which direction to turn, I showed up at Edwin Axelrod's home to pay my last respects. As might be expected for a high-priced, shady lawyer, he lived in style. The waterfront place on Diamond Head Road was two stories of slate cement stucco with large, gabled windows. Unfortunately for Axelrod, he couldn't take the elegant digs, expensive car, or money with him. Presumably, that left it all to the wife.

I rang the doorbell. It was the lady of the house herself who answered the door. I believe Ridge had told me last night during our heated debate that her name was Isabella and that she was indeed a fashion model, as I had once imagined. She certainly fit the bill: beautiful, tall, and sleek. She was wearing an outrageous floral print sheath and platform slides. Her long red hair was draped over one shoulder and her bold blue eyes looked swollen from tears.

She glared at me. "You! How dare you show up at my house!"

My guess was that she remembered our brief meeting at her husband's office. And yet I sensed there was much more to her hostility.

"I think there's been a mistake..." I told her and waited to see what came next.

"You're damned right," she blasted, her voice coming alive, "and *you* made it when you started sleeping with my husband!"

"Now wait just a minute—" I said and actually felt some relief that her anger was misplaced. "I don't know who you think I am, but I guarantee you I wasn't your husband's mistress. I'm a private investigator—"

Isabella Axelrod sighed while checking me out. She seemed less interested in my casual outfit of shirt and shorts than my overall physical appearance in deciding if I fit the bill as the possible mistress. Evidently she knew her husband was fooling around, if not with whom.

A moment or two passed before she asked suspiciously: "What do you want?"

"I'm investigating the death of Carter Delaney," I told her. "He was..."

"I know who he was," she interjected.

In that case, I got right to the point. "I think his murder might somehow be connected to your husband's death—"

Isabella stared at me for a full minute before saying: "Come in."

I was led through the foyer to a spacious living room filled with traditional furnishings and exotic art. A carafe of brandy sat on a table beside a half-filled glass. Isabella picked it up and sipped mechanically.

"Would you like some?" she asked.

I shook my head. "No thanks. I need to keep a clear head during my investigation."

She shrugged and sat on the sofa, folding her legs beneath her. I took the liberty of sitting in the chair closest to me.

"They said it would never work," she said reflectively. "A young, good-looking runway model and an older, handsome criminal defense attorney. I mean, what did we have in common, right? Well, we proved them wrong—at least in the beginning..." She wet her lips with brandy.

My insatiable curiosity about people and places from all walks of life prevented me from saying do us both a favor and keep your personal trials and tribulations to yourself. After all, I knew a little something about becoming involved with the wrong man who seemed right at the time. Obviously, it helped her to have someone to talk to about this.

"I'm a very jealous woman," Isabella freely admitted. "I've been with men who had other women hanging all over them. I couldn't deal with it. Edwin knew this when we got married. All I ever wanted from him was to be honest with me...no secrets and no affairs. I deserved to be respected. Having very different careers and working hours made it easy for him to cheat on me. I actually thought our love and trust would keep him faithful." She laughed cynically and sipped her drink. "Then I overheard Edwin on the phone one day talking to some bitch who talked about how good he was in bed. I wanted to kill him—and her!"

It was a feeling I could very much relate to—at least in theory, I thought. I hoped that was the extent of her pain and resentment as well.

"Edwin swore to me it was over," Isabella continued, "and I believed him." She sneered. "What a fool I was to think that he was any different from other men who only cared about what was in their pants—"

"Maybe he was telling the truth—about it being over," I offered, trying to give Edwin Axelrod the benefit of the doubt for her sake.

"When I saw you at his office, I thought you were the bitch he was sleeping with." She gazed at me with lingering suspicions. "Of course, he denied it. Then you show up here today now that Edwin's dead. What else could I think?"

"I'm very sorry about your husband's death," I told her compassionately. "I went to see him regarding the case I'm working on."

Her eyes narrowed. "What did Edwin have to do with the death of Carter Delaney?"

I had to be careful here. Both men were dead. There was no reason to bring more pain to the living if it could be avoided. Yet I couldn't escape the thought that these deaths were related in some way.

"One of your husband's clients was a man named Kazuo Pelekai," I said. "He was found dead last night in his car—the apparent victim of foul play. Before that, he was being investigated by the P.A.'s office for everything from drug trafficking to the murder of Carter Delaney..." I shifted my body and looked at her face. "I think your husband may have put himself in danger by working for Pelekai—"

Isabella's lower lip trembled. "Are you saying Edwin was killed by this man...Pelekai?"

"Or maybe one of his associates," I suggested, feeling there was no other way to put it. "I believe there's a good possibility that your husband's doings may not only have cost him his life, but Carter Delaney's as well."

Isabella frowned and drank more brandy. "I once told Edwin his drive and ambition would get him killed," she said, teary-eyed. "But I was only kidding—"

"The police think your husband's wound may have been self-inflicted—" I told her frankly, noting that a gun he owned was found near the body.

"No way—" she insisted. "Edwin was *not* suicidal. He wouldn't have taken his life—not without any warning..."

Maybe you just didn't know your husband as well as you think you did, I mused, immediately realizing the irony of that thought, as I had apparently fallen into the same trap with Carter. *Join the club.*

But that hardly meant I believed Axelrod killed himself any more than I believed Carter had, even though it appeared that they had.

If Isabella Axelrod knew anything more, she was in no condition or frame of mind to divulge it. I left her to her mourning and went from one recent widow to another.

* * *

I caught Darlene just as she and Ivy were leaving the house in what appeared to be a big hurry. Darlene was carrying a duffel bag that looked overstuffed. I honked my horn to get their attention. It did, and probably the whole neighborhood as well.

I wasn't about to let Darlene skip town before this thing had been resolved.

"Going somewhere?" I asked, placing myself between them and the BMW.

"Skye," Darlene said in a jittery voice. "What are you doing here?"

"I came to see you." It seemed obvious enough to me.

"What for?" she asked innocently.

I looked at Ivy, who smiled up at me as her pigtails bounced against her ears. It was my first good look at the little girl who, under vastly different circumstances, could have been my own.

I smiled back just as her mother said: "This is my daughter, Ivy—"

"Hi, Ivy," I said sweetly, trying to hide the awkwardness I felt and Darlene was no doubt enjoying. Ivy had Carter's eyes and smile as well as a more dainty version of his nose.

"Skye is someone your father knew a long time ago," Darlene told her, making me seem older than I was. I wondered if Carter had ever planned to tell his daughter about our life together as husband and wife that had once been just as important to him. Or had he planned to pretend that part of his history never existed, except for when it suited him to remember?

"Hi, Skye," Ivy said politely.

I looked at Darlene and said: "I need to talk to you about a certain defense attorney—"

225

Her brow creased with uneasiness. "Wait in the car for me, honey," she told Ivy. "I'll be just a few minutes—"

I watched Carter's daughter skip to the BMW as if not a care in the world, and couldn't help but wonder what this entire mess would do to her over the long haul. Particularly as she learned more about her father—and mother.

Speaking of which, Darlene looked about as fearful as I had ever seen her. "I heard about Edwin," she muttered while moving away from the car toward the house. "It's starting to get creepy. I'm mostly scared for Ivy. That's why I'm taking her to stay with my sister for a while—"

"Do you know anyone who would want to kill Carter, Kalolo, and Edwin?" I asked point-blank. Not to mention Pelekai, I thought.

She sighed. "I've thought about it. But I honestly can't say anyone comes to mind who would have reason to do such a thing."

"Were you still seeing Edwin Axelrod after Carter died?" I asked, locking eyes with her in assessing whether or not there were possibly further implications from the affair— such as murder.

Darlene flashed me an annoyed look. "Absolutely not!" she said. "We both agreed it was best to end it as quietly and painlessly as possible."

"Did anyone else know about your affair?"

Darlene fluttered her lashes. "You mean like his wife?"

"I mean anyone," I reiterated, as the reporter Liam Pratt came to mind.

She pursed her lips and said: "Just you—" She paused and added: "It wasn't exactly something to brag about..."

I considered that maybe I was way off base here. Despite Darlene being the common link between the victims, each could have easily died independent of one another. But did they?

I asked her: "Did Axelrod ever ask you about Carter the businessman...or former prosecutor?"

Darlene stared at the question before responding. "He might have. Why?"

"Did you ever give him any information you had on Kazuo Pelekai?" I asked.

Darlene shot me a cold stare. "Are you suggesting Edwin was using me to get information from my husband?"

I nodded. "It's a very good possibility," I told her.

She did not take the news well. "Look, Carter and I may have had our problems—okay, we had some big problems—but I would never have sold him out by giving away any tidbits concerning his professional life, past or present. Besides, Carter didn't believe in bringing his work home—figuratively or literally. And I never encouraged it."

"I had to ask," I said, giving her the benefit of the doubt.

She studied me. "Why?"

"Because people are dying all around us, Darlene," I pointed out, "and I have a vested interest in making sure that *we* don't end up on that list, too—"

That was at least partially true. The other part had to do with solving Carter's murder—the first murder that tied us together. I was pretty sure Darlene knew more about it than she was letting on.

She sighed and said: "I made a mistake—maybe a few—and I'll pay for it for the rest of my life. But I never knowingly did anything that I thought might get Carter or anyone else killed."

Knowingly? I thought. What about unknowingly? I couldn't help but wonder.

I told her: "It's probably a wise move to get your daughter out of harm's way. And if I were you, I think I'd seriously consider hiring a body guard, just until you can be sure you're not on someone's hit list."

Darlene raised a brow. "Are you offering your services?"

"No," I responded without hesitation. "I'm a security consultant and private investigator, not a bodyguard. Sorry."

"And I'm a woman trying to put her life back together," she stated with determination. "I'm not going to give in to

227

fear and things I can't control—at least where it concerns my health and well-being." Her look of defiance weakened. "But protecting my daughter is a different story—"

"Then think of your daughter," I urged, "and protect yourself. She'll thank you someday."

Darlene gave me a look of resignation. "If there's someone out there who wants me dead, there probably isn't much I can do to prevent it," she said. "I'm not going to spend the rest of my life looking over my shoulder." She smiled faintly before saying: "Maybe we'll both get lucky and you'll catch whoever is committing these murders before either of us is targeted—"

"I wouldn't count on that," I told her. "Luck doesn't apprehend murderers. Private investigators don't either, for the most part, though not necessarily for lack of trying." My pessimism gave way to motivation in catching a killer, and I told her, for both our sakes: "I won't stop trying to do right by Carter, even if he didn't always do right by us—"

I left Darlene to carry on with her plans and went to the office for a short time, then home. My tropical fire ant problem had apparently gone the way of the dinosaur and I hoped to keep them at bay, certain that Ollie was in complete agreement.

I eased my stress and strain by running with him and, later, soothing my body in the bathtub. It was the first time I had been able to bring myself to use it since Carter's corpse was left there for me to find. I decided it was time to conquer the distaste it left in my mouth and try to enjoy the things I'd worked hard to achieve.

In bed, I watched a DVD. It was a suspense thriller that often showed the killer's viewpoint. He enjoyed playing mind games with his victims before he killed them.

I couldn't help but wonder if I was dealing with a similar scary villain in real life...

CHAPTER 46

The following day, I left home just before noon and drove the short distance to the Waikiki Shopping Plaza on Kalakaua Avenue to pick up some office supplies.

After that, I stopped by the post office. No sooner had I headed to my car, which was parked on the street, when I heard the rev of an engine. I turned just in time to see a vehicle barreling toward me at a high rate of speed. It took only a second to realize that this was *not* a driver out of control, but one who knew *exactly* what he or she was doing.

Someone was trying to run me down!

I barely had time to dive out of the way, much less see who the driver was, or go for my .40 caliber revolver that was safely tucked away in my purse.

At the last possible moment before impact, I lifted myself off the ground and hurdled atop my hood as the car raced past me with tires screeching. Unable to brace myself or grab onto anything, I bounced against the windshield then fell back onto the street, hitting my head on the pavement. The last thing I remember was seeing a grayish black cloud of pollution trailing the car and the license plate number RKL 497, before blacking out...

I awoke with a splitting headache to Ridge's smiling face. "Welcome back, Skye—" His smile was replaced with a scowl. "You gave me one hell of a scare there!"

"What happened?" I asked groggily before I realized I was in a hospital bed.

"You tell me," he said.

Another voice to my left said: "You suffered a nasty bump on the head, Ms. Delaney—"

With a great deal of discomfort from the neck up, along with other aches and pains, I swiveled my face to see the person behind the voice was a middle-aged African American man wearing standard hospital garb. A stethoscope hung from his neck and he was holding a chart.

"I'm Doctor Ellison," he said, crinkling his black eyes. "A passerby saw you on the street and called 911. An ambulance brought you here to the Waikiki Medical Center ER. We called Mr. Larsen as the person you asked to notify if something happened to you—"

I was glad to know that Ridge was there to offer comfort and support. I put a hand to my throbbing temple. "Just tell me, Doctor," I moaned, "will this headache get better before it gets worse?"

"Yes," he assured me. "You were very fortunate. A mild concussion is the official diagnosis. Hopefully, you'll be back on your feet in no time." His expression changed. "As a precautionary measure, we're going to keep you here overnight for observation. I'll give you something to ease the pain..."

He did, and it seemed to be working.

Ridge grabbed my hand, getting my attention. "Was it a hit and run, Skye?"

I swallowed, nodding. "I think someone tried to kill me—"

His brows furrowed. "Who?"

"I don't know," I managed. "The car was...a dark color, older model—"

"Did you see who was in it?" Ridge persisted. "Male? Female...?"

"Never saw the driver—" I hated to say, feeling as if I had somehow let him and myself down.

"She should get some rest now," the doctor intervened politely.

"This is *official* police business," Ridge told him, and flashed his I.D. for apparently the first time. "Whoever did this will probably try again—unless we get to the bastard first."

"Put a police guard on her if you want," Ellison said, "but I must insist that you come back later if you want to ask her more questions—"

While they argued, something inside my head clicked. One of the first things I learned at the Academy was memorizing license plate numbers.

"Ridge—" I squeezed his hand and muttered: "RKL 497."

* * *

"Looks like that son of a bitch Antonio Ramirez was the one who tried to run you down," Ridge said angrily after picking me up the next day. "We traced the plate number to a car he owns. That's the good news. The bad news is that Ramirez is still on the loose. We put out an APB. We'll get him—"

"But why would Antonio Ramirez try to kill me?" I asked, surprised at this revelation. His alibi for Carter's death had checked out. I looked out the car window at the passing palm trees and businesses and then turned to Ridge's profile.

"I don't know. Maybe you rubbed him the wrong way during our visit to the construction site," he suggested. "Or it could be that Ramirez was using you to get even with Delaney for putting his brother away. Who knows what set him off to go after you."

I tried to picture Antonio Ramirez, but my head was still throbbing despite the effects of extra strength Tylenol. Given his size and muscular build, it didn't seem like he would choose a car as his method for attacking me. Besides, killing me would seem to go against the grain of the Jesus and church theme he had spouted. While I hardly considered myself to be a pushover, if Ramirez had wanted me dead, he probably could have gotten the job done with his bare hands much more efficiently than the hit and run method. *So why didn't he try?* I asked myself before asking Ridge the same question.

"We'll ask him when we pick him up," he said simply. "My guess is that when it got right down to it, Ramirez didn't have the balls to take you on without the protection of a car while he did his dirty work."

"Perhaps," I said thoughtfully. "Or maybe he's not the person who tried to run me down."

Ridge made it clear that he didn't want to hear a point of view that could let Antonio Ramirez off the hook. "Are you saying you think we're after the wrong man?"

I pondered the question. No one would have faulted me if I'd accepted that my assailant had been quickly uncovered, if not yet apprehended. But the more I thought about it, the less I believed Antonio Ramirez was the person who nearly put me out of commission for good even though it contradicted my memory of his license plate number.

I was now starting to question my memory. "You know it's possible," I told Ridge, "that I may have gotten the plate number wrong. Maybe the L was really an I or the 9 a 6—"

He scratched his head, looked at me sideways, and said: "I don't think so. The car description you gave matched Ramirez's car. If that isn't proof enough, the man is on the run." He looked into my eyes. "If you were guilty of nothing more than mistaken identity, would you go underground?"

"Probably not," I admitted. But since Ramirez was already a suspect in Carter's murder, I could envision him panicking at the thought of being sent to prison for a hit and run that he may have had no part in. Of course, that still didn't explain why another killer would use his car, unless

Ramirez was being set up. I kept these thoughts to myself for now, not wanting to get Ridge riled up again.

The worst thing about being in the hospital, even for a day, was that I missed my dog. Ridge had kept him fed during my absence, with help from Natsuko. I could hear Ollie barking as we pulled into the driveway beside my car, which Ridge had driven back from the scene of the crime.

"I'm keeping my eye on you," he declared, "until Ramirez is apprehended."

"Anything you say, *Detective* Larsen." I smiled at him, happy to have his company at a time when I was not fully recovered from banging my head on the street and, as such, more vulnerable than I was willing to admit.

We entered through the side door and were met by Ollie. He was in a barking mood. Obviously, he had missed me as much as I did him.

"He must be hungry," I told Ridge when it became apparent that Ollie's barks went beyond being glad to see me.

"I fed him this morning," Ridge said defensively.

I tried to calm Ollie down and he nearly bit my hand. "What's wrong, boy?" I asked. He barked back as if I were suddenly his enemy. "Something's wrong, Ridge—" I said intuitively.

Ollie ran down the hallway, barking relentlessly.

"Wait here!" Ridge ordered. "Somebody might be in the house—" He removed his .38 from a shoulder holster and began walking down the hall toward the dining room and living room.

The tension in the air was suddenly thick enough to slice in more than once place. I removed the Smith and Wesson from my purse and followed Ridge. Was Antonio Ramirez actually laying in wait to take another crack at me? I wondered. Or were we up against something or someone else?

I heard Ridge say "Oh, damn!" after he had gone into the living room.

"Ridge?" I called out, and approached cautiously, my head still pounding painfully. He stepped out just before I got there, holding the .38 at his side. His face was sullen.

"What is it?" I asked. Ollie ran out of the room, barking and huffing.

Ridge hedged, as if the words would not come out, prompting me to see for myself.

"Don't!" Ridge said to deaf ears as I squirmed past him and looked in the living room. My knees nearly buckled as my eyes looked up—

A stark naked Antonio Ramirez was twirling by a rope around his neck from the ceiling fan...

CHAPTER 47

On the coffee table beside some neatly folded clothes that presumably belonged to Antonio Ramirez was a typed suicide note, in which he confessed to the murders of Carter Delaney, Edwin Axelrod, and Kalolo Nawahi. According to the note, Ramirez blamed Carter for his brother's incarceration and had planned his revenge for a long time, including what he described as the perfect alibi. The note indicated that Axelrod and Nawahi's murders were just meant to confuse the police.

Ramirez made no mention of the attempt on my life, but did say that it only seemed fair that he end his life where this whole thing began.

"I had a gut feeling about him all along," Ridge claimed as the victim was carted off to the morgue.

Me, too, I thought, glancing at the overturned chair that Ramirez had obviously been standing on before hanging himself. But apparently my gut feeling was wrong. What type of person used the church and Jesus as pawns in a multiple murder scheme? I wondered. Was Antonio Ramirez truly that calculating and clever? Or was there much more to this story than met the eye?

Once again, my house had been turned into a police den of crime scene technicians and potential homicide investigators. This time the general feeling was that it was a mere formality to a case that, for all intents and purposes, was now closed. Given Ramirez's size and stature, murder had all but been ruled out, as it would have practically taken Hercules to wrap the rope around his neck, lift him up, and hang him from the ceiling fan.

For me, and Ollie, it would take a lot longer to get over the trauma of having our residence invaded by the sights, smells, and sounds of murder times two. Right now, I'd just settle for a little relief from the headache that had returned, no doubt brought on by the distressing events of the last hour.

Ridge told me: "Ramirez must have figured we were onto him and decided to save us the trouble of putting him away." He scratched his chin. "He obviously found a way past your security system again."

This, in and of itself, was disturbing to me. What good was a security system if it could not keep out the bad guys or at least alert the authorities in a timely manner.

"I'm just glad it's over," I said. Deep down inside, I knew it would never be over for the families of the ones Ramirez murdered. I thought of Darlene and Ivy, as well as Isabella Axelrod, and found myself grieving along with them all over again.

Kawakami, who looked as if a load had been taken off his shoulders, interrupted us. "I'd say the asshole did us a favor by killing himself," he said. "Saved the taxpayers the cost of a trial." He eyed me. "Ramirez won't be breaking into your house anymore and you don't have to be burdened by Carter Delaney's death anymore either."

I agreed that the weight had been lifted somewhat. But something about the entire equation still bothered me.

"Doesn't this all seem a just a bit too pat?" I said, standing between the two detectives. They both rolled their eyes simultaneously at the mere suggestion. "First Ramirez tries to run me down, then he comes to my house to kill himself? Oh, yes, but not before making sure he had *typed* a confession to several murders that would possibly let someone else off the hook. And can any of us really believe that Ramirez managed to break into my house a second time, shut off the alarm, and tame Ollie all by himself?"

I knew I was going out on a limb, but it needed to be said by someone who had a nose for something that stunk to high heaven.

Kawakami used a dirty handkerchief to wipe his nose, and frowned at me. "Will you listen to what the hell you're saying? This psycho murdered Delaney and threw in a couple of others just for effect. When the screws began to tighten, Ramirez put a rope around his neck and hung from it." He stuffed the handkerchief into his back pocket, and said condescendingly: "Now do yourself a favor, Skye, and don't try to be a cop anymore when you aren't one."

I'd forgotten what an ass Kawakami could be. Now I remembered why I never saw fit to date the man a second time. I glared up at him and said brusquely: "Lay off, Henry. Who says I want to be a cop again? I don't, thank you very much. But that doesn't mean I left my brains behind with the badge. I want Carter's killer just as much as you do or anyone else. I'm just not sure we have him. So don't patronize me—especially in my own house!"

Ridge intervened. "Okay, okay, let's all calm down for a minute," he said. "We're the good guys here. Remember? Why don't we wait until the autopsy report comes in before we start pointing fingers and saying things we'll regret."

Kawakami grinned sheepishly at me. "Sorry, Skye. I didn't mean to take it out on you. This isn't personal. I just want to see this damned thing over and done with so we can all move on. As far as I'm concerned, all the pieces of the puzzle seem to fit solidly. Ramirez is our man—"

"I hope you're right, detective," I said. "If he is our man, I'd be interested in knowing how and why Antonio Ramirez chose to single out Edwin Axelrod and Kalolo Nawahi as part of this intricate plot to murder Carter. I really don't see the connection there unless their deaths were part of some larger conspiracy..."

Both Ridge and Kawakami seemed stumped by that one. I certainly didn't claim to have the answers. I theorized that perhaps Antonio Ramirez had somehow found out about Darlene's affair and drug use—and put that together with his hatred for Carter. Axelrod's and Nawahi's murders could have simply been thrown into the mix just to keep me and the police off balance. Or was it simply made to look that way?

* * *

Ramirez's vehicle was found in a ditch about a mile from my house. Police speculated he ran off the road, couldn't get back on it, and decided to walk the rest of the way. After all, he wouldn't need the car anymore after killing himself.

I was leaning more toward the theory that someone else could have strategically left the car there, leaving nothing to chance in confirming Antonio Ramirez's guilt. Proving this suspicion would be much more difficult, particularly if no corroborating evidence surfaced.

Still shaken by the most recent death to occur under my roof, Ollie and I spent the night at Ridge's. It seemed like we were becoming regular overnight guests at his place lately. Not that Ridge was complaining. On the contrary, he liked the idea. Maybe too much. That's what scared me. I felt as safe and secure with Ridge as I had with anyone, but still wasn't ready or willing to give up my independence anytime soon.

That didn't mean Ridge's companionship was not a blessing in disguise, especially during times like these when a good friend meant more to me than a good lover.

"And I thought being cooped up in a hospital room was bad," I muttered in his bed as two more painkillers began to work their way to my head.

Ridge was holding me. "It could've been worse," he pointed out. "If Ramirez had his way, you'd be dead right now—"

At least that was the general consensus. I only wished Antonio Ramirez was alive to confess to that and his other alleged crimes, rather than having to rely on a piece of paper that couldn't be interrogated.

Ridge added: "Who knows how many other victims there might have been if you hadn't gotten his plate number before you passed out."

I looked up at him and asked: "Who knows for sure how many victims did not die by Antonio Ramirez's hand?"

Ridge didn't respond, but he was clearly pondering the notion.

* * *

Two days later, I was back at my house. I was having my locks changed and my security system replaced with what I hoped would be a much more reliable system to keep killers out and keep me and Ollie safe.

Afterward, I put things back in order as best as possible with the help of Natsuko. My headache had been absent for nearly twenty-four hours now—a good sign that I was definitely on the mend. Rather than tempt fate against doctor's orders, I resisted the desire to run or swim. Instead, I lifted weights and tried to keep my mind off the events that had kept me preoccupied.

As if.

By two o'clock, Antonio Ramirez's autopsy had been completed.

CHAPTER 48

The Medical Examiner, Doctor R. Mitsuo Isagawa, looked exhausted after three postmortems in a row, including Antonio Ramirez's.

"They seem to be coming in droves," Mitsuo complained, while leading Ridge, Kawakami, and me into the examination room where Ramirez's body still lay, partially covered by a sheet. "Must be something in the air that's driving people to do crazy things."

Kawakami balked at that suggestion, saying: "Why the hell do we always make excuses for every bad thing that happens? Don't blame the air. It's about time homicidal assholes were held accountable for their own actions."

"That doesn't mean some of them weren't given a nudge in committing the crimes," I said, leaving open the possibility that Ramirez could have been working on behalf of someone else, including his brother, assuming he was actually a multiple murderer.

Ridge asked Mitsuo what we all wanted to know: "Did Antonio Ramirez kill himself?"

"The evidence says he did," Mitsuo replied evenly. "He died from a broken neck, caused no doubt from the pressure applied around his neck from hanging—"

"Any chance someone else could have killed him?" I asked. "And made it *look* like suicide?"

Mitsuo slid on his examination gloves and began to manipulate Ramirez's thick neck as if he were a giant doll. "There's no reason to believe he was a victim of foul play," the medical examiner said. "I find no evidence of fresh abrasions or bruises on his arms or legs to indicate resistance. And there were no drugs in his system to suggest this might have played a role in his death." Mitsuo looked me in the eye. "In my judgment, the decedent caused his own fate—"

"Thanks, Doc," said an almost gleeful Kawakami. "That jives with the physical and circumstantial evidence he left behind."

"Then it's settled," Ridge agreed. "Ramirez killed himself to avoid prosecution."

"So it looks like Antonio Ramirez was Delaney's killer," Kawakami surmised.

"It certainly appears that way," Mitsuo said. "The DNA results will presumably corroborate that."

"I think it's safe to say the whole city of Honolulu will rest a little easier now," Ridge said, clearly satisfied that they had their man.

"Wish I could say the same," complained Mitsuo, removing his gloves. "People on the island somehow seem to find their way to the morgue too much these days. Why do you think I haven't had a vacation in almost two years?"

Ridge frowned, Kawakami half-smiled, and I kept a straight face as my mind was elsewhere. I was still having trouble with the suicide and killer conclusion, in spite of the strong indications of such on both fronts.

"I have one more question for you, Mitsuo," I said. "How is Ramirez's cause of death different from Carter's? They both had their necks broken. I'm obviously not a medical examiner, but how can you be so sure one died of suicide and the other was a murder victim?" The question made sense, at least to me.

241

Mitsuo regarded me with amused eyes. "It's not really all that difficult, Skye. But then, like you said, you *aren't* trained to be able to detect the differences. Fortunately, I am."

I could almost read Ridge's and Kawakami's minds saying: *Leave it alone, Skye.* But I couldn't. At least not before being able to better understand how two deaths that seemed remarkably similar were technically distinct.

Mitsuo put the gloves back on and began moving the head and neck of the deceased. "In Carter's case, the mortal injuries he suffered were consistent with those of a person strangled and then drowned. With Ramirez, his death had all the earmarks of a person who died as the result of a broken neck caused by two hundred and fifty pounds hanging from it." He looked at me sympathetically. "Satisfied...?"

Not quite, I thought. I looked at Ramirez's exposed upper body—his arms and shoulders. There were some signs of injury—like the wound on his shoulder— but no clear evidence that Ollie had dug a hole, or two, into his flesh recently.

"Does he have any injuries consistent with a dog bite?" I asked Mitsuo.

He scanned our faces, sniffed, and looked at the victim, pulling the sheet down. Ramirez's body resembled something akin to a road map, with discolored scars and contusions every which way. "You can see for yourself—this man was a walking disaster. Yes, it's quite possible he's seen a few dog bites in his day. Probably ran into a few walls, too—"

Is this the man Ollie bit? I asked myself, second-guessing what was staring me in the face and not really sure why. I decided to hold my tongue till the DNA tests on Ramirez were completed and compared to the DNA that Carter's killer left behind.

* * *

That afternoon, Sumiyo Ishimoto from the crime lab phoned me with the results, having already presented them to Ridge and Kawakami.

"There is a positive match with Antonio Ramirez's DNA and the blood of the person your dog bit," she said. "Ramirez was in your house the day Carter died and was bitten, leaving behind his AB negative blood. Also, the fingerprints on Ramirez's suicide note belonged to him. Given the circumstantial evidence, I'd say you have your killer and the case is solved."

I could hardly argue the point, all things considered. Everything led right to Ramirez as Carter's murderer. Yet I still couldn't help but wonder if he might not have been a fall guy for someone else. Or, I wondered, was I just reaching for something when the evidence clearly indicated otherwise?

I brought it up to Sumiyo, who responded: "Yes, it's always possible that Ramirez had an accomplice, but there's no DNA evidence to support it. I'd say he was a lone ranger, looking for some payback and finding it."

"Ramirez went through a lot of trouble to do this," I said musingly, "and got little for it. It doesn't seem like it was worth it if his brother is still left to languish in prison."

"Who's to say what extreme measures a person is willing to go through to make a lethal point?" Sumiyo said. "Carter is dead and maybe for Ramirez any collateral damage, including to himself, was more than worth it."

"Maybe you're right," I told her waveringly. "Either that or we're still missing something...or someone."

"Don't torture yourself over this, Skye" she said in a concerned voice. "We've all done our jobs to the best of our abilities, with help from Antonio Ramirez. Carter couldn't ask any more of us than that. Neither should you—"

Knowing that Ridge and Kawakami felt the forensic evidence cemented their case against Ramirez, I resigned myself to the conclusion that he was responsible for the murders of Carter, Kalolo Nawahi, and Edwin Axelrod. Even Kazuo Pelekai, whose murder was still under investigation, may have been the unfortunate victim of

Ramirez's twisted vengeance, though he didn't take credit for that one.

There were still some unanswered questions in my mind. But my objectivity in this case was very much in doubt. I had let it become too personal.

The time had come to call it quits and get back to being a private investigator without a personal agenda.

Later that evening, Ridge took me out to dinner for what was billed by him as us starting all over again. He seemed determined to help me put Carter out of my mind and life once and for all. It seemed like an uphill battle, but I was willing to at least put forth the effort.

CHAPTER 49

Carter's will was going to be read at his attorney's office. Now that the official police investigation into his death had been closed and the expected chief beneficiary cleared of all suspicions, the will could now be read.

I was surprised that I was invited, the presumption being that Carter had left me something. I wanted nothing from him that I didn't already have, which included good memories. But curiosity caused me to show up, much to the chagrin of his widow, who seemed to think I was going to somehow walk away with everything she believed was rightfully hers.

Neil Schmidt had been Carter's attorney since before Carter and I were married. They had attended law school together and remained friends and friendly competitors, in spite of veering off into different branches of law and social circles. Neil had a successful law practice and an office on Merchant Street in the high rent district downtown. At forty-one, he was no taller than five-five and slightly built with short dark blonde hair parted to the side.

"Aloha, Skye!" he said in a deep voice, unbuttoning the jacket of his designer suit.

"Hi, Neil," I said, and shook his hand.

A look of sadness washed over his face. "I wish we were meeting again under better circumstances—"

"So do I," I said, then felt obliged to add: "Carter's life was not in vain."

Neil nodded. "I agree," he said solemnly. "Carter knew how to live life as it should be. More than anyone I knew, he was relentless in going after what and who he wanted—and usually succeeded..."

Whatever Neil may have meant, his words were not exactly endearing to me or likely to my successor as Mrs. Carter Delaney. Darlene was standing near a wooden conference table at one end of the long office. She pressed her lips together tightly and gave me an impatient look.

I nodded in polite acknowledgement.

As far as I knew, outside of Ivy, Carter had no other living relatives. An only child, his parents had died in a car accident when he was thirteen, forcing him to be shuttled between foster homes until he reached adulthood. No doubt this would work in Darlene's favor and she would presumably get all of whatever Carter left behind, as would his daughter.

We sat in cream-colored leather chairs on opposite sides of the table as Neil took a chair at the head. His briefcase was open on the table beside a pitcher of water and some drinking glasses.

"Can we please get on with this," Darlene whined nervously.

Neil raised a brow at her, then me. "Yes, of course..." He removed some papers from his briefcase and said: "As the executor of Carter's estate and as his attorney, I've been appointed to read his last will and testament and see to it that it is carried out according to his wishes. None of us expected it would be this soon..." He paused, glancing at the papers and then back to each of us. "There's no easy way to put this, so I'll just get right to it," Neil said. "Carter's business was in big trouble when he died. As you know, the economy has been in the doldrums of late and is still struggling to regain its footing. Internet-based companies have been hit especially hard where it concerns international trade. Carter's liabilities far exceeded his assets. In other words, Carter was a step or two away from filing for bankruptcy..."

Darlene batted her lashes in disbelief. "You're telling me that *all* of the money he invested in the company is gone?"

"Just about," Neil said sadly. "I'm sure you know that Carter had a serious gambling problem." He carried on before she could respond. "Unfortunately, he often dipped into his business profits and assets to cover his debts. But the creditors are still there waiting to be paid what Carter owed them—"

None of this came as a surprise to me. After all, it was obvious that Carter was in real trouble when the gambling came to light and Darlene was forced to come up with the funds to try to bail him out of a difficult and dangerous situation. The businessman and the gambling addict were one and the same—meaning they either rose or fell together. Unfortunately, Carter got in over his head in both arenas and destroyed much of what he had in the process.

From the look on Darlene's face, not even a payoff of three million dollars in insurance money appeared to be satisfactory as a parting gift from Carter.

But Neil wasn't through with his surprises.

"The house will have to be sold to cover Carter's outstanding debts," he said bleakly.

Darlene stared at him wide-eyed. "What—?"

"I'm sorry, but there is no other choice other than to try to protect what's left for you and your daughter." He looked at me. "There's still something in this for you, Skye."

I wasn't holding my breath at this point, wondering what was left. I did find it somewhat amusing that Darlene was taking this so hard, as if she were somehow entitled to far more than she ever brought to the marriage—which it seemed like she was getting.

"Fortunately, between selling off the assets of Carter's business and the house itself, it should wipe the slate clean," Neil said. "I don't think you'll end up in the poor house, Darlene, especially with the generous insurance policy Carter made sure he had in the event of his death."

Darlene sneered at me, but seemed to now be counting her blessings. She asked Neil: "So do I need to move out of my house now?"

He smiled faintly. "In time, yes, but not overnight or anything." After winking at me, he turned to the papers before him and said: "Now, back to the will... The bulk of Carter's estate, minus that used to pay off creditors—including outstanding stocks and bonds, an old coin collection, paintings, and an account he set up to continually subsidize his daughter's trust fund—goes to Ivy. He also updated his life insurance, making his daughter the beneficiary of two-thirds of the amount—"

Darlene reacted to this, clearly not expecting that last statement. I, for one, was happy that Carter had at least put Ivy ahead of himself in securing her future—even at the expense of his wife, who may have had other ideas about spending his money.

Neil turned to Darlene and continued. "These assets, including the insurance payout, are to be converted into cash as soon as possible, then added to Ivy's trust fund, which I will administer until she reaches the age of twenty-five. A second account will be set up in Ivy's name that will be available to her when she turns eighteen."

He stopped and took a drink of water. "As Ivy's mother and legal guardian, Darlene, you'll have access to any funds deemed necessary to maintain a reasonable standard of living for her. Money will also be available for any emergencies that might arise regarding Ivy—"

Darlene narrowed her eyes at him. "So I get nothing but one-third of the insurance money?"

Neil leaned back in his chair. "Actually, you get all the furniture, jewelry, and other household items not already stated, as well as any stocks, mutual funds, and bank accounts that were in your name," he answered coolly. "And, with all due respect, Darlene, your portion of Carter's insurance money amounts to a million dollars. That's not a bad piece of change, considering—"

Darlene grunted with tight lips. I waited more than patiently to see what Carter had seen fit to will to me in his unpredictable way.

"There is one other thing Carter left behind for you, Darlene," Neil said, removing more papers from his briefcase. Darlene's eyes lit up with a ray of hope. "He was aware you had a drug problem..."

I watched Darlene's face suddenly darken.

To me, this was an indication that Carter probably also knew about Kalolo Nawahi. Could Carter have also known about Edwin Axelrod even before he had hired me? While this didn't make sense, not much did where it concerned my ex-husband and the inner workings of his mind.

Neil went on: "To that end, Carter was able to set aside funds to be used at a drug treatment facility of your choice, for you to receive as much care as you are willing to get for up to ten years following his death—"

Darlene avoided my eyes as she digested what Carter had quite literally delivered to her from the grave. Clearly he'd given this much thought, and was most concerned about protecting his daughter's best interest, even if it meant his wife just might have to get used to a less extravagant lifestyle. At the same time, I felt that Carter had at least cared for this woman more than she'd ever believed. In sponsoring drug treatment for her in death, he was giving Darlene a way to help herself and their daughter that he apparently couldn't do in life.

"Carter also instructed me that if there was anything left, he wanted to set up a foundation to help fight substance abuse and gambling addiction..." Neil caught the surprised look on my face and said: "He knew he had a gambling problem, but couldn't lick it. Guess this was his way of trying to help others caught in the same vicious trap."

Carter continued to surprise me in a positive way. It was as if he was trying to make amends after the fact for a life in which he'd made some regrettable, and often baffling, errors in judgment.

"Now for you, Skye..." Neil said, gazing at me with a smile.

I poured myself a glass of water and tasted it as the suspense mounted regarding the fate or fortune Carter had in store for me.

Neil removed something wrapped in brown paper from under the table. The paper was removed, revealing a 12 x 18 inch custom-framed oil painting. It was a picture of Carter and me on our wedding day.

"He had this made for you from an old wedding photo he kept in his wallet," Neil said, handing the painting to me. "Carter wanted you to have something to remember him by on what he considered to be one of the most special days of his life."

A touch of nostalgia overcame me as I remembered the moment in time that truly seemed like someone else's moment. We both looked so young, happy, and in love. It was supposed to be the first day of the rest of our lives. But it didn't quite work according to plan.

"Thanks, Neil," I said, trying not to get too emotional. "It's a nice way to remember Carter—"

His eyes crinkled as he smiled. "You two did make a pretty nice couple, didn't you?"

Darlene pouted. "Why the hell did he ever bother to leave you in the first place when he obviously couldn't get you off his mind...right up to the very end?"

I was barely able to refrain myself after her outburst. *Talk about ungrateful*, I mused. *I get a painting with sentimental value, and she walks away from this a millionaire.* I was getting damn tired of being the bad guy in this twisted three-way scenario of sex, lies, infidelity, drugs, and gambling. It seemed like a good time for me to vent some unresolved feelings I had for Darlene to her face.

"If you take a good look at yourself," I barked, "you just might reach the conclusion that *you* had something to do with me giving Carter his walking papers and, in effect, him giving you yours—" It wasn't a knockout punch, but I did deliver her a well deserved stinging jab or two.

And felt much better for it.

Ridge was waiting for me in the car after the show had ended. "What the hell's that?" he asked of the painting, which I placed across the back seat, face down.

Something told me that showing it to him right now wasn't a smart move. It was likely headed to my attic for cold storage and invisibility. Right now I didn't need to be reminded of days gone by, especially the recent ones.

I flashed Ridge a little smile and said: "Let's just say that as far as bequeathed items go, it's not something that will allow either of us to retire any time soon—"

"Too bad," he said, frowning. "I had visions of you coming out of this with a fortune, asking for my hand in marriage, and both of us retiring to a house on the beach in Maui."

I laughed and told him: "Keep dreaming. You never know what might be waiting around the corner—"

Retiring with riches did sound nice, I thought. But funding that retirement through Carter's last will and testament and untimely demise did not set well with me. I doubted it would have for Ridge either.

Marriage, though, was a different proposition altogether, I thought. And, frankly, it scared the hell out of me. My last marriage had left me with a bad impression of the institution.

When and if the urge came around again, Ridge seemed like the perfect choice to walk down the aisle with, assuming he really saw me as marriage material.

But that was something to consider for another day, I thought.

CHAPTER 50

Even though Carter's murder had been solved, I still had some lingering questions that needed answered. And Liam Pratt seemed like the one person who might be able to help me fill in the blanks. He knew about the relationship between Edwin Axelrod and Kazuo Pelekai and may have discovered Axelrod's affair with Darlene. I wondered what else he had uncovered that could possibly connect Carter's death to the others and Ramirez's suicide to the alleged suicide of Axelrod.

I dropped by the offices of the Honolulu Press where Liam worked, hoping to catch him there. I walked up to the front desk in the lobby.

"How can I help you?" a twenty-something Polynesian receptionist asked.

"I'm looking for Liam Pratt," I told her. "Can you tell me where his office is?"

"Yes, I can tell you, but you won't find him there," she said. "Liam's on assignment. You just missed him."

Oh, hell, I thought. *When I finally do want to see him, he makes himself scarce.*

"Can you tell me where he is?" I asked. "It's important..."

She studied me the way a jealous woman might, almost making me wonder if Liam was bedding the pretty young woman.

"My name's Skye Delaney," I said, deciding to put my cards at least partially on the table. "I'm a private investigator. Liam and I have been working together on a case..." I considered this to be true in a roundabout way, even if he didn't know it yet.

She gave me a thoughtful look. "Oh yeah, I read about you and all the crazy stuff that's been going on at your house."

"Yes, definitely *crazy*," I told her, but I wasn't looking to turn this into some girl chat right now.

She seemed to read my mind. "Well, I'm not sure exactly where Liam is, but I can give you his cell number, if you don't already have it."

Actually, I did and told her so.

After I got back into my car, I phoned Liam Pratt, putting him on speakerphone.

He answered on the first ring. "Skye," he said, as if we were longtime buddies. "Believe it or not, I was just thinking about you."

"Oh really," I said. I didn't even want to imagine the exact nature of those thoughts. I recalled our last meeting and the mild flirting that seemed to be going on, more his way than mine.

"That so hard to believe?" he asked. Background noise suggested he too was driving.

"Actually, no," I admitted, considering the source.

"It's not what you think," Liam said mysteriously. "I was hoping we could talk. Guess you felt the same way..."

"Maybe I did," I conceded, as he now had my full attention. "Why don't you go first?"

"All right," he said. "I've been doing some digging into these recent deaths that appear to be connected to Carter Delaney and, to tell you the truth, I'm not really satisfied with the official findings—" Liam paused as if gathering his

253

thoughts. "I found a common thread between Delaney, Edwin Axelrod, and Antonio Ramirez that I think is worth checking into."

"I'm listening..." I told him.

He continued. "A man named Trevor Baldwin worked for Delaney and, most recently, Axelrod, as a driver, bodyguard, and all around errand boy," Liam informed me. "According to my sources, Baldwin is a forty-five-year-old Persian Gulf War vet who carries some psychological baggage from his tour of duty and a bitter divorce. Delaney allegedly fired him for stealing money. Although he was no longer employed by Axelrod, a witness saw Baldwin coming from the building the day Axelrod was killed."

"Interesting," I said, while remaining skeptical that this information was tied to Axelrod's death. The police had not labeled Baldwin as a suspect in Axelrod's death nor had they indicated that Baldwin had any connection to Carter's murder. "But what does that prove, other than Trevor Baldwin couldn't hold onto a job and he may have visited the building that day?"

"For one, it gives us someone—besides those already noted—who could've had it in for either man," Liam answered equably. "But here's where it gets even more interesting. I had my man on the force run Baldwin's name through the system. He spent time in the joint for attempted murder. And guess who he roomed with for a while?"

"Adam Ramirez," I replied. It seemed to fit when I put the pieces together.

"Bingo!" Liam yelled into the phone. "Antonio Ramirez's brother. Doesn't that strike you as just a little bit too coincidental?"

"How about a lot too coincidental," I told him, as the improbable connections raced through my mind. "Frankly, it does seem almost too weird to be true."

"I know," Liam concurred, "but the facts speak for themselves. I found out that Baldwin was also charged once with breaking and entering, but it never went to trial after the victim mysteriously disappeared. I admit that one thing may have absolutely nothing to do with the other in these scenarios and happenings. But, when you put it all together, it could be that Trevor Baldwin is a ticking time bomb on the loose..."

"Even if I were to believe that Baldwin is a threat to society and may have killed Axelrod," I said, "Antonio Ramirez's DNA was a positive match to blood found on my dog when he bit someone in my house the day Carter was killed. There was no indication that Ramirez had a partner in crime or was there to stage his suicide."

"So maybe Baldwin did a damned good job to make it appear that way," Liam speculated. "Stranger things have happened."

It seemed like this case had been full of strange twists and turns, I thought. So why not another?

"Are you on your way to talk to Baldwin?" I asked Liam, conceding that this turn of events could be much more than a wild goose chase.

"Not exactly," he said. "The man's been hard to track down. Seems like he never stays in the same place too long." Liam cleared his throat. "However, I've got a lead on a woman who supposedly knows Baldwin. I'm on my way to see her right now. Her name is Natsuko Sasaki. I think you know her..."

My heart skipped a beat in that moment of shock. *Natsuko Sasaki,* my mind repeated as if I'd heard him incorrectly. My housekeeper!

What did she know about any of this? I wondered. Was Trevor Baldwin Natsuko's boyfriend, in spite of her supposedly strong anti male sentiments? I refused to believe that she could possibly have had anything to do with Carter's death.

At least not until I heard it from her. Natsuko's apartment was not far. I preferred to discuss this face to face with her, while hoping that Liam was way off base.

"And what was it you called to talk to me about, Skye?" he asked, snapping me out of my trance.

I told him, which amounted to the same reason he had called me. But now there were new players involved in what had become an increasingly complicated and potentially dangerous game of life *and* death.

I finished with: "I'll meet you at Natsuko's..."

CHAPTER 51

Natsuko lived in a one-bedroom apartment on Hibiscus Drive. Her eyes betrayed astonishment as I stood at her door. I had apparently beaten Liam there and saw no reason to wait for him.

"Can I come in?" I asked. This was my first visit there, though I'd taken Natsuko home once when her car broke down.

She stepped aside without uttering a word.

From where I stood, I took a quick scan at the sparse furnishings that included a small wooden desk with papers and an open textbook on it.

I refocused on Natsuko, deciding that she was alone. She wore no makeup and had on a print dress and thongs. She flashed me a befuddled look.

"What are you doing here?" she asked. "And please don't tell me you just happened to be in the neighborhood—"

Not quite, I thought. "I need to talk to you, Natsuko," I said with a catch to my voice.

"What about?" she asked.

"Why don't we sit down?" I suggested for some reason, though I was eager to get this over with.

"Okay," she said uneasily. "Do you want something to drink?"

I passed, and sat down next to her on a worn out couch.

"You caught me in the middle of studying for my psychology exam," Natsuko told me. "But it's okay. I needed a break anyway."

I faced her and asked candidly: "Do you know a man named Trevor Baldwin?"

Her face betrayed her surprise. "Yes, I know him. Why?"

I hesitated, not wanting to accuse her of anything if she was innocent. But I sure as hell was not leaving there till I got some answers about Baldwin.

I told her: "I think it's possible he might know something about Carter's death."

Natsuko's eyes widened. "Trevor...?"

I nodded and said: "I have it on very good authority that Baldwin was once employed by Carter and fired for stealing." I waited a beat before continuing. "He's also been in trouble with the law—"

I wondered just how much she knew, or didn't know, about Trevor Baldwin.

"I know Trevor has had some problems," Natsuko said. "But what does that have to do with Carter's death? I thought the police already decided it was that man—Antonio Ramirez—who killed him and some others..."

"The police may be wrong, Natsuko," I said sharply, while trying not to point fingers—at least not at her. "I need you to tell me *everything* you know about Trevor Baldwin and if you told him anything that he could have used to break into my house."

She rolled her eyes and sneered. "So you think I helped him get inside your house to kill your ex and..."

I sighed. "To tell you the truth I don't know what to think," I responded. "I only know that this is not going to go away. Please help me out here..." *And maybe help yourself at the same time*, I thought, assuming she was somehow caught in the middle of a murder plot.

Natsuko seemed to gather her composure before saying: "I'm not dating Trevor, if that's what you're thinking. We just hang out together sometimes. He's actually dating my friend Akiko."

"Did she or Trevor ever ask you who were you working for or anything in specific about me?" I pressed her.

Natsuko's face twitched before she responded. "Come to think of it, there might have been a couple of times when your name came up. But it was nothing important. Just little things..."

Little things have a way of becoming big things, I thought, beginning to see a disturbing pattern emerging here.

"Did they ever ask you anything about my security system?" I asked.

She shook her head. "Never," she insisted. "I'm not that dumb. I would never give anyone your security codes, Skye. You have to believe that."

I did. But something told me that they might have wormed as much information as they could out of Natsuko for reasons she would never have suspected.

"Was Carter's name ever brought up in relation to me, before he was killed?" I asked.

"No, not that I recall," Natsuko said. "Like I said, Akiko and I only talked about small stuff regarding my work. Mostly questions like if you were easy to get along with, or did I mind taking care of Ollie. I usually only talked to Trevor when Akiko was around, and not much then."

"Did either of them ask anything in specific about Ollie?" I wondered, knowing he had encountered an assailant twice, but attacked only once.

"I think one time Akiko asked me if he bites," Natsuko replied. "That's about it."

I contemplated that for a moment or two, speculating that if Baldwin had been in the house with Antonio Ramirez when Carter was killed, he could have purposely instigated the dog into attacking Ramirez to either set him up or keep Ollie at bay while Baldwin murdered Carter. It could have also been practice for how to deal with Ollie if Baldwin had accompanied Ramirez to the house the second time around.

I looked into Natsuko's eyes and asked: "Where can I find Trevor Baldwin?"

She didn't hesitate. "I don't know where he lives. But Akiko lives in this complex. We met here and it's the only place I've ever seen Trevor."

That was a step in the right direction, I thought.

Just as I was leaving the apartment, Liam Pratt showed up with a frown on his face.

"What happened to you?" I asked, not bothering to speculate.

"There was an accident," he moaned. "Traffic was backed up for miles. Guess I picked the wrong way to go." He paused. "Did you talk to her yet?"

"Yes, I did," I told him.

Liam looked perturbed that I had beaten him to it.

"So what did she say?" he asked anxiously.

"More than I expected," I said. "Let's take a walk and I'll fill you in—"

CHAPTER 52

A few minutes later, we were at the door of Akiko Higashi. According to Natsuko, she lived with her three-month-old daughter Eva, and Trevor Baldwin was reportedly the father. Liam and I were both eager to talk to Akiko, each having our own agenda with a common goal of getting to the truth, which increasingly seemed to center around Trevor Baldwin.

We knocked on the door several times before it was finally opened. It took me maybe two seconds to recognize the face before me. She was the receptionist at the Manoa Aloha Clinic on Punahou Street that I visited as a possible place where Carter's killer might have gone for treatment after being bitten by Ollie.

Immediately I began speculating... Could Trevor Baldwin have shown up at the clinic to get medicine or bandages from his girlfriend so he could treat Ramirez's wounds from Ollie's bite? If so, Akiko could have easily made sure there was no record of it. And it likely would have gone unnoticed by the busy doctor on duty.

Akiko stood there in her bare feet wearing a blue tank top and cut-off jeans. It was clear from her expression that the recognition was mutual. She was cradling a baby, who looked at me with mild curiosity.

Akiko stared, but waited for me to speak first. I glanced at Liam, who was still clueless, and back again.

"Are you Akiko?" I asked, though I had little doubt.

"Yes," she confirmed.

"My name's Skye Delaney," I told her. "I think we met once before at the Manoa Aloha Clinic."

She gave a slow nod of acknowledgement, and Liam raised a brow.

"I'm a private investigator. And this is Liam Pratt, a reporter with the Honolulu Press. We're looking for Trevor Baldwin."

Akiko assessed us uneasily, then said: "He isn't here."

I took her at her word, taking the opportunity to find out what we could before confronting Baldwin.

"Do you mind if we come in for a few minutes?" I asked.

She fluttered her lashes. "What for?"

"Baldwin might be in a lot of trouble," Liam told her. "And *you* could be, too. The police will likely be coming your way next. I think the smart thing would be to talk to us first—"

I could see why Liam had gone into reporting. He had a way of getting his point across and making you feel as though he was on your side.

It worked, as Akiko Higashi invited us in.

Her apartment was a carbon copy of Natsuko's. Only it was less tidy, more furnished, and reeked of marijuana.

"You want to sit down?" Akiko asked nervously.

We sat on an old sofa, while Akiko, still holding her baby, remained standing.

I sighed and then got right to the point. "Natsuko's my housekeeper. But I'm sure you know that—"

"Yes," Akiko admitted. "What did she tell you?"

"Enough to know that you and your boyfriend—Trevor Baldwin—may have used Natsuko to get information about me, my dog, and my house that could have led to multiple murders starting with the murder of Carter Delaney."

Akiko's eyes grew with fear. "I didn't have anything to do with any murders—"

I wasn't so sure about that. "You might have to prove your innocence to the police," I told her.

She kissed her baby fretfully. "I never expected any trouble. Trevor told me he worked for Carter Delaney and that it was Carter who wanted him to learn some basic stuff about you. No one was supposed to get hurt—"

"But more than a few people did get hurt," I said. "And not just the dead." I glanced over at Liam and he took the lead.

He asked Akiko: "Did you know that Baldwin spent time in prison for attempted murder?"

"No," she said. "He never told me that."

"Yeah, there are probably a lot of things he didn't tell you," Liam said, "like the fact that he was fired by Carter Delaney for stealing and was once a cellmate of Adam Ramirez."

The baby started to wail. "You made her cry," Akiko said, rocking her gently.

I gave Liam a "cool it" look, though he was only trying to clue her in as to the type of man she had let into her life and what he was capable of. The reality was that there was still no proof that Trevor Baldwin was a brutal killer or that Antonio Ramirez had not acted alone in Carter's murder and the others. Right now, Akiko was the one person who could make the pieces of the puzzle fit for the police to take it seriously.

I tried a different angle with her once the baby was quiet again. "Did Trevor ever come to you at the clinic for medicine or dressing to treat an injury or a dog bite?"

The question seemed to throw her for a moment. Holding her daughter close to her chest, Akiko answered slowly: "Yes, he said a dog had bitten his friend and he needed my help. I gave him what he wanted."

I couldn't help but think again of Akiko's words: "*No one was supposed to get hurt.*" If Baldwin was behind the deaths, I thought, then he clearly had every intention of hurting certain people and didn't give a damn who he had to walk over to achieve his lethal objectives.

I gave Akiko the weight of my stare, and demanded: "Where can we find Trevor Baldwin now?"

"I don't know," she said in a shaky voice. "We stopped seeing each other right after—"

"Get smart for once in your life, Akiko," barked Liam. "We both know that Baldwin still comes to you whenever he wants some action. If this man's who I think he is, he's already killed at least three people and certainly won't have any qualms about killing another, especially if he feels threatened by someone who may know too much about him—"

Realizing that she had no other options as Liam's harsh message hit home, Akiko gave us an address for Trevor Baldwin. I wasn't really interested in seeing her go down with him. Like me, she had no doubt been taken in by a smooth talking man whose charms would come back to haunt her.

"One other thing," I told her, "if you hear from Baldwin, be smart and don't mention our little conversation or otherwise tip him off. It could be a matter of life and death—yours."

We left her on that note and now had to hope we could find Trevor Baldwin before he either skipped town or decided to target someone else for death.

CHAPTER 53

Trevor Baldwin lived in a cottage three blocks from Akiko's apartment complex. While Liam knocked on the door, I kept a hand in my purse in case I needed to go for my gun in self-defense.

It never came to that. Either Baldwin wasn't answering or he wasn't home.

"My guess is that he's onto us and has fled to parts unknown," Liam said, leaning against my car.

I wasn't so sure about that, but kept it to myself. "Well, at least we know who we're after."

"Yeah, Baldwin can run, but he can't hide," Liam said, "as cliché as it sounds."

I nodded while still trying to process the connection between Carter, Trevor Baldwin, Edwin Axelrod, and Antonio Ramirez.

Liam's cell phone rang. "It's my editor," he said. "I need to get this."

"Don't let me stop you," I told him and glanced up at Trevor Baldwin's house.

Liam was off the phone in a minute. "I've gotta go," he said, frowning as if we were in the middle of a date. "My editor wants me back now. He wants a story with everything I've got so far, which is plenty."

"Wouldn't it be better if you waited till Baldwin was under lock and key?" I asked.

He shrugged. "Maybe. But since neither of us knows how long that will take, the news can't wait."

I was inclined to agree to some extent. Maybe writing about Trevor Baldwin as a murder suspect would help flush him out in the open.

Liam and I went our separate ways with a promise to keep in touch on this recent turn of events and maybe even work together again in the future, should our paths cross. I had gained a whole new respect for the man, but was happy to keep it on a professional friendship level at this point, though he seemed to want more. I wasn't ready to give up the good thing I had going with Ridge anytime soon.

* * *

In my car, I phoned Ridge and gave him the run down on what we'd learned. I hated to break it to him that the case he thought was solved might not be after all.

"You and Liam have been busy," Ridge said unkindly, "doing police work."

"It's what we do, more or less," I told him. "Besides, I couldn't exactly come to you until I had something to go on."

"I'm not sure you do," he said. "It may be a bit of a stretch to think that Baldwin was the puppeteer for this string of murders, especially when the solid and circumstantial evidence points toward Antonio Ramirez."

"It fits," I said tersely. "I was never totally comfortable with Ramirez's suicide note or some of the other aspects of this case. I think Trevor Baldwin can fill in the blanks, assuming we find him."

Ridge sighed loudly into the phone. "If he really is responsible for killing Delaney and others, why don't you leave it to the police to handle from this point on," Ridge said firmly.

I was sure he already knew the answer, but told him anyway. "Because it's something I need to see through to the end."

Ridge didn't try to pull rank on me as a police detective or boyfriend. Nor did he back away from something that could reopen his case and tie up loose ends.

For my part and for Carter's sake, I hoped that having the man I believed to be a killer—Trevor Baldwin—in custody could give us both a little more peace and a resolution to the case that went beyond Antonio Ramirez.

* * *

"I've seen Trevor Baldwin before," I told Ridge while looking at the suspect's mug shot.

"Where?" he asked, peering at me as we stood by his desk.

"He was at my house the day Carter was killed, posing as a journalist," I said. "The bastard asked me what happened, as though he didn't have a clue. I never gave him much thought at the time, because I had other issues on my mind." Suddenly my mouth became a perfect O, as another memory surfaced. "I also saw him at the Whaler's Club when I had lunch with Liam Pratt. I thought then that he was kind of creepy, staring at me from the bar. But I ignored it, focusing instead on getting whatever info I could from Liam..."

"Damn," Ridge muttered, shaking his head. "The asshole's been stalking you as part of his sick game."

Kawakami approached us and said: "That's all interesting, Skye, but I still think it's pointless to try to tie him to our multiple murders." Kawakami frowned as he looked at Ridge and then me before continuing. "There's nothing that positively places Baldwin at your house at the time of Delaney's or Ramirez's deaths. No DNA, no fingerprints, no living witnesses. For all we know, everything else you dug up or think you did on Baldwin is purely coincidence."

I wasn't going to backpedal on this one. Not with the stakes so high. "Will you listen to yourself, Kawakami?" I said harshly. "It sounds like you're more interested in keeping this case closed for good than finding out the truth. How the hell much more information do you need in that thick skull of yours before you open up to the very real likelihood that Trevor Baldwin is the man responsible for Carter's death, among others?"

"A confession would be nice," Kawakami said.

"So maybe we can get a confession when we find him," I told him.

"Hold that thought," Ridge broke in. "As far as I'm concerned, there's clearly enough probable cause here to get a search warrant for Baldwin's residence. Hopefully, a judge will agree and we can pay the suspect's house an official visit. Who knows? Maybe we'll even find him there."

Half an hour later, equipped with the search warrant, Ridge, Kawakami, and I headed over to the home where we believed Trevor Baldwin lived.

With the very real possibility that he was armed and dangerous and possibly still on a mission to kill, Ridge requested a police backup unit, which had yet to arrive.

As with my prior visit with Liam, there was no indication anyone was home. I thought about Liam's belief that Baldwin was on the run. My gut instincts told me that he was still in Honolulu and no less a threat.

"I say we check it out," said Kawakami. "Hell, we can take him if he's unlucky enough to be in there. Worse for him if he gets in our way..."

While we sat in the car waiting for backup, Ridge said: "The guys ought to be here any minute. No sense taking chances."

"If I get a say," I offered tentatively, "I agree with Kawakami on this one. Baldwin doesn't even know we're onto him, if Akiko Higashi was smart enough to keep her big mouth shut. As far as he's concerned, everyone believes Antonio Ramirez is the guilty party. Case closed. If we wait much longer, it could cost us the element of surprise, assuming Baldwin is inside destroying evidence. Then who knows what might happen?"

Ridge seemed to contemplate it, and finally said: "What the hell. Let's go for it. Carefully—"

We left the car, not looking for a fight, per se, but ready to do battle if we had to. Kawakami knocked on the door. Ridge and I did not take out our weapons, but kept our hands on them, just in case.

The door opened after several knocks and a Filipino woman in her thirties stood there.

"Yes?" she asked with an accent.

Ridge identified himself, flashing his badge. "We're looking for Trevor Baldwin."

"He isn't here," she said, brushing a few strands of dark hair from her face. "I haven't seen him for two days."

We all exchanged dubious glances.

"What's your name?" Ridge asked.

"Maria," she responded.

"Maria what?"

"Enriquez," she responded.

"Are you his lady, Ms. Enriquez?" Ridge asked.

"No, just a friend," she said. "I look after the place when Trevor's away."

"Is anyone else inside?" Kawakami asked.

"No," she said quickly.

Ridge glanced my way and back. "We've got a warrant to search the premises." He showed it to her.

She fluttered her lashes. "What are you searching for?"

"Evidence in a murder investigation," he said brusquely. "As long as you stay out of the way, you can remain in the house."

She nodded meekly, and looked at me. I gazed back, wondering if she had any idea about her friend and the threat he posed to her.

We all went inside.

Mindful that Baldwin could actually be in the house, we kept our eyes open and instincts sharp. The place was a mess, as though the occupants could care less. Wearing latex gloves, we padded across dingy carpeting looking for anything that would tell us something meaningful and/or be admissible in a court of law.

In a downstairs room, I spotted a laptop computer on a glass table and immediately thought of the suicide notes that Carter and Antonio Ramirez allegedly wrote. There was a printer on a stand nearby.

"Ridge! Kawakami!" I called out.

Kawakami came running in, gun drawn. "What is it?"

Don't worry, it's not the boogie man, I thought, smiling. I nodded at the laptop and printer and said: "A hundred bucks says this computer and printer were used to create Ramirez's supposed suicide letter, not to mention Carter's faked last words—"

Kawakami frowned and put his weapon away. "I'll hold off on that bet for now."

I think he was starting to come around to the real possibility that Trevor Baldwin may have been up to his neck in this case.

We heard Ridge beckon us and followed the sound of his voice to a back room. Entering, we saw Ridge and Maria Enriquez, who he had used as an involuntary tour guide.

"Well, look what we've got here..." hummed Ridge.

The room had an arsenal of semiautomatic and automatic weapons, along with enough ammo to fuel a small army.

"Wonder how many of these he has a license for?" Kawakami asked jokingly.

"Obviously, he was prepared for any situation," I said uneasily. I recalled that Liam had mentioned Baldwin was a Gulf War vet. I wondered if he'd lost it somewhere between then and now.

Ridge looked at his reluctant host and asked: "Do you have any idea what Baldwin planned to use these for?"

"I never talked to him about this stuff," she said nervously. "He never offered to tell me why he kept so many weapons, except to say they were for protection."

"Protection, my ass," growled Kawakami. "He's the one that people need to be protected from."

"What's in there?" Ridge asked Maria, pointing at a closed door in the back of the room.

"I-I don't know," she stammered. "Trevor always keeps it locked."

"Well, maybe we should see what's behind door number one," Kawakami said humorlessly.

"Yeah, I agree," Ridge said.

It took a crowbar and some determination to pry the door open. We went into what appeared to be a darkroom and cut on the light. There were several black and white pictures and color enlargements clipped to a line. The first one I honed in on was a close-up photograph of Darlene and Edwin Axelrod kissing passionately. I had to admit that it was a much better picture than my own photos of the two former lovers. The second photograph was also of the adulterers in an even more steamy display of lust and loins.

Then my eyes rested on a picture that Ridge saw at the same time, prompting him to say: "What the hell..."

It was a photo of Ridge and me in living color on a day where we got wild and crazy and decided on the spur of the moment to get naked and intimate at Ridge's house.

"This sick bastard has really found some wicked ways to get his kicks," Kawakami said.

I think I was more embarrassed than Ridge. And I think Kawakami was more embarrassed than Ridge or me.

"Try not to stare *too hard* at it, Kawakami," I teased.

Ridge ripped the picture down. "He was in *my* house?"

"I think I can relate all too well," I told him sympathetically. I looked at the picture again. From the angle, I realized it could have been taken through an opening in the blinds from the outside, without either of us being the wiser.

"Just who *and* what are we dealing with here?" Ridge asked angrily.

"I'd say we've got a peeping Tom who murders people on the side," I suggested, suspecting it went even further than that.

My eyes scanned the other photos on display. Most were of me alone, with Ollie, more with Ridge, and even one of me with Carter in the doorway of my office.

"I'll look around some more out there," Kawakami said tactfully. "See what other interesting stuff the asshole's got lying around."

We watched him leave before Ridge asked me: "Why you—why us? What the hell's going on here, Skye?"

I decided to tell him what I couldn't bring myself to do before now, as I put two and two together. "I think Carter hired him to spy on me..."

Ridge knitted his brows. "What the hell for?"

I hunched a shoulder. "Who knows?"

"Why don't you take a guess," he pressed.

Well it had to come out sooner or later, I thought. After sucking in a deep breath, I said: "I think Carter developed an obsession for me that somehow got out of hand. He must have paid Baldwin to take pictures, only Baldwin kept some for his private stash—"

I saw no need to tell him about the journal at this point. As far as I was concerned, it should have been buried with Carter.

Ridge set his jaw, looking confused. "So you're telling me that Delaney and Baldwin were in this together?"

I responded: "Only to a point, I think. Carter certainly had nothing to do with what happened after his death. But Baldwin worked for him, apparently doing whatever little jobs Carter had in mind—till he caught Baldwin stealing and fired him. I think that he may have killed Carter out of revenge and killed the others to cover his tracks—"

Ridge ran both hands across the top of his head and said: "This whole thing is crazy."

I agreed. "I'm sorry, Ridge," I said sadly. More than he knew.

"Yeah," he snorted. "We'll talk about it later—"

The forensic investigation team took over and more evidence was discovered linking Trevor Baldwin to Antonio

Ramirez, including a first aid kit and a sterile gauze roll with possible DNA from Ramirez, as well as circumstantial evidence connecting Baldwin to the death of Edwin Axelrod and Kalolo Nawahi. But it was the association between Baldwin and Carter involving me that was most unsettling. I wondered if Carter even had a clue as to what he was getting himself into by intruding into my life and Ridge's for reasons that made little sense, eventually costing him his life.

Ridge confiscated the more explicit photos and negatives of me and us, while Kawakami showed some class by turning his back to the whole thing. Meanwhile, the police had put out an APB on Trevor Baldwin. They believed he was still in town and, based on his impressive collection of weapons, he was described as a loose cannon willing to kill anyone who got near him.

* * *

Trevor Baldwin had been very clever, I thought. My home had been bugged and I assume the same was true for my office.

"This must be how he managed to stay one step ahead of the game," I told Ridge as we sat in my living room sipping wine. Outside, was an officer Ridge had assigned as my twenty-four-hour home and property guard. Inside, he had joined Ollie in protecting me from the man Ridge called a voyeuristic psychopath. "Trevor Baldwin had to have known about my initial meeting with Carter and our last scheduled appointment," I continued. "Then he and Ramirez must have followed him here to my house. But Baldwin couldn't have known at the time about Carter's blood type, which wasn't public info, until he overheard us talking about it at some point. The fact that Antonio Ramirez happened to have the same AB negative blood type was probably purely coincidental, but made him a perfect scapegoat nevertheless to get Baldwin off the hook. Almost—"

Ridge sipped his wine and then asked: "But why didn't Baldwin just blackmail Delaney or Edwin Axelrod? He probably had enough secrets on both men to bury them if he

273

wanted to, figuratively speaking, while still keeping the money coming in."

"Maybe he found a higher bidder for his services," I suggested.

"You mean like Kazuo Pelekai?" Ridge asked.

"Why not?" I argued. "Once Baldwin had damaging information against Darlene *and* Carter, it wouldn't take much for him to discover someone who stood to gain from it. But Pelekai may have seen Trevor Baldwin as an unstable personality who could be more useful taking out Carter altogether—"

Ridge nodded in agreement and said: "Too bad we may never be able to prove it, unless Baldwin suddenly develops a conscience when we get him in custody—"

"I still haven't quite figured out why Kalolo Nawahi and Edwin Axelrod had to die," I muttered, staring into my wine. "Baldwin obviously knew about their connection to Darlene. He must have used them to throw off the investigation and me—"

"Maybe," said Ridge. "But I wouldn't put it past Kazuo Pelekai to have gotten rid of Axelrod himself since he probably considered him more of a liability than an asset. And maybe he took out Nawahi, too, as a smalltime competitor he could do without."

I couldn't dismiss his logic, even if my instincts told me that Trevor Baldwin probably also had a hand in their deaths.

We didn't go to bed till after midnight. Even then, restless tossing and turning replaced any semblance of a peaceful sleep.

It wasn't until the following morning over breakfast that conversation about the revealing photographs and Carter resumed.

Ridge said with an edge to his voice: "What I'd like to know is what the hell else did Baldwin discover about you and me that he spoon fed to your ex?"

"Whatever he learned," I said thoughtfully, "I'm sure it wasn't very fulfilling for either of them."

A full minute went by before Ridge asked: "What did Delaney hope to gain by spying on you?"

"I doubt it was to win me back," I told him reassuringly, scooping up a spoonful of Shredded Wheat. "Knowing him, though obviously not as well as I thought I did, Carter probably viewed this as his own private game of voyeurism and nostalgia all wrapped in one not so neat package, where he made up the rules as he went along. He probably thought he could control it." I paused to eat some more cereal. "Only he went too far," I continued, "and it started to control him instead—"

"That may be great for a psych class," Ridge said, "but the way I see it, Delaney knew *exactly* what he was doing. He knew he'd lost a good thing in you and used his money and power to get back whatever part of you he could." Ridge sipped his coffee and continued: "He was a mass of contradictions: a successful attorney and even more successful businessman on the one hand and a jealous, domineering, gambling, obsessive, weak loser on the other. As this damned thing has unfolded, Delaney comes across as something akin to a modern day Dr. Jekyll and Mr. Hyde..."

"I think you're right...and it cost him dearly," I said sadly, still trying to come to terms with it.

Meanwhile Doctor Frankenstein's monster was still very much on the prowl.

CHAPTER 54

He'd spotted the roadblock ahead and sensed something wasn't right. Then he'd heard the following message on the radio: "We've got an APB out on Trevor Baldwin, age forty-five, Gulf War vet, suspected of being involved in a number of murders... He's considered armed and *extremely* dangerous—"

He'd known it was just a matter of time before they—no, Skye Delaney—put all the pieces together.

She was good at her job, he thought. Just like Carter Delaney had said.

Trevor blamed his current predicament partly on the company he kept. None of those stupid bitches could be trusted to keep their mouths zipped, leading Skye and her detective boyfriend straight to his door.

Now he was on the run. He'd been prepared for this moment from the very beginning. It was up to him now to do what he had to do before the trigger-happy cops got to him first and took him down.

Trevor drove around in a car he'd stolen after ditching his last night. He wanted Skye Delaney now that everything was out in the open. But how? They were probably guarding her twenty-four-seven.

He couldn't even eavesdrop on her conversations anymore now that they'd discovered the bugs.

What would you do Carter if you were in my shoes? Trevor thought to himself. *Oh, but you were once, weren't you? It was your idea to spy on your ex-lady and report back to you her every move—and who she moved with.*

I did the grunt work and you repaid me by firing my ass, he thought angrily. *Did you think I'd let you get away with that, especially after what I had on you?*

Hell no! You got what you deserved—just like Axelrod and that bastard Ramirez. All of you tried to screw me over.

Now it's your turn to pay the piper, Skye, Trevor told himself. Borrowing something his mother always used to tell him, he said aloud: "Where there's a will, there's a way."

He would find that way.

Skye Delaney, you owe me one, he thought. *And I intend to collect!*

But first, he needed somewhere to hide out. Lay low for a while.

And he knew the perfect place...

CHAPTER 55

After three days of round-the-clock protection, I did a reality check and decided I wasn't ready to give up my freedom by being a virtual prisoner in my own home. Not to mention my work as a security consultant and private investigator was starting to suffer. My reliability was on the line and I had bills to pay. Besides, I was a big girl and used to taking care of myself.

If Trevor Baldwin was smart, he would already be halfway to Timbuktu, I thought, since every law enforcement officer in the state was looking for him. But most dangerous felons were anything but smart in the final analysis. I had to assume that he was still hanging around Honolulu waiting to add me to his collection of corpses. If so, I refused to remain a stationary target for him even in the continual company of Ridge and Ollie.

Ridge suddenly remembered just how stubborn I could be and reluctantly gave in to my desire to return to work. It helped that he also had a job to go back to and he wasn't being paid to baby sit me twenty-four hours a day. Not that he was complaining. That was left for me to do.

Ridge insisted that his officer-bodyguard remain close by wherever I went. Under the circumstances, I could hardly object.

That afternoon, I took Ollie with me to the office. I figured it never hurt to have him tag along as an added safety measure. At least until Trevor Baldwin was behind bars. Officer James Yayoshi was just outside the door if we needed him.

I had played catch up on the computer for little more than an hour when Ollie suddenly jumped to the floor from the chair he was comfortably occupying and bolted for the door, barking and growling.

"What's wrong, boy?" I asked, figuring that he must have been spooked by something. Or someone. I wasn't taking any chances so I grabbed the 9-millimeter from my purse and waited.

Ollie continued to bark at the closed door, jumping up against it. I grabbed his collar to try to restrain him even as I called out to the officer: "Everything all right out there, James?"

When he failed to answer, I knew something was very wrong.

Before I could react, the door burst open, knocking me to the floor and the gun out of my hand. I watched Ollie go on the attack, but he proved no match for the brute that lifted him in the air and flung him against the wall, knocking Ollie out cold.

I went for the gun. Trevor Baldwin was quicker, kicking it outside my reach with his sneaker. Suddenly, I was cornered by a cold-blooded killer who I assumed planned to make this my last day on earth.

"Did you think that cop or your stupid mutt could keep me from getting to you?" Baldwin scowled at me, making him that much more intimidating.

Bald and at least six-foot-four, the man was all muscle. Inside his jeans was a pistol, which he now took out and pointed in my direction. It was a .357 Magnum, no doubt loaded and ready to kill.

I was worried about the condition of my dog and the officer assigned to protect us both.

"What did you do to Officer Yayoshi?" I asked, glaring at the culprit.

"I made him wish he'd been on vacation when he was told to watch your back," Baldwin bragged. "He's not dead, if that's what you're asking, but he's going to have one helluva headache when he wakes up. I don't have any quarrel with the man, other than him getting in my way. I took care of that."

I carefully got to my feet, aware he was watching my every move intently. "You got your revenge against Carter, Edwin Axelrod, and killed Antonio Ramirez," I told him, figuring there was no reason to sugar coat it. "What do you want with me?"

He grinned. "I want you dead," he snapped. "If it hadn't been for Delaney making me chase after you like your damned dog, I probably wouldn't be in this mess..."

"Who are you kidding?" I taunted him. "Whatever dirty work you did for Carter, I'm sure he paid you handsomely for it. It was your own greed that got you fired. Probably the same reason Axelrod gave you the boot. I don't know what you had against Kalolo Nawahi or Antonio Ramirez, though I suspect Ramirez was merely a convenient patsy. Killing me is not going to right all the wrong moves you've made, Trevor."

I figured my best plan of action at this point was to stall for time by getting him riled up.

"Maybe not, *bitch*," he spat, "but at least it'll make me feel better by ending your misery. You just kept digging and digging till you got what you wanted. Happy?"

"You got what you wanted, too!" I told him, glancing at Ollie, who was still out cold. I hoped he didn't have internal injuries from the assault. "Everyone who betrayed you is dead now, Trevor. My investigation was never about you. It was about me and Carter, and why he refused to leave the past where it belonged. I needed to find out for my own peace of mind. If you walk out that door right now, you can go anywhere you want and I won't try to stop you. Otherwise you're just digging a deeper trench for yourself with no escape—"

He chuckled and said: "The trench is already dug and I'm halfway in it. But before I go, I want to finish what I started..."

I flashed him an exaggerated stare, my heart pumping madly. I knew this was the moment of truth. Attacking the brute with a .357 pointed at my face was suicidal. If I was going to die, I wanted to at least be able to have a proper funeral with an open casket.

"So why not finish it like a man, Trevor?" I dared him. "Do you really need to shoot me? Why not strangle me like you did Carter and Ramirez? Or are you afraid you can't take me?"

He threw his head back and laughed boisterously. "Who said anything about shooting you? This was just to get your attention." He moved the gun up and down for effect, and then tossed it to the floor. "You and me, we're going to have a little fun, before I wring your pretty neck—"

Trevor Baldwin approached me full of confidence—the type of poise one gains when strangling two people with his bare hands, among other violent crimes. I noted that Ollie was beginning to stir, but knew I couldn't count on him, Ridge, or anyone else to bail me out of this one.

When Baldwin got close enough, I threw both fists at his face, hitting him solidly with a left and right hook. He shook them off as though merely tickled, grinning broadly.

"You've got to do better than that," he said crookedly. "Like this—"

A fist came at me too fast to duck, landing flush on my jaw. I went down like an imploded house. Dazed, I felt myself lifted back to my feet as if weightless. As another blow approached, instincts made me turn my face away, so that the punch was only grazing. I felt blood trickling from my nose, while getting back my senses.

An overconfident Baldwin tried to grab my neck, getting air instead as I managed to duck. At the same time, I slammed the heel of my shoe into the side of his knee, instantly dislocating it.

He wailed like a big baby, and screamed: "You bitch!"

I made sure I earned his rage as my fists went after his face again, throwing uppercuts, while bobbing and weaving like a middleweight champ. It was like hitting steel, as the blows seemed to bounce off his body and reverberate back to me.

Putting his weight on one leg, Baldwin still managed to wrap a large hand around my throat. I had no intention of waiting for him to tighten the noose. I gripped his shoulders and lifted my body up so that I could head butt him while simultaneously slamming my knee as hard as I could between his legs, and again.

It worked on both counts, as Baldwin grunted and moaned, his grasp loosening enough so that I was able to go for his windpipe, pounding my fists against his throat. He released me while he backpedaled, gasping for air.

I was taking no chances that this asshole was down and out. Staying on the offensive, I lunged at Baldwin and again went to work hitting him squarely in the nose several times until it broke. Then I smashed my fists into both cheeks with everything I had.

Just when I thought I had gained the upper hand, Baldwin swung wildly and caught me on the jaw. I managed to stay on my feet, but was seeing stars as he dragged himself forward. Before I knew it, he had both hands around my neck, literally lifting my entire body off the floor like in a bad horror movie.

I felt myself losing the battle and consciousness, when Ollie came to the rescue. At full speed, he dove into the air like a flying dog and landed squarely on the back of Baldwin, clamping his powerful jaws into the side of his face.

Baldwin shrieked and released me, while trying to fight off a determined Ollie. I knew now that it was my turn to save my dog. I went after Baldwin again, kicking and throwing punches wherever I found an opening. There was enough blood to go around.

We all went down to the floor, with me on top of Baldwin, and him on top of Ollie. In my attempt to win the battle, I never saw that Baldwin's outstretched arm had managed to grab hold of his gun.

"You're dead, bitch," he moaned. "So is the mutt."

Not quite.

In the process of going for the gun, Baldwin had rolled off Ollie just enough to allow him to dart over and dig his teeth into the man's wrist, forcing him to release the gun and yell, as if it would make a difference to his pain.

"Good boy," I called out, and slammed a fist flush into the slack part of Baldwin's face, putting him out for the count.

I was still on top of my would-be killer, trying to catch my breath, and counting my blessings that Ollie and I would get through this ordeal in one piece, when Ridge stormed in, gun first, with several officers accompanying him.

"What the hell took you so long?" I teased him, knowing just how close I'd come to never having this moment.

Ridge grimaced. "I thought Yayoshi was on top of the situation," he said. "When the officer didn't check in like he was supposed to, I knew something wasn't right."

"Well, I think Ollie and I managed to clean up your mess," I said with a sigh, feeling exhausted and pretty sore.

He smiled thinly. "Looks like it. Are you and Ollie all right?"

"Better than him," I replied, gazing at the man beneath me. I looked at Ollie who was still gripping Baldwin's limp wrist between his teeth and said: "You can let him go, boy. He won't hurt us ever again."

Ollie obeyed and we both released our hold on Trevor Baldwin so the authorities could take him into custody. I crawled over and hugged my dog, knowing he had been willing to make the ultimate sacrifice for me, and vice versa. He licked the side of my face and seemed to say, "Don't worry about me, I'll survive."

"So will I," I told him, and looked up at Ridge. "How's James?"

"A little shook up with a king-sized headache," he said. "Other than that, the guy's a hard one to put down for the count. Much like you and Ollie."

Ridge helped me to my feet and we hugged, as if afraid to let go of one another. I knew this was but the first step toward putting what we had back on the right track, without past haunts to derail us.

CHAPTER 56

There was an elderly woman tending to geraniums planted around a gravestone. A young couple walked arm in arm by me in obvious grief from the loss of a loved one.

My own emotions were mixed as I stood before Carter's grave. I read the words on his marble headstone:

CARTER DOUGLAS DELANEY

A Man Who Believed In Family

And Stood For The Law

I wasn't sure just how true those statements were. But I applauded Darlene for honoring the memory of her husband as best she could for their daughter, if nothing else.

I feared that somewhere along the line, Carter had forgotten all he once stood for and aspired to be. And in the end, it cost him his life and much of his legacy.

It had been three months since Carter's death. Trevor Baldwin had recovered from the mauling he took from Ollie and me and had been formally charged with the murders of Carter Delaney, Edwin Axelrod, and Antonio Ramirez. Baldwin's DNA was discovered outside my house, but close enough to put him inside, while Ramirez's DNA was found in Baldwin's cottage. Circumstantial evidence had more than filled in the blanks to tie Baldwin to the string of killings, along with attempting to murder me twice, breaking and entering, and a number of other charges. The prosecuting attorney's office had all it needed for a sure conviction. Meanwhile, the investigation was still ongoing in tying Baldwin to the deaths of Kalolo Nawahi and Kazuo Pelekai.

The one sure bet was that Trevor Baldwin would never again be able to hurt a living soul in the free world.

I held a dozen violets in my hand. Carter had once presented me with the same when he asked me to marry him. It was the memories of a time gone by that had brought me here on this overcast afternoon. Only it was the more recent past that cast a dark shadow over everything else between us.

My life was finally starting to return to normal, thanks in part to therapy sessions with Whitney. But some lingering thoughts continued to haunt me like a bad dream.

"Why couldn't you have let me go when you were alive?" I asked Carter out loud. "It might have saved many people undeserved grief and you, your life. I was never yours to worship or hold onto," I said to his headstone. "Whatever we had, you threw away. You should've been man enough to leave it at that and give your second family a fighting chance."

I could only hope that, with time, healing would come for Carter's daughter and even his widow, who deserved better, in spite of her own weaknesses.

Suddenly it no longer seemed important what my ex-husband's state of mind had been during his downward spiral. I could not and would not let him bring me down with him.

"These are for old time's sake, Carter," I said softly. I was about to put them on his grave when, at the last moment, I decided instead that they would look nice around the geraniums the old lady had prettied up for her dead husband.

Ollie had wandered off to a grave on the other side of the cemetery, as if he was in tune with the soul of the person buried there. I made eye contact and he came running.

Ridge was waiting for us by the car. He gave me an understanding smile. I gave him a long hug and said with finality: "Let's get on with our lives."

"You sure?" he asked with a catch to his voice.

I thought about it for less than a second, smiled at him, and replied: "Positive—"

# # #

Bonus excerpts from the bestselling medical thriller
MURDER IN MAUI: A Leila Kahana Mystery by R. Barri
Flowers

MURDER IN MAUI
A LEILA KAHANA MYSTERY

PROLOGUE

The handgun was loaded methodically. Time for payback.
Now they would know what it felt like to be humiliated. And
only then could some peace of mind come.

And just maybe a life again.

First things first. There was a job to do and the doer was
determined to exact some vengeance against those deserving.

Stuffing the gun in a pocket, the soon-to-be-killer
downed the rest of a glass of liquor before heading for the
door.

It was a relatively quiet evening by Maui standards, what
with the constant throng of tourists practically taking over
the island. This was a good omen. No need to draw undue
attention or have to take out someone who didn't deserve to
die.

The doer got into a vehicle and began the drive down
Mokulele Highway toward the South Shore.

Arriving in Wailea, the car was parked not far from the Crest Creek Condominiums.

Then came the wait, certain they would show up. After all, their routines had been studied and memorized.

Ten minutes later both arrived in separate BMWs. The tall, handsome man left his car first and casually looked around as if lost before heading toward a condo.

The woman waited an appropriate amount of time before stepping out of her car. She was attractive and leggy with long blonde hair.

She joined the man in the condo.

It didn't take much to imagine what they might be doing inside, having already witnessed it firsthand.

She was the loud type; while her lover was more focused on rough actions speaking for him.

Glancing at a watch, the doer decided it was time to get this over with.

Moving quickly toward the condo, the doer resisted the temptation to look around in the dim light, knowing this small impulse alone might cause someone to hone in on a passing stranger.

Pausing at the unit and listening carefully for any sounds within, there was nothing perceptible due to the thick walls, which would work well for the purpose in mind.

The gloved hand turned the doorknob, slowly opening the door.

Inside two goblets of wine sat on a table in the living room. Clothes were strewn about the hardwood floor as if they couldn't get them off soon enough. Muffled sounds could be heard upstairs.

The doer climbed the steps, moving steadily. The master bedroom was just down the hall. Laughter and moaning grew louder, along with the frenetic movement of bodies.

The two were on the bed naked having sex. She was on top, galloping like a stallion, while he had one hand clamped firmly on her breast and the other gripping a buttock.

Removing the gun, a few brisk steps toward the pair followed. Before they were even aware of another presence in the room, it was too late. Bullets were systematically pumped into the pair until the killer was satisfied there was no life left in the room other than one.

CHAPTER ONE

Leila Kahana had been with the Maui County Police Department for seven years, working in the Criminal Investigative Division as a detective and composite sketch artist. She'd joined the homicide squad three years ago and had seen her share of murder victims in various types of positions, ranging from fetal to awkward to dangling. But none made her olive skin flush like the present victims. A Hawaiian man and white woman, both in their thirties, were naked and locked in coitus; the woman slumped astride the man.

Identified through their driver licenses as Doctors Larry Nagasaka and Elizabeth Racine, both had been shot at point blank range in the head and the woman had bullet wounds in her back. The two were literally lying in a pool of their own blood.

The call had come in this Tuesday at 8:30 p.m. with a report of gunfire at the Crest Creek Condominiums, one of the new and expensive developments in the exclusive Wailea Resort. Neither victim lived at the residence that, according to records, was owned by the Medical Association of Maui.

"Looks like they went out with a bang, no pun intended," her partner, Detective Sergeant Blake Seymour, said as a police photographer took pictures of the decedents.

Leila winced, hoping Seymour didn't notice how uncomfortable she felt seeing the victims locked in the sex act. Not that she had anything against sex, other than being without for the past six months. It just seemed like some things should remain private and not exposed for everyone to see. Or at least not a bunch of gawking law enforcement personnel.

But then Leila didn't imagine the pair knew they would be murdered at the worst possible time. Or best, depending on how you looked at it.

"I guess we can pretty much rule out murder-suicide," she said, as there was no murder weapon found anywhere near the bodies. Not to mention they were shot multiple times and in difficult positions, making it all but impossible that either victim could have been the shooter.

"I agree. Not unless one or the other was a glutton for punishment and Houdini at the same time."

Leila wrinkled her nose. "There was no sign of forced entry either. And it doesn't look like anything was taken. Once you get past their messy remains and clothes scattered around, the place is immaculate. Not exactly evidence of a burglary."

Seymour flexed his latex gloved hand and lifted a shell casing, dropping it in a plastic bag. "Someone invaded the place all right, and found exactly who they were looking for. The question is, under what circumstances and who got the jump on the lovers?"

Leila made it a point to never try and get inside a killer's head too soon. The evidence had a way of leading them down the right path, even if less than straight and narrow. She looked again at the victims.

"No reason to believe they were expecting company. Obviously it didn't deter the killer. Whichever way you slice it, this was definitely personal."

"Sure looks that way. Whoever did this definitely wanted to make a statement. They didn't have a fighting chance."

"So we'll fight the fight on their behalf."

Leila stepped aside as the photographer took pictures of the corpses from a different angle. She believed the killer not only wanted to execute the pair, but humiliate them, too.

She instructed other CSI members to document the crime scene including identifying, collecting and processing any possible physical evidence.

Following Seymour downstairs, Leila couldn't help but wonder if anyone ever used the place other than for sex. If only her house were as tidy. Or maybe that would make it seem too artificial rather than a place to live.

She noted the door key on a cabinet off the foyer. "I'm guessing one of the victims used this to get in. Probably left the door unlocked and that's how the killer got in."

Seymour looked. "Yeah, you're probably right. Still, you never know. If the killer had a key, he or she might have tossed it aside, no longer needing it once the deed was done." He said to a nearby CSI, "Dust this key for prints."

"Sure thing."

Seymour did a quick scan of the area. "Would've helped if they'd had a first rate security system."

Leila blinked. "Maybe the association didn't feel one was needed."

"A costly error in judgment, though something tells me the victims were here on their own time taking care of business, so to speak."

"Yeah, right." She rolled her eyes.

Seymour managed a weak smile.

Leila approached Officer Tasia Gould. "Who called this in?"

"A neighbor." She lifted a notepad. "Barbara Holliman."

"We'll need to speak with Ms. Holliman."

"And anyone else in the immediate area who was home when the call came in," Seymour added. "Someone must have seen the shooter."

Tasia nodded. "That's usually the case, even if they didn't realize it at the time."

Leila looked up at Seymour, who was nearly a foot taller than her five-four with most of it muscle. "You think this is an isolated incident?"

He shrugged. "Guess that will depend on why someone wanted the doctors dead while caught in the act."

Leila refused to speculate on motive beyond the obvious that the killer knew the doctors. Not till they had more to go on regarding the victims.

And perpetrator.

* * *

Leila sat in the passenger seat as Seymour drove. Both were trapped in their own thoughts about the latest case to bring them out into the night. For her part, Leila never considered one investigation to be any less or more important than the next. When dealing with human beings and loss of life through violence, all cases deserved their best efforts.

She glanced at Seymour's profile. He was nice enough looking, if not the most handsome man she had seen. His salt and pepper hair was cut short and he'd recently grown a mustache, which Leila hadn't decided if she liked. They had been partners for two years and she still didn't know him very well. At times he could be moody, witty, or a million miles away.

Seymour was currently separated from his wife. Leila suspected he wanted to get back together with her, but tried to pretend otherwise. She wasn't sure what to tell him, having no experience in that department.

At thirty-two, Leila had never been married. Born in Hawaii to conservative Polynesian parents who believed it was her duty to marry an established Polynesian man, Leila wasn't opposed to marriage as much as being with someone she didn't love. That included her last boyfriend, who had turned out to be a real jerk.

Leila preferred to be on her own for now till someone came along who really made her want him.

She looked again at her partner. "Why are you so quiet over there, Seymour?"

"Just thinking about disappointing my daughter." He paused. "I was supposed to pick her up for the night. Then duty called."

"Is it too late now?"

"She's probably asleep."

"She knows you're a cop. I think she'll understand." Easy for her to say.

"Yeah, I suppose." Seymour sniffed. "I still hate letting her down."

"So find a way to make it up to her."

"I'll think of something."

Leila's mind returned to the grisly crime scene. They were on their way to notify next of kin before the press could. This was one of the hardest parts of the job, along with tracing the winding path that had culminated with a double murder.

* * *

The address they had for Larry Nagasaka was in nearby Kihei. It was a beachfront estate surrounded by swaying palm trees in a gated community. Seymour could only imagine what a place like this went for. Certainly way out of his league.

Apparently the doctor wasn't entirely at home here though, considering he'd chosen another location to have sex.

The door was opened by an attractive petite Asian woman with long raven hair, almost as though she'd been expecting them.

"Yes?"

He identified them. "And you are...?"

"Connie Nagasaka."

"Is Dr. Larry Nagasaka your—?"

"Husband. Yes." She frowned. "What is this about?"

"Could we please come in?" Leila asked.

Connie met her eyes and nodded. She led them into a large foyer. "What's happened to Larry?"

Seymour cleared his throat. "I'm sorry to inform you that your husband's dead."

A hand flew to her mouth. "How?"

It was always the initial reaction Seymour tried to gauge in determining if such news came as a total shock.

"He was shot to death."

"Where?"

"At a condo in Wailea."

Connie's nostrils flared. "Was he with *her*?"

"Who?"

"His lover."

Seymour glanced at Leila, deferring to her.

"You knew your husband was having an affair?"

"He made no secret of it. Neither did she."

Leila glanced at her notes. "Two people were shot to death tonight. Your husband and a woman named Elizabeth Racine."

Connie started to cry. "I told Larry she wasn't worth it. He never listened to me."

"Mind telling us how you spent your evening?" Leila asked.

She sneered. "At home. By myself. I've gotten used to it."

Seymour chewed on his lip. "Do you know anyone who would've wanted your husband dead?" He was still trying to decide if she belonged on that list.

"Maybe Liz's husband, Kenneth," Connie answered matter-of-factly. "Few men can tolerate a cheating wife."

* * *

Leila eyed Seymour after they reached the department issued dark sedan. "She wasn't exactly a grieving widow."

"Not everyone takes the news the same."

"Especially when you have an adulterous husband who happens to be bringing in what has to be big bucks."

Seymour opened the door. "Think she did it?"

Leila imagined Connie pumping bullets into the lovers. "Anything's possible. Or maybe someone did the job for her."

"Like Kenneth Racine?"

"Hey, stranger things have happened. Maybe he'll save us all some trouble by fessing up."

She wasn't holding her breath. From Leila's experience, most homicidal spouses were anything but accommodating. They usually preferred to blame everyone else for their problems, including the victim.

Or, in this case, victims.

Seymour pulled into the parking lot at Maui General Hospital where Doctor Kenneth Racine was on duty as medical director of the Behavioral Health Unit.

Leila hated hospitals, an emotion born from fear of having her tonsils removed as a child and added to by the death of her father ten years ago after spending the last two months of his life in a hospital bed.

They were directed to the third floor, where a nurse pointed toward a forty-something, tall man with thick gray hair. He seemed agitated after snapping his cell phone shut.

"Dr. Kenneth Racine?" Leila asked.

"Yes?"

She lifted her I.D. "We're detectives with the Maui County Police Department. Could we have a word with you in private?"

His brow furrowed. "Look, if this is about those parking tickets, I swear I'll pay them. Things have just been a little crazy around here, you know?"

"We're not traffic cops," Seymour said curtly. "This is a homicide matter—"

Kenneth's head snapped back. "My office is just over there..."

They followed him to the office, where he left the door open.

"You said homicide?" He looked at Seymour.

"Afraid we have bad news. Your wife, Elizabeth, was murdered."

Kenneth's eyes bulged. "That's not possible! Liz is at a seminar in Honolulu."

Leila blinked, wishing that had been the case for his sake and hers. "We believe a woman found shot to death at a condo in Wailea tonight is in fact Elizabeth Racine."

He lifted his cell phone and pushed a button. "Yes, I need to speak to Elizabeth Racine. She's a guest there." A few moments passed. "What do you mean there's no one registered there by that name?"

Leila regarded Seymour. She wondered if Racine's reaction was mainly for their benefit.

He hung up, eyes downcast. "They said she never checked in, even though she had made a reservation."

Leila supposed it had been smart to cover her tracks. That was, until someone made certain they ran out for good.

"Larry Nagasaka was also murdered at the condo," she said.

"Larry—" Kenneth gulped. "Are you telling me my wife and Larry were having an affair?"

"Sure looks that way."

"That bloody bastard."

Leila didn't disagree, but that was beside the point. "You had no idea your wife was seeing another man?"

Kenneth sneered. "Isn't the spouse always last to know?"

"Not always," said Seymour. "We need you to account for your whereabouts tonight."

"You're kidding, right? You think I actually had something to do with this?"

"Wouldn't be the first time a vindictive spouse offed his wife and lover."

Kenneth took a step backward. "Look, I loved my wife and would never have wanted her dead, no matter what. I've been working my ass off here since three o'clock trying to keep this unit together."

* * *

"His story seems to hold up." Seymour stood beside Leila in the elevator.

"Even in a busy hospital, people can sometimes see what they want to," she said.

"True. Wouldn't be too much of a stretch to believe Racine could've taken a break from his duties to get rid of a cheating wife and her lover."

Leila ran a hand through her hair. "Aren't doctors supposed to be in the business of saving lives?"

Seymour gave her a deadpan look. "That may well depend on whose life it is."

He drove on the Honoapiilani Highway to West Maui where Leila lived.

"Do you want to get a drink?"

Leila didn't look his way. "Tempting, but I think I'll call it a night, if that's okay. It's been a long day."

"You're right, it has been, and that's fine."

"Another time?" She faced him.

"Yeah." He turned to look at her and back to the road. A few minutes later Seymour dropped Leila off at home. "See you tomorrow."

"Count on it." She gave a little smile and waved.

Seymour drove off, thinking she was probably the most levelheaded cop he knew, including himself. And also the best looking, which may have been the problem. He loved her new hairstyle, a short bob with sloping edges. Of course he kept his compliments in check, not wanting to make either of them uncomfortable in what was a good working relationship. Partnering up with Leila might not have been his first choice, but she'd earned his respect and taught him a few things along the way.

Seymour took the Kahekili Highway to the place he was renting in central Maui. Unlike the resort areas on the west and south sides of Maui, there wasn't much here to excite tourists. The fact that real people like him lived and worked in central Maui made it more to his liking, aside from living alone for the time being.

He would've preferred going to the house he once shared with his wife, Mele. That was before he screwed up, got caught, and was kicked out four months ago. She had yet to file for divorce, but since there was virtually no real communication between them, he feared it was only a matter of time.

When they did talk, it was mostly about their eight-year-old daughter, Akela. They had adopted her when she was less than a month old after learning that Mele was unable to have children. Akela was the one thing in his life Seymour was most proud of. He hated having to disappoint her. But he was a cop and had been for twenty of his forty-six years. Someday Akela would understand that people like him were needed to go after the bad guys in the world. Or at least within Hawaii. Until then, he would continue to try and balance the things most important to him.

Seymour thought about the crime that left two doctors dead. There was nothing more to be done tonight other than hope they caught a break and made an arrest.

As to what drove the killer to taking the two lives was pure conjecture at this point. But it didn't mean he wasn't up to some guesswork. Obviously the victims thought they had the perfect place for their affair.

Well, they were dead wrong.

They had ticked someone off. Or maybe one had been targeted and the other was just collateral damage.

Either way, a killer was on the loose and that was always cause for concern for you never knew what one might do next after experiencing their first kill and finding it agreed with them.

* * *

MURDER IN MAUI: A Leila Kahana Mystery is now available in eBook through Kindle, Nook, iTunes, and in audio from Audible.com, Amazon, and iTunes.

# # #

Bonus Excerpt of R. Barri Flowers' bestselling hard-boiled
thriller

DEAD IN THE ROSE CITY
A DEAN DRAKE MYSTERY
(available in print, eBook and audio book in Audible,
Amazon, and iBookstore)

CHAPTER ONE

I'd just stepped out of the restaurant, the greasy food still
settling in my stomach, wondering if I was ever going to get
out of the Rose City, when I saw her approaching with a tall
man. I did a double take, barely believing my eyes, but
trusting the sudden racing of my heart.

It was *her*—Vanessa King. Still as gorgeous as ever. How
many years had it been? Ten? Eleven? Too many to even
want to think about. Yet that was all I could do at the
moment, especially when she was the best thing that ever
happened to me. And I'd thrown it all away for reasons I
couldn't explain.

If only I could turn back the hands of time, things might
have turned out differently. Me, Vanessa, and all the joy we
could bring to each other.

The day we met years ago was forever ingrained in my mind for more reasons than one...

* * *

The dictionary defines fate as "unfortunate destiny." Once upon a time, I didn't buy into forecasts of doom and gloom, much less associate it with my life as a private eye and even more private individual. But then I took on two seemingly unrelated cases and one bizarre thing seemed to lead to the next and even I began to wonder if I was somehow tempting fate.

Before I begin my fateful tale, let me introduce myself. The name is Dean Jeremy Drake, or D.J. for those close enough to be called friends or kin. Otherwise it's simply Drake. Some call me a pain in the ass. Others see me as a half-breed with an attitude. I prefer to think of myself as a forty-one-year-old, six-five, ex-cop turned private investigator who happens to be the product of an interracial affair.

My parents, who have both since gone to heaven, couldn't have been more different. My father was Jamaican black, mother Italian white. But for one steamy night they found some common interests and ended up with me for their trouble.

I admit I can be a pain in the ass with an attitude, or a gentle giant with a perpetual smile on my square-jawed face, depending on which side of the bed I wake up on. But that's another story. Let's concentrate on this one for now.

It was raining like the second coming of Noah's Ark on that day at the tail end of July. I was sitting in my Portland, Oregon office, my feet on the desk as if they belonged there. The Seattle Mariners were on the tube playing the Oakland A's in sunny California. With three innings to go, the Mariners were getting a major league ass whipping, 11-0. To add insult to injury, there was a rumor that the players were planning to go on strike next month.

Who the hell needed them anyway? I'd had just about all I could take from greedy players, and owners who never seemed to tire of bleeding the fans dry. For me, this was merely a tune-up for the mother of all sports—football. The exhibition season was due to start next month in what might finally be a winning season for the Seahawks, my adopted team and a three hour drive away on a good day with light traffic.

The Mariners had finally gotten on the scoreboard with a solo shot when I heard one knock on my door and watched it open before I could even say come in.

A tall, chunky, white man entered wearing a wrinkled and dripping wet gray suit. He had a half open umbrella in one hand that looked as if he had forgotten to use it, a leather briefcase in the other. "Nasty out there," he muttered, and let out a repulsive sneeze.

"Tell me about it," I groaned. You didn't live in a city like Portland if you expected sunny, dry weather year round, though a soaker like this was pretty rare in late July. I was still partly distracted by the game, when I asked routinely: "How can I help you?"

That's when he walked up to me, stuck an I.D. in my face, and said: "Frank Sherman, Deputy District Attorney for Multnomah County—"

Only then did it dawn on me that I knew the man. Or at least I used to. Like me, Sherman was an ex-cop in his early forties. He had made that relatively rare jump from law enforcement to criminal law, while I had chosen private investigation work as my answer to justice for all. The closest I'd come to law school was the B.A. I'd earned in Criminal Justice from Portland State University. This hardly made me in awe of the man before me. He had gone his way and I had gone mine. Right now, it looked as if our ways had converged.

"Narcotics, right?" I asked, taking my feet off the desk.

He nodded proudly, and ran a hand through wet, greasy dark blonde hair. "And you were homicide?"

"Seems like two lifetimes ago," I exaggerated. In fact, it had been six years since I turned in my badge and the stress and strain that went with it for a lesser, more independent kind of misery. That Sherman could identify my department meant he had done his homework or my reputation preceded itself. I chose to believe the latter.

"At least we made it out on our own two feet." Sherman looked down on me with big blue eyes and a twisted smile. He was heavier than I remembered him, by maybe fifteen pounds. No, make that twenty. I turned off the TV to give him my undivided and curious attention. I did maybe a quarter of my work for the D.A.'s office, but I almost always went to them rather than the other way around.

"So is this a social call?" I asked, but seriously doubted. "Or have those unpaid traffic tickets finally caught up with me?"

He lost the twisted smile, and said directly: "I'd like to hire you, Drake—on behalf of the State. Mind if I sit?"

I indicated the folding chair nearest to him—a flea market pickup that was a bargain. "I'm listening..."

Sherman laid the briefcase on the desk, opened it, and removed a folder. "It's the dossier on Jessie *The Worm* Wylson," he explained, handing it to me. "He's wanted in connection with the sale and distribution of narcotics and methamphetamines. This bastard is personally responsible for most of the drugs poisoning our city and turning our kids into junkies!"

I looked at the face of a bald, dark-skinned black man on the dossier. It said he was thirty-five, six feet tall, and one hundred and seventy-five pounds. Wylson was a resident of Portland and had been in and out of jail most of his life for an assortment of drug and theft charges.

Even if I believed he was the scum of the earth, I had trouble buying that this one dude was behind most of the drugs floating about the city. In my book, that distinction belonged to the Columbia drug cartels and the rich Americans who made getting drugs into this country as easy as addicts getting crack on the inner city streets.

"Why do they call him The Worm?" I had to ask.

Sherman shrugged. "Heard someone gave him that name while he was in the joint, probably because he always seems able to worm his way out of trouble." He scowled. "Not this time."

There was something sinister about Sherman's, "Not this time." I took another look at Jessie The Worm Wylson, before shifting my gray-brown eyes to the man on the other side of the desk. "If I find him—which I assume you'd like me to do—what makes you think he won't manage to slip away again?"

Sherman shifted somewhat uncomfortably. "It's a chance we're more than willing to take," he said evenly, "provided you can locate his ass. If I have my way, once he's in custody, Wylson will be in a cheap, wooden box the next time he gets out." He sneezed then wiped his nose with a dirty handkerchief. "So what do you say, Drake, will you take the case?"

I glanced once more at the dossier and the man called The Worm. It seemed like a simple enough investigation. But I knew that no investigation ever turned out to be that simple, especially when it involved the district attorney's office. In fact, finding anyone on the streets of Portland could sometimes be like searching for a hypodermic needle in an urban jungle.

For some reason, I found myself hesitating in jumping all over this case. Like most P.I.'s, I liked to go with my instincts. And, from the beginning, there was definitely something about the case that rubbed me the wrong way. Maybe it was the surreptitious meeting with a member of the D.A.'s office outside the D.A.'s office. Or perhaps it was uneasiness in taking on an investigation that I presumed was still active with the Portland Police Department. Experience told me that they didn't take too kindly to meddlesome private eyes muscling in on their territory.

Sherman seemed to be reading my mind. "If you're wondering why you instead of one of our regular investigators, the answer is simple. I want this asshole off the street! I was told that you do things your own way, and not always within the guidelines you learned as a cop. We both know that sometimes the guidelines can be a bitch when it comes to justice for all." He sucked in a deep breath. "I'm willing—unofficially—to do whatever it takes to find Jessie Wylson. Of course, the D.A.'s office will cover all of your regular fees and expenses."

The private investigation business had been fairly good to me by the standards of most trying to make a living as dicks for hire. I managed to stay one step ahead of my debts and have some money left over for recreation. But business had been lean of late and the bills never went on holiday. I could hardly afford to pass up a cash-paying reliable client, assuming that at least a minimal standard of acceptability was met. This one seemed to qualify, though barely.

"Can I keep this?" I held up the dossier, which was my way of saying I was on board.

Sherman smiled. "I was counting on it." He stood and pulled a card from his pocket, handing it to me. "Keep me informed, Drake. If and when you find him, I want to be there to personally slap the cuffs on."

I wanted to remind Sherman he wasn't a cop anymore. But I gave him the benefit of the doubt that old habits died hard, and said: "I'll be in touch."

Once the Deputy D.A. left me all by my lonesome, I turned the TV back on. Mercifully for the Mariners, the game was over. Final score: A's 14, Losers 3.

* * *

The sun had begun to peek through the clouds by the time I left my downtown office which was not far from the Riverplace Marina. It was on the third floor of a building that seemed to house everything from a psychic hotline office to a Jenny Craig weight loss center. I wasn't complaining though. The rent was affordable and most of the tenants tended to mind their own business.

I was wearing a jogging suit that fit well on my six-foot-five body and my Nike running shoes. People asked me all the time if I ever played basketball. I usually responded truthfully with, "I was lousy at basketball, but give me a baseball bat and I can hit the ball ten miles." That almost always left them speechless.

I liked to think that I was in pretty good physical condition for the forty and over crowd. Jogging was my forte, so to speak, these days. It was a carryover from my days on the force. Before they brought in all the high tech exercise equipment to keep everyone lean and mean.

I half-jogged, half-walked the two miles on the street parallel to the Willamette River, till I reached my apartment building. It was not far from the Hawthorne Bridge—one of several bridges that connected the city that was separated by the river. Since Portland was so beautiful and pedestrian friendly, I favored being on foot to driving or light rail.

Home for me was an old brownstone on Burnside Street. It was old, but comfortable. Most of the residents fit the same profile: single, divorced, or widowed *and* available, over thirty-five, and professional in some capacity.

Just as I was entering the building, exiting was another tenant who I seemed to pass by every other day lately. I didn't know her name or anything about her, but I liked what I saw. She bore a strong resemblance to Halle Berry, only she was better—and sexier!

She looked to be in her mid-thirties with jet-black curly hair that grazed her shoulders, cool brown eyes, and an oak complexion. She had a streamlined, petite figure that I could imagine cuddling up to on a lonely night. If there were such a thing as my ideal woman, she was probably it.

Though my mouth always seemed to go dry whenever I got near her, I managed to utter: "Hello."

She gave me a faint smile in return, perhaps flattered, but obviously unimpressed. I tried to convince myself that she was just having a bad day. Some other time, pal.

I climbed three flights of stairs before I reached my one-bedroom apartment. It was pretty much what you would expect of a single, male, private investigator: not particularly tidy, cluttered, bland, and sorely in need of a woman's touch. The "right" woman just never seemed to come along and volunteer her services.

I showered, shaved, and stepped into one of two cheap suits I wore on the job. This one was navy blue and the most broken in. I combed my short, black hair that was sprinkled with more gray than I cared to admit. Since high school, I'd had a thick coal black mustache. It was probably the best part of me and hung just over the corners of my mouth, tickling me whenever I yawned.

Dinner was some leftover KFC drumsticks, canned pinto beans, and milk. Afterwards I caught a bit of the news on TV, glanced at the front page of the *Oregonian*, and pondered my newest case.

* * *

Pioneer Courthouse Square was the place to be if you wanted to mingle with your neighbors and tourists alike, be right in the heart of downtown Portland, and catch some of the city's best free sidewalk talent.

Nate Griffin had made a name for himself as the Rose Clown, in reference to the annual Rose Festival held in the city. He did everything you expected of a clown and more, including cartwheels, telling bad jokes, and giving an often distorted, comical history of Portland. Nate also happened to be my best street informant ever since my days on the force. Sometimes he was helpful, other times helpless. At twenty-nine, he had succumbed to a life mostly on the streets after off and on bouts with alcohol and drug abuse, and failed opportunities to better his life.

The Rose Clown was in full costume and makeup when I saw him on the Square working his magic on anyone who cared to watch and listen. Nate was tall, lanky, dark, and bald. One wouldn't recognize him when looking at the clown in a baggy outfit, white curly wig, green painted face, and big red nose.

He acknowledged my presence with a half-hearted nod. I dropped a few dollar bills into his bucket that was sparsely filled with mostly dimes and quarters. He finished a terrible rendition of a rap song before giving me a moment of his time.

"They love you, Nate," I told him encouragingly, "even if your singing stinks."

"It's all in the ears of the beholder," he said, smiling and showing off a gold front crown. Then he looked into his nearly empty bucket and seemed to do an about face. "Guess I could use some work on my chords."

Guiltily I dug into my pocket and came out with a couple more dollars, dropping them into the bucket. "Maybe this will help—"

He wet his full lips. "Thanks, D.J. Times are tough these days."

"For *all* of us," I said with a sneer.

He peered at me suspiciously. "So what brings you my way?" He chose to answer his own question, fluttering his false lashes. "You probably missed seeing my pretty face!"

"Don't believe that for a minute," I said firmly. "I'm not into clowns, pretty or not." It had been about six weeks since I'd come his way. If there was anyone who could find out where Jessie Wylson was holed up, it was Nate and his seemingly endless network of street contacts.

I removed the photo of The Worm from my pocket and laid it on Nate's palm. "Know him?"

He studied the picture as if it held the secret of the universe. "Should I?"

"His name is Jessie Wylson. They call him The Worm."

"Ugly dude," commented Nate bluntly, his brow furrowed.

For once we agreed on something. Nate was still staring at the photo when he asked: "Why you looking for the man?"

I decided to be straight with him. "He's wanted by the D.A.'s office for drug trafficking, among other things."

Nate scratched his fake nose, then sniffed like it was clogged with a white powdered substance. "So why come to me?" he asked, as if he hadn't a clue.

"I need to find him." My mouth became a straight line. "And I need *your* help—"

Nate's eyes popped wide. "Don't know the man. Don't want to know him, 'specially if he's got the D.A. on his ass. Sorry." He handed me the photo as if glad to be rid of it.

I had a feeling he was holding back on me, but didn't press it—yet. "Ask around anyway," I insisted. "Maybe you'll get lucky."

"Can't make no promises," he hedged. "But I'll give it my best shot—for you."

"I'll check back with you in a couple of days."

"That soon?" He rolled his eyes. "What do I look like, a miracle worker?"

Gazing at the Rose Clown, that wasn't exactly the first thing to come to mind. I told him: "The sooner you give me what I want, the sooner I'll leave you alone—for a while."

Nate went back to what he arguably did best and I headed to my favorite nightclub, satisfied that I had at least put the wheels in motion to find the man known as The Worm.

CHAPTER TWO

Jasmine's was located right on the Willamette River. The jazz supper club was owned and operated by Gus Taylor, Vietnam vet, friend, and the ninth wonder of the world. He hovered somewhere in the neighborhood of three hundred pounds on six feet, three inches of flab. His salt and pepper beard was thick, as were his brows over large brown eyes. His head was shiny bald like Mr. Clean.

Jasmine's had the best jazz in town. Gus had named it after his late wife who was his pride and joy. I couldn't remember a time dating back to my days as a rookie officer when I didn't come to the club and leave feeling genuinely uplifted. Tonight was well on its way to following suit. The featured singer looked like a young Diana Ross, but had a voice that sounded much more like Billie Holiday than Ross ever did in "Lady Sings the Blues."

"What's shakin', D.J.?" The boisterous voice was none other than Gus himself, who often doubled as bartender, waiter, janitor, and security guard.

"She is!" I declared from my stool, while my eyes remained riveted on the singer who called herself Star Quality.

"Don't even think about it," Gus warned me. "She's too hot for even you to handle."

"I wouldn't doubt it," I said, finishing off my beer.

"How 'bout another?"

"Why not?"

Gus filled two mugs. "Why don't you come and work for me, D.J.?" he said as if he really meant it.

I raised a brow. "You mean you want me to *sing*?"

"Not if I wanna stay in business," he quipped. "I was thinking more along the lines of security."

I looked at him like he was half crazy, though I suspected he was dead serious. "Thanks, but no thanks, Gus. I'm afraid I'm not cut out to break up bar brawls."

"Don't knock it till you've tried it," he said. "You hang out here almost as much as I do. Why not put your talent to good use?"

"I thought I was," I responded with serious sarcasm, and tasted the beer.

Gus leaned at me from across the bar. He could tell that I was a little pissed. "Don't get me wrong," he said apologetically, putting froth to his mouth. "I'm not knocking what you do to earn a living. We need some of our own doing the private eye bit. 'The Man' sho ain't gonna bust his ass to find out whodunit, especially not in the part of town where most of us live. But you, my man, could do better than that. And I could use a man with your background and guts to help keep law and order around here. Think about it, D.J. That's all I'm askin'."

I already had thought about it, but saw no reason to tell him at that moment. Good intentions aside, I didn't quit the force to wind up checking I.D.'s for the proper drinking age. "I'll think about it," I lied.

He left it at that and went to jaw with another patron. I refocused my attention on Star Quality and became lost in her velvety, soulful voice.

* * *

The Worm's last known address was a house on Thirty-Third Street and Drummond, an area in Northeast Portland that was known more for its crack houses and gang bangers than its law-abiding citizens.

That next morning I paid the house a visit, figuring I might hit the jackpot the first time around and catch The Worm with his pants down. Not that I really believed I could be that lucky. If it had been that easy to locate Jessie Wylson, Sherman could have—and probably would have—done the job himself.

Wearing my alternate P.I. suit, this one dusty brown, with a tan shirt and thin brown tie, I rang the doorbell. It seemed that dressing the way people expected detectives to dress—somewhat rumpled and sleazy—made it easier to get a little cooperation from those least apt to give it.

There was a beat up Olds Cutlass in the driveway. From the looks of the house, with its peeling paint and overgrown lawn, it was as if no one had lived there in years.

I heard a rustling noise inside. It sounded more like a snake than a worm. But I was taking no chances. I placed my hand close to the .40 caliber Glock I kept between my waist and pants. I had never been accused of being trigger-happy as a cop or P.I., but that didn't mean I wasn't ready and willing to confront any dangerous situation that came my way.

The door slowly opened. A walnut-skinned woman in her early thirties stuck her face out. Her short, permed dark hair was highlighted with blonde streaks. The way her sable eyes squinted like taking a direct hit of bright sunlight suggested that I had disturbed her beauty sleep. A terrycloth white robe was loosely wrapped around her voluptuous body, revealing enough cleavage for my eyes to get sore.

"What?" she asked brusquely.

"My name's Drake," I said tersely. "I understand Jessie Wylson lives here."

Her brow creased. "He ain't here. Ain't seen him for weeks."

I glanced around skeptically and then back at her. "Who are you?"

She batted her lashes as if to say *Who's asking?* "Used to be his girlfriend."

"Anyone else home?" I asked guardedly, my hand still within reach of the Glock.

"I live by myself," she hissed.

"Do you have a name?"

She hesitated, regarding me suspiciously, before saying in a higher octave: "Nicole."

"Nicole, do you expect me to believe that even a low-life drug dealer like The Worm would dump a lady as fine as you?" I figured that would elicit a meaningful response.

She gave me a coquettish grin and seemed genuinely flattered. Then her face became an angry machine. "I dumped the bastard after he stole from me—every chance he got."

"Maybe the biggest mistake of his life," I offered, almost feeling sorry for her. "Do you know where can I find him?"

Her nostrils ballooned. "You askin' the wrong person. I'm not his damned keeper—not anymore." She sighed raggedly. "If there's nothin' else, I got things to do."

I was not altogether convinced that she had no knowledge of Wylson's whereabouts, but gave her the benefit of the doubt—for now. "Your ex-boyfriend's wanted on drug charges," I said coldly. "I'm not a cop, but I've been hired to bring Wylson in if I can find him." My eyes sharpened on her. "If you know where he is, you'd better think twice about keeping it to yourself. He's not worth going to prison for." I slipped my card in her cleavage for a perfect fit. "Give me a call if you hear from Jessie or happen to remember where he's hiding out."

* * *

By afternoon I had finished up some paperwork from a previous case. I rewarded myself by running. There was an unexpected joy in feeling the stress and strain course through my entire body as I pushed myself to go the extra mile, so to speak.

I took the long way home—about four miles along the river—leaving me exhausted and regenerated. I finished my run by cooling down and walking about the last quarter of a mile.

As I approached the front of my apartment building, I noticed a cab pull up to the curb. *My ideal woman*, the attractive lady whose name I still didn't know, got out of the back seat. She was wearing a gray business suit that flattered her nice figure. She reached in the back seat and came out with a painting that seemed nearly as tall as her. With obvious difficulty, she began to carry it toward the brownstone.

"Let me help you with that." I took full advantage of the moment, catching up to her in looping strides. *Maybe this was the break I'd been hoping for to get to know this angel.* I grabbed the painting before she could say no thanks.

"Thank you," she said in a shaky, but appreciatively soft voice. "I think this one was just a bit too much to handle."

I looked at the painting. It was a scenic landscape of Mount Hood and the surrounding area. I was not exactly a connoisseur of the arts. I wondered if she was the artist. The apartments in our building hardly seemed large enough to hold such a painting.

"Where to?" I asked. For one of the few times in my life, I was actually intimidated by someone. Her attractiveness, grace, and sensuality really did a number on me.

313

"I'm in 427," she said with a slight smile that revealed small, straight white teeth and thin sweet lips.

She even smelled good, as I got a whiff of her perfume. Definitely not the cheap stuff.

We took the elevator up and neither one of us seemed to have much to say. For my part, saying the wrong thing seemed worse than saying nothing at all.

"Do you live here?" she asked, seemingly out of courtesy, and apparently oblivious to the fact that we had been practically bumping into each other every other day for the last two months.

I nodded. "Third floor."

She smiled ingenuously. "Thought I'd seen you before. I suppose it's a good thing you came along when you did."

"If it hadn't been me, it would have been someone else," I muttered like an idiot.

She gave me a look to suggest that she agreed.

The elevator doors opened and I followed her to the apartment.

"Just set it there," she pointed to an empty wall in the living room.

I did and we stared at each other for seconds that seemed like hours. I started to ask her if she wanted to go for a drink, but something told me I wouldn't like her answer. So I kept my mouth shut. There was plenty of time to get to know this lady. *Why rush a potentially good thing?*

"Well, I'd better get going now." The words crept from my mouth as if they were stuck in cement.

She did not argue the point. "Thanks again. Maybe I'll see you around."

I nodded miserably, and left without even finding out her name or telling her mine.

At the mailboxes, I discovered that her name was Vanessa King. It seemed to fit her. This was another possible step in the right direction for me.

* * *

DEAD IN THE ROSE CITY: A Dean Drake Mystery is now available in print, and eBook through Kindle, Nook, iTunes, as well as audio from Audible.com, Amazon, and iTunes.

# # #

Bonus excerpts of the bestselling police procedural and legal mystery JUSTICE SERVED (A Barkley and Parker Thriller) by R. Barri Flowers

JUSTICE SERVED
A BARKLEY AND PARKER THRILLER

PROLOGUE

She hid under the bed, carefully controlling her breathing. She didn't move, not even a twitch. Her pink dress was dirty from the pine hardwood floor and her pink shoes were scuffed. The curls of her raven hair billowed around her head like a halo. She could see their shoes, moving around as if dancing to a tender love song.

Only she knew it was no dance.

And it was no love song.

She heard the sound of his fist as it smashed against her mama's cheek. Her mama immediately crumpled to the floor like a rag doll, dazed and moaning. Blood spilled from a corner of her swollen mouth like a red stream.

Her mama's face ballooned, her cheek shattered from the blow. One eye was swollen shut, protruding like a golf ball. With her good eye, mother and daughter made eye contact in a moment of sorrow and sheer terror.

She wanted to help her mama and save her from him. But she knew that she would be no match for his brute strength and drunken rage. In that moment of mental connection, her mama told her to remain still as the night so that she too would not face the fists and battering he had inflicted upon her.

With all of her willpower she closed her eyes tightly; her instincts telling her nothing would ever be the same again. Not that she ever wanted things to be.

Not this way.

Not with him.

When her eyes opened, her mama was no longer on the floor. She had been dragged to her feet and thrown onto the bed like a sack of soiled clothes.

"Bitch!" She heard him roar like a lion, hovering over her mama as if her shadow.

Then he hit her again. The blow must have been tremendous, for her mama's dentures went flying across the floor like a bird, landing harmlessly beneath a chair in the corner. She was pounded several more times. Her mama's blood curdling screams had turned to faint whimpers.

Then the bed suddenly sank to the point where she thought she might be crushed or cut by the jagged springs nearly touching her. It was all she could do not to make a sound, though inside she was crying as loudly as she could muster.

He had gotten on the bed with her mother.

"This ain't over, bitch," he spat. "Not by a long shot!"

She listened as she heard him unbuckle his pants.

"I'll show you to smart mouth me. When I'm done with you, you'll know who's boss, and who ain't nothin' but a damned ugly assed whore!"

She could hear some rustling noises, heavy breathing, and groans—the last coming from him by the wicked deepness of it. She couldn't bear to think of what he was doing to her mama. But she knew it was something awful. Something that would make her curse him even more than she already did.

When he was finished, she heard him roll over. Moments later he was snoring like a bear, the sound coming from deep within his throat, punctuated by labored breathing. She could hear no sounds from her mama, but suspected she was too afraid to even breathe—afraid he would wake up and continue hurting her.

She was also afraid. After waiting there paralyzed with fear for what seemed like an eternity, she nudged her way beneath the springs till she was out from under the bed. Her pink dress was covered with dust and blood from where her mama had fallen.

She stood up, intent on taking her mama away from him forever. But it took only one look at her to know this would never be. Her face was almost unrecognizable—horribly discolored and at least twice the size as normal. Her clothes had been ripped apart, exposing a frail thin body, marred with marks and bruises both fresh and from other beatings he'd inflicted upon her. Her legs were spread wide, blood oozing from between them, seeping onto the sheet like red dye.

Her mama's eyes were wide open, as if held that way by toothpicks. Whatever life was in them had vanished forever.

Beside her, he lay naked in a drunken sleep, his breathing erratic and uncertain.

She felt the hatred in her build like steam in an engine. This was softened only by the love for her mama and hardened again by her feelings of helplessness and guilt.

She climbed atop her mother's battered, broken, and bloodied body and lay there with her thumb in her mouth like it contained magical properties. It was as if she would be rocked to sleep and would wake up and find that everything was all right.

Deep down she knew that would never be the case. He had seen to that.

She began to hum a song she made up on the spot, somehow soothing her, no longer caring if he woke and hurt her as he had her mama.

After all, she could feel no greater pain, bleak darkness, or emptiness than she felt at the moment.

CHAPTER ONE

Judge Carole Cranston sat on the bench and banged her gavel. The courtroom immediately came to order on this late July afternoon. She was a no-nonsense judge who only wanted to expedite things as quickly as possible from trial to trial, preferring to be in the comfort of her condo overlooking the Willamette River in Portland, Oregon. It was especially nice at this time of year when the summer breeze came in and the sun bounced off the water as if too hot to remain in one place. She was reminded of trips to the Bahamas where she had fallen in love with Grand Bahama Island in particular. She could imagine herself maybe one day retiring to the Bahamas, Jamaica, or even Hawaii, and drink in its beauty and perennial sunshine each day for the rest of her life.

Carole returned to the present, realizing that at thirty-five years of age and three months, she was hardly able to begin thinking about retirement just yet. *I wish.* Not when she had a job to do—no matter how maddening and disillusioning at times—and people who depended on her to dispense justice to the best of her ability.

She turned her espresso eyes on the prosecutor. His name was Julian Frommer. He was in his early thirties, but looked about twenty-one with dirty blonde hair a bit too long, and a small goatee that looked almost taped under his chin. His wool navy suit was ill fitted on a tall, lanky frame.

"Are you ready?" she asked him routinely.

"Always, Your Honor." He pasted a flirtatious smile on his lips.

But Carole had not even noticed as she turned her attention to the defense. George McArdle, fortyish, African-American, and built like a house, was already on his feet and showing off a three-piece tailored gray suit. His closely cropped dark hair had a slightly crooked part off to the side. He acknowledged her with a twinkle in his eyes.

"The defense is ready to present its case, Your Honor."

She nodded and looked at the defendant. Roberto Martinez—a thirty-six-year-old, muscular, Hispanic construction worker—had been charged with beating his live-in lover half to death. The medical report said that she had sustained multiple fractures, including a shattered nose, broken jaw, broken arm, and broken leg. But she would live. And so would the memories.

Martinez grinned crookedly, as if to say: "It would have been more fun had you been on the other end of my fists, *Your Honor.*"

Carole glared at him. She could feel the tiny hairs stand on the nape of her neck. But this was invisible to those before her who saw only the cool, calm, and collected attractive judge. Her russet colored individual pixies curved under her chin and onto slender shoulders, contrasting a beautiful butterscotch complexion. Beneath the black robe was a tall, shapely body with long, runner's legs.

She faced Julian Frommer again. "You may call your first witness, Counselor—"

* * *

It turned out his first witness, the victim, was a no-show. She was going to be wheeled in from the hospital where she was still recovering from her injuries. She had apparently had a change of heart and now refused to testify against Martinez. The State's case further began to unravel when it was revealed that the only other witness was a known drug dealer whose testimony came as a result of a plea bargain that would keep him from doing hard time.

Meanwhile the defense had produced witnesses who would testify that the defendant was seen at work at the alleged time of the assault. It was a shaky alibi at best that left a window of opportunity for Roberto Martinez to have committed the offense and returned to the job. But given that the victim was unwilling to refute this, the prosecution had little choice but to go along with George McArdle's request that the charges be dropped.

And neither did Carole, though this pained her more than she was willing to admit. The thought that a scumbag batterer like Martinez should get off so easily was disturbing. But then, that was the system for you. Justice often needed help to be dispensed properly.

Looking Roberto Martinez straight in the eye, Carole announced unaffectedly: "The charges have been dropped. You're free to leave, Mr. Martinez."

He grinned lasciviously, gave his attorney a hearty bear hug, and headed for the door without so much as a slap on the wrist.

Growling at Julian Frommer, Carole snapped: "I would strongly suggest that in the future you not waste the court's time—or mine—with a case you were clearly unprepared to make!"

On that note and without giving him a chance for a lame response, she headed for her chambers, disappointed that another woman beater, who was obviously guilty, had found a way to beat the system. Much in the same way he had his lover.

* * *

At Portland General Hospital, Lucie Garcia winced from the pain that wracked her entire body like it was being assaulted all at once. This in spite of the painkillers she had been given. They told her she was lucky to be alive. She didn't feel so lucky.

The Hispanic twenty-three-year-old rolled her large ink-black eyes, as if to ward off danger. Her brunette hair splayed across the pillow soaked with perspiration. An irregular line of blood had seeped across it from her mouth, which had been cut and was swollen to twice its normal size. A tube was helping her to breathe. Her fractured bones were held together with pins and casts. The rest of her was held together through sheer willpower.

She thought about Roberto. She'd been told he had been released from custody. Without her testimony, the case had gone out the window. Like a parakeet freed from its cage.

When it came right down to it, Lucie knew she couldn't testify against Roberto. Though she was afraid of him, and the beatings had become more frequent and more violent in recent months as his alcohol abuse grew worse, she loved him. She couldn't help it anymore than a mother could help loving her son, no matter what he did to hurt her.

Roberto was the only man she had ever loved. The only one who didn't run away at the first opportunity another piece of ass came into view. For that she was grateful. The rest just came with the territory as far as she was concerned.

Still, Lucie wondered what awaited her when she got home. Would Roberto take it out on her because he had been in police custody? Would he want her back now that she was badly bruised and broken and didn't look anything at all like the pretty Latina who had captured his attention in the beginning?

Lucie winced again before the sedative began to take effect and she drifted off into a restless sleep. Her last thought was that maybe she would awaken and find it had all been an awful dream.

Deep down inside she knew otherwise.

CHAPTER TWO

Roberto Martinez was counting his blessings as he sat in the bar getting drunk. He had been staring at twenty to life, according to his Afro American public defender. He figured that he'd be lucky if he ever saw the light of day again while he was young enough to be able to appreciate it.

But the devil must have been watching over his shoulder. Here he was out amongst the living again, and there wasn't a damned thing anyone could do about it.

He thought about his old lady. Yeah, he'd beaten the hell out of her. But, dammit, she deserved it. They all did.

Especially when they opened their big mouths too much and their legs too little. It was the only way to keep them in line. All whores needed to be kept in line, one way or the other.

Roberto Martinez finished off his last shot of whiskey before winking at the sweet looking black broad wearing shades in the corner while imagining what he could do with her, then moseying out of the bar. The night was cool for this time of year and darker than most. Stars seemed to have disappeared, as if relinquishing their place in space for other solar systems.

Roberto had half staggered about a block when he heard footsteps behind him. He turned and saw a tall, stacked, dark skinned woman with a blonde wig of box braids almost on top of him. He remembered she was the broad in the bar sitting all by her lonesome at the end of the counter. Only she was without the sunglasses, so he could see her eyes. They were deep, dark, enchanting. Just like the bitch herself.

"You looking for some action, honey?" she asked in a voice that sounded vaguely familiar.

He studied her. She had on a tight red dress that hugged every curve of her statuesque body, red gloves, and stiletto shoes. She was obviously a hooker. Why the hell not? It wasn't like his old lady was at home waiting to greet him or anything.

He grinned. "Yeah, I'm looking for some action, baby. How much will it cost?" He figured she was worth maybe twenty. Twenty-five if she was real good to him.

"Keep your money," she said curtly. "Let's just say I'm in a generous mood tonight."

Roberto regarded her uneasily. Was this some kind of a setup or something? Were they trying to get him back behind bars? Trying to trick him into doing something stupid on account of what he did to Lucie and got away with it?

"You ain't a cop, are you?" he asked tentatively.

She placed a hand on her rounded hip. "Do I look like a cop to you, sugar?"

Roberto grinned again. "Not like any damned cop I've seen," he had to admit.

"Then why are we wasting time here jawing?"

He felt at ease again. His libido was admittedly in need of a quick fix.

"Yeah," he said. "Why are we? Your place or mine?"

"Neither." She pointed toward the alley. "In there."

He looked into the darkened alley. It was hardly the ideal place to get laid. But who was he to argue? He could get his rocks off just about anywhere.

"Lead the way," he told her.

He followed the whore to the back of the alley, where she leaned up against a wall and urged him on.

"Come and get it, big boy," she teased.

Roberto could hardly contain himself as he rushed towards her. He only noticed at the last moment that she had picked up something with lightning quick speed and swung it hard at his head. He felt the impact as his skull cracked, sending him to his knees. The pain cut through him like a sharp knife. Make that a dozen sharp knives.

"How does it feel?" she asked him, a suddenly wicked edge to her voice. Before he could even think past the pain, much less respond, she struck him again with what he now suspected was a wooden bat. This time it connected across his back, smashing into his spine, paralyzing him. "Does it feel good, asshole?"

She swung the bat like an All Star baseball player, landing flush against his right cheek, dislodging his jaw and most of the teeth on that side of his face.

"Isn't this what you like to do to women, Roberto?" she spat, clubbing him across the top of the head, crushing his skull. "Well, how about a taste of your own medicine, you bastard!"

She swung again and again, each blow shattering another part of him, sending blood, bone, brain, and body pieces flying everywhere.

By the time she was finished, he was long dead. But it didn't matter, for she received great satisfaction to see to it that even in death he would never be whole again. Just like the lover he had beaten to a pulp.

She tossed the bloodied bat atop the corpse. Then she removed her wig, gloves, dress, and shoes. She put them in a duffel bag, slipped on some jeans, a sweater, and tennis shoes, leaving Roberto Martinez's remains to rot like raw meat.

* * *

JUSTICE SERVED (A Barkley and Parker Thriller) is now available in eBook through Kindle, Nook, and iTunes, and in audio from Audible.com, Amazon, and iTunes.

# # #

ABOUT THE AUTHOR

R. Barri Flowers is a bestselling, award winning author of more than fifty books, including mysteries, thrillers, romance, young adult, true crime, and criminology. Recent mystery fiction titles include MURDER IN MAUI: A Leila Kahana Mystery, DARK STREETS OF WHITECHAPEL: A Jack the Ripper Mystery, DEAD IN THE ROSE CITY: A Dean Drake Mystery, KILLER IN THE WOODS, STATE'S EVIDENCE: A Beverly Mendoza Leal Thriller, JUSTICE SERVED: A Barkley and Parker Mystery, and teen mysteries, DANGER IN TIME and GHOST GIRL IN SHADOW BAY.

Recent true crime titles by the author include SERIAL KILLER COUPLES, THE SEX SLAVE MURDERS, and MASS MURDER IN THE SKY: The Bombing of Flight 629.

Mr. Flowers is the recipient of the Wall of Fame Award from Michigan State University's renowned School of Criminal Justice. He has appeared on the Biography Channel's *Crime Stories* and Investigation Discovery's *Wicked Attraction* series.

The author is busy at work on his next mystery novel, SEDUCED TO KILL IN KAUAI.

Connect with R. Barri Flowers online through Facebook, Twitter, YouTube, LinkedIn, MySpace, CrimeSpace, and at www.rbarriflowers.com.